SECRET REMAINS

ALSO AVAILABLE BY JENNIFER GRAESER DORNBUSH

The Coroner

God Bless the Broken Road

Forensic Speak: How To Write Realistic Crime Dramas

WITHDRAWN

SECRET REMAINS

A Coroner's Daughter Mystery

Jennifer Graeser Dornbush

CROOKED
LANE

NEW YORK

Copyright © 2020 by Jennifer Graeser Dornbush

All rights reserved.

Published in the United States by Crooked Lane Books, an imprint of The Quick Brown Fox & Company LLC.

Crooked Lane Books and its logo are trademarks of The Quick Brown Fox & Company LLC.

Library of Congress Catalog-in-Publication data available upon request.

ISBN (hardcover): 978-1-64385-122-8
ISBN (ebook): 978-1-64385-123-5

Cover design by Erin Seaward-Hiatt

Printed in the United States.

www.crookedlanebooks.com

Crooked Lane Books
34 West 27th St., 10th Floor
New York, NY 10001

First Edition: January 2020

10 9 8 7 6 5 4 3 2 1

To the underdogs, victims, widows, orphans, adoptees, crime fighters, sisters, best friends, and long-lost loves . . .

PROLOGUE

Day broke and the sun began to warm the thin layer of frost off the forest floor as the contractor waved to the backhoe operator to fire up the beastly machine. The crew was just beginning excavation on the first parcel of land in a brand-new housing development just inside Freeport city limits in Pinetree Slopes—named appropriately for its long rows of tall white pines planted in a reforesting effort some twenty years earlier. Now many of the pines lay fallen to make way for construction.

The two-story, four-bedroom house would have a full basement, which meant several tons of earth needed to be hauled away. It would take a full week to prep the land for the concrete pouring.

The growling backhoe plunged its scoop into the earth, grinding its way through the first layer of rich, dark-brown soil.

The contractor's face lit with satisfaction. He had been crafting and creating this dream for several years now. Today it was becoming reality. In a year or two, several dozen homes would spring up in this idyllic wooded setting. Couples would move in. Families would grow. Children would ride bikes down a sidewalk that at the moment existed only on paper. Parents would gather on lawns to share gardening tips, recipes, or local gossip. A community was being born right before his eyes.

As the sun rose higher in the morning sky, creating bright tunnels of light between the rows of trees, something caught the eye of the contractor in the freshly dug hole.

He waved his hands frantically at the backhoe operator. The beast sputtered to a stop, leaving a silent void.

Rushing into the shallow pit, the contractor fixed his gaze on something unearthed from the broken ground. He knelt and brushed away the cool, moist soil, his eyes growing wide as he unearthed a slender gray bone.

1

D
r. Emily Hartford sat nervously at her father's side. He was lying helpless on a stretcher in the back of the ambulance as they raced down the two-lane country road to Freeport Hospital. Had she not stopped by to say goodbye on her way back to Chicago, he might have died right there on the kitchen floor. Thank God she had.

His heart rate was dropping, and he was going in and out of consciousness. She knew from the sweat beading on his face, his increased breathing, and his recent stint in the hospital for a heart attack that he was having another one. And it took everything in her power not to push the paramedic aside, grab the defibrillator paddles, and take charge. *Just be there for him. He needs to see you calm.*

She held tight to her dad's hand, glanced out the windshield, and saw Nick Larson, the county sheriff, leading the way in his squad car, flashers swathing a red-and-blue path to Freeport Hospital. Nick had been with her at her dad's house when she'd found him lying in the kitchen. And he had stayed with them until the paramedics arrived and packed Dad into the ambulance. She was so grateful she hadn't been alone.

"Em?" mumbled Dr. Robert Hartford from under his oxygen mask.

She snapped her gaze back to her father, struggling for his life. "Dad. I'm here." She removed his oxygen mask for a moment and pressed her ear close to his mouth. "What is it?"

"I'm not gonna make it this time," he said in a wispy voice.

"That's not true. Hang in there. There's a surgeon waiting for you at the hospital."

Doc, as he was known by locals, not only held a thriving family medical practice at his home office but had also served as Freeport County's coroner for over thirty years. He shook his head ever so slightly. "No, Em. Don't waste his time."

Emily put the mask back on her father so he could get more oxygen into his system. "It's not a waste. We're going to do emergency bypass, and in a couple weeks you'll be back in your orchard fertilizing the trees for spring. Okay?"

He struggled to lift his hand to his mouth. Emily understood that he wanted to speak again, and she removed his mask. "Your mother had cancer when she died," he sputtered out in short breaths.

"No, Dad. She died in a car accident. Remember?"

"She had terminal cancer, and she didn't tell us." Tears started to flow from his eyes.

"Are you saying Mom died from cancer?"

"No . . ." A breath caught in his throat, and he began to wheeze.

Emily quickly replaced the mask over his nose and mouth. He wasn't making sense. Just like when she'd found him on his kitchen floor twenty minutes earlier, babbling about how it was his fault his wife had died thirteen years ago.

It had been an accident. Deer versus car. The police had confirmed it. But Emily had found evidence to prove otherwise. Her mother's blue slipper under a bush near the crash site. What had Mom been doing driving her car in slippers? It was unlike her. But Dad had refused to investigate, and they'd drifted angrily apart. At sixteen, hurt and grieving, Emily had run to Chicago to live with her Aunt Laura. She'd finished high school and immediately enrolled in pre-med at the University of Chicago. She was now three years into her surgical residency. Emily hadn't been to Freeport since she'd left at sixteen. But a week ago, her father's first heart attack had sent her rushing back after her long hiatus.

"Breathe, Dad. Breathe."

He tried, but had trouble sucking in the air he needed. Emily noticed his gray skin taking on a bluish hue. If he didn't get into surgery as soon as they got him to the hospital, she would lose him.

"How close are we?" Emily asked the paramedic.

"About three minutes," he said.

"Can you get the driver to go faster? Please!"

"Sit back, please," barked the other paramedic, who was standing by with the paddles and monitoring her father's sinking heart rate. Her dad's eyes rolled back.

Emily slapped his arm three times. "Dad! Dad! Wake up! Come on!"

It worked. Doc's eye fluttered open. "Just a few more minutes, Dad. Focus on me. Focus on breathing. That's all you have to do."

His eyes darted back and forth, finally landing lazily on Emily's face.

"That's it. Good. Good. Look at me."

He started to talk again, but she couldn't understand him with the mask over his mouth. She leaned over again and lifted it a few inches from his face.

"The day . . . your mom died . . . I was meeting . . . a woman . . ."

Emily felt the ambulance jostle as they made a corner. They were here. Thank God.

The ambulance rolled to a halt, and she heard the driver open the front door and slam it shut.

"I need to get him ready to exit," the paramedic said, unlocking the gurney wheels. Emily stayed firmly in place, still grasping her father's hand.

"A woman? Who? Dad?" Emily gasped. "What woman?"

"Mom . . . loved you. I love you."

The other paramedic touched Emily's arm and gently removed her hand from her father's.

"We have to take him now." The back doors flew open. Emily instinctively gripped her father's gurney. But as soon as she did, the cold metal was ripped from her palms and the wheels dropped to the ground and snapped into position. The paramedics rolled the gurney toward the ER entrance, where three hospital staff were waiting to assist their patient inside.

What woman? What was he talking about?

Emily froze for a moment, unable to jump from the back of the ambulance. A sudden drop in adrenaline made her legs go to jelly. She took a deep breath, and when she looked up, Nick had parked behind the ambulance and emerged from his patrol car to meet her. He rushed over and offered his sturdy grip, and she grabbed his forearm. He lifted her from the back of the ambulance and led her through the emergency room entrance.

Emily was in a foggy dream state as they traveled into the waiting room. Nothing was normal. Not the sounds. Not the smells. Not the staff or other patients. Where was Dad? Her eyes darted around the room, frantically searching.

She felt Nick's grip again, leading her to a curtained area. One of the nurses at her father's bedside looked up from her mask, and Emily recognized those eyes immediately. Jo Blakely, her best friend. She was a floater nurse at Freeport Hospital and had been the first to call her when Dad had had his initial heart attack.

Emily knew once she looked into Jo's grief-stricken eyes. "He's not going to make it, is he?" she whispered.

Jo didn't answer. She just motioned for Emily to come closer. Nick let go of Emily's hand as she moved toward her father's bed.

The staff were working hard in their efforts to stabilize him. An eerie foreboding swept through the space as Emily entered and saw one of the doctors on duty prepping the defibrillator. Dad was slipping into unconscious, and Emily took his hand again.

"Dad, I love you." She choked out the lump in her throat and kept her focus on her father's chest as he released a breath. *Please don't go now. We have twelve years of catching up to do.*

The heart monitor blipped a weak rhythm as a nurse continued compressions and another one by his face squeezed the bag mask over his mouth and nose.

Emily looked up at the doctor in charge. Their efforts were in vain, but they kept trying. Emily knew he was gone. "It's okay. You can stop."

The doctor looked at Emily but kept charging the defib paddles.

She didn't have the authority to make the call, but she couldn't stand watching this torture. "I'm his daughter. Please. Stop."

When they didn't, Emily dashed over to the defib machine and switched it off. The nurses in the room stood still, unsure how to respond. Their eyes landed on the doctor in charge and then back on Emily.

"I'm calling it," she said in a defeated tone as she glanced up at the large clock on the wall.

"You can't call time of death," said the doctor in charge.

She went on in a breathy, desperate voice. "Time of death, thirteen sixteen." She looked around the room. Everyone was staring at her. "He's gone. He's . . . dead." Her voice cracked and broke.

The doctor nodded and called out, "Time of death, thirteen sixteen."

He then turned to Emily, putting a hand on her arm. "I'm very, very sorry. We all loved your father."

Emily's throat constricted as she stared at her father's lifeless body. The staff began to remove tubes from him, then carted away machines and exited the space in a silent parade. Nick and Jo stayed with her.

"I'm so sorry, Emily. I don't know what to say," said Jo, gripping Emily's hand with a tight squeeze. "I can't believe he's gone."

Neither can I.

She wasn't able to voice the reality.

Here she was, thirteen years after the death of her mother, again in the emergency room of Freeport Hospital, now with a dead father. *How can this be happening?* She and her father had just started to reconcile after a long hiatus of estrangement. Her body went cold and quivery, and she couldn't get it under control. Nick and Jo's supportive grips were the only thing keeping her from buckling to the floor.

Emily let out a long sob. Why had she waited so long to return home?

2

Five restless nights later Emily lay awake watching the sky from her bedroom window in the house she'd grown up in. She couldn't sleep. Hours passed, and mercifully the jet black slowly changed to midnight blue tinged with orange as the sun rose on the day of her father's funeral.

Emily crawled out of bed to take a walk around the property, a fifty-acre farm and orchard. She wandered across the harvested wheat field that her father had rented out to a local farmer, and through the small orchard of apple and peach trees he had planted that were almost past their prime. The dew was heavy on the tall grass and soon soaked her tennis shoes and pant bottoms. She had a hard time following her thoughts, so she stopped fighting them and let her mind drift as her senses absorbed the earthy odor and the cool morning air, which had dipped to around forty degrees. Soon the swirl of thoughts presented themselves as a string of questions.

What did Dad mean by 'meeting a woman'? Was he having an affair? Did Mom know? Why didn't she tell me about the cancer? Did this other woman somehow contribute to Mom's accident?

When Emily returned to the house, she found Cathy Bishop, Dad's new wife of just six months and third-generation owner of

Bishop and Schulz Funeral Home, in the kitchen boiling eggs for breakfast. Emily's stomach turned at the thought of food, but that's how people fed their grief here in Freeport. She would be expected to eat, or pretend to, anyhow.

"I know you're not hungry, but you need to eat something," said Cathy, correctly guessing the thoughts behind the look on Emily's face. "It's going to be a long day. Three bites."

Emily nodded and sat at the kitchen table. Cathy brought her a mug of coffee and a hard-boiled egg. She sipped on the bitter black brew, so deadened inside that she did not even make the effort to add her usual sugar and a dash of cream.

"I want you to know that I've decided to move out of the house," Cathy declared after Emily had taken her first bite of egg.

"No. No. You don't have to do that. This is your house now."

"Technically, it's probably yours. We never got around to making a will together."

Emily wasn't surprised by this. Even Emily hadn't known about her father's marriage until recently.

"I'm not kicking you out. Besides, I don't even know if I'm sticking around Freeport now." She had arrived in Freeport less than two weeks ago to attend to her father after his first heart attack. She hadn't intended to stay long, because she had a surgical residency in Chicago . . . and a fiancé, Brandon. Well, ex-fiancé. They had been engaged for a week before things took an odd turn. The same day she arrived in her Freeport home, Senator Dobson's daughter, Julie, had been killed riding her horse and Dad had begged her to assist on a medical examiner case. Just like the old times when Emily was a teenager, assisting as junior coroner.

At first, Emily begrudgingly agreed to help him, but she soon found herself engrossed. It turned out to be a homicide case, and she quickly became bent on cracking it as the familiar, old passions for investigation kicked in from the years when she and her Dad had solved cases together.

Emily rubbed her healing ribs, a lingering reminder that the Dobson murder investigation had almost cost her her life. But she had found the killer. The Dobson case had invigorated Emily in a way she hadn't felt since she had worked side by side with her dad in death investigations.

"It doesn't feel right to stay. I'll be out by the end of the week," said Cathy.

"Back to the funeral home?" asked Emily. Cathy owned the large red brick Victorian home in downtown Freeport that served as a funeral parlor and upstairs residence.

"Yes. I rented it out, when your father and I got married, to a young couple. Fortunately, they understand my need to have the place back."

"Cathy . . . please stay here. The place is huge, and there's no reason we can't both be here. Besides, I'll be having to get back to Chicago sometime soon."

"I just can't. I need to move on." Cathy wagged her head. "Fresh start." She took a seat at the table, slid two hard boiled eggs onto a plate, and broke them with a fork. "My son, Ben, came into town last night," Cathy said, taking a seat at the table. "He's bringing the hearse by in a half an hour to take me to the funeral home. You're welcome to ride with us."

"Nick said he would pick me up. But thanks."

Emily forced down two more bites of breakfast and went up to her room to slip on Jo's black A-line dress. All of her stuff was still in Chicago. When her father had his first heart attack, she had rushed from her shift at the hospital, dressed only in jeans and a blouse, to drive four hours north to Freeport upon getting news from Jo. Since that horrible call, Emily hadn't had a single moment's time to return to Chicago, where she lived, to retrieve her things, which was now proving very unfortunate because Jo was tinier than Emily and the dress snugged her chest and hips. Emily had to wriggle the fabric into place to keep it from riding up. *My own father's funeral, and I don't even have my own dress.*

After things settled down, she would need to get to Chicago to pick up her belongings from the brownstone that Brandon, her ex-fiancé, had purchased for them. The bombshell engagement in the doctors' lounge, complete with a two-karat diamond ring adorning the top of a peanut-butter-and-jelly cupcake (her favorite!) had come just moments prior to news of her father's first heart attack. After checking in on him, Emily had launched into Julie's death investigation. The week following she had been consumed with Julie's case. Stepping into the coroner's shoes after 13 years took up every ounce of her energy. When she surfaced, she realized Brandon had not exactly been the model of support. She had barely heard from him. He was consumed by his own burgeoning surgical schedule. How on earth would they be able to make a life together if he couldn't even be there for her during her father's crisis?

When Brandon did finally drive up to Freeport and meet her father for the first time—a few days before Dad's second heart attack—she had been surprised at how different they seemed from one another.

In the short time she had been absent from their life in Chicago, Brandon had bought them a brownstone and moved everything from her city apartment into the new place without even telling her. And he had begun plans for their wedding reception with the help of his controlling mother. Again, without any consent from Emily. It was more than she could take. She didn't want her life ordered and arranged. She wanted a say in it. She wanted an equal partner, a best friend, someone who would drop everything to be by her side, especially in her time of greatest need. Brandon was too little, too late.

Her feet had grown cold, and she'd given the ring back. Their breakup had been abrupt and hurtful for both of them. Now, in all the trauma over her father's sudden passing, she hadn't even thought to call Brandon to tell him her father had died.

How easy it was for someone who had been in her life every day for the past couple of years to slip her mind so quickly. Still, the pain tugged at her heart when her mind wandered to the good places their relationship had taken them. Emily decided she would chalk up her oversight to sleep deprivation and grief.

Emily brushed out her hair and twisted it into a smooth bun. She applied four bobby pins and a spritz of hair spray. From her mirror she could hear the hearse pulling into the driveway. Cathy's son, Ben, exited and headed toward the front door, but his mother met him in the drive. When she saw him, she broke down and he gave her a long hug. Emily felt a lump in her throat. Despite their very short marriage, Cathy had really loved her father. She was now twice a widow and it just didn't seem fair. After a moment, her son led her to the hearse and opened the door.

Emily turned back to her image in the mirror. She feared she looked stark and bookish with her hair pulled back, but she hadn't had the energy to wash, dry, and style it properly. Everything about the last two weeks had drained her, including her own short hospital stay after being struck down during a chase to catch a killer. Thankfully, her shoulder, jaw, and rib injuries had been reduced to dull aches that required only a single ibuprofen this morning to relieve them.

Emily dabbed her lips with coral lipstick and searched for her red jacket. She headed downstairs to wait on the front porch for Nick, then sat on the same chair where she and her father had shared a slice of apple pie just a few days before he died. Emily thought about the house, the property, the home office. She wasn't looking forward to dealing with it all.

Nick's squad car pulled into the driveway, and she rose to meet it. When Nick got out of the car, Emily's lips parted as she caught her breath. He looked handsome and dignified in his dress uniform.

"You look really stunning," said Nick. "I don't know if that's the right thing to say on a day like this, but . . ."

Emily gave him a small smile. "You're kind. I look like a tired library lady."

Nick reached out to take her hand. She was grateful for the chivalrous gesture, especially as she maneuvered her way in the four-inch heels—another wardrobe borrow from Jo—that were two inches taller than she was used to.

Nick drove them onto the two-lane county highway that led toward Bishop and Schulz Funeral Home in the center of Freeport. Neither spoke for several miles until Nick's radio scratched, breaking the silence.

"All units, I'm requesting a ten-thirteen at Pinetree Slopes. Please respond," chirped a dispatcher on the other end.

Nick grabbed the radio receiver.

"What does that mean?" said Emily. "Is it urgent?"

"It means they need emergency assistance."

Nick pressed the transmit button. "This is Sheriff Larson. Can you advise further?"

"Negative. Waiting on more information," said the dispatcher.

"I need more info. What are we dealing with?"

After a moment, the dispatcher said, "They called in a nine-eight-oh-seven."

"What's that?" asked Emily.

"Suspicious situation." Nick pressed his radio button down again to signal dispatch.

"What does that mean exactly?"

"It's code for a lot of things we don't want to announce over the airwaves."

"Like?"

"Like . . . like maybe a HAZMAT situation, or animal at large."

She knew he was lying by the way his glance shifted out the driver's side window as he said it.

The radio crackled and the dispatcher's voice belted out, "We may have a ten-fourteen. Out."

"A suspicious death," Emily said with an air of confidence.

"I shoulda figured you knew that one," Nick said as he nipped the cuticle skin off his left thumb with his teeth. There was one code Emily knew well. It was 10-14, request for a medical examiner.

"I'll send a local police officer."

"Nick, if you need to go there, I understand," said Emily, remembering all the times her father, Freeport's coroner for over thirty years, had been called to a death investigation case during the most inopportune moments and important events of their daily lives—band performances, the middle of a church service, and always, always during holiday dinners.

"I can't. It's your father's funeral."

"Drop me and come back," she said.

"He was my friend, too. I'll let some of the other guys handle it."

"They'll be calling for me next," she mused, "and they'll have to wait."

Nick made the request for another officer, and they rode in silence. Emily's thoughts started to drift to the call, and she wondered what they had found. How many bodies? In what condition? A small smile formed on her lips. *How absolutely fitting that death would interrupt your own funeral. Nice nod, Dad. I get you.*

"What are you smiling about?" Nick interrupted.

"Mom always joked that Dad would be late to his own funeral."

Nick pressed on the accelerator pedal, and they sped toward Freeport.

"What is Pinetree Slopes, by the way? It wasn't here when I lived in Freeport," said Emily.

"Freeport's hope for urban revitalization. They just broke ground."

"No one's actually living there yet?"

"No."

"So, if no one's living there, who's dying there?"

Nick glanced over, and Emily met his eyes with a smug look.

"You are still definitely your father's daughter."

3

Emily and Nick arrived at Bishop and Schulz Funeral Home and, ironically, couldn't find a place to park in the overfull lot, so Nick pulled the car under the large overhang at the front entrance. Emily could only imagine how many people were packed inside. Cathy was probably in there frantically setting up more chairs in the back instead of allowing herself to play the part of grieving widow.

Emily realized just at that moment she hadn't prepared anything to say. The last few weeks had been a blur, and cobbling together any string of thoughts or decisions had been almost beyond her abilities. She would have to wing it and just speak from her heart. It wouldn't be too hard to praise the younger version of this man who had lovingly raised her and formed her into the surgeon she was today. It was the older version of Dr. Robert Hartford who was the enigma. Especially in light of his last words to her. She would play it safe and focus on the father of her youth.

"I'm just gonna park it here. What are they gonna do? Arrest me?" said Nick.

Emily grinned at his joke.

"Don't move," he said, getting out of the car. Nick went around to her door, opened it for her, and helped her out. He took her arm and opened the right door of the double doors.

"It's going to be okay. Freeport loved your dad."

Did they? She wished she could know that part of him now.

"You'll probably get to hear lots of stories today that will fill in some details that you've missed." Nick had read her mind.

"Yeah." She would get to know better the father she had abandoned . . . and who had emotionally abandoned her after her mom's death.

"Emily?" said a voice behind her. She turned to see Brandon rising from a high-backed chair in the corner.

"Oh my goodness. Brandon. You're here." Her hands dropped limply to her sides, and she could feel the corners of her mouth turning down into a frown. This was a surprise, especially since their last words to each other had indicated they were over.

Cathy shuffled in from a side room and grabbed Nick by the arm. "Nick, I could use your help with something for a second." The two of them disappeared into the side room.

Emily turned to Brandon, who embraced her. He smelled amazing, and she melted comfortably into his arms like she had a thousand times throughout their relationship. "I'm sorry I didn't let you know about Dad."

"Don't worry. The way we left things . . . you had a lot on your plate."

"Nice of you to come up." She forced a small smile.

"Are you okay? Of course you're not. Stupid question." He was nervous—a trait she had never seen in him before. "I'm so sorry about your father."

"Thank you." Emily nodded and swallowed the lump growing in her throat.

"I know this is really weird timing, but as soon as I heard about your father's passing, it got me thinking about how little time we have on this earth, and that . . . that I'm sure, one hundred percent, that I want to spend the rest of it with you."

Emily pulled away and looked into his eyes. Was he serious? Now? Of all times and places?

"I'm about to bury my father," she whispered.

"I know. And that's why I feel so urgently about this. I love you, Em. I don't want to wait another minute. I had to be here for you. To tell you that I'm willing to do whatever it takes."

"This is not the right time, Brandon." Her unease shriveled up, replaced by a warming sensation of disgust squeezing her rib cage. *Is this what a panic attack feels like?* She had heard them described this way by her patients.

"I've got a year left on my contract with Northwestern. After that, the sky's the limit. We can go wherever you want."

"Anywhere but Freeport. Isn't that what you mean?" she pressed. She had introduced the possibility of settling in Freeport when he'd come to visit during her father's recovery, but he had shut it down. Brandon was a city boy, through and through. Freeport's small-town way of life was a joke to him.

"Why limit ourselves? Why not try a place that's new to both of us?"

This was a new twist.

"What about the brownstone? Your parents? The city?" Emily had learned that Brandon's loyalties lay with his beloved life in Chicago. She was just the pretty add-on.

"Just come back to Chicago and we'll figure it all out together."

"Clearly I'm not in the right state of mind to make that decision. You understand that, right?" This babbling, begging version of her former fiancé added to the surrealness of the day. Her thoughts began to swirl again, impervious to capture. *Is this really happening right now? Where are Nick and Cathy to save me from this conversation!*

The piped-in organ music further contributed to the silent-movie melodrama of the moment.

"Okay. Okay. We can move to Freeport," he blurted out. "I'll see if I can get out of my contract early. I'll start a practice here. I can make this work." He grabbed her hands and held them to his chest. "Please, Em. I miss you."

Emily's eyes blinked wide with overwhelm. "I don't know what to say." She exhaled and felt her rib cage release a little pressure. "I have no idea what the future holds. I have no idea how long I'll be here. If I even want to stay."

"You have to return to Chicago. To finish your residency."

"I guess. Maybe." She should. Right? She had worked so hard for it. Only two more years to go.

The side door swooshed opened and Nick stepped into the lobby. "We had to get some more chairs from the cellar," he said, his eyes landing on Emily's hands as they slipped from Brandon's. She detected Nick's perturbed look as he lasered his focus on Brandon. They faced each other, caught in the awkwardness of the moment.

"We should get Emily seated," said Nick.

Brandon's nervousness was replaced by an annoyed expression, but before he had a chance to take the conversation further, Cathy whisked in with a professional stride from a side door in the lobby that connected to the main viewing area where her father's casket lay.

"Okay. We're ready. You?" Cathy took Emily gently by the shoulders.

"No one's ever ready for a day like this."

Emily knew from the dampness around her hairline that Cathy had been working overtime on Dad's funeral. That's what you did in small towns—you pitched in because you had to. But she knew Cathy didn't mind; she wouldn't have been satisfied sitting around feeling gloomy and depressed while every guest around reminded her how gloomy and depressed she should feel.

"You're amazing. Thank you for making this so special. I know you're hurting, too." Emily gave Cathy a little squeeze and noticed tears filling her eyes.

She quickly brushed them away with the back of her hand. "You should see all the arrangements inside. Like a botanical garden in there. Your dad would've loved it."

"It's too many for us to take home. Can you bring some to the nursing home and hospital? They love the fresh flowers," said Emily, the lump returning.

"Absolutely. Come on. I have a seat for us and Nick in the front," said Cathy in a quiet tone.

"Ms. Bishop. My condolences."

Emily noticed Cathy glance over her shoulder as Brandon came between them and gave Cathy a firm handshake.

"Brandon, if I would have known you were coming, I could have set an extra chair for you in front. But I'm afraid it's full down in front. You can slide in in the back."

Emily could read Brandon's disappointment, but she knew Cathy was protecting her. She felt Cathy's gentle tug as she pulled her away from Brandon and Nick. Emily didn't care in the moment what they said to each other, to her, or where they sat. She grabbed tightly onto Cathy's warm, strong arm, a safe and sturdy haven. That's all she needed right now to get through the next few hours.

4

After the funeral, the guests proceeded to the veterans' hall in downtown Freeport for the reception Jo Blakely and friends had prepared. Emily wanted a few minutes alone with her father before Cathy closed the casket. They would do a private burial the next morning at the cemetery, and her father would be laid to rest next to her mother, Mary, who had passed thirteen years ago.

Nick and Brandon hung back and helped Cathy load the floral arrangements into the hearse so they could deliver most of them to the hospital and nursing home. Cathy closed the French doors to the viewing room so Emily could have privacy.

Emily stepped up to her father's casket and touched his cold, rubbery hands folded across his abdomen. Hands that had done so much in their lifetime. Hands that had taught her so much.

"Dad, I don't think I ever thanked you enough for everything you did for me." Her voice hiccupped, and she cleared her throat. "I'm sorry I ran away, and I'm sorry for the lost years in between then and now. I know we can't ever make those up. I regret that." She drew in a couple of deep breaths to try to calm her nerves, which were quaking. "I'm really confused by what you told me. And I'm really scared about what I might find. But I know it's important, and I know you wanted to give me the truth. I just wish you were here to explain it." So many conflicting emotions were trying to sort their way to the surface. "I want you to know I'll look into it. I hope what I find doesn't . . . I don't even know how to put it . . . I just don't want to think badly of you again. And I'm afraid that what I find might do that."

She stopped, utterly exhausted. She let her head drop as a little sob shook her chest. "I thought we'd have more time. I'm gonna miss you, Dad."

Her body convulsed with grief, and tears blurred her vision. She stepped away from the casket and fell into a plush armchair to the side. After a good amount of tears had fallen, she reached for the tissue box on the side table. Cathy always kept the place stocked in tissues. Emily wiped her face, figuring her mascara had created dark blotches under her bloodshot eyes. She would have to use the bathroom to wash them the rest of the way off before heading to the veterans' hall for the reception.

She gave her nose a good blow and took several more inhales and exhales. Soon Cathy would be in, ready to shuttle her to the reception, where she would have to face the masses who loved her father. She would have to sit through endless stories about the kind of father she had never gotten to experience. How beautiful it was that there had been so many who respected and adored him. But *should* they respect him? And would they continue to, once they found out about this other woman? How would they feel about their beloved Doc then? How would she feel?

"Em? Can I get you anything?"

Emily turned to see Brandon by her side. He would be tethered to her all day if she didn't say something now.

Can I just send him away? No, that would be rude.

"Yes. You can do something. Please don't ask me anything more about our relationship today. Soon I'll come down to Chicago and we can discuss it more when I come to get my things. But on my terms."

"I'm here now, and I want to be with you."

"I know. But I need some time."

Brandon did nothing to hide the distressed look on his face. He nodded, then turned on his heel and padded out. She heard the doors click shut and let out a sigh.

After a few more moments of silence, there was a soft knock. Emily turned her head toward the back of the room and saw Nick's urgent face poking around the door.

"Em, I'm so sorry to interrupt. Do you have a minute?"

"It's okay. I was just finishing." She didn't bother to get up. She was too drained to move.

Nick opened the doors further, and Emily saw a police officer standing behind him. They entered in silence.

"What's going on?" Emily said as they positioned themselves in front of her. She sat up a little straighter.

"Em, this is Officer Matthews. He's the police officer I sent to Pinetree Slopes," said Nick.

"Nice to meet you."

"Likewise, Dr. Hartford. And my condolences on your father's passing. He was a great man and a pillar of this community."

"Thank you for paying your respects," said Emily as she rose to shake his hand, before realizing her own were full of soiled tissues. She drew her hand back.

"He's not here just to pay respects," said Nick.

"Oh?" Emily's inquisitive eyes searched the officer's.

"It's about the call from Pinetree development."

"The ten-fourteen?" asked Emily. "Can it wait?"

"The contractor over at Pinetree found something this morning when they broke ground on a new house. It's obviously a bone of some kind. We're just not sure if it's human or animal."

"I had them halt all excavation efforts, but we need you to make an identification," said Nick.

"I . . . Nick . . . Please . . . I don't think I can . . . I'm not an anthropologist," stuttered Emily, who as a surgeon and medical doctor was qualified to act as medical examiner in her father's stead. And her recent success in the Dobson death investigation had proved her astute for the job. But bone identification was an entirely different science. This day was getting stranger and stranger.

"We need to get to this before sundown," said Nick. "If it's something other than animal bones, we don't have the resources to secure the scene overnight."

"And the construction boss has been harassing us all morning about how this is delaying him and costing him a ton of money," added Officer Matthews.

Emily wanted to moan, *My dad just died. I don't give a hoot about your greedy boss.*

"Please, Em, you're the only one I trust on this," Nick said into her ear. "And obviously, the only one in the county qualified."

"What time is sundown?" she asked, knowing that October evenings were growing shorter and shorter.

"Sun sets around five thirty, in a little more than four hours."

"Okay, here's what I can do," said Emily mustering some thoughts together. "I suspect you already cordoned off the area?"

"They did," said Nick.

"I need to attend my father's funeral reception. In the meantime, take all the photographs you need and collect all the evidence you can without touching the body—I mean, bones. I'll make my appearance at the reception for an hour, then meet you at Pinetree Slopes."

"That seems fair," said Officer Matthews. Emily didn't care about fairness. This was pushing the limits. Even for her. She hoped this was just a very inconvenient false alarm that would become a minor speed bump to her day.

"Emily? I'm heading to drop off the flowers now," called Cathy from the doorway. "Everything okay?"

"Ah, yes. Thank you. I'll see you at the reception." Emily gave her a weak smile.

"I don't mean to rush you, but I need to lock up after everybody."

"Of course. I'm ready. We're ready," said Emily.

"After you," said Nick, indicating that the officer needed to exit first.

Emily turned and took a few steps back toward her father's casket. Nick stayed at her side, wrapping an arm around her, and she felt truly comforted. The grief would linger for a while. She knew that from her mother's death.

They turned from Dr. Robert Hartford's casket and walked slowly together in reverence until they were under the awning outside near the hearse. Brandon's car was still sitting in the lot. He was in the driver's seat, eyes locked to his phone, not looking up.

"What do you think about those bones?" said Emily as Nick opened the passenger door of his squad car for her.

"I hope they are from a deer," he said.

She glanced up at Nick, surprised to find his face drained of color.

5

A little before three PM, Emily and Nick arrived at Pinetree Slopes. Cathy had helped her slip out the back door of the reception after she had greeted a good share of the guests. Even Brandon, who was schmoozing a group of her dad's doctor buddies, hadn't seen her go.

She and Nick pulled up to the site, where an officer stood guard on the opposite end of a single plot-sized perimeter sectioned off by yellow caution tape. Emily exited Nick's patrol car, still in Jo's heels and black dress. After three wobbly steps over the gravel driveway, Nick reached out and grabbed Emily's arm to steady her. This wasn't gonna work.

"Do you maybe have an extra pair of tennis shoes or boots or something in the trunk?" she said.

"I do, but they're going to be huge on you."

"Not sure I have a choice. I'll never make it in these, and we just don't have time for me to go back home to change." The weather had shifted from a beautiful, cloudless day to a fairly stiff wind coming from the north. It had dropped the temp a good ten degrees, and the sky was filling with bottom-heavy, dark-gray clouds. They still had several hours of daylight, but this storm would beset them in less than an hour, Emily was certain.

Nick pulled out an old pair of golf shoes and dirty socks. Emily stuffed the socks into the tops of the shoes and slid her bare feet in. She pulled the laces as tight as she could, but still the shoes barely snugged around her narrow size-seven feet. To walk, Emily had to lift her feet a little higher than usual, but she was able to clod her way toward the home site.

Only she and Nick entered the cordoned area. Someone had planted a stake with an orange plastic flag at the site where the bones had been found. Emily and Nick made their way over as the wind picked up and a flicker of lightning flashed, sending a shiver along Emily's arms. She began to count, a habit from her childhood. *One Mississippi, two Mississippi, three Mississippi, four Mississippi, five Mississippi, six Mississippi . . .*

A faint rumble of thunder sounded in the distance. They were racing against time. The storm was only about one mile away.

"Rain's coming soon. Does anyone have a tarp we can set up?" she called out to the officers and construction crew who had lined up along the perimeter to watch.

"We got one!" one of the crew yelled back, running off to fetch it.

Emily turned back to the site. The first thing she could see was a mandible and partial cranium jutting out from the crusty, red soil. Her eyes wandered south from the skull and spied several phalanges. Long, like fingers; definitely not toes. Nothing else protruded from the earth. Emily knelt down, immediately soiling the hem of the dress. As she bent over to brush away some of the dirt around the skull, the bodice of her dress tightened across her rib cage. She tried to exhale carefully but felt a tiny rip at the side seam. *Sorry, Jo. I'm gonna owe you a new black dress. Hope you weren't too attached to this one.*

She gently swept away the dirt around the mandible until she could see that it was attached to the calvarium. The teeth were in near perfect condition.

And definitely human. She knew there were differences between the shapes of the male and female jaw, but she wasn't trained well

enough to make this call. They would need to get a forensic anthropologist for an official determination.

"Nick, we're going to need something to collect this." She looked
up at him with a straight face.

"Not a deer, huh?"

She shook her head. "Human."

He paused for a moment, and she noticed again the color drain-
ing from his face.

"You okay?" She might have expected this look at a more grue-
some death scene, but there was nothing gory about a couple of teeth.

"Yeah. Yeah. I've got evidence-collecting kits and a roll of heavy-
duty trash bags in the car."

"That'll have to do. Oh, and a small shovel and a paintbrush
would be ideal."

"I'll see what I can find. Maybe some of these guys have brushes."

Nick raced back to the squad car as Emily continued to carefully
excavate. Soon she had the entire skull exposed, except for the back,
which was still resting in the dirt. She could also see that the skull
was attached to a vertebral column. They were lucky. A full skeleton
would make identification easier.

The lightning flashed again overhead, and thunder rumbled
again, growing closer. Louder. Two construction men returned with
a blue tarp and began to stake the ground to install it.

"Careful, please," Emily instructed. "We have no idea if this
body is fully intact. Bones may be spread nearby."

Still using her hands, Emily scraped away at the dirt clinging to
the neck bones. She noticed a fissure in two of them. Until further
examination at the morgue under good light and perhaps a magni-
fying lens, it would be impossible to know if the fractures had happened at death or after death.

The construction guys were now struggling to secure the posts
for the tarp, fighting against the wind whipping through the construction site, harpooning sticks and leaves through the air. One of

them held the edge of the tarp while the other secured it to the poles. Emily hunched her back toward the wind as Nick ran up with his arms loaded with equipment. He laid everything out a few feet from where Emily was working. By now the tarp was overhead and the thunderclaps were rolling in one behind another. One of the construction guys ran over with a handful of paintbrushes and a small shovel. Emily thanked him and she and Nick got to work, gingerly but quickly, digging and sweeping away at the bones.

"You realize the county is going to need to hire a forensic anthropologist," said Emily after they had uncovered cervical bones and a shoulder blade.

"How long do you think this body has been here?" he asked.

"I don't know, honestly. It could be several months to many years, since it's fully skeletonized. The bones are in fairly good condition. That could mean it's younger or that it was buried deep enough that the critters weren't able to get to it."

They worked for a few more minutes in silence. Emily could tell something was troubling Nick by the way he held his brow furrowed in concentration. His brushstrokes were soft and swift, but Emily noticed a slight quiver in his hands.

"Do you feel okay?" she said when he stopped and sat back on his heels with a big exhale.

"No. I'm . . . I'm kinda queasy," he said, rocking back to a cross-legged position on the ground. The wind howled above through the treetops, pelting more small branches and leaves onto the tarp.

"Are you going to be sick?"

"No . . . it's not that kind of sick."

"Low blood sugar, maybe?"

Lightning flashed closer, illuminating the whole site. The crack of thunder that followed made Emily jump. They were losing time. She needed him back to work. "Take a couple deep breaths and get back in here, Larson. The storm's about to hit, and we need to get this outta here."

"I know. I know. I'm sorry." Nick drew in a breath and squatted again. "It's just . . . I think I know . . . who these bones belong to."

"What?" Emily yelled through the wind.

"Sandi Parkman."

"Who?"

"A girl from high school. Do you remember?"

"Not really." The name was vaguely familiar, but she couldn't place her.

"She went missing ten years ago. I'm just wondering if this might be . . . her."

"These exact bones? How can you be so sure?" Emily challenged. Until a forensic anthropologist examined them, they would not know for certain if the bones were male or female, how old they were, or from what race of people the bones belonged. From what she could tell so far, they looked small, not adult sized. But she was not a bone expert, and it would be crucial to get a complete and proper identification in case this investigation ended up in court. Always good to have an expert second opinion.

"I just have a feeling," Nick yelled back.

Sandi Parkman. A vague recollection gathered in her mind.

"Was she the girl who lived in the little run-down house down the street from you?" Nick had grown up in the country so "down the street" really meant a quarter mile to the next residence.

"Yeah."

"What would Sandi's bones be doing out here?"

"You never heard what happened?" His voice rose above the wind.

Emily shook her head without looking up. They had uncovered the skeleton to the hip bones, which Emily found detached from the femur. She started to place the bones in the thick black garbage bags Nick had brought.

"Well, I guess this would have been two years after you left Freeport. She left home one spring day after school, and no one ever saw her again," said Nick.

Emily made a quick calculation. Emily had left Freeport when she was sixteen. That was the last time she had seen Nick, too. Now she was newly twenty-eight.

"That's awful. I'm sorry."

"You know I used to take her home from school now and then. She was a sophomore and I was a senior, and she didn't have her driver's license. But a lot of times her boyfriend would drive her, you know? This one day she came up to me at my locker after lunch and asked if I could take her home after school."

Thunder cracked louder overhead and shook the ground, rattling Emily's organs.

This is turning into one nasty storm. Emily picked up the pace on her digging. No anthropologist would have approved of her technique, but she didn't want rain or wind washing away any potential evidence.

"I drove her home that day and . . . and never saw her again," said Nick. His digging paused again as he stared at the femur bone emerging from the soil.

"You're making pretty big assumptions here. Keep those to yourself until we get the bones identified. They may not be Sandi's remains at all."

Emily wanted to impress on Nick that he shouldn't start any rumors a hungry press might pick up on and feed from like they had with the Julie Dobson case. Speaking of the press, she was surprised they hadn't descended on their investigation already. This was a juicy discovery, and storm or no storm, hungry news hunters would be eager to swarm in. Perhaps Nick had learned from the Dobson case and demanded this stay under wraps.

A bolt of lightning zapped the forest floor fifty feet from their makeshift tent as a deafening crack of thunder gave her insides another good stir. They had to hurry.

Emily glanced over to Nick's section again. He was still digging away around the right femur. Emily lent her help, and they were able to slide the bones securely into a bag.

"We don't have much time," Emily yelled, wedging her shovel into the dirt on the outside of the right tibia that had emerged from the soil. Rain entered their shelter sideways, carried by the wind from the north. The temperature had dropped another five degrees, hovering just above the freezing point. Emily shivered in Jo's short dress and her red jacket. She put it out of her mind and kept digging.

Nick and Emily huddled in the center to keep cover, guarding the collection kits and trash bags of bones the best they could on their laps. The water streamed into the crevices and craters where the bones had been, creating a massive, muddy puddle around Nick and Emily. Wet and cold, her shoes now covered in slippery mud-clay, Emily resigned herself to the elements and inwardly celebrated their successful excavation. She hugged her arms around her sides and felt another tear in the seam of Jo's dress under her red jacket. It was already completely ruined by mud, so what did one more tear matter? Besides, she could breathe more easily now. She looked at Nick, who seemed far away in his thoughts as he clawed at the muddy ground to extract another bone.

The wind howled above them and the trees shook down leaves and branches. She glanced up at the sky. The grayish-green clouds churned in a circular formation above them. Nick followed her gaze, his eyes widening with alarm.

"We need to get out of here," Nick yelled over the rush of wind. "We're gonna get killed."

"Keep digging!" She was able to release the tibia and handed it to Nick to place in the bag. The foot was buried deeper, and she had to excavate with more care and precision. Working in tandem, they made tiny stabs with the tip of the shovel while Nick brushed away the dirt. Soon they were able to loosen the foot.

Then an eerie stillness broke over the woods. And a faint scream, like a fast-approaching train, pealed in the distance. She and Nick exchanged a panicked look. They had only minutes to clear out before the twister touched down.

* * *

They had just enough time to make it to Nick's patrol car with the bones when the tornado's fully formed funnel dipped down over the treetops, snapping thick branches like toothpicks and hurtling them through the forest like javelins.

"Get down!" Nick shouted as they both flattened to the floor of the patrol car, and he covered Emily's head and back with his torso the best he could.

Branches plunked and thudded all around outside Nick's patrol car. Emily tried not to imagine how much damage was being inflicted and prayed none of the trees would fall and crush them.

The tornado's terror lasted less than a minute, but it felt like an hour. Then, as if someone had turned off a turbofan in a warehouse, the wind instantly stopped. Emily and Nick didn't move a muscle as they listened to the last few small, stray branches tumble from heights to plink against the patrol car. Soon it was quiet. A sliver of sun and a bird's chirp finally drew them from the patrol car, where they got the first look at the damage.

Nick went immediately to check on the construction workers, but they found all of them had already evacuated the site to seek shelter. *Smart guys.* Emily scanned their surroundings and spied their tent tarp wrapped around the cab of the backhoe.

Branches—full tree limbs—littered every square inch of the forest floor. More stunning to her was that oddly patterned patches of full-grown trees lay felled in a crisscross arrangement all around them. Nick's patrol car had been narrowly spared.

She and Nick picked a path toward the site of the bones where they had been just minutes ago. A giant oak tree lay across it. They shared a terrified, grateful look. They had been lucky to survive. Really lucky.

"All your limbs intact?" Nick asked.

"Pun intended," said Emily, and they shared a nervous laugh.

They looked over the bone excavation site in silence.

Emily could tell he was thinking about Sandi.

"Do you think she ran away?"

"I told myself that because she had it rough. Jealous, controlling boyfriend, tough home life. In my mind, I guess I wanted to believe she left to find a fresh, new start," said Nick. Emily could tell from the distance in his look that his mind was replaying the memories of that day.

"What did you do when you learned she was gone?"

"Not enough."

She let the moment hang, hoping he might expound on his memories. When he didn't elaborate, she broke the silence. "Once we can get this body to the morgue, we'll need to arrange for a forensic anthropologist."

"What's that?" She had drawn him from his thoughts. "Why do we need that?"

"Because I'm not a bone expert. You need a forensic anthropologist on this case. Someone who can properly identify the victim. I know bodies. Not so much old bones. University of Michigan has a great program. Give them a call and have them send their best and brightest," she said, wiping a strand of wet hair away from her forehead. She must look a mess. "Nick, I cut my father's funeral short for this. And tomorrow I bury him. I'm taking the day off. And maybe the rest of the week." Her furrowed brow sent him the message.

"Fair enough. I'll call." He was snippy and distracted, a common defense mechanism for hiding one's true emotions.

"I know how you're feeling about this, Nick. I can't imagine the burden you've been under."

"I just know it's her."

"It might not be," she tossed back at him, then softened some. "You have the power to do something really important here, because that body belongs to someone who's been missing for a long time. Sandi or not. That's a detective win-win, right?"

"Let's get the remains to the morgue," said Nick.

This was Nick at his raw core. A practical protector. A fighter for the underdog. A relentless champion for the vulnerable. She wished she had trusted him with her secret when she was fifteen. Things might have turned out so differently if she had.

As Emily looked west to a bright-red-and-orange sky that held a sinking sun, its last light filled the woods and made the raindrops on the fall leaves glow like twinkle lights. She was kissed by a memory of something her father used to say. "No matter how grim the day, there is always beauty if you just open your eyes to it."

6

Nick and Emily safely delivered the bones to the morgue that evening. Then Nick drove Emily home, and she crept quietly into the dark house. Cathy was already long asleep. Emily trudged upstairs past a note Jo had left on the kitchen table about soup in the fridge. She drew a bath, where she soaked for an hour before collapsing into bed.

The next morning, Emily woke up with one thing, and only one thing, on her mind. Where was her mother's real autopsy file? She needed to know the details of what she had been missing all these years.

But there was no time. She had to rush to the cemetery by nine AM. They were burying her father in a private ceremony for her, Cathy, and Aunt Laura, who had come up from Chicago overnight.

* * *

After leaving the cemetery, Emily went straight to her father's empty home. Cathy was at Bishop and Schulz taking care of business the rest of the morning, leaving Emily in the house alone. She kept expecting to hear her father clacking away on his computer from the office or shuffling about in the kitchen cupboards. But it was, of course, silent.

She went into her father's office and sat at his desk. She pulled open the long center top drawer and riffled through it, looking for a small key that she hoped would open the locked file drawer on her right. Finally, she removed the drawer and dumped its contents onto the desktop. The key plinked out. Small, worn, tarnished brass. She slid it into the keyhole and turned left.

It didn't take her long to find her mother's "hidden" file. It was only two pages in length. Simply stated, with clear handwritten notes over front and back diagrams of a human figure. *Manner of death: accidental. Cause of death: transection of cervical spine at level of cervical vertebrae two due to single vehicle automobile collision.* Below that the medical examiner had noted incidental findings: *carcinoma of the pancreas.*

My mother did have cancer! How long did she have to live? Emily didn't remember her mother feeling sick or complaining about being tired. She could easily have hidden it from Emily, though. Emily had been fifteen and busy day and night with her studies and high school activities. And obviously she'd hid it from Dad, too. How had it been possible to keep such a secret?

Her father's words came back to her. There had been another woman. The details had been eating him up all these years, Emily was certain. What could have been so devastating or so embarrassing or so guilt-laden that he couldn't tell her sooner? Or maybe he had wanted to, but she'd never come back home or returned his phone calls to make amends. So much lost time.

Emily slid the death report back into the manila folder and placed it in the file. She'd started to clean up the contents of the drawer and place them in a more organized manner when the doorbell rang. She glanced out the office window, which overlooked the driveway, and saw a white, newer Ford pickup truck. It wasn't the kind she often saw farmers driving—those were rusted out, dented, their paint peeling off. This truck belonged to someone who had means and liked to show it off. She jotted down the license plate quickly. Her father had run his general medical practice and Freeport County's medical examiner's office from his home office. And death wasn't always a friendly business.

The doorbell rang again. She went to the front door and peered through the peephole. On the other side she could see a Caucasian male, about sixty, bald, dressed in jeans and blue collared button-down. He didn't look threatening or angry or anxious. He glanced down at his shoes—loafers—and then back at his truck. He rang the bell again, and Emily opened the door a crack.

"Hello, may I help you?" she said.

"Hi, Emily? I'm Hank Wurthers. Friend of your dad's," said the man, taking a step back from the door out of respect.

"I see. Something I can do for you?"

"I'm also a Freeport County commissioner. And I know this is probably poor timing and all, but in light of the body that was found at Pinetree Slopes yesterday, we need to know if you'll be taking over your father's coroner duties on this one or if we need to hire this out."

Emily opened the door and stepped out. "Oh, I see. Yes. I started working on the case yesterday with Sheriff Larson."

The coroner was an elected position. The medical examiner was a hired gun. Her father had been serving in both capacities, and for thirty-some years, the commissioners hadn't had to give it another thought. He was a one-stop death investigation shop that saved the county hundreds of thousands of dollars because they didn't have to pay for both positions separately.

"Will you be continuing in your father's duties as coroner on this case?"

"Um . . . yes. I will," said Emily, wondering what was brewing beneath all this.

"Good. For now. But we are going to open up the position for county coroner at the next board meeting. As you probably remember from working with your dad, county coroner is an elected position.

So, if you want the job, you need to throw your hat in the ring. Do you think you'll be sticking around Freeport to do that, young lady?"

"I'm not sure. When's the next meeting?"

"Three weeks."

"I know my father's passing was sudden and has put the county in a bind here. I told Sheriff Larson the county's going to need to hire a forensic anthropologist to get an ID on the victim."

"You'll have to run that expenditure through the commissioner's office."

"What? How long will that take?"

"You can submit before then, and we'll take it up at the meeting."

"There's a bagful of bones in the morgue right now that need to be identified."

"We have protocol. Third Thursday. Courthouse, room two-oh-seven. Seven PM. Until then, you're allowed to operate in the position of coroner for this case and this case alone, under probation, until we elect the right guy."

Allow? Guy? Probation? Oh, no. Dad had never had to ask permission to do his job.

"I want to hand this over to an anthropologist who can make the proper identification," said Emily. "That has to happen now."

"You can argue that with the commissioner's board in three weeks."

Emily just stared in disbelief. She couldn't decide which offended her more: his chauvinism or his ignorance. Emily wanted to slug him, but she smiled politely and stepped backward into the doorway. "Thank you for informing me."

"I'm just saying, that anthropolygist's fee is gonna come outta your pocketbook if the commissioners don't approve it."

Anthropolygist?

"My father always undercharged the county for his services. Did you know that?" Emily asked, bracing herself in the doorframe. "His rates were at least half what bigger-city medical examiners charge. And he didn't charge you extra for his elected title, either."

"He did this county a great service. He will be greatly missed."

Hank glanced over his shoulder to the driveway. "Is that your peashooter over there?"

"My car?"

"Yeah, the deathtrap. If you're planning to stay up here, you're gonna need something more rugged to get around in. Stop by the dealership. I'll set you up with a good deal."

With that, Hank stepped away and sauntered back to his truck.

Emily felt anger surge as she stayed planted by the door to watch Hank Wurthers and his fancy pickup truck pull out of the driveway. Hank would have never treated her father this way. After his white truck drove out of view, she slammed and locked the door.

Wait. What was she getting herself all worked up about? Yes, things were up in the air. True, she needed to move her things out of Brandon's new townhouse and find a new place to live. Yes, she should finish her residency. But Dad had built a legacy, one she, as a teenager, had always thought she would carry on. And now she could. Did she want to?

Stop spinning. I don't need to decide this all now.

Like she'd always told her surgical patients, it was best not to make any big decisions after a traumatic event. And oh how the past few weeks had been full of them. Her breakup with Brandon. Her dangerous foray back into death investigation. A new case on her hands. Her father's passing. And now her mother's secret to unravel.

She decided to escape it all under the cozy retreat of a down comforter.

7

Emily was wakened from a deep sleep by her phone ringing. Bleary-eyed, she pulled it out from between the couch cushions and checked the caller. It was Dr. Claiborne, the supervising doctor she had been working with in Chicago since she began her residency.

"Hello, Dr. Claiborne," she said, clearing her throat. "How are you?"

"I'm fine, Emily. But I'm quite concerned about you." His tone held genuine care, and she immediately felt soothed by the familiar sound of his voice. He had been a father figure to her during the last three years of her residency. "How are you doing? I am sorry to hear about what happened with your father. The medical community lost a great one."

"Thank you. Yes. It's been rough." She couldn't pretend with him. He would see right through it.

"I suppose you have a good deal of things to take care of now in Freeport?"

"Um, yes, I suppose I do. Although I don't think I know the half of it yet."

"Do you know when you're planning to return to Chicago?"

She paused to clear the cobwebs from her sleepy brain. "Oh, I don't really . . . have any idea. It's been a whirlwind around here. I'm still adjusting to the fact that he's gone."

"Yes. I'm sure. And . . . well, I hate to be the bearer of any more distressing news, but unfortunately I am compelled by the hospital's human resources department to remind you that you've used up your sick time and vacation days since you've been gone. Your paychecks will stop at the end of this week. Of course, you can apply for family medical leave. Up to twelve weeks."

"Okay. Yes. I could . . . I guess I'm not sure if that's enough time."

"I thought that might be the case. You realize that will put you behind in your residency. Maybe longer if you have to wait for a spot to open up."

It was a very good possibility. Dr. Claiborne's mentorship was always in high demand.

"Oh? Yes, of course." A little panic rose in Emily. She still had two years left.

"And if you're not coming back for a while, I'm going to need to fill your spot as soon as possible."

"Right."

A gnarled pit grumbled from the base of Emily's stomach. *Is that nerves? Or hunger?*

"When do you need to know?" she asked.

"The sooner the better."

Emily didn't have the brain energy to process the dilemma that had just been thrown into her path. She felt she needed more clarity about her father's estate, the secret about her mom's death, and the Pinetree Slopes case before she could answer intelligibly. Her silence prompted Dr. Claiborne to jump in with a solution.

"Emily, why don't you do this. Apply for short-term leave. That'll give you thirty days to figure this out and you won't lose your spot.

Reach out to me in a week or so after things settle and you have a better picture, and we'll go from there. Sound good?"

"Yes," she answered immediately. "You always know how to keep things simple."

Emily hung up the phone and slipped on her tennis shoes. She needed fresh air. And something to eat. She headed to her father's small orchard to search for a late-harvest treat. She had picked a few small apples and wandered back toward the front porch when Nick's squad car pulled up the drive.

He joined her, and she handed him an apple. They sat in silence, gnawing away at the crisp fruit. Emily didn't have the vigor to start a conversation, so she was grateful when Nick spoke first.

"I think I may have found an anthropologist. Dr. Charles Payton," he said. "He's available to come up day after tomorrow."

She thought the name sounded like it belonged to an older, distinguished gentleman. "He's from the University of Michigan?"

"Yeah. At first he was going to send up a grad student. But after I told him a bit more about the circumstances, he offered to do the examination himself. He's a tenured professor, and he's got a ton of credentials. Not that I understand any of them."

Emily smiled. "Great. You're getting the best, then," she said, eating her apple down to the core. "Dr. Payton will do the official autopsy and help you make an ID. Then you and one of your detectives can take it from there."

"You'll stay on this case, right?"

"There's not much I can do."

"It's not every day we find bones in the woods," he said, and Emily could read the tension and urgency in his tone. "You're good at this. I want all hands on deck for this kind of situation."

"It may not be a criminal case, Nick. It's very possible it could be Native American remains. Or an early settler who first logged those woods. They were here long before us."

"Please, Em. Just stick with me for a bit on this one?"

She studied the pleading crease forming above his brows.

"You didn't sleep a wink last night, did you?"

He shook his head.

"You believe strongly that those bones belong to Sandi Parkman, don't you?"

"I do."

"Be straight with me. Why?"

"I talked to Shirley Parkman about it." Emily didn't like the sound of involving a family member just yet, but she knew Nick could be a loose cannon when he was nervous.

"You have to keep this under wraps. What did you say?"

"I told her they were human, that we didn't know anything, and that if we discovered anything connected to Sandi's case, we would contact her."

"And of course she said, 'Thank you, Officer,' and skipped out of there?" Emily couldn't hold back on the sarcasm.

"Em, she thinks about her daughter every single day. Bones turn up in a deserted forest ten years after Sandi disappears and yeah, she's gonna be a touch curious."

Emily relented. He had a point. Who was she to judge a grieving parent's motives?

"However, I did ask Mrs. Parkman to submit a DNA sample. If those bones belong to Sandi, we're going to need to get a DNA match."

"And did she?"

"Readily. I did a buccal swab."

Talk about getting ahead of one's skis! Emily held back her comment, realizing how emotional this case was for Nick. She didn't want to make him feel bad just because he was overexerting his compassion and sense of justice. And if Shirley Parkman was willing to give up some cheek cells because it made her feel better, what harm was it? This led her mind to twist around one of Nick's comments about Sandi when they'd been digging under the tent.

"Did you tell anyone else?" she pressed.

"No, of course not." He was earnest.

"Nick, I'll help you with this case, but if these bones do turn out to be Sandi's, I need to know something right now."

"Anything."

"What's haunting you? There's no way you could have known this would happen to Sandi."

He leaned his forearms on his thighs and put his head between his hands. He drew in a long breath, and as he exhaled, he looked out across the lawn.

"James VanDerMuellen and I were on the baseball team together. Do you remember him? He would've been a senior when you were a sophomore."

"Vaguely." Her sophomore year of high school had been a blur until she had run away to Chicago late second semester to live with Aunt Laura.

"Well, Sandi had been seeing him for at least a year, maybe longer. And I got the feeling he was filming her . . . you know . . . having sex."

"You got a feeling? Nick, no one gets that as a feeling. Either you know or you don't."

"Okay . . . I heard some guys talking about it in the locker room."

"Talking about what, exactly?"

"That there were sex videos of her."

Videos? Plural? Disgusting!

"I hope you said something to someone."

Nick shook his head. "The day she disappeared, she asked for a ride home from school. I said fine. We were neighbors, and it wasn't unusual for me to drive her home. She was pretty quiet on the ride home, which I just chalked up to a bad day or the fact that her stepfather had just gotten out of prison. I felt bad for her. I always got the feeling no one was really looking out for her or her younger sister, Tiffani. I always felt like I played the role of older brother for her."

Emily nodded. She didn't recall hearing too much about the Parkman girls when she was younger and living at home. And she didn't remember Nick mentioning much about them either. But then again, she hadn't frequented Nick's part of town even when they were dating—he usually came over to her house.

"I asked her about the videos. Just, you know, did she know about them. That I had heard they were circulating the school. She acted really, really shocked."

"What do you mean?" asked Emily.

"She said she didn't know about them."

"How could she not know?"

"James is a snake!"

"Do you think she was lying?"

"It didn't seem like it. She seemed really scared and upset."

Emily couldn't move a muscle as Nick revealed his final conversation with Sandi.

"I asked her if I could do anything."

"What did she say?"

"She begged me not to do anything. She had already testified against her stepfather and put him in prison for sexual abuse. How would it look if she were caught starring in sex videos?"

"But she said she didn't know? Was she being forced?"

"I don't know. She begged me to leave it alone."

"What did you do?"

"I told her it wasn't her fault and that I would help her figure something out. When we got to her house, I pulled in and she jumped out of the car before I had even stopped it. She ran to the house and slammed the door."

"And that was the last time you saw her," Emily said in a hushed voice as Nick's regret came together in her mind.

"I sat there for a minute in my car. I thought about going to the door. But I didn't. I just backed up out of the driveway and went home. I couldn't eat. I couldn't sleep. I just wanted to help her. The next day she didn't show up for school. And then the next, and . . . then . . ."

Emily stared at Nick, not sure how to react to his confession. She had so many questions. But now was not the time to interrogate him. He was stinging from the memory.

"You've been holding this in all these years?"

Nick nodded and stood up. He shook his body in an odd little jig, like he was trying to brush off a layer of sawdust from his legs. He clapped his hands together and turned to her with a forced smile that showed Emily he was trying to ignore the images his brain was conjuring up.

"Look, we still don't know if those are her bones. But either way, I'll help you. Okay?"

"Thank you." Nick cranked his head left and right as if stretching out a sore muscle in his neck and then turned to Emily with a lighter tone. "So, hey, I didn't come here to stir up bad memories. What I really want to know is if I can I take you to dinner. You need more to eat than an apple."

"Nick, I'm really beat. I won't be much good for company."

"We don't have to talk. I just want to . . . to do something nice for you."

"Dropping by was nice," she said.

"I want to do more. Let's grab a bite."

"Look at me. I'm a mess. And I have no intentions of changing or brushing my hair," she said in her stretched out in yoga pants and sweat shirt.

"In that case, we could order in?"

"That actually sounds kinda nice. I'd love a good ramen bowl."

"Pizza or Chinese? We're still very limited here in Freeport."

"Pizza. Everything."

"Even mushrooms? You used to hate mushrooms."

"I've changed."

"Yes, you have." Nick pulled out his phone to order. "But Em, sometime when you're feeling more up to it, I'd really like to take you out."

Out? Like out-out? Was he asking to date her?

He broke into her thoughts. "I was hoping we would maybe . . ."

"Pick up where we left off?" she offered, wanting to air this out.

"No. Start over. Fresh."

"I like the sound of leaving the past in the past. But I come with a lot of baggage right now." She smiled, trying to redirect the old feelings for him that were beginning to arise.

"Twelve years is a long time. I may have racked up some baggage myself," he said with a sly look.

"I think we just unpacked a little," she said, thinking of Sandi and knowing there was probably a whole nother suitcase full of non-Sandi stuff.

"I guess we find out if you're willing to try," Nick said.

"Slowly."

"Slowly. So, Friday then. Let's head to Rock River."

Rock River was the biggest city near Freeport, an hour away, with shopping malls, several universities, a sporting arena, and a world-class symphony.

"Can we go for ramen?"

"I have no idea what that is, but as long as it's not from the sea, I'll try it."

Emily couldn't help but let out a laugh. His palette hadn't changed a bit in twelve years. Meat with a side of meat. Good ole midwestern fare. Good ole midwestern Nick. It was nice to be home.

8

Emily's body shuddered and went into a cold sweat when Gerard Blatts, her father's estate attorney, read her father's will to her the next afternoon. "What? Who?" She managed the guttural response from her clenched throat.

The attorney reread the statement. "'I leave my grandfather's watch and all my stocks and bonds to Anna Johnson.'"

"Who is Anna Johnson?"

"Your sister. Well, half sister, technically." Mr. Blatts handed her a sheet of paper with Anna's full name and address, phone, and email.

"I don't have a half sister," she said, handing it back. "I've never heard of this person in my life."

"Your father never explained the logistics of it."

"Logistics?" What an obtuse statement.

"Your father never told me who her mother was or when it happened. I don't even know how old this woman is. I literally have no other details other than that address and what she's entitled to via your father's last will and testament."

"You mean she could be younger than me?"

"Maybe. It's possible. I really don't know."

Emily's theory about her father's potential affair was spooling questions in her mind. And then it hit her. Anna was the "other woman." But had it been an affair or not? Had her father produced another offspring before he was married to Mom? Or had it happened during? Mom and Dad had been married eight years before Emily was born. She had to admit she didn't know a lot about their marriage before she'd come into the picture. It seemed odd that neither of them had ever mentioned Anna to her. Had Mom known? If Mom hadn't known about Anna, then why would Dad have kept it a secret from her?

But what if she *had* recently found out before her fatality? That coupled with her secret terminal cancer . . . Well, that was enough to put anyone over the edge—the edge of an embankment along a windy, two-lane road where she crashed to her death. A thought bolted through Emily. What if Mom's accident had actually been a suicide? A queasiness churned up in her stomach. That would explain why Dad had wanted to keep her mother's cause of death from her all these years.

"Why didn't he tell me any of this before he died?" she asked, a hollow feeling emptying her chest cavity. And then almost immediately answered herself in her head. *He tried to tell me.*

"I was instructed very clearly never to contact Ms. Johnson. That is your job."

"Me? Oh no . . ."

"Your father stated in his will that he wanted you to reach out to her. I think he hoped you two might foster a relationship down the road."

"I don't think so," she said, tension constricting her voice. "That's asking a lot. Too much."

"Are you angry about the way things have been divided? Because we could contest this will, based on—"

"Angry? No. In shock? Definitely." The will stated that Emily would retain the bulk of her father's estate. The house. Vehicle. Bank accounts. Retirement funds. Besides, even if Dad had left her nothing, she would never have asked her father for anything. She had survived estranged from him thus far. And she could survive without his estate. But confusion riveted her. Another huge enigma. How many more would she have to uncover as things went along?

"Did my father have contact with her? Did he know her?"

"I don't really know. He didn't mention any direct contact. So I'm guessing not. At least not recently."

"I don't understand. How am I supposed to just call this woman up out of the blue and tell her that I'm . . . her long-lost—This is ludicrous!" She couldn't bring herself to say *sister*. It was too strange.

"I'm sorry. I know this piece of news is hard to swallow."

"What do I do?"

"Give yourself a little time. But not too much. If you don't inform her within thirty days, I will be compelled to send a certified letter. And if that happens, I suspect you'll find her knocking on your front door shortly thereafter. So if I were you, I'd take the reins on this."

"Can you arrange a meeting for us? Maybe here. Somewhere neutral?"

Mr. Blatts shook his head. "I'm sorry, Dr. Hartford. The instructions were explicit. I am not to reach out to her."

Emily sighed and rose from the high-backed leather armchair. She paced to the window of his office that overlooked downtown Freeport. Thirty days. The last thing she wanted was legal trouble.

"Have you ever had any cases like this before?" Emily asked, hoping for his advice.

He shook his head. "Put yourself in her shoes. You've never known your biological father. You've always wondered about him. Hoped to meet him someday. How would you receive the news?"

Emily was suddenly flooded with compassion for this Anna Johnson. Here she had been, yearning for family connection all these years. Emily folded up the piece of paper and slid it into her coat pocket.

"How much is she getting from the stocks and bonds?" Emily asked, thinking about all the years Anna had been cheated out of knowing their father.

"If she sold them today . . . roughly half a million."

A thought flitted through her brain: *Is this guilt money?* She quickly dismissed it. Dad had always been a generous and fair man. He must have known enough about Anna to know she needed the money. This was her father's desire and she must respect it, even if she didn't understand it.

"There are instructions in this envelope for Anna on how to access the funds," said the attorney. "I know this is a difficult time, and I'm here if you need me."

"Thank you."

She took the envelope and left his office. As she stepped onto the main street of Freeport, suddenly it hit her. She had a sister. Maybe this wasn't a bad thing. She had always wanted a sister.

Emily pulled the paper out again and looked more closely at the address. Rock River. This whole time, her flesh and blood had been just an hour away. A sudden sadness overwhelmed her, filling her with a tangible, tight pain. Her sister would never know the amazing father, Dr. Robert Hartford, of her youth. Just as Emily would never be able to know the father of the last twelve lost years. No amount of inheritance could ever make up for that.

9

"You have a sister? Holy moly!" Nick exclaimed from the morgue sink as he shook the excess water off his hands and reached for a paper towel. Emily had asked him, once again, to please assist her by taking pictures during the autopsy examination with Dr. Charles Payton, who had yet to arrive. Nick had eagerly agreed. After his help with the Dobson autopsy, Nick knew the ropes and she didn't have to instruct him on how to angle up the camera equipment over the body.

"It's a half sister."

"How old is she?"

"I dunno. Not sure if it happened before or after he married Mom."

"Tricky. Have you called this Anna yet?"

"I'm still trying to figure out what to say."

"I wonder if she's as smart and driven as you are."

Emily appreciated the offhanded compliment. "I don't know how I feel about her. Or how to approach this."

"Meet her at a neutral place. Wait. Maybe it would be better if she came up here to see the house? You can show her photo albums of your dad, where he worked."

"Maybe. It might be a lot to take in. I have no idea how she'll react. What if she hates me?"

"That's ridiculous."

"What if she wants to sue me for more of my dad's estate? What if she's bitter and angry?"

"Stop, Em. You're spooling over nothing."

He was right. Emily pushed the fears aside. She needed to focus on the task at hand, because Dr. Payton would be arriving any moment. "Hank Wurthers told me I needed to get board approval before hiring this forensic anthropologist. What do you think about that?"

"The county commissioners are overstuffed windbags. They like to piss on territory that's not theirs. Don't mean to be crude, but I call it like I see it. Hank and his buddies on the board like to lord their so-called power. They forget they're servants of the people."

"Hank says they're putting the coroner position up for public vote. Although I can't imagine who else is going to apply who's actually more qualified than me."

"So does that mean you're staying here in Freeport?"

Emily glanced up at Nick. His face registered a glowing hope.

"I'm putting a pin in that decision." Emily finished arranging the bones on the stainless-steel table. "I got a call from Dr. Claiborne, and I'm also under some pressure to make some decisions about finishing my surgical residency. Going back to the pace, the pressure . . . just feels a bit overwhelming right now."

A knock at the door halted their conversation.

"Door's open," hollered Nick.

Emily took one look at the tall, sandy-brown-haired man entering the morgue and almost gasped out loud. He couldn't have been older than thirty-five. He had the body of a soccer player and the even, dark tan of a surfer. Lean legs in skinny jeans. Tight torso under his slim-fit white button-down with sleeves rolled into cuffs. And tall. Had she mentioned tall? He towered a good three inches over Nick. And probably four over Brandon.

"Hello. I assume I'm in the correct location. I'm Dr. Charles Payton, the forensic anthropologist from the University of Michigan."

"Pleasure to meet you. Thanks for driving all the way up," said Nick.

"Hi, I'm Emily," she said.

"Dr. Hartford, right?" he asked.

"Yes, yes . . . Dr. Emily Hartford. That's me." Why did she sound like a child answering roll call? She was suddenly and painfully aware of how untidy she must appear. Her hair covered by a net. Her thick, black rubberized apron tied loosely around her middle, doing nothing for her figure. And faded jeans that she hadn't washed in three weeks.

"I was expecting someone with crow's feet and gray hair," she joked.

He smiled at her, easing her nervousness. "Hopefully I'm still a good decade away from that."

Amazing. Those pearly whites were nearly blinding. She snapped out of her thoughts.

"My condolences on your father's recent passing." He continued reaching out his hand for hers, but instead of shaking it, he held it for a moment in a gesture of consolation.

"Thank you," she managed, before her words got choked off by that mounting lump in her throat that seemed to rise at very strange moments. The lump softened, and she could swallow it away. She held on to his warm hands and inhaled a light, earthy scent. His cologne—something organic based. After just the right amount of time, so things didn't feel awkward at all, he released his grip.

"Well then, shall we get started? Sheriff Larson prepped me on the details of where you found the remains. I'm assuming this is our person?" He moved toward the table.

"Yes, this is her," said Nick.

"Or him," corrected Dr. Payton.

Emily handed him a black apron and box of latex gloves. "Nick—Sheriff Larson—will be taking the photographs. I'm here to assist if you need anything at all." *There's that willowy kid voice again.*

"Thank you both. I'll need measuring tools and forceps," he said, moving into place at the top of the skull. "And if you wouldn't mind taking notes, it goes much faster. If you don't feel offended by that."

"No, of course not." Emily's voice jumped ahead of any judgments she might have had about being treated like a glorified secretary.

For several hours the three of them went meticulously through every centimeter and crevice of the remains. Emily was fascinated with the process and the level of detail Dr. Payton put into examining the bones. There were areas of the bones she hadn't realized had names. The science of anthropology took human anatomy to a new level for her that afternoon.

There were nine places where they collected hair remnants. Emily had, of course, noted this upon excavation, but she'd left the hairs to be collected during the official autopsy. She placed them individually in glass vials, marking them with the exact location they had been found on the skeleton. Most were found attached to minuscule skin remnants on the skull. There was one lodged under the third fingernail of the left hand.

After all the measurements and notes were recorded, Dr. Payton stepped back and removed his mask to reveal a calculating face. They all remained quiet as he processed the exam, flipping back and forth between notes and rechecking the surface of several bones. Finally, he spoke.

"The victim is Caucasian in ancestry. Probably between fifteen and nineteen years old. Height estimated around five feet.

He paused. Emily waited on pins and needles. She glanced over to Nick. The color had again washed from his face, and she knew what he was thinking. So far, this sounded like a description of Sandi Parkman.

"There is blunt-force trauma to the neck, right ribs, and skull. It's clear to me that this person was the victim of trauma resulting in homicide."

Emily had also noted that when they were retrieving the bones, but had held back from saying anything to Nick about it. She hadn't wanted to feed any worry he already held until it could be confirmed by someone who had more experience with skeletal remains.

Nick pressed against the wall of the morgue for support. "It's her. I know it."

"I'm not entirely sure this skeleton is a she."

"What? Why not?" asked Emily.

"Sex is determined by looking at size and architecture of the bone structure. For instance, the pelvis of a male is more oval shaped, while the pelvis of a female is more heart shaped. The angles are different because females give birth. And ninety-two percent of the time, males have larger bones than females."

Nick's pressed lips told Emily he was agitated by the doctor's answer.

"Well, what can you tell us now? Heart or oval?" Nick said.

"I can't say definitively without more time to measure and compare," Dr. Payton said.

"We'll be eagerly awaiting your results," said Emily.

"How long will that take?" asked Nick.

"A week or two."

"At the rate you're charging, is there any chance you can speed it up?"

Emily shot Nick a look: *Stop it.* Then she turned to the anthropologist. "Thank you, Dr. Payton. Is there anything else we can do for you before you head out?"

"I'm awfully hungry. I hear Delia Andrews runs a great bakery here. Care to join me?"

"How do you know about Delia Andrews?" Emily said with surprise. Delia was a former FBI agent and longtime friend of the

Hartford family. During Emily's impromptu death investigation just a week earlier when she had been torn from her surgical residency in Chicago to tend to her father after his first heart attack, Delia had helped Emily and Nick identify the rare tool used to kill Julie Dobson.

"I've read a lot of her papers. Her work with the FBI on tool identification is landmark. But I'm sure you know that already. I suspect she's a bit of a local celebrity."

Only for her cinnamon rolls and bear claws.

Delia had kept a low profile during her FBI years and had traveled a lot internationally during her years on duty. In retirement, Delia didn't talk about her FBI experiences. Emily assumed those cases were still classified.

Several years ago, Delia had left the FBI and slipped back into small-town life in Freeport, where she had elevated pastries to a mouthwatering, edible art form. She was definitely better known for those than for her academic articles.

"Yes, she owns Brown's Bakery. On Main Street. I can take you there," said Emily. *Did I really just offer that?* "I mean, not that you can't find it on your own. Freeport's small, and there aren't any other bakeries in town."

"I'd love for you to show me," said Dr. Payton with a look that lingered on Emily. Twitters and tingles jumped through her insides as if she were a star-struck thirteen-year-old. *What's wrong with me?*

"Then let's get this body put back to rest for safekeeping," said Emily, trying to keep it professional.

"Do you still need me, Em?" Nick said from the corner of the room as he packed up the camera equipment. Emily's eyes jumped to his. She had almost forgotten he was there.

"I think we're good here. Thanks for your help," her voice chirped at him.

"Sheriff, I was wondering if you could download those pictures and put them on a jump drive for me," said Dr. Payton.

"Make a copy for me, too," Emily added as she and Dr. Payton covered the bones with a protective tarp. She didn't mean for her request to sound condescending. "Please." But Nick snapped a glare at her.

"Just to confirm, Emily, you aren't releasing the body yet?" asked Nick.

"Of course not. We don't even know who it is," said Emily. There was that tone again.

Nick breezed by and handed her the camera with one word. "Here." Then he exited promptly.

Emily hoped Dr. Payton hadn't heard the tension between them.

Dr. Payton turned around from where he was washing his hands, shaking the water off.

"Where did Sheriff Larson go?"

"Emergency call," Emily fibbed.

"I owe you for bringing me such a fascinating case study. It's not often I get out onto the field anymore, given my teaching load and lab responsibilities."

Emily smiled and removed her apron and hairpiece. *Bringing him a case study.* Interesting choice of words. To someone in this community, these remains had once been their daughter or son. Not an academic study.

A text pinged Emily's phone. Cathy. Darn!

"Ah, hey, about that offer," she said to Dr. Payton. "I forgot I promised a good friend that I'd help her with something today." Cathy had hired a moving truck and was moving back into her apartment above the funeral home a few days sooner than planned.

"I'm sure I can find Brown's Bakery on my own," said Dr. Payton, peeling off his gloves and tossing them into the trash bin. "But I was looking forward to it. Hopefully our paths cross again soon."

Emily nodded. "Enjoy your lunch. And be sure to take some bear claws back to your department."

"Good tip. It'll keep me in their good graces."

"They'll consider you a hero," she laughed.

"Hope I don't get too used to the view atop the pedestal," he joked in return, but there wasn't a shred of pretention in his tone.

He opened the door for her, and Emily noted a twinge of disappointment forming. It might be nice to spend a little more time getting to know a forensic anthropologist, especially one this easy on the eyes.

10

"It must be strange to be back in your old house," said Emily as she lifted a box labeled *kitchen appliances* onto a countertop in Cathy Bishop's Victorian apartment above the funeral home.

"Doesn't feel right. Nothing feels right here anymore," said Cathy, exhaling as she set down a weighty box.

Emily opened bare cupboard after bare cupboard. "Where do you want the dishes? By the sink? Or maybe closer to the kitchen table?"

"It doesn't matter. I won't be here long." Cathy stopped and looked at a surprised Emily. "I'm selling the business. House and all."

Emily's mouth gaped. "You can't. It's been in your family forever."

"My heart's not in it. Your father's funeral was my last. A beautiful bookend to end a satisfying career."

"That's so sudden."

"Not as sudden as you think. Your dad and I were starting to talk retirement. This just seals the deal for me."

"What will you do?" asked Emily.

"We had been entertaining the idea of going to Arizona. And I still like that plan. I talked to Ben when he was here for your father's funeral, and he and Lily will host me for the winter. They love it there, and I think I could handle three hundred and sixty-five days of sun."

Ben was Cathy's oldest son and Lily was his wife. Ben was five years older than Emily. When her mom had passed, he'd already been a couple of years into college across the country, so they didn't know each other all that well.

"I can't see you sitting poolside every day, Cathy." Emily smiled.

"I've always wanted to take up golf. Or tennis. Or—"

"Please don't say shuffleboard."

Cathy laughed. "I was going to say aqua aerobics."

"I am trying to imagine you with a pink swim cap and a bunch of blue hairs splashing around to eighties pop."

Cathy laughed again and handed Emily a box labeled *fridge magnets*.

Emily gawked at the label. How many magnets could one fridge hold, exactly?

"Put them back into the moving truck."

"We just took them out."

"I know. But I just had a wild hair of an idea. I'm going to drive straight to Phoenix. Today!"

"Cathy, are you sure?"

"What am I waiting for?"

"This is a really big decision to make after just . . . well, you know what they say about making a big decision after . . ."

"I know. And I say it all the time to grieving family members. And yet here I am, not taking my own advice. It feels right, Em. Feels like time for a change. Especially with winter setting in soon. I don't want to be boarded up and gloomy the next six months. Your dad wouldn't have wanted that either."

Emily nodded. Come to think of it, she was facing the same plight. She was alone, too, now that Brandon and nuptials were no longer part of her future. This winter she would either be boarded up in her father's home or all alone in some gloomy studio apartment in Chicago. Neither sounded too inviting at the moment. "Are you going to list it or put out word at the mortuary school?" Emily wondered how difficult it was to sell a funeral home business.

"Hmm, mortuary schools. I hadn't thought of that. Grab a newbie grad ready to spring fresh into the field. 'Freeport, perfect place to bury the dead and raise a family.' This ad is writing itself," she said, humor lifting her voice. "Great idea, Emily."

Emily wasn't pleased that her brainstorm had helped Cathy get one step farther out of Freeport. The Bishop family had been a staple of Freeport for three generations. Why had Ben broken the chain? She wondered if Cathy felt resentment over his choice to become a software engineer at a tech company.

"Now, what's this about having a new sister? Anna something-or-other?"

"Johnson. So, I take it you didn't know?"

Cathy shook her head. "Your father never said a peep. I wish he would have. I supposed she might have liked to attend the funeral."

Emily hadn't thought of that.

"What does she look like?" asked Cathy.

"I'm not sure."

"You haven't Facebook-stalked her, huh?" Cathy asked.

"I'm not on Facebook."

"Oh, that's right. Your generation is more into Instagram."

"I'm not on any of it."

"Good for you. Waste of time. Have you tried calling her?"

"Working on it," Emily fibbed. She wondered how quickly she could change the subject.

Cathy turned to face Emily. "You need to call her. Soon."

"I'm waiting for the right words."

"The right words, huh? In these kinds of situations, it's best to be honest and clear. 'Hi, Anna. I'm your sister Emily. I have something for you from our father that I think you'll want. When do you want to meet?'"

"Ah yeah . . . something along those lines." Emily had always known a more couth Cathy, but she kind of liked this freer version.

"I'm losing my filter, dear. Probably another reason I should retire."

"You've been through a lot."

"We both have, but I get to walk away from it. You have your whole career ahead of you," said Cathy, looking out the open kitchen door into the driveway. "I assume you'll be heading back to Chicago. So, it looks like with your father's death, both his legacy and mine are coming to a close."

"I haven't decided." Emily followed her gaze to where the moving truck stood open, stacked floor to ceiling with boxes and furniture. Thank goodness they hadn't unloaded all of that before Cathy made her declaration to skip town.

"If you leave now, who's going to take care of the funeral arrangements while you're waiting on someone else to buy the business?" Bishop and Schulz was the only funeral parlor in Freeport.

"I've got a friend who owns a mortuary association in Rock River who might be able to cover," Cathy said, heading out the door with a box to reload into the moving truck. Emily trudged after her with the magnets.

"I'm gonna give Ben and Lily a call right now and tell them I'm on my way." Cathy tucked the box securely between two taller ones and wandered back into the house, her cell phone pressed to her ear.

Emily crawled into the back of the truck and found the perfect crevice to nestle the precious magnet collection into where it wouldn't get smashed. She scanned the boxes of Cathy's belongings.

The world she had grown up with was shifting fast, right out from under her. She knew her father would have supported Cathy's decision. He would have wanted her to be happy.

Just as Emily was about to jump from the back of the moving truck, her phone rang from the pocket of her jeans. The screen said *No Caller ID*, but curiosity prompted her to pick it up.

"Hello?"

"Hi? Is this Dr. Emily Hartford?"

"Yes, this is she," she answered in a professional voice. "How may I help you?" Was this one of her patients in Chicago? She tried to place the voice. It was female. Sweet. And a bit apprehensive. In fact, the voice sounded a bit like . . . her own.

"This is Anna Johnson."

Emily's throat went to her gut.

"I'm your . . . your dad was my . . . this is so strange. I don't really know how to put this."

"I do," Emily spit out. "You're my sister."

11

Two days later, Emily slid a watch box across the café table to Anna, who was more petite than Emily and had her long auburn bob smoothed into place.

"He wanted you to have this," she said, lifting her fingers off the box and folding her hands in her lap.

Anna's wardrobe was straight from Bloomingdale's. A Chanel bag hung from her chair. She crossed her legs so that one of her cropped leather boots stuck out from under the table. Emily felt awkward and tomboyish in her fleece sweat shirt and jeans next to her sophisticated—and clearly older—sister.

Anna took the box with her taupe gel-painted nails and turned it around in her hands for a moment. She jiggled open the box and looked inside.

"It was his father's. Our grandfather's. He got it in Germany during the war. I guess I've often wondered if maybe he stole it from a German soldier." She released a nervous laugh.

Anna smiled at the contents. "It's quite lovely. A beautiful token. But I don't feel very attached to it. Are you sure you wouldn't rather have it?"

"It's not mine to have," said Emily. "Neither is this." Emily handed her a white envelope that held Anna's inheritance.

Anna gave her a quizzical look as she unfolded the papers. She skimmed over them, but her face registered the same expression. "Sorry, I'm not really sure what I'm reading here."

"Oh, well, it's my—our—father's stock portfolio. He willed it to you," said Emily, looking for Anna's reaction. "His attorney told me it's worth about half a million dollars."

"Oh. My." The papers slipped from Anna's hands, and her eyes grew wide. "It's . . . I didn't even know the man."

Emily wasn't sure what to say. She actually felt the same and had struggled to quell the resentment that kept surfacing.

Anna slid the paper back across the table to Emily. "You must feel really resentful about this. I can't . . . I can't be the cause of that."

"I don't. I'm not," said Emily. "Legally it's yours. I can't take it back."

"We don't need the money."

Clearly! Emily caught a glimpse of Anna's three-carat diamond wedding ring that matched the one-carat studs in each ear lobe. She slipped the envelope back toward Anna and laid her own thread-worn wallet between them so Anna couldn't slide it back.

"I wonder . . . is it guilt money? For never showing up that day."

"What do you mean?"

"Did you know your father and I had been communicating for about a year before your mother died? I searched him out when I was twenty-three. I was newly pregnant with Flora, my oldest, and I was feeling those strong maternal feelings and was desperate to know more about my biological parents. I was placed for adoption when I was a baby."

"How did you find them?" Emily did the math. Anna was thirty-five years old, which meant their father would have been about seventeen when Anna was born. That was a lot of responsibility for a senior in high school. Emily could understand how her father could have reached the decision to place his own flesh and blood with adoptive parents. Years later, though, it must have haunted him. Dad loved kids, and he and Emily's mother had always wanted more. But they weren't able.

"I talked to the adoption agency first. They rejected my request because it was a closed adoption. So I did one of those online DNA tests. And the results pulled up my mother's name. Apparently she had done one, too, which is why it was in the database."

Emily detested how few secrets there were in this world anymore. Everyone's personal business was on display for anyone to discover at the click of a mouse. This was exactly why she shunned social media. And she would continue to protect as much of her privacy as she could.

"When I contacted my bio mom, she was actually elated. Even though she had a wonderful life, husband, more kids, she had always thought about me and wished she had chosen an open adoption. But it was a different time and she wanted to move on in life with no strings attached."

"Was she the one who told you about Dad, then?" asked Emily.

"She did. My mom's name was Angela," Anna replied.

"Was?"

"Yes. She passed away about five years ago from a stroke."

"Oh, I'm terribly sorry." *Could life have doled out any more grief for this poor soul?* Any doubt, worry, or resentment she had been holding on to about her half sister melted away. Anna's lot had been a hard one, but from her upbeat tone and bright expression, she had found a way to make lemonade from lemons. Emily liked this survivor attitude. It seemed in many ways they were cut from the same cloth.

"Angela and Robert were a summer fling," said Anna. Emily found it strange that she referred to her parents by their first names. But then, they were just another set of people to her, not the mom and dad who'd raised her. "They met when their families were staying at a resort on Mackinac Island. After the summer, Angela went back to their home in New York City and Robert went back to . . . where was he from, again? I don't even remember anymore."

"He and his family were from Chicago," Emily offered. "My grandparents have both passed, but Dad's sister, Laura Hartford Pennington, still lives in the city."

"Well, when Angela found out she was pregnant at the beginning of her sophomore year, she didn't tell Robert at first. Then, after a couple weeks, she called him and told him about the baby but that her parents had made her have an abortion."

"Oh my goodness!"

"You can imagine how shocked Robert was when I showed up in his life two decades later claiming to be his daughter."

"I'm guessing he didn't believe you," said Emily, knowing her father's penchant for investigation.

Anna laughed. "No. He did not. He insisted on paternity testing. Which I happily agreed to. I sent him my DNA results. A couple months later he reached out with the results to his test, and it confirmed that we were a match. He agreed to meet me one spring morning for breakfast after I dropped my girls off at school."

"Your girls?"

"Yes, I have two now. Flora, twelve. And Fiona, eight."

I have two nieces!

Emily nodded. This whole thing had been going on behind her and her mom's backs. Both of them going about their daily business, school, activities, meals. Neither aware that a whole melodrama was unfolding beneath them. One that would have disrupted their perfect little trio forever. And perhaps in the nicest way. She couldn't imagine her mother would have been upset about a child created years before she'd ever met Emily's father. She knew Mom would have welcomed Anna into their family.

"What happened when you met?" Emily asked.

"We never did." A sadness overshadowed Anna. "He got called to your mother's accident before our meeting. And he never showed up."

"How . . . how do you know that?" Emily's emotions took a swift kick to the gut.

"I did a little investigation of my own. I tracked the obituaries in your hometown paper. I knew he investigated deaths and I thought I'd be able to piece it together. Your mother's death was the only one listed in the next week's paper. I never heard from him after we scheduled that meeting. I didn't want to reach out because I knew he hadn't told you. Or your mother. I had to respect that."

Emily struggled to comprehend what was happening. The morning her mother had died. The blue slippers she was wearing at the scene. She had rushed from the house so quickly she hadn't even bothered to slip on her shoes. She must have suspected something was amiss. She was following him. Spying on him.

"Where were you and my fath—our father—supposed to meet that morning?" Emily asked.

"The Rose Café." Emily knew the location well. It was halfway between Freeport and Rock River. A tidy shack along the main highway that served home-cooked breakfasts and lunches, recipes passed down from Great-Grandma Rose, who had lived in the shack a hundred and fifty years ago, feeding loggers who worked to clear the forests that provided lumber for Chicago's big boom after the great fire.

What's more, Mom's accident had happened less than a mile from Rose's Café. Which meant . . . there hadn't been a deer in the road like the police had stated in their official report. Mom had been majorly distracted. In her distraught state of mind, she had made the most common driver mistake.

"Emily, are you okay?" Emily's eyes traveled from her lap to Anna's eyes. She realized she had been quiet for a long moment. She felt cold from the inside to the exterior of her skin and through her scalp.

"I think my mother knew about you," she said in almost a whisper. "I think she thought you were his . . . that he was having an affair."

"An affair? What would give her that idea?"

"She rushed from the house that morning with her slippers on. She was . . . I'm guessing she felt desperate because she believed her husband was cheating on her. And she hadn't told him about the cancer."

"Your mother had cancer?"

"I only recently learned this myself," Emily said.

"But the paper said she died in a vehicle fatality."

"She did. It came up during the autopsy and my father hid it."

Anna took a sharp inhale. "I don't know what to say. I feel like this is all my fault." Her voice started to stutter as if she were holding back emotion. She sipped in little gasps of air.

"It's not your fault, Anna," said Emily. There were so many secrets. So many misunderstandings. So many lost years. It was all a huge, mistaken tragedy. She looked up and saw Anna's soft, loving eyes looking back at hers, baring their own measure of guilt and sorrow. Here they sat, sisters, together over coffee. Trying to make sense of family mistakes, unspoken hurts, and hidden mysteries.

"I am sorry," Anna said. "I've always wondered about you. And I've always wanted to meet you."

"Why didn't you . . . I mean, reach out again after mom's death?" Emily asked.

"I was waiting for Robert to make the first move. I didn't really know what would be the best timing. Then Flora was born, and my whole life changed. A few years later, Fiona came along. I guess life just . . . it's not that I didn't want to know you and Robert, but the more time passed, the more I figured he had changed his mind. That he didn't want to know me anymore."

"I won't pretend to know what you've been through—"

"What we've both been through," Anna interrupted. "I understand if you never want to see me again." She gathered her Chanel bag.

Emily looked at the stock certificate lying on the table between them. There was a lot to process from their conversation. But one thing was obvious—nothing Anna had done in this drama was her fault. She was just as much a victim of circumstances as Emily was. Perhaps they could build something from the ashes of their charred pasts.

"Please, stay. Our food should be arriving any second," she said, not wanting the meeting to end. "I would love to hear more about my nieces."

12

Emily left her meeting with Anna brimming with emotion. She couldn't go home to that empty house. She had to talk to someone she trusted. Cathy was on the road and not answering her phone. Jo texted that she was midshift and couldn't talk.

Emily called Delia. And within ten minutes she was at her doorstep being swept in with a tight hug. Delia led her to the kitchen, where a plate of homemade turkey and baked potato was waiting for her. Over their leisurely comfort meal, Emily relayed every single detail of her talk with Anna and her hypothesis about her mother's death.

"So what do you think? Does it make sense?"

"Sadly, it does, doll," said Delia, starting a kettle for tea. "The one thing I don't understand is why your father held this back from you all these years."

"I know. It would have made things between us . . . resolvable. We could have avoided all those lost years when I was in Chicago."

"Your dad was under an immense burden of guilt himself. People do unimaginable things when they're torturing themselves with it. He knew how much you loved your mother. It can be hard to get out from under. But please try. He loved you very much. The emotional distance between you two never changed that."

Emily knew she was right. She'd run away from home because she was in pain. How much pain had that added to her father?

"I'm going to try to stop guessing and guilting," Emily stated. "I know it'll never serve me. From this moment on, I'm going to embrace the good things in my life. My last few days with my father and Anna are two of those."

Emily believed she could actually feel a shift in her being. Delia smiled at her as the kettle screamed from the stovetop.

"Believe me, love, that is the best decision you could have made. The whole world is going to look different to you now that you're out from under the shroud of the past." She turned down the gas dial and poured two mugs of hot water. "Isn't it lovely that you've been given a second chance at family? I only wish your father could have lived long enough to enjoy both of his daughters . . . and granddaughters."

She saw the tears well up in Delia's eyes, which caused a wellspring in her own. They both shed a few tears as they sipped their after-dinner mugs of tea.

"I hear you entertained a fan recently?" said Emily, wiping under her eyes with her napkin, eager to change topics.

"A fan?"

"Dr. Charles Payton?"

"Oh yes, he cleared me out of bear claws."

Emily laughed. "That's not what I meant."

"I'm surprised anyone's still reading my crusty old papers," said Delia.

"Don't be modest. You could write the textbook on tool marks. Hey, maybe you should. Good winter project."

"Funny, Dr. Payton suggested the same thing. Did you two talk about this?"

"No."

"I'll admit it felt nice to be flattered, even though I do believe his motive is purely to pry."

"What do you mean?"

"He was asking about some prior classified cases, but I sent him home without any supper."

"Do you think he's harmless?"

"He's hungry."

"For what?"

"For his breakthrough case. The one that will earn him international acclaim and engagements."

Emily nodded. Nothing was ever veiled from Delia.

"And he's hungry for you."

"Ridiculous." Emily dunked her green-tea bag back into her mug and poured more hot water over it.

"He wanted to know about you growing up here. What you were like as a kid. Did you always have an interest in forensics."

"That sounds like small talk."

"And if you were seeing anyone."

"He asked you *that*?"

"In so many words."

Emily plunked her tea bag into a bowl Delia had set between them.

"I may have told him you were single. Again."

"Delia! Now is not the time."

"Now is *exactly* the time. Get out there, doll. No one's asking you to marry the guy."

"I thought you wanted me to get together with Nick." Delia had almost pushed them together during their first murder investigation. Had she misread Delia's intentions?

"Nick's great. So's Charles. Play the field a little before you lock it down." So, Delia was on a first-name basis now with Dr. Payton? He must really have charmed her, because she was usually more formal about professional names. "You've been through a lot lately. It's okay to sprinkle in an ounce of fun between all the worry. I speak as someone with dating regrets."

Delia with dating regrets? She had never married. And to Emily's knowledge, never come close. "I want to change the subject and talk about that," Emily suggested with a wry smile.

"No, no, doll. Not tonight. Not over tea and the heavy surprises of your day. That is a conversation best served over a couple good cold brews."

Fair enough. Emily was so glad she had stopped by. Talking to Delia over the past few hours had lightened her spirit and calmed her worries. As the minutes had ticked by, she'd been grateful she didn't have to sit alone in her father's—well, now *her*—big home. She looked at the clock. It was nearly eleven PM. She yawned, realizing how thoroughly exhausting the day had been.

"I was thinking today about those bones found in Pinetree Slopes," said Delia, reheating her tea with the kettle. "I'm aware that there is chatter going around about them belonging to Sandi Parkman. But I remember an incident a few years back now. Maybe eight or nine. There was a boy, I think about fourteen years old, who went out hunting with his dad in that same area and never came home."

"There was? What happened?"

"They never found his body. His father claimed he had left the boy to run into town to get something for them to eat, and when he got back to the site, the boy was gone. The police were called out. This was right before Nick became an officer. I think he was probably still a cadet in training. But they couldn't find anything. No evidence of him being taken or killed. He just vanished. Like that."

"And the parents? The family? What did they do?"

"The mom moved with the little brother shortly after the incident. Rumor was that she was too distraught to continue living in Freeport. I heard they divorced about six months later."

"And he never showed up."

"Never."

"Was the father a suspect?"

"For a short time, because he was the last person to have seen the boy."

"Was there legitimate motive?"

"Who's to say? Rumors flowed that he had accidentally shot the boy and then disposed of his body out of fear and shame."

"There were gunshots heard?"

"Of course. But it was hunting season. Everyone and their cousin's brother's best friend's neighbor had a blind in those woods. But there were records of him buying food at the market during the time he said he was in town."

"He had an alibi. That complicates things," said Emily.

"People can fudge an alibi. Or perhaps he created one after he shot the boy?"

Emily nodded. This certainly put a new wrinkle into the case. She would bring it up to Nick and have him look into the boy's file.

"I just mention it because, well, no one else has. And it would do no good to start a witch hunt for the wrong witch."

"Thank you. You always know how to keep things in perspective," Emily told her. Knowing the sex of the remains would be crucial now in pointing them in the right direction. And, of course, the DNA results would be the capstone. Until then, there was no use speculating too much.

Emily took her last sip of tea as an image of Dr. Payton's infectious smile drifted to the forefront of her mind and that twitter and tingle returned. His interest in her had captured her curiosity.

13

After three days of being cooped up in her father's house taking care of estate stuff, Emily was ready to get out of Freeport for a little while. Nick was coming over to drive them to Rock River for ramen. Date night, he had called it over the phone to confirm. Emily had quickly tamped down his rhetoric with her own term—dinner with a friend. It was way too early to start putting labels on any future relationships. She still felt the sting of her recent breakup with Brandon.

Nick pulled up and Emily dashed out the front door. When she got into Nick's car, he immediately handed her a jump drive. "Here. Before I forget. I've been meaning to drop these off. Pictures from the autopsy," he said. She took the drive and slipped it into her purse.

"Thank you. Did you send a set to Dr. Payton, too?" she asked, sliding her seat belt across her lap.

"Oh, him. Nah."

She shot him a look.

"Of course I sent them." He grinned. "But please tell me you can see right through his tactics."

"Tactics? Come on, Nick. You make him sound villainous."

"He's a career climber and he's using you and this case to get to the next rung."

"You're just jealous."

"He's using Delia, too."

"That's what Delia said. In so many words."

"I think he thinks that if he can get on Delia's good side, then she'll do something for him. Professionally speaking."

"Don't worry about Delia. She's wise to that. And so am I."

"Are you?"

Emily shrugged off his comment and turned her focus outside, where late-October leaves blanketed lawns in red-yellow-and-orange mosaics. The early-setting sun was cresting over the browning corn and wheat fields. Farmers were bringing in their last harvest. Frost was forecasted tonight.

"If Delia gives him a good word, he'll get a huge feather in his academic cap. There's nothing wrong with that," Emily said after mulling it over.

"He's already full professor at U of M. Why does he need another feather?"

"It's a competitive field filled with competitive intellects." Emily eased back into the passenger seat. But what would Nick know about that? He had chosen a sleepy sheriff's life in a place where rising up the ranks required minimum friction. Emily's mind drifted to the long ramen noodles and hot broth she would soon be slurping down. So soothing. A taste of Sunday study nights in Chicago.

"I can prove he's using you and Delia." Nick's tone was challenging, and she knew he wouldn't let it go until he made his point. "First point of proof. Motive. He wants department chair status before forty," said Nick.

"How can you prove that?"

"He's already achieved tenure, which usually takes professors half a life-time. He needs widespread acclaim to seal the chair deal."

"Like I said, he's ambitious. So's everyone else in his field."

"If he can get Delia on board with an endorsement, bam-o. The golden ticket."

"Ticket to where, exactly?" she said with a tired sigh.

"To . . . speaking engagements . . . grants . . . book deals! Knighthood!"

Emily let out a laugh. "I am genuinely entertained by your fabrications," she said.

"Mark my words. He's coming on hot and fast. Like a wildfire. And he's going to burn right through you. Pull the pin on that extinguisher and get ready."

Emily had known a ton of doctors just like him in med school. He was one of those guys who puffed their feathers out like a peacock at first to get you to look at them. And then once you did, they backed down and turned sweet and soft and even a little insecure.

"Second point of proof. Opportunity—"

"Oh, we're still doing this?" Emily grinned.

"I'm just getting started."

His playful tone relaxed Emily. She was starting to like this game.

"He was totally playing you to meet Delia. He could have sent one of his students or assistants. No. He came up here himself."

Emily's attention drifted from images of peacocks back into the middle of Nick's ongoing diatribe.

"Third point of proof. Means. He already knew Delia owned a bakery. He wanted you to suggest it so he could tell Delia you sent him there."

"How can you know he would know that I would suggest Delia's bakery?"

"Em, come on. It's the only decent café in town."

"Delia didn't seem bothered by his assertive questioning. She loved the attention," said Emily.

"Fourth proof! See! He's got her mesmerized by his charm, too!"

"That one I'll give you. She calls him Charles!" And they both laughed. "But for your information, she sees right through him."

"Aha! Corroborating testimony!"

"When are you planning to make the arrest, Sheriff?"

"Besides, I think he knew back at the morgue if that skeleton was male or female and he's just stringing us along," said Nick.

"I disagree. I couldn't tell either from just looking. It can be challenging to differentiate when the skeleton is not fully grown into their adult frame. Was Sandi tiny?"

"Yeah, she was petite."

"How petite?"

"I dunno, five foot? People were always surprised to learn she was in high school because she looked like she was in junior high."

"There you go. Her pelvic structure might have looked more kidlike. Not that I'm suggesting those bones are hers. I'm just saying. I don't think he was pulling one over on us."

Emily's hunger was taking over her interest in Dr. Payton's witch hunt. She didn't see him as a threat. He was a brilliant scientist and they needed him to help identify the Pinetree Slope bones. He would do just that.

"Okay, Sherlock, let me throw this wrench in your case theory. Delia told me about a fourteen-year-old boy who went missing in that same area at hunting season about eight or nine years ago. They never found him or a body."

"I'm a step ahead of you, I got a few tips on the hotline about that," said Nick.

"What'd you find out?"

"I looked up his file. Eddy Morton is the boy's name. I'm planning to do a search on the national missing-persons database to see if there has been anything new, maybe from another state. You never know. Sometimes these kids pop up later."

"See. Those bones could be Eddy's," said Emily. "That's why we want Dr. Payton to be extra careful here."

Which would be better—finding out that the bones are Sandi's or Eddy's? It was horrible to think about either one. A real *Sophie's*

Choice scenario. She looked over at Nick. He was signaling and glancing in his mirrors to enter the freeway. She waited to speak until Nick was safely in the far-left lane to continue.

"Did the police ever talk to you about Sandi's disappearance?" she ventured.

"Of course," said Nick, eyes glued to the road.

"And what was the outcome?"

"I mean, I told them basically what I told you. I said she was really upset about those alleged videos and that she wouldn't talk to me."

"And they let you off? I mean, you said you were the last person she saw."

"They held me overnight. They grilled me about our relationship. About my alibi. My parents hired an attorney, and somehow it all got worked out by morning."

"What was your alibi?"

"I went right home after I dropped Sandi off, and I hung out till my parents got back from work. Maybe around six thirty."

"What were you doing at home during that time?"

"A number of things, probably. Homework, TV, shooting hoops."

"Probably?"

"I don't have a clear recollection of that afternoon."

Emily didn't get it. To this day, she could recall everything she had done the morning of her mother's accident. When she'd gotten up—6:05 AM. What she'd been wearing—jeans and a short-sleeve sweater and her favorite tan leather ballet flats. What she'd had for breakfast—half a bagel and orange juice. How she'd gotten to school—bus. Her first class of the day—geometry. Who'd been sitting in front of her—her best friend, Jo. When she'd gotten called to the principal's office to get the news—11:20 AM, between third and fourth periods.

Emily looked up as they approached an overhead street sign. "That's your exit. McClintock Street. Two miles."

Nick started to maneuver the car, a lane at a time, across four lanes of traffic.

She could see why the police couldn't have made any arrests at the time without any physical evidence of the video or witness testimony. But Nick had been told there was a video. Where had the breakdown been in the evidence-recovery process with the police? Had they searched James's house? Sandi's house? Lockers? Computers? Phones? Or had it just suddenly vanished?

"Do you really think those videos existed?" Emily asked. "Or is it like when guys brag that they went to third base with a girl and then it comes out later from the girl that he was too chicken to even try and kiss her?"

"Who knows? I think so, based on how Sandi reacted when I brought it up. But everyone who knew about the video lied to the cops about its existence," said Nick. "Guys are apes sometimes."

"That's your excuse?" Her wounding shot caused him to fall silent.

"Me included. I should have said something right away."

Nick gripped both hands on the wheel and clenched his jaw. And drove.

More and more and more silence flooded between them. Overflowing buckets of silence pouring out and filling the car until neither could move through the thickness.

Silence. The greatest sin of omission.

Emily was almost choking from it until Nick's voice plumbed an air hole into the deep silence.

"I don't have an excuse, Em. I left senior year ridden with guilt and regret." The pressure valve opened; the silence released with a swoosh. "The only way I could deal with it was to get my badge. I thought it would make me feel more in control. But every year that has passed, I'm just more imprisoned with guilt. I stuff it down, but it gurgles back up like rotting sewage."

"We still don't even know if those bones are Sandi's."

"At this point, it'll be worse for me if they're not," said Nick.

Point taken. Sandi or no Sandi, Nick needed to win this battle.

"Let's take a look at the timeline again. School got out at three. Sandi asked you for a ride. And then you dropped Sandi off . . . when?"

"Probably close to four. But before that we both kinda lingered with friends after school, and then I drove her to McDonald's to get a Coke before I took her home."

One thing that seemed unanswerable was what had happened to Sandi between four and six. Had she left with someone else after Nick dropped her off? Had someone else come to the house? Who else had known about the videos? And how exactly were they tied to her death, if at all?

"He's been out there all this time. Living like nothing ever happened." Nick's voice grew tight.

"Who?"

"James." Nick said.

"You think he killed her? Why?"

"Maybe the fact that he got the heck outta Freeport as soon as he graduated and he's never been back."

"I know someone else who got the heck outta Dodge," Emily reminded him, trying to lighten his mood. "People have their reasons. Doesn't mean murder's behind it."

"I just got the feeling there was something shady there," said Nick.

"Fair enough. But what about the facts? Did James have an alibi for that afternoon?" Emily asked.

"He said he went home after school. Even his folks testified. His mom said he came home around four. His dad said they all ate dinner together about six thirty, and then James left for a friend's house to do homework a little after eight."

"And you don't believe that?"

"His parents both worked. How would they know if their son was home after school?"

"What would be James' motive?" Emily asked.

"That's why it's been a mystery for ten years, Em." He launched a missile of frustration at her.

"Didn't you say she was on the outs with her stepdad?"

"She basically put him in jail."

"That sounds like motive to me." Emily rubbed her growling belly as they exited the freeway. "We're not going to solve this tonight. Let's focus on ramen. Since this is your first time, lemme explain how it works."

"How it works? Uh-oh. Sounds complicated. You sure I'm gonna like this?"

"I'm not sure at all. But you asked what I wanted to eat." She grinned.

Nick feigned a nervous look.

"Hey, it's just broth, noodles, meat, and veggies. Simple."

Nick sailed through the green light at the end of the exit ramp and turned left.

"Okay, should be about two blocks up on the left. They have a parking lot in the back," Emily said. "You choose your broth, meat, and veggies. You can also get an egg or tofu." He made a face at the suggestion. That wasn't going to happen. "All of the ramen dishes come in a big bowl. Like a soup."

"We drove all this way for a bowl of soup?"

"Well, kinda. I mean, it's hearty. You eat it with a wide-mouthed flat spoon."

"Isn't that an oxymoron?"

"You'll see what I mean. You need a flat spoon so you can scoop up the noodles and meat. And don't worry about slurping or food hanging out of your mouth. That's all part of it."

"Sounds very romantic."

Emily laughed, and her eye caught the name of the restaurant painted on a red awning. "Oh, there. It's right over there with the little tables outside. How cute! It's not too cold to sit outside, is it? In Chicago, Brandon and I always love to eat outside. There was this one café that kept heaters on outdoors through Christmas so you could—" She stopped, realizing her blunder in bringing up the ex. "Sorry."

"No, no. It's okay. I mean, it's pretty recent history. I can't expect you to just forget it. It's a part of who you were . . . or are. But it would be helpful to know where you stand with Brandon."

She could tell he was trying to keep it light. But she knew it'd been bothering him since Brandon showed up at the funeral unannounced and proclaimed his undying devotion with the most inappropriate timing in the world. It was so unlike him to be that incongruous that Emily knew he was truly, truly serious about them getting back together.

"We broke off the engagement."

"Yes, but then he showed up at the funeral home drooling all over you. Didn't look over to me."

"I'm going back to Chicago soon to see what I can work out with my residency status and pack up my stuff. I told Brandon that we'd grab a bite and we'll talk about what happened at the funeral home."

"Does that mean you're moving back to Freeport permanently?"

"Don't read into that."

"If you go back to Chicago, will you guys get back together?"

"I don't know." She was weary of the third degree.

"On a scale of one to ten, ten being most likely, where do you think you would place your answer right now?"

"Nick. Enough."

They were now parked outside the ramen house, and patrons were streaming past on their way to the brothy goodness inside.

"Must be really good if all these people are here," Emily commented into the uneasy silence between them. "Glad we made reservations."

"Em, I'm just going to put this out there. I know this isn't supposed to be a date or anything, but I want to keep seeing you. Like, officially," Nick blurted out.

Whoa. Too much. Too soon. Too strong. Now she was just plain hangry. "Let's just eat some ramen. Please?" She swept him with a broad smile and got out of the car.

14

The next morning, Emily was in her father's office, tasked with organizing a mountain of paperwork and weighing the pros and cons of selling or shutting down her father's medical practice, which he ran alongside the medical examiner's business. Pro: Shutting it down would be way less work for her. Con: The people of Freeport needed all the doctors they could get. When her father was alive, he'd been one of eight full-time practicing physicians for a county population of ten thousand. One less in town and everyone would be feeling the difference.

Pro: If she sold it, she could reap the profits and pay off medical school loans. Con: It might take a while to find the right fit. Idea: She could quit residency and immediately take over her dad's practice.

Her phone buzzed with a text from Brandon.

When r u coming back?

That was Brandon. Direct and to the point.

She texted back: *Not sure.*

He replied: *Haven't cancelled Palmer House yet.* Their wedding venue.

Her: *That's only 2 months away. You have high hopes.*

Him: *We could always elope. How does Grand Caymans sound for Christmas?*

This was a very out-of-the-box suggestion for someone who loved spending money on experiences and events.

Her: *Cancel Palmer. Get your money back.*

Him: *Does this mean Cayman's a go?*

Her: *Let's talk this over face-to-face.*

Him: *So . . . when r u coming.*

He would be relentless until she gave him an answer.

Her: *Maybe next weekend?*

Him: *Can't wait. Securing dinner reservations. TTYL.*

And just like that, he was offline. Totally engaged one second, completely MIA the next. That pretty much described their dating life. When he was there, it was magical. And when he was gone, it felt . . . hollow.

She sighed, took a sip of her now-lukewarm coffee, and went to check her emails. One from Nick had the subject line *Morton Boy Not It.* Uh-oh. What had he found? She clicked the link Nick had attached. Up popped a recent police report from Coral Gables, Florida, about Eddy Morton—or rather Gabriel Dade, his pseudonym. The report stated that his mom had convinced a distant cousin to "kidnap" her son during the hunting outing and hide him away with a family from the cousin's church in Florida until she could safely relocate, because the boy's father had been beating them for years. The mother was afraid that if she reported it to the police, the state would take her son away or her husband would find a way to kill her and the boy before justice could be administered. Mom and son had it all worked out. On the morning of the hunt, fourteen-year-old Eddy purposefully forgot to bring their cooler of food, sending the father into town for something to eat. Meanwhile, the cousin showed up to take Eddy away without a trace. Mom spent the next six months playing the elaborate role of grieving parent until she could safely get out of there. Emily wondered how many beatings she had to survive during that time.

Then, Mom cooked up her own little witness protection plan. Brilliant. They were discovered only when Eddy went to register to vote four years later and conflicting identification documents started to churn up. A gracious judge allowed Gabriel to give up his lie and become Eddy again. For the price of community service, he'd avoided jail time. And as it turned out, his dad had continued down a bad path and overdosed three years earlier, so Mom and son did not have to live in fear any longer. While the story was tragic, it meant that the bones found at Pinetree Slope were not Eddy's.

Emily clicked out of her email when her phone rang. There was that number from lower east Michigan. This time she recognized it and a little zing pinged up her spine.

"Dr. Payton?" she said, standing up to stretch and holding in a yawn.

"Dr. Hartford. So good to hear your voice," he said.

"Likewise."

"I'm calling about the Pinetree Slopes remains. I have some more information for you. Is now a good time?"

She was still dressed in her pj bottoms, sweatshirt, no bra. Hair wound into a messy bun on the top of her head. She hadn't even bothered to wash her face this morning. After this call, she would jump in the shower and then try to get through at least one more of her father's file drawers before noon.

"Now's great."

"Wonderful. I can deliver them in person if you come let me in. I'm at the front door."

What? He's here? Emily glanced out the large windows of her father's office. Sure enough, there was Dr. Charles Payton waving at her from the driveway. She ducked out of sight.

"Sorry, didn't mean to catch you off guard," he said apologetically. "Cute jams, by the way."

Had he just complimented her on her pajamas? *Aaaagh!*

"Bonus of working from home," she covered.

"Sorry I caught you unprepared."

Yup. Exactly. He was the kind of person who asked forgiveness instead of permission.

"Give me just a minute?"

* * *

A face wash, fresh jeans, and a hair brushing later, Emily and Dr. Payton sat on opposite couches in her father's office. Between them on the coffee table Emily had cleared of books and manila folders, Dr. Payton opened a large trifolded paper. On it was a blown-up photographed image of the skeletal remains from Pinetree Slopes.

"We prepare this with all our cases so we can clearly demonstrate our discoveries to victims' families, detectives, attorney, juries, judges. It becomes very important once it goes to trial. And I'm guessing it will."

Emily found his swagger slightly attractive. She liked a man who was clever and down to earth . . . and prepared.

"Were you able to identify the sex of the bones?" asked Emily.

"I was. But with some difficultly. And it was impossible with the naked eye. That's why I blew up the images for you. Let me explain what you're looking at. One way we determine this is by the size of the pelvic girdle. Which can be tricky, because before pubescence, the male and female pelvis can be hard to differentiate. But I was able to identify the starting formation of a heart shape and a ventral arc."

"Ventral arc?" asked Emily.

"The ventral arc is a slightly raised ridge of bone across the inferior and lateral central surface of the pubis and joins with the medial border of the ischiopubic ramus. And we only see this in females." He traced the shape of the blown-up image on the x-ray with the tip of his pen cap.

"The victim is a she?"

"Yes. And based on the epiphysis in the long bones, which is not quite fused in this victim, I believe she is between twelve and fifteen years old."

"How do you know that for sure?"

"Fusion is completed as we grow into adulthood. Usually after age eighteen."

Emily nodded. "You're sure?"

"I am. But if that's not enough to convince you, you can use the victim's DNA results and see if they match the sample Mrs. Parkman supplied."

"Do you know the status of that sample?"

"It's in the queue at our lab."

Emily nodded. More wait-and-see.

"One more thing that I noted. I'm sure you already noted this, but there's periosteal trauma to the vertebrae in the neck and the hyoid bone," said Dr. Payton.

"Confirming she was choked."

"Yes. Asphyxiated. A horrible way to die," said Dr. Payton with a sigh. He pointed to the locations on the paper where the trauma had occurred. "I blew these up too so you would have them for trial."

Emily's stomach sank as she looked at the remains. "Thank you for your thorough attention."

"Any thoughts about who might have killed her?"

Emily wasn't about to show her hand. "Sheriff Larson's looking into it."

Dr. Payton handed her an envelope. "My invoice for services rendered."

"I'll submit these to the county right away." She remembered her father complaining about how slowly the wheels of the county clerk's office moved when it came to reimbursing or paying invoices to him. What kind of delays would she run into with this one?

If the county balked, Hank Wurthers and his buddies would have to fight the U of M on this one. And surely they would lose.

Dr. Payton rose from the couch and scanned the room.

"So this is how he did it."

"Did what?"

"Run a thriving medical practice for the dead and the living."

Emily looked around the office. It was a typical office. Desk. Couches. Bookshelves. File cabinets. "I guess so. He didn't actually house the dead here. Sorry if that's disappointing to you."

Dr. Payton laughed. "There's that gallows humor."

"Dad actually ran his practice from the garage. Had it turned into a three-room clinic. Would you like to see it?"

"I'd love to."

Emily showed him into the clinic through the waiting room, which held a couple of chairs, an end table, and a kid's table. "Dad didn't keep his patients waiting long, so there was no reason to have much up here."

She led him through the three separate rooms. There was a lab area with a sink and supplies, where he and his attending nurse could prep charts and medications. Walking Dr. Payton through here, she realized how simple it was compared to bigger-city medical clinics. Who would she find to take over such a small operation? It would take a special buyer to move in here. Maybe an artist who wanted a big studio or a large family who home-schooled? Maybe a newly married doctor who wanted to plant his career and his family in a safe, quiet town, like her own parents had dreamed of?

"It's very cozy. Very, I don't know . . . Little Hospital on the Prairie." He was pleased with his own joke. Emily found it endearing.

"Dad does—did—well here. His practice is—was—thriving. Sorry. It's hard to . . ."

"No, it's okay. I understand." He put his hand on her arm, and it immediately had a calming effect.

"It's a little unconventional having the clinic in a garage, but it was nice having him home so much when I was young and my mom . . ." Emily stopped short. She put her hand to mouth and turned away as her eyes filled with tears.

"Dr. Hartford, it's okay. I know your mom passed when you were fifteen."

She glanced at him over her shoulder with a bewildered look. "Please, call me Emily."

"And likewise. Charles, please." His smile disarmed her. "I don't mean to sound like a stalker, but I admit, I was curious about you," said Dr. Payton.

"So you Googled me? Stalker," Emily joked, but she wasn't surprised. It was the layman's background check. Besides, it wasn't difficult to find the old newspaper articles online about her mom's accident.

He gave an apologetic shrug. "You fascinate me more in real life."

Emily deflected the flirtatious remark. "My mom managed his office. Bookkeeping. Appointments. Ordering supplies. She loved having Dad's office here. She made lunch for him almost every day."

"Sounds like the perfect life and the perfect wife."

"She was. And mother, too," Emily added as her thoughts drifted off to those days before the accident when she would come home after school to find her mother in the clinic, happily chatting it up with patients as they came and went. Mom and Dad were a team. She healed with hospitality. He healed with medicine.

"Emily, would you join me for dinner later?" Dr. Payton broke into her memory. Emily's gaze went to the clock on the wall. It was 9:35 AM.

"Are you planning to stick around Freeport that long?"

"Yes. I think I'll stay to see some sites."

What sites? She just smiled and nodded. "That's not going to take until dinner."

"I may while away a few hours at Brown's Bakery. Delia is a great storyteller."

So that *was it!* She hated that Nick might be right about this one.

"The baked goods were a hit, then?"

"Gone in sixty seconds," he laughed. "My colleagues told me I couldn't return without more."

93

"What's your intention with this case?" Emily blurted out. "Do you want to use it in your research work?"

"You sound upset about it," said Dr. Payton, without missing a beat.

"Not angry. Just curious." Her face flushed in anger.

"I'm always looking for interesting cases. It's in my blood. It's what I do. You understand that."

"Yes, I do, but—" Emily frowned. "It's just . . . this is not your case per se."

"You hired me. I'm as much part of the case as you are."

"You're a consultant. I'm acting ME. I hold the files and permissions."

"Whoa, I didn't mean to ruffle feathers. I'm not going to steal anything here. I just find what's going on here is a little more interesting than what usually comes across my desk day to day." He raised an eyebrow her way. "You're more than meets the eye, Dr. Emily Hartford. And I do find this case research-worthy. But that's not the only reason I came here. I have a proposal for you."

"For what?" *At least we're being honest now.*

"I'll tell you over dinner."

"Why not just tell me now?"

"No. I want to leave you with something to be curious about all day. And I want to be sure you'll show up tonight."

She was both annoyed and intrigued with his little game.

"Drop your shoulders," he instructed.

"What?"

"Your shoulders are raised."

Emily's attention went to her shoulders. The muscles were tense. It was where she carried all her stress. Dr. Payton came over and raised his hands over them.

"May I?"

She nodded. He began to knead the taut muscles, and Emily cringed at the discomfort.

"I feel a lot of resistance. Don't try to fight it."

She tried to relax her shoulders, but each time he pinched her muscle between his forefingers and thumbs, a sharp pain pricked down her spine.

"I'm not a professional massage therapist, but you are full of knots," he said.

"It's been a rough couple weeks," she said.

"You're holding it all up here. Close your eyes."

She did. His thumbs worked out a knot on either side and the pain lessened. As she began to relax under his healing touch, any remaining annoyance drained. And she found herself looking forward to dinner.

15

Later that afternoon, Emily made a trip to the sheriff's office to talk with Nick about Dr. Payton's findings. But Nick had some findings of his own to announce.

"The lab called this morning with the Parkman DNA comparison study," said Nick.

"That was fast. And? What are we looking at?"

"They're a match. Sandi's DNA contain the same twenty-one DNA loci points as her mother's," said Nick, running his hand over the edge of Dr. Parkman's oversized poster of skeletal remains.

"Oh Nick. You were right." But she was devastated for the Parkman family. And a bit regretful that she had doubted Nick's instincts.

"With Dr. Payton's and your assessment of how she died, we're conclusively looking at a homicide case, and we can officially announce it."

"Have you contacted Mrs. Parkman?"

"No, not yet. I'm not sure what to say. How do I tell her that the mystery of her daughter's disappearance is unhappily over?" Nick stretched his hands across his forehead as if he were trying to press out all his stress to the edges of his face. People failed to acknowledge that the discovery of hard truth was actually the primary cause of wrinkles.

"I don't think it's going to be big news to her. She can bury her daughter in peace now."

Nick didn't respond, his eyes glazing over her shoulder. Emily knew guilt and regret were rearing their ugly heads.

"I'll go with you. We'll tag-team this, like we did with the Dobsons," Emily offered.

"Yeah, that's a good idea. I'll set up a time to talk with her."

"Did it ever occur to you that maybe her stepfather made the videos? I mean, since no one claimed they saw them or knew about the source?" It might be a stretch, but they had to consider every strange, offbeat theory.

Nick shrugged. "She had a restraining order against him. He couldn't go near her."

"Right. But people don't always obey those orders. Did you ever see him with Sandi after he got out?"

Nick thought about it for a moment. "I saw him waiting outside school a few times."

"Maybe it's worth looking into?"

It was sickening to think about, but there might be a way to connect the dots.

"Maybe." His voice and attention drifted.

"Nick, do you think you ought to get yourself some protection?" said Emily.

"I carry a badge and a gun."

"No, I mean legal protection."

"Why?"

How could he not see it? "You were the last person to see Sandi before she died."

"That we know of. Other than the killer."

"Yes. And now that this is a murder case, you're going to be questioned again."

"How is that going to look when I lawyer up at the same time we announce Sandi Parkman's homicide?"

"I'm just saying, get on the offensive."

"They have my statement on record."

"But you have no alibi."

"I have an alibi. I was home."

"Alone. No one saw you." Emily didn't mean to come off so accusatory. "I understand this is awkward and awful. But if you're innocent—"

"I. Am. Innocent." He punctuated each word.

"James claimed he was home all afternoon, too. But no one actually saw him at home. You see? It just doesn't look good for your defense." Emily hadn't meant to talk in hypotheticals. It was a clinical habit. Instead, she kept putting her foot in her mouth. "A good defense attorney will make sure the world knows that."

"You already have me convicted."

"No, Nick, that's not what I'm saying. I'm thinking proactively here. Once you release the manner of death, the media will bite. It's a juicy news story. And just like the Dobson case, it will reach far beyond the rural borders of Freeport County and seep into the media feeds all across the state. And it won't take but a blink of the eye for fingers to come pointing at you. 'Freeport County Sheriff Larson a Teen Sex Offender and Killer?' I can hear the thousands of mouse clicks all over the state of Michigan. Not something you want to get back to the state police post. They'll send in their own investigators and you'll be taken off the case and detained."

"Okay, settle down. I get your point," said Nick.

But she wasn't sure Nick would do anything about it, and it troubled her. She had seen her father become the victim of a witch hunt during a seedy death investigation of a domestic violence homicide that had left scars on him and his reputation for years.

"Think of it like hiring a publicist who's going to extinguish all the fiery darts so you can concentrate on getting this case solved."

"They'll take me off the case," Nick admitted, taking a seat behind his desk. His brow crinkled. Emily drew in a breath and calmed her tone. That was it. He felt solely responsible for finding Sandi's killer.

"You have nothing to hide. And soon, this will pass. I promise."

"It will pass even quicker once we find the killer."

"*We?*"

"You're in it now, Em. I need you."

"You don't need me for this. You'll probably get a slam dunk with the stepdad. He's got guilt written all over him. There's really nothing more I can do as acting medical examiner on this case, but I would advise that the ME's office hold on to Sandi's remains for a while."

"What reason can I give Mrs. Parkman as to why she still can't have her daughter back?" Nick had that pinched tone to his voice that conveyed he was trying not to get upset.

"We may get a request for another forensic examination. Either the prosecutor, defense, or both. We wouldn't want the Parkmans deciding to cremate and then lose all our evidence."

"Always thinking ahead."

"Saving you grief you didn't know you had coming," Emily teased. The mood lightened.

"I know this sounds weird, but I don't want to be alone tonight," said Nick. Her eyes flitted to his with a startled expression.

"No, that's not what I meant. It's just that since I have to break the news in the morning, I could use the company to help me process all this."

"I wish I could, Nick," Emily said, truly feeling for him. "But I promised Dr. Payton I'd have dinner with him later."

"Hey, I thought you weren't into dating right now."

"It's not a date."

"He drove all the way up here. It's a date."

"It's not a date," she insisted again.

"Sounds like a date."

"It's dinner at the country club. Nothing romantic about that."

"Did he make a reservation?" Nick questioned with a wide-eyed look.

"I assume so."

"Then it's totally a date." There was triumph in his tone.

Emily sighed. "Semantics aside, let's catch up first thing in the morning to go over your statement before you release it?"

"No, no. It's okay. I know you're super busy."

Emily shrugged. *So this is how you're going to play it? Fine.* "And the attorney?"

"I'll think about it."

Nick's face went a little gray. She had seen that sick look on her father's face before, too, when he was talking to his attorney over the phone. It was sinking in with Nick how serious this could be. Emily hated that he was going to be thrown to the dogs tomorrow.

Emily took the poster-board images of Sandi's remains and sent Nick a little wave as she headed out of his office and through the sheriff's department. A chilly breeze cut through her thin shirt again, reminding Emily that her winter wardrobe was still in Chicago at the brownstone Brandon had bought for them. On her way home, she would stop at Jo's to borrow another dress for dinner tonight.

Date. Pleeease. It's not a date.

That little ping zinged up her spine again. *Is it?*

16

Emily valeted her Nissan Leaf at the country club entrance and found Dr. Payton waiting for her in a chair near the door of the lobby. As soon as he saw her, he hurried to greet her. She was quick to note how sharply dressed he was in his tweed jacket, slim dark denim slipped over brown leather boots.

"You look amazing." He bent to her cheek with a European double kiss. It threw her off for a second, but then she went along with it.

Emily was grateful she had dressed up for the evening. She was in Jo's charcoal pencil skirt and red silk blouse. Her freshly washed hair was down and styled, and she had found a pair of her mother's old earrings in a jewelry box on the top shelf of her father's closet. She felt good. The best she had in over a month.

He led her to the table—a three-top? With Delia already seated?

"Hello, doll. I hope you don't mind. After patronizing my establishment all afternoon and gushing over my pastries, how could I say no to this? Besides, I haven't had a man ask me to dinner in longer than I care to admit."

See, Nick? This was definitely not a date. But she couldn't help feeling a little let down.

Emily reached down to give Delia a hug. "I always love seeing you."

They all took a seat as the waiter arrived with a water pitcher and menus, which he set in front of each of them.

"Red or white?" asked Dr. Payton, snatching the menu.

"Red," Emily and Delia confirmed in tandem.

Dr. Payton took the liberty of ordering one of the more expensive bottles, and the waiter scuttled toward the bar.

"Don't leave me in suspense any longer," said Emily. "What's this big thing you want to ask me?"

"I was telling Delia earlier today that we're expanding our anthropology department to add more courses in forensic investigation, and I'd like you to consider applying for the job."

"Is that an academic position?"

"Yes, about fifty percent professorial, and the other fifty percent is built around lab work that comes into our office from the state police posts."

"I'm pretty sure I'm not qualified." Emily nearly laughed out loud. "That's why we had to call you up here."

The waiter returned with the red wine and opened the bottle. He poured a sample into Delia's glass, and she took an approving sip. Then he filled each glass a third of the way to the top and hurried off.

"I think you should hear Dr. Payton out. It's worth considering his offer, doll," said Delia, raising her glass in a toast. "To new opportunities."

They clinked goblets as if they were already celebrating her acceptance. Emily felt her gut tighten.

"I'm a surgeon. I've never even taught before. And I'm not a bone expert," said Emily.

"You're good with people. A natural teacher. And we'd give you the courses and training you need to catch up on the anthropology side." He pressed her with a serious look. "You know anatomy, Emily.

You understand how people are put together. How they live and move. And what happens to them when they die."

"I've never really considered an academic career," she stated plainly.

"It's a nice life," said Delia. "I sometimes wish I'd transitioned into academia. Would have left a lot less battle scars." She smiled and took a sip of her wine.

Emily didn't believe for an instant that Delia would have been satisfied at a university. She was a field agent through and through. Adventure and wanderlust were her lifeblood.

"I don't know. I've put a good amount into my surgical training," she said.

"And that will all be counted to your benefit when you apply."

"This is a huge shift in direction."

"Think of it more like exploring a new branch on the same tree."

"I'll give you a raving recommendation," said Delia.

Emily wondered why Delia was so in favor of this opportunity. "I always thought you were rooting for me to return to Freeport."

"I'm rooting for you, period. You have the chops for surgery. I know you do. But Emily, forensics is in your DNA. You've known that since you were thirteen and doing autopsies with your dad."

"That's brilliant, Emily," said Dr. Payton. "I can't wait to hear more about the young Emily Hartford, working the morgue instead of attending football games."

"I went to football games," she said flatly, and buried her eyes in the menu. She resented the fact that on the deepest level, Delia had hit a sore spot. Defenses rose in her mind. At sixteen years old, Chicago had been Emily's only outlet. Emily would not apologize for her Chicago choices. She'd been hurting and no one would listen to her. Her father had checked out, refusing to investigate Mom's death. Delia was traipsing across the Middle East or Europe or Asia or wherever on FBI assignment. Emily hadn't had anyone back then. How could Delia know how desperate and lonely Emily had felt?

She couldn't deny that running to Chicago had changed the course of her life. All she had wanted to do was prove to her father that she was fine without him. She would get his attention by excelling in the area of medicine he had given up after a surgical procedure went afoul. Now the sting of that childish decision would be with her the rest of her life. Even though her father had eventually applauded her venture off the forensic trail, he had been proud of how it had broadened her horizons and opportunities. And branching out had helped Emily get a new perspective and attack life in a productive manner. But she'd never known, until recently, how much Dad had missed her and been deeply hurt by her absence. And she hadn't realized how much she'd missed home and forensic investigating with her father and connecting over cases.

"To the future," said Dr. Payton, raising a wineglass in another toast.

"The beautiful, beautiful future," said Delia.

"And the beautiful women who make it happen," said Dr. Payton. He passed his glance from Delia to Emily and held it there.

Emily kept her lips in a taut grin and said nothing as she clinked her glass to theirs. She took a sip and mentally shrugged off her worry thoughts. The present offered enough challenges. Better not to borrow more from tomorrow.

But she had little reprieve, as Delia started right back in again. "Emily, I don't mean to harp, but let me make a plug for university life. It's a lot less stressful than being a surgeon. And it fosters a good schedule for having a husband and kids."

Emily choked on her second sip of wine and sent Delia a mortified glare. "That is *not* on the table right now."

"But it will be. Sooner than you think," said Delia.

"Oh, are you getting married?" said Dr. Payton with a slight sinking tone.

Emily glanced to where her engagement ring used to be. "No, I'm not."

"She just got disengaged," Delia piped in. "Is that a word? I think I made that up. At any rate, she's single."

Dr. Payton feigned surprise.

Emily shot Delia a sharp look. "There's a lot of stuff up in the air right now," she said, trying to recover gracefully. "Drink your wine, Delia."

Dr. Payton divided the rest of the bottle of wine into their three glasses and turned his attention to Emily. "What do you think, Emily? Is it at least something you'd consider?"

She wasn't sure how much of herself to give away, but she'd better say something before Delia overstepped.

"I've got a lot of distractions these days."

"Yes. She'll consider it," said Delia.

Oh Delia, can you please keep your trap shut?

Emily buried her head in the menu again, biting her lip lest she regret the words rolling to the tip of her tongue. *Steak, salmon, or ribs? Wait. That mushroom risotto looks tempting. Where is that waiter?*

"Freeport is a great little city. Reminds me of my own hometown," Dr. Payton said, changing the subject.

"Does it? Where was that?" said Delia.

"Wilshire, Vermont. You won't find it on a map. It's just a dot off the interstate in the middle of the Northeast Kingdom. Population three hundred."

"Wow, that's more like a pinprick," said Delia. "I once knew an FBI agent who lived up in northern Vermont. Commuted to Washington, DC, every week. Said it was the only way he could stay sane on the job."

"There's nothing like small towns to come back to nature and one's true self," said Dr. Payton, turning to Emily.

"That's why I came back. It's ideal here," said Delia. "Think about it, doll. The clock is ticking."

Emily shot her a look. *Stop. Please!*

"Have you ever thought about keeping your house here as a vacation home?" asked Dr. Payton. "Many of our professors have vacation homes up north."

"That might make the decision more palatable," said Delia, flagging down the waiter for another bottle of wine. "You don't have to give everything up. Work there. Weekend here."

"What sites did you get to see today?" said Emily, changing the topic with a plastic smile.

"I never made it out," said Dr. Payton with a laugh toward Delia. "There was too much going on inside Brown's Bakery."

Another busy day of town gossip. She could imagine Dr. Payton charming the customers and making new friends. She wondered if people knew he was the forensic examiner working on the Pinetree Slopes case and if people's curiosity had gotten the better of them. And if he had given in to their inquiries.

"Have you two decided what to eat?" Emily asked, setting her menu aside.

"Roast chicken. I'm a simple eater," said Delia.

"Rib eye. I'm simple, too." Dr. Payton turned to Emily. "And you?"

"The braised salmon sounds good," said Emily, feeling braised herself.

"Emily, I do hope you'll at least consider my offer. I'd be happy to show you around the department and campus. How does next week look?" Dr. Payton softened his gaze.

Thankfully, Emily didn't have to answer because the waiter showed up with a bread basket.

17

Emily was exhausted from the emotional ping-pong of the evening, yet she wasn't ready to go to her empty home, so she zig-zagged through Freeport's neighborhoods as her thoughts turned to the Parkman case. And to Sandi's last ride. Had she known she was in trouble? Had she been bound and gagged in her final hours? Did she know her attacker? Was she even conscious? What thoughts of terror would have been racing through her mind? Had she tried to escape?

Emily shook herself free of the horror thoughts. She was passing the entrance to Pinetree Slopes and had a strong urge to pull in. Because of the storm, she hadn't really taken a good look at the entire area when they were excavating. And even though it was dark now, she wanted to get a sense of the place at night. It was most likely that the killer had waited to dump the body until after dark.

Her thoughts reeled back to her questions. What sort of obstacles would he have encountered? There had been no roads ten years ago leading to the development. It was just a dense woods back then. How far off the main road would the killer have had to carry the body? And why here? Did it carry some meaning to the killer? To Sandi?

Emily's Leaf bumped along the gravel drive. The estate was so new that they hadn't paved the roads yet. A few parcels of land had been cleared in preparation for building, but only the plot where they had found Sandi was under construction. The rest was virgin land marked in flags.

Sandi's parcel, she would call it, since she didn't know who had bought it. And would the owners still want it now that a body had been found on the property?

As she came around a bend, she noticed a set of headlights pointed away from her into the woods about a quarter mile up. Emily instinctively shut off her lights and slowed to a stop. Thank goodness her electric vehicle was silent.

From her vantage point, she could see that it was a black Lexus parked on the edge of Sandi's parcel. Was it the developer? The owner? A pair of lovers seeking privacy?

She thought she saw two people in the car, but she couldn't tell if they were male or female. She couldn't tell their age or ethnicity. They were just dark shadows. Heads bobbing in quiet conversation. She was having a hard time making out the license plate. Emily pulled out her camera and zoomed in to capture an image, but when she looked at it on her phone, all she could make out was a dealer plate. The car was brand-new. Maybe that was of benefit here. How hard could it be to track down a brand-new Lexus? It had probably just been registered with the secretary of state.

She texted the picture to Nick. And waited. Hoping they hadn't see her. Hoping she wasn't placing herself in any danger.

Emily backed up out of view and headed down the gravel path out of Pinetree Slopes. She didn't turn her headlights on until she turned out onto the main road heading home. She called Nick, and he picked up on the second ring.

"Did you get my text?" she said right away.

"Yeah, it just came through. What is it?"

"Dealer plate from a vehicle loitering around the site where Sandi's remains were found."

"That's really odd."

"I thought so."

"What were you doing there?" he asked. "Date get cut short?"

"I think I lost my bracelet during the dig."

"So you went to look for it in the dark?"

"While it was on my mind," she said defensively, suspecting he wasn't buying her fib.

"Are you still at the site?"

"No. I'm heading home. I just thought you should check it out."

"I will. I'll head over right now," said Nick.

"What time are you going to Mrs. Parkman's tomorrow?"

Emily could hear him gathering up his car keys, heading into his garage, and getting into his truck.

"Not sure exactly. I'll text you in the morning."

"Sounds good."

"So, how was the big date?"

"It wasn't a date."

"Two bottles of red wine? Sounds like a date to me."

"You were spying on me?"

"My friend Becky Matthews waits tables there."

"Who's that?"

"Officer Matthew's little sister. Well, not so little. Twenty-one. Had to bust her for a DUI on her twenty-first."

"Ouch," said Emily. "Small towns."

"Sometimes I hate playing the bad cop."

"Good night, Nick," said Emily as she hung up and pulled into her driveway. She wondered what Mrs. Parkman would be doing tonight—the last sleep she would ever take not knowing where her daughter was. Emily thought of her own mother and father, resting together under the maple tree at Freeport Memorial Cemetery. They had chosen Freeport out of all the places they could have lived. A nice, safe place to settle down and raise a family. The perfect child-hood. Just miles away, Sandi had been suffering a terrifying exis-tence. Life was not fair.

To what degree was Shirley Parkman guilty of the sins of omis-sion? It seemed almost certain she had turned a blind eye to what her husband was doing to her daughter. The need for love and a roof over her head perhaps had trumped her protective motherly instincts. How sad that these sins of omission had destroyed her and her daughters. Perhaps Shirley Parkman was hiding still more from them.

18

"Did you find out anything on the Lexus?" Emily said the next morning after Nick picked her up so they could drive to Shirley Parkman's house together.

"Not much. By the time I got over there, it was gone. I tried to look up registration, but there have been no new Lexus' of that make and model registered to anyone in Freeport County in the last year."

"Out-of-towners."

"Probably," said Nick. "So I widened the search to all of Michigan. There were about a hundred Lexus' registered near the Detroit area in the past month. Only three of the model you photographed."

"Any names you recognize?"

"Contrary to the fact that I've never lived anywhere but Michigan, I actually don't know every resident in the state," he chided with a light tone. Emily smirked. "But to answer your question, no. I didn't recognize anyone on the list, and none of them sent up any red flags for past criminal arrests."

"Can you question them for an alibi?"

"Under what probable cause? 'I saw your car in the woods'?" He snickered. But Emily didn't think it was funny this time.

"You can come up with something. Trespassing on private property?"

"Relax, will you? It's probably a developer or maybe a visiting architect. A lot of people from Detroit are starting to build summer homes up here."

"Since when has Freeport experienced a building boom?"

"The county clerk said she's getting flooded with building permits."

Emily knew she should have gotten closer and tried to get photographs of the people inside. "Who visits land in the dead of darkness?"

"Who goes looking for a bracelet in the dead of darkness?" Nick challenged back. "Did you find it?"

"I did. On my dresser at home," she fibbed.

She didn't want to get in it about Dr. Payton's offer, the awkward dinner conversation, and how she needed to unwind before facing a lonely, empty house.

"I told you after the Dobson case, a heroine makes no promises to quit sleuthing. It's in my blood."

"I thought you were looking for a bracelet," Nick volleyed back, glancing over with a smirk. He saw right through her.

"Well, at least you called me this time," he continued, referring to the way she had left him out of certain investigative trails on the Dobson case.

He slowed as they came up to the Parkman place. They needed to shore up their strategy.

"I think you should tell her about Sandi's cause and manner of death," she suggested.

"And I think you should, Dr. Hartford," said Nick, stressing the word *Doctor*.

"You were a family friend. It'll be better coming from you."

* * *

The small, two-bedroom home with a single-car attached garage was falling apart. Emily took in the broken gutters, peeling exterior paint, and a roof that needed to be replaced.

Shirley Parkman was unable to come to the door to let them in. She was grossly overweight and seemed glued to the couch with the TV blaring six feet in front of her. She waved Nick in and Emily followed, accosted by the smell of old frying oil and mildew.

When Nick gave her the news, Mrs. Parkman didn't seem very surprised at all about the bones belonging to Sandi. In fact, Emily noticed a touch of relief wash over her face when she handed her the death certificate. She even gave a sad smile when Emily relayed that they would have to hold the body just a little longer for the investigation.

"It's okay, really. At least I know she's in a safe place. And that'll give me a moment to figure out some arrangements."

Emily then remembered that Cathy Bishop had breezed outta town toward her new desert life. "Bishop and Schulz Funeral Home will be under new management soon. I can call you later with the new contact information," said Emily.

"Yes, that would be good. I guess I never really planned her funeral. I didn't want to believe she was really . . . gone."

Emily offered her condolences. She saw Mrs. Parkman's eyes travel to the word *homicide* written plainly under *manner of death*. Emily thought it best to give her a minute to digest the news.

"Homicide," said Mrs. Parkman. She spoke with a steady voice, not surprised at all by the verdict. "It's very strange to see it in writing."

"I want you to know that we're investigating this very actively," said Nick. "We're starting to piece together the events of her last day."

"You were part of that last day. Weren't you the last one to see her alive?" Shirley made a struggling effort to reach for a soda can atop a stack of magazines on the coffee table. Nick got it for her.

"The killer would have been the last one to see her alive," Nick corrected.

"Oh, Nick, I know you didn't kill my Sandi. You were a good friend to her. Like a brother."

"I've never really talked with you about Sandi's death," said Nick.

"No hard feelings. I wasn't exactly a social butterfly after she disappeared."

"What do you think happened?"

"I've thought about it a lot over the years. Sandi was not a real happy teenager. She had been through a lot with her stepdad. As you know."

Nick nodded. Emily hoped this might be the moment Mrs. Parkman opened up about her troubled marriage and any suspicions she might have about her ex.

"Sandi was depressed. I know that. But not enough to be suicidal. She had plans for community college. Cosmetology. She was a survivor."

"Can you think of anyone who would want to kill her? Nick pressed gently.

"I don't know." Mrs. Parkman shook her head, getting lost in her thoughts. "I feel responsible, partly."

"Responsible for what?" asked Nick, scooting to the edge of his seat.

"For just not being around. I should have known."

"Known what?" asked Emily.

"I was working a lot back then. I just wasn't paying attention."

She knew she had been an absentee parent. She felt the guilt. Emily didn't blame Mrs. Parkman for keeping her thoughts to herself all these years, especially if the killer was in close range. But now that her daughter had been found murdered—now was the time to come clean.

"Are you saying you're somehow responsible for your daughter's death?" said Emily. Nick shot her an acidic glance.

"No. Not directly." Mrs. Parkman looked horrified, and Nick quickly stepped back in.

"We're not accusing you, Mrs. Parkman," Nick offered apologetically.

"I suppose I should have said something a long time ago. But I was scared. Scared of him." She stopped. Her lips pressed together and her gaze went to her feet.

"Her stepfather?" said Emily.

She nodded. "Sandi put him in prison with her testimony. I stood by her, silently, but I never said in court that I knew this was going on under my roof. Truthfully, Sandi never said a word to me about the abuse. It was Tiffani who first told me about what was happening to Sandi."

Emily nodded. She was proud of Shirley for owning up to this difficult admission.

"After her stepfather got out of prison, did he exhibit behavior that would indicate he wanted revenge?" asked Nick.

"Absolutely. He was furious at her for putting him away. He came out and started stalking her."

"What about the restraining order?" said Nick.

"Didn't matter. He came after her. Me. Tiffani. Police couldn't always be there to enforce it, so I told Sandi never to be anywhere alone. Not school. Not home."

"But you said you were working a lot of hours. How could she not be at home alone some of the time?" asked Emily.

She choked out her answer in a gravelly voice covered in guilt. "That's why I feel responsible. I couldn't protect her from him. The second time."

Emily and Nick let a moment pass for Mrs. Parkman to compose herself.

"Mrs. Parkman, where were you the day Sandi disappeared?" said Nick.

"Waitressing at Orion's Belt." Emily knew the place; it was an all-night diner on the edge of town. "I got home about seven thirty, after the dinner rush. Tiffani was gone, too. I kinda panicked at first."

Emily nodded. "Had either of the girls left a note?"

"No. But that wasn't unusual."

"Where did you find Tiffani?"

"At a friend's, spending the night. I just figured Sandi was doing the same, and I was so beat from my day that I fell asleep on the couch. I woke up the next morning to a call from the high school that Sandi had missed her first two classes."

"What's the name of the friend?" asked Nick.

Mrs. Parkman stopped to think. "She was a mousy girl. Kinda scraggly. Don't remember the name. It's all kinda fuzzy in my memory now."

"Where is Tiffani living these days?" asked Emily.

"An apartment at Cedar Heights."

Emily detected a slight vagueness in her answer and pried a little more.

"Is she married?" said Emily.

"God, no."

"How did Tiffani take Sandi's disappearance?" asked Emily.

"Devastated. Sandi was very protective of her. You know, especially after the whole thing with their stepdad. She was convinced that he killed her."

"What made her think that?"

"She never really said. But she was really pent up about it. I just kinda let her work it out, because Tiffani was always really shy. She liked to read. To study. Not like Sandi. But after Sandi . . . her whole life changed. She got real rebellious."

"How so?" said Emily.

"Started running around with guys a lot older than her. Skipping school. Dropped out at sixteen."

"I heard you kicked her out of the house." Nick's voice quivered as he clearly struggled to control his emotions. Emily shot him a quick glance, hoping to catch his look. But he bent his head and in a swift motion used his thumb and forefinger to swipe away the wet under his eyes.

"I couldn't control her no more." Mrs. Parkman shrugged. "Wait till you have kids. You'll see. Sometimes they have to learn from the school of hard knocks."

It made Emily feel awful to hear about a mother just giving up on a daughter who had clearly been traumatized by several major life events. She was immediately grateful that her own parents had cared so much. Well, at least until Mom's accident. And Tiffani, poor thing. Here was girl with a promising future. At least academically. She could have risen above her circumstances.

"Mrs. Parkman, thank you so much for talking with us. Again, my deepest sympathies." Nick rose. "We should get going. I'll keep you updated as I can. And if you hear or see anything or think of anything that might help the investigation, please reach out. Okay?"

"What am I supposed to do with this? I already know she's dead," said Mrs. Parkman, glancing back at the death certificate.

"It's for your own personal records," said Emily.

Mrs. Parkman laid it on top of a stack of junk mail next to the magazine pile.

"I don't got money for a fancy funeral."

"Bishop and Schulz can work with even modest budgets."

"I don't have a budget at all." An acrid lament hung in the room.

Emily vowed right there to make sure Sandi got the kind of burial she deserved.

As they left, an achy feeling rooted in Emily's gut. Tiffani. Such a troubled life. A criminal stepdad. A sister missing. A mother who was unable to care for her emotional needs. What a mess.

"We should see what we can do about raising funds for a proper memorial service," said Emily.

Nick nodded. "I'll put the word out at the department."

"I'll tell Delia. She can spread the word at Brown's."

They pulled away from Mrs. Parkman's house, thinking about these two loyal sisters, suffering together and then viciously torn from each other. Sandi and Tiffani had shared lots of secrets. Secrets that were meant to go to the grave. Because that's what sisters did. Tiffani knew the truth about Sandi. Or at least enough of it to have dramatically affected her after Sandi's disappearance. Keeping secrets did that. They changed you, for better or worse. If Tiffani did know something about her stepfather's role in Sandi's death, that could be pivotal to this investigation.

The secrets of sisters. Emily had always thought it was cool that sisters had the upper hand on what was really going on in each other's lives. She had seen it in her friends' sibling relationships and had always been a little envious.

And then it dawned on Emily that *she* had a sister now.

"I was reading through Sandi's file again last night, and the step-dad was never listed as a suspect," said Nick.

"That's so strange. I mean, it seems so obvious. He has the most motive."

"I agree. But he wasn't listed because his time card showed he was punched in for work during the time of her disappearance."

"He could have been punched in and then left work early, conveniently forgetting to punch out," Emily suggested.

"It's definitely possible," Nick said.

"Did anyone talk to his boss? His coworkers?"

"There are no statements from them. You have to remember, at the time, he wasn't being questioned for murder. Most people thought she was a runaway."

A runaway who'd told no one she was leaving. Left no notes. Took no clothes or purse. Had a bad home history, a jealous, controlling boyfriend, and a sex offender for a stepdad. There were so many red flags! But no one was paying attention to these details of a poverty-stricken teenage girl's life. It wasn't fair, and it wasn't right. If Emily stayed in Freeport, she wanted to do something to help young women understand how to protect themselves and value themselves so they didn't end up in a clandestine grave.

"You wanna grab a bite to eat?" Nick asked her.

"Can't. Tonight's the commissioners' meeting."

Nick hummed the opening bars of the *Jaws* theme. Emily chuckled, getting his implication. She was diving headfirst into a sea full of sharks.

19

"This Dr. Payton you hired sent us a bill for three grand," said Hank Wurthers, who was heading the board of commissioners' Thursday-night meeting. He was sitting next to a skinny grandpa type with rough, wrinkled hands that belonged to a farmer used to counting every penny and nickel. The seating area was spotted with a couple dozen townspeople awaiting their turn to speak on a particular issue of personal concern.

"That's his fee," Emily defended from a podium facing the table of commissioners. "And it's not out of range."

"We can't pay this," said a man with a crooked toupee sitting on the end of the row of tables.

"It's a difficult case and growing more difficult by the day. Dr. Payton's services have already saved this county time and resources."

"Do you have a cause of death?" said crooked toupee.

"I do, but I cannot release it publicly," said Emily.

"Well, let's not belabor this case too long, shall we?" said a teacher type with a clip-on bow tie. "We can't afford to waste county resources on cases like hers."

His derogatory tone pricked at Emily. "What do you mean, *like hers*?"

"It's no secret that this girl was troubled . . . and caused trouble," said clip-on bowtie teacher. Emily didn't like his assessment of Sandi. Teachers like bow tie lived with their heads in ivory towers and were quick to lump the "troubled" in with those "in trouble."

"I'm not sure how that affects my professional duty to this case?" *Or Nick's. Or the county's. Murder is murder.* And bow tie's argument was not justified, no matter how ill-reputed or irresponsible the victim. Besides, based on what Emily knew about Sandi thus far, these claims were untrue. He had no idea what that girl had lived through.

"I think what's being expressed here is that sometimes these things just aren't worth the hassle," said Hank.

These things? Had he just referred to a murdered young woman as a *thing*?

"What about *these things* is concerning to you?" Emily stepped carefully, but kept a firm tone.

"Her death was a long time ago," said skinny gramps. "Ain't no use bringing it all up again and charging our taxpayers for it."

"Oh yes, let's not waste any money on justice for one of our own, precious young people. What if this had been your daughter?" said Emily, trying to keep her voice in diplomatic range.

"We all know this was a girl who took an unfortunate wrong turn, and we're sorry for her loss, but we all know how she got there, and I for one, don't think we, and by that I mean the good citizens of Freeport County, should have to foot the bill," said clip-on bowtie teacher.

"Especially for something that happened ten years ago," added crooked toupee.

"You're making a lot of assumptions considering you don't know the facts of her case," said Emily.

"Ms. Hartford," started skinny gramps.

"Dr. Hartford," she interrupted.

"Some kids are prone to sad demises," he continued.

"Sandi's sad demise, as you call it, was not her fault. She didn't asked to be raped by her stepfather over and over. She didn't ask for a mother who was scared and couldn't protect her. She didn't ask for poverty."

The entire room sat up on edge.

"It'll do the whole community a great deal of good if you just release the report and let the cops do their job," said Hank.

"Just shove it aside into the cold-case cabinet, right? Just another case you can't fund. What message does that send to our teens today about their value in our society?" said Emily, their ignorance and indigence grating on her.

Out of the corner of her eye, Emily saw a young man in the front row of the audience jotting something down in a notepad. Probably press. Emily almost groaned aloud. After the run-ins she'd had during the Dobson case, she wanted nothing to do with drawing media attention. She needed to right this ship. Now. Or she would find herself in a gale storm with a broken sail.

"Are you going to pay Dr. Charles Payton or not?" Emily demanded.

Hank murmured with his fellow commissioners and then turned to Emily. "We'd like to see a twenty-five percent reduction in his fees," he said.

"You'll have to take that up with him." She stood her ground.

"Will you be running for county coroner, Miss Hartford?" asked clip-on bow tie.

"Dr. Hartford," she corrected again. "I'm not sure yet."

"Then why don't you rest your grand cause for justice until you're a little more sure. You millennials have a lot of passion but come up very short in the way of action."

"Who else is running?" asked Emily, quivering with fury inside.

Hank paused, searching his board for their permission. Once granted by several nods, he revealed, "Melvin Rotsworth and Roger Phizter."

Emily didn't know who these men were, but Delia would. Delia would also know how she should handle this stingy, judgmental group of men. This is what she would be facing if she stayed and took the position, which she felt assured she could win. Was the battle for her father's position one that she wanted to fight? Was it worth the fight? It had worked for him. They would have to respect her and listen to her. And they would need to provide the funding a proper coroner's office required. This wasn't some idyllic dream she'd had when she was thirteen, working side by side with her father. He had showed her the importance of proper investigation in finding and convicting criminals.

The people of Freeport County had been blessed with a thorough, compassionate medical examiner in her father. Someone who had cared about justice more than the bottom line.

"'Societies get the criminals they deserve,'" she said, quoting one of her favorite French forensic doctors, Alexandre Lacassagne. It was a mantra her father had often stated when he was working on a particularly challenging death to remind him of the importance of thorough and objective investigative work.

These men hadn't deserved a coroner like her father. But Freeport did. Would Melvin and Roger be worthy of the task? She had her doubts.

"I'm not sure what that means, Ms. Hartford," Hank said. "But I think we need to move on to other business."

Emily didn't budge from her spot. "It means . . . that this community will only be as good as the evil you allow to prevail within it."

She paused and let her gaze travel to each face. The group of white men shifted their glances to one another or to their paperwork in front of them. None was able to look her in the eye. There was nothing more to do or say at the moment. Frustrated, Emily spun around and marched toward the back of the room. It was only as she was about to exit the auditorium that she heard a ripple of clapping break out from the room. Tossing a look over her shoulder, she saw the tiny crowd on their feet, directing their applause at her.

20

"Who are Melvin Rotsworth and Roger Phizter, and what do you know about Hank Wurthers and the county commissioners?" Emily asked Delia as she set down two beers and two bear claw pastries on the kitchen table. It was after nine o'clock, and Delia was in her pj's already. She routinely had to rise at three AM to open the door of Brown's Bakery. Emily sunk her teeth into the flaky, cinnamon-y goodness and chased it with a pale ale from Mash Up, a local brewery. The perfect pairing.

"Melvin Rotsworth moved here a couple years ago with his family to start a plumbing business in Freeport. Rots-No-More."

"Horrible name," said Emily with a mouth full of claw.

"Terrible. But business is good, and from what I hear, he does good work. And Roger Phizter is a pharmacist."

"And do either of them have coroner experience? My guess is no."

Delia shook her head.

"Then why on God's green earth do they want to run for county coroner? Neither one has a medical degree, so they'd still have to farm out the autopsies to a medical examiner. Which means the county would be paying double fees. With me, like Dad, they'd get two in one. One-stop shop. Besides, both those men are working full-time already. It makes no sense."

"It's simple politics, Em." Delia broke off a piece of pastry and popped it into her mouth. "Melvin and Roger are making a power play."

"How's that?" Emily groaned.

"In a lot of counties, the coroner position is a stepping-stone into local politics. Get elected coroner, do the job for a couple years. Gain local recognition and then run for another office up the food chain, so to speak."

"Ridiculous. You can't play with people's lives and deaths like that."

"Doll, that is exactly one of the reasons your dad stayed in his position for so long. He knew no one else cared as much as he did or could do a better job. He didn't play their political games. Don't let them walk all over you. Demand to be paid fairly. And demand justice."

Speaking of. "Delia, I wondered if I could ask you a favor."

"Always."

"Mrs. Parkman doesn't have the funds for a proper funeral for her daughter—"

"Say no more. I'll start a kitty at the bakery. And all tips will go in as well."

"Thank you so much, Delia. Now, we just need a new funeral director."

"Have you heard from Cathy?"

"Only that she arrived safely to Ben's house. I'm taking the lack of news as good news." Emily licked cinnamon off her fingers and chugged down the last swallow of her ale.

"You're doing a great job, doll. Your dad would be really proud. Don't let those old codgers get you down. They have no idea how important it is to maintain justice in the community—and what it takes to do it properly," said Delia triumphantly as she pushed her almost-untouched bear claw over to Emily. Emily smiled and took the pastry. She was ravenous.

"Have you thought about Dr. Payton's job offer?"

"It's a request to apply," Emily mumbled through her mouthful of bread.

"Semantics. He sees something in you that he wants."

"He has eyes only for you," Emily joked. "And your cinnamon rolls."

"He'll have to take a number, like the rest of the men waiting in line for my sweets."

Emily laughed and felt the tension release in her shoulders. "What about settling down here? Taking on Melvin and Roger?" she mused.

She considered Delia's life. Delia had given her life to the FBI and had forgone marriage and kids. Not that she'd ever seemed lacking without them. Her life was complete and fulfilled, and she had expressed that to Emily on numerous occasions. She was not defined by her lack of marriage or children. Emily knew that whatever she chose, Delia would support her one hundred and ten percent.

"I don't know, Delia," she continued. "It's hard to wrap my mind around university life. I've just never thought of myself as the teaching type."

"You stay, and you'll never leave."

"You live here."

"I came back. I had a life first. Besides, you're a natural teacher, Emily. You always have been. You get that from your dad, too."

Emily's memory flashed to the many times in the operating room when Dr. Claiborne had handed her the reins to instruct a student doctor on how to make a clean incision or sew up a chest cavity.

"Here, you help a community. There, you influence generations from all over the world," said Delia, with a keen eye toward Emily.

Emily had never considered that angle before. Delia had a point. Where would her talents be more useful and effective? On the field?

Or teaching those who would be going onto the field? And which could she weather better—university politics or Freeport politics? It wouldn't hurt to at least explore the opportunity at the University of Michigan. Especially since it had come knocking at her door, delivered in such a genteel package.

"He's not bad to look at, is he?" said Delia with a sly smirk.

Emily laughed. "He's definitely my type."

"Brains, brawn, and beauty. I got you." Delia glanced over and checked the time on the microwave. "Oh, goodness. I have to be up in five hours. If I don't get my beauty sleep, I end up sprinkling salt instead of sugar on the doughnut twists."

That was Emily's cue to head home, but instead she reached for her bag.

"Oh, I almost forgot." Emily pulled out her laptop. "Do you have a quick minute to take a look at something?"

"Please tell me these are from the Pinetree Slopes case." Delia's voice sprung up with that old, investigative excitement.

"You don't think I would leave you out of the loop, do you?" said Emily as she opened the images from Sandi's autopsy. "And don't worry, Nick is okay with this." She told a little white lie. Easier to ask forgiveness than permission.

"I can tell you're lying, Miss," Delia said. "You pursed your lips just now when you told me."

Emily sighed. There was nothing she could put past Delia. Which made her the perfect asset and ally. "I just want a second opinion on these fissure lines. It's within my rights to consult a consultant."

"I won't disagree. I'm just remembering what a row it caused with the Dobson case."

"Nick saved my life. We have an understanding now."

Delia accepted this answer. Emily scrolled through the files until she found the ones she was looking for.

Delia slipped on her reading glasses as Emily turned the screen to her view. One of Delia's many specialties at the FBI was forensic tool examination. Delia flipped through the series of X-ray images.

"Damage to the neck vertebrae and hyoid bone. Classic strangulation injuries," she muttered, her eyes scanning the film of Sandi's skull and neck. Delia clicked the mouse, and the screen changed to an image of Sandi's ribs and midvertebral section. She slid her glasses down her nose and shook her head.

"What is it?" Emily asked.

"If I've seen it once, I've seen it a thousand times. See the fourth and fifth left rib? Look closely."

Emily leaned in as Delia ran the point of a pen across a series of small fissures.

"Common blunt-force-trauma injury," Delia said with a sigh. "Right under the heart."

"The question is, which injury did her in first—heart or neck?" said Emily.

"Beaten and strangled." Delia drew in a deep breath and leaned back in her chair. "Hard to know which came first. More importantly right now, what caused it?"

"And that's why Dad came to you," Emily said.

"From time to time. He knew when to ask for help," Delia said with a comforting tone. "And I'm here for you, too."

Emily followed Delia's gaze back to the screen.

"It wasn't a sharp object," said Delia. "Something more narrow and rounded. Like a crowbar or pipe."

"Those are a dime a dozen. It'll be impossible to locate the murder weapon. Especially ten years later," said Emily.

"Could be," said Delia. "Best to focus on other evidence. There's always another path, right, doll?"

Yeah. But why was it always so hard to find the trailhead?

Delia rose from the table, taking the two empty beer bottles and setting them in the sink.

Delia turned back to look at Emily. "It must be lonely in your house now."

Her house. Technically. Yes.

"You going to be okay heading home tonight?"

"I'll be fine."

Home. Was her father's house still—or rather, now—home? Where was home?

21

The next day Emily holed herself up at home to take a much-needed break from the world. She ignored her emails and turned off her phone. And she slept. Emily couldn't remember when she had slept so much and for so long. A full ten hours. With a catnap in the afternoon. It felt delicious. The fogginess lifted and her brain cleared. She no longer felt so overwhelmed when thoughts about the future drifted in. The shock of her father's death had dissipated into a numbing reality. She allowed herself a few overdue sobbing sessions. Everything about her little retreat was restorative.

She spent time going through her father's estate and researching the U of M's anthropology department. From everything she could find in her search, she concluded that it seemed well-funded. Advanced. Multicultural. And respected worldwide. Since there was no forensic anthropology focus in place yet, Emily wondered who would be heading up the program and what exactly she would be expected to bring to the table. On the surface it seemed a bit daunting, seeing as she had neither the training nor the experience. She wasn't afraid to forge new paths, but she had a lot of questions welling up in her mind about the position. And why Dr. Payton had asked her, of all people.

Yes, she was suspicious, as any good investigator would be. Why her? Why now? These were core questions in any criminal investigation.

By the following day, after lunch, Emily finally pried herself from her laptop to take a long walk around the property, soaking up the last autumn smells and sun. Seeing her father's apple tree, she decided on the spot to spend the rest of the afternoon resurrecting her mom's apple pie recipe. She'd never had time in Chicago to make pies, and Aunt Laura wasn't exactly the culinary type. She plucked a dozen apples off Dad's apple tree, went inside, and dug through her mom's old recipe box, shoved in the back of a cupboard with cooking sheets and baking tins layered in dust. She found what she was after. The prized apple pie recipe.

But first, coffee. She brewed a pot and was pouring herself a mug when her doorbell rang.

"Hey, look at you! No more dark circles under your eyes," Nick blurted out when she opened the door.

"Nice greeting," She swung the door open so he could enter.

"It was a compliment. You look good. Rested."

She just waved him in. "Coffee?"

"Always." He followed her into the kitchen.

"To what do I own the honor of your visit?" she said with a chirpy voice.

"Just some updates on the Parkman case," Nick said, scooping a full two teaspoons of sugar into his coffee. "I have a lead on something, and I was wondering if you wanted to take a drive with me."

"I was going to make a pie today," she said, proudly spreading her hands like a game show hostess over the apples and prepared baking supplies lined up on the counter.

He nodded. "Those are big plans, Betty Crocker. But I think you'll find my idea more appetizing."

"Oh? What did you have in mind?"

"I found Sandi's stepdad, Gordon Ghetts. Landed himself back in prison three years ago for breaking and entering and attempted robbery. I'm heading over to question him. Come with me."

Emily's eyebrows raised as she took a sip of her coffee. She glanced down at her mother's grease-stained, handwritten recipe card and felt a familiar twinge in her memory. She was fourteen and in the kitchen with her mom, who was peeling a large bowl of fresh apples. Emily held the recipe card in one hand and was gathering ingredients from the cupboards with the other when her father entered and announced there had been a boating fatality on the lake. Did she want to join him or stay with her mother making pie? Of course she had wanted to tear off her apron and rush out the door. But she had promised her mother she would help her make pies to freeze for Thanksgiving. She was about to say no when her mother interjected, giving her permission to go with her father. Emily didn't have to be told twice. Off came the apron. She slapped the recipe card down next to the apple bowl and gave her mom a quick hug.

"So what's the verdict? Coming or not?" said Nick.

Emily glanced up at him as he pulled her from her thoughts.

Mom would understand. And the pie would taste just as good tomorrow.

"I'll grab my jacket."

* * *

The scrunched-up expression on Gordon Ghetts's pockmarked face told Emily that a cop and a blonde woman in a red jacket were not the visitors he had been expecting. They took seats across from him. After introductions had been made, Ghetts, whose charcoal-gray eyes kept shifting from Emily to Nick and back, belched out one question.

"So you think I did it, don't you?"

"Did what?" Nick asked. Emily gulped inside. They hadn't said a single word about Sandi Parkman or her being dead or murdered.

"Why the hell else would you two be up here? I hear things. This ain't Antarctica. I get the news. I know Sandi's bones been found."

"Her remains have been recovered," said Nick in an unflinching, professional tone.

"Well, I didn't do it."

"Why would you lead with that?"

"Because I know this ain't no social call. You both cops?"

Emily had agreed that Nick would lead the questioning and she would be there strictly to answer anything that came up related to the medical forensic facts.

"I'm Dr. Emily Hartford. Medical examiner."

"I understand your defensiveness, but I'm not accusing you or anything, Mr. Ghetts." Nick was so calm. "I just wanted to come down here to ask you a few questions, as we're trying to piece together some details of the day she disappeared. Where were you the day Sandi disappeared?"

"Nowhere near her," Ghetts sputtered.

"Then where?" Nick pressed.

"Work."

"Working where?"

"The sand mold factory."

"From when to when?"

"I started at eight and we got out around five."

Nick nodded. Emily knew those times correlated with his time card. Nick had gone back through old factory records.

"What did you do after work, Mr. Ghetts?"

"What I always did. Went for a drink with the guys."

"Where?"

"Local bar."

"Which one?"

"Silver Slipper."

That was using the term *bar* loosely. Emily held back a grimace.

"You sure you went to work the day Sandi disappeared?"

"Yes. I'm sure. Do I need my attorney?" He folded his arms across his chest.

"You know your rights. You want me to call him? I will. We'll get him here and I'll wait all day if I have to. All weekend and all week, if that's what it takes. And we'll just pick up where we left off."

This gave Ghetts pause. Emily held in her breath, waiting to see what he would do next.

"That won't be necessary. I ain't got nothing to hide, 'cause I ain't done nothing."

"Except sexually abuse an innocent young girl." Emily betrayed her cool. Nick shot her a look.

Ghetts lurched forward in his chair. "I didn't lay a hand on that girl!"

A guard stepped over, and Ghetts leaned back.

"She made all that shit up because she wanted attention. She was messed up in the head," he growled.

"You must have been really angry at Sandi for turning you in."

"She lies really good." His voice bled with sarcasm.

"I don't think Sandi was lying about what you did to her," said Emily.

"Did you even know her?" Ghetts barked back.

"Some people say they saw you were hanging around the school a lot after you got out of prison," said Nick.

"Yeah. I did. And you wanna know why? Because Sandi didn't know how to choose guys and she didn't know how to keep her legs closed."

"Are you saying you were trying to protect her?" Emily's voice took on an incredulous tone.

"Sandi always had a boyfriend. Or two. She liked to play the field. She liked those jock types."

Emily and Nick shared a quick glance. Was he telling the truth? Was there a side to Sandi Nick hadn't seen? Or didn't want to admit?

"Do you remember any names?" Nick asked.

"Shit, no. There was too many. But I know faces. Don't think I don't recognize you, Officer Larson," Ghetts sneered.

"I never dated Sandi. We were friends. Neighbors." Nick was laser focused, but Emily could see he was getting hot under the collar.

"Sandi had a lot of 'just friends,' if you know what I mean."

"Who?" asked Nick.

Ghetts sat back, thinking. "She was always yapping about this one guy. They would talk for hours on the phone."

"You remember his name?" asked Emily.

Ghetts shook his head. "The guy was a carrot top."

"He had red hair?" Emily wanted to clarify.

"Yeah," said Ghetts.

"What was this guy like?" asked Nick.

"I dunno. Never came around the house. None of them did."

Nick shook his head. Emily knew he wasn't buying this.

"Did you ever violate your restraining order?"

"I never went near her."

"You were seen at the high school."

"I never went near her," he repeated, louder.

"You sure? 'Cause I'm finding it hard to believe you were just stalking her for the sake of watching her."

Ghetts clenched his teeth like he was biting back some response. Emily could see Nick's frustration growing as he tapped his heel against the chair leg. She discreetly reached her hand under the table and placed it on his leg to get him to stop.

"Did you ever videotape the stuff you did to Sandi?" Nick went in heavy.

"I never laid a hand on that girl," he laughed, but Emily noticed that his eyes drifted to the wall left of them. And then to the floor. After a second, he looked through them.

"I never taped anything. You got that?"

"You already served your time for what you did to Sandi. I'm not here about that. I don't care about that now," said Nick. "But she turned up missing shortly after you were released. So, I'm just putting two and two together."

Ghetts's breathing shallowed, and he turned back to Nick with a grim face.

"How'd she die?"

Nick turned to Emily, who inhaled and looked Ghetts in the eye.

Ghetts pressed. "What happened to her?"

"She was beaten and strangled."

Ghetts's gaze bounced to the ceiling, and he let out a long sigh.

"You damaged her. You sent her down this path," said Nick.

"I wasn't in my right mind," he said after a moment, his gaze drifting inside himself. "Booze. Meth. Takes a man and guts the humanity right out of him."

"That's a cowardly excuse for destroying a young lady and her family."

"I always wanted the chance to . . . tell her . . . that I was sorry for what happened."

Emily froze. Was he for real? Nick kept his eyes trained on Ghetts.

"What did happen?" said Nick in a steady, hushed tone.

Ghetts waved his hand at the guard to signal he wanted to leave. The guard came over and led him away. Nick and Emily watched as he trudged out of the visiting area. At one point, he reached his shoulder up to his face and wiped something from his eye. Was it tears? Or just a ruse?

*　*　*

"Who's he talking about? The carrot top?" said Emily as soon as they stepped out the prison doors.

"Ross Geldon," said Nick with his eyes locked ahead on the parking lot. "Rosy Ross, we used to call him."

"I don't get it," said Emily.

"Roses are red. Ross had red hair, and his face would get all beet red when he was embarrassed or mad."

"Rosy Ross. That's kinda mean."

"Nah. Everyone had a nickname. It was a badge of honor."

"Guys are weird."

"You had a name, too."

"What? No. I never had a nickname."

Nick laughed. "Oh yes, you did."

"What was it?"

Nick nodded. "You honestly never knew?"

"Tell me. Come on." She punched him playfully in the arm.

"Doctor Death."

"That's so demeaning!"

"No, it makes sense, 'cause you wanted to be a doctor. And you worked with your dad on dead bodies." He grinned.

"Ridiculous. People actually called me that?"

"Yes. People liked you."

"No, they didn't. Only Jo." Emily was secretly pleased. She had a nickname! "Who started calling me that?"

Nick grinned and opened the passenger door for her. Emily crawled into his squad car.

"I'll never tell."

"Spill it, mister." She propped the door open with her leg so he couldn't close it on her.

"I did."

"You're ridiculous," she said, releasing her leg. "And kinda mean." He smiled and closed the door. She couldn't help but giggle. *Doctor Death.* She had to admit it was a good fit and had an intimidating ring to it.

Nick joined her in the car, and they took off as the sun was setting.

"Do you believe Ghetts?" she asked.

"I believe he's guilty of the sex crimes. The murder? I don't know. You?"

"His time card is pretty solid evidence. If you could find some coworkers who remember seeing him that day, then maybe I'd be willing to clear his slate."

"I'm already on it. But it hasn't been easy to find these old-timers. A lot of them have passed away."

"Did you know Sandi and Ross were so close?" asked Emily.

"I did not. And I'm rather suspicious about that claim. I don't remember seeing any statement from him in Sandi's original case file."

"I don't remember you having a nickname in high school."

"I got it junior year. You were gone."

"What is it?"

"I'm not telling you."

"I'll just ask Jo." She shrugged and picked up her phone to call her best friend.

"Settle down, Doctor Death." Nick put his hand over the face of her phone.

"I think it's time to retire that name."

"I birthed it. I'll decide when it needs to die."

Emily laughed. They drove for a moment in silence.

"It was . . . Nick the Prick."

"That was your nickname? That doesn't sound endearing."

Nick shrugged. "I was always standing up for the underdog. And that pissed off the bullies. And now, this uniform now pretty much guarantees my nickname for life."

"Well, you're not. Just so you know." Emily regretted that she had pushed the issue. Confident, popular Nick. She would never have guessed this to be his sore spot.

"I'm starving." It was a two-hour drive back to Freeport.

"We'll have to settle for fast food because we have one more errand to run." Nick turned into the drive of a burger joint.

"We do?" said Emily, noticing a rumble in her belly. "Where?"

"Lyndon."

Lyndon was a half hour east of the penitentiary. "What's there?"

"You'll see."

22

"I'm standing by the alibi I gave ten years ago. I was at the gym after school with James and Landry. You can ask them," said Ross Geldon when Nick and Emily found him working sales at a used car dealership in Lyndon.

"I did ask Landry," said Nick. "He said you left early. How early?"

"I don't know. I was there till James was."

"Give me a guesstimate. When did you leave the school gym?"

"Or what? You're going to arrest me?" Ross let out a huge sneeze. "Sorry, caught a cold." He reached for a tissue in his pocket and blew his nose. "I know you don't have any evidence on me, Nick. You only care now about Sandi because it's your job."

"That's not true. I tried to help her." Nick raised his voice, and Emily noticed a middle-aged salesman drinking hot cocoa from a dispenser in the waiting area turn a quick glance to them. Other than him, they were the only three people in the place. It was now eight o'clock on a Saturday night. Emily noted that this was definitely the best time to buy a used car if you wanted a salesman's full attention.

"When did you last see Sandi?" Nick asked.

"Best guess, four thirty," said Ross, tossing the dirty tissue into the trash and reaching for another one.

"What was your relationship to Sandi?" asked Nick.

"Friends."

"Did she ever talk to you about her relationship with James?"

"James was toxic to her," hissed Ross, wiping his sniffling nose into the fresh tissue.

"How?"

"He just bullied her. Forced her into things she didn't want to do."

"Like what?"

Ross crossed his arms and glanced outside. "Hey, man, it's water under the bridge, right? Nothing we can do now."

"Yes, there is. We can try to find out who killed her. So speak up. What do you know?" said Nick.

"I know what you know."

"I don't think so. I think you know more," pressed Nick.

"The video, you moron. Don't you remember?" Ross said, throwing his hushed voice away from the prying ears in the waiting area.

"Of course I do. But I never saw it. Did you?" Nick turned to Ross with an indignant look.

Ross shrugged.

"Does that mean you did?" asked Nick.

Ross began to strum his fingers lightly on his arms. Emily knew this as a classic sign of anxiety. Ross knew something more about that video.

"What was on that video, Ross?" Nick asked.

"Stuff."

"Be a little more specific."

"Stuff she didn't want anyone to know about."

"She told me she didn't know about the video," said Nick.

Ross shook his head, "She did. She knew."

"If what was on that video was so bad, why didn't you do anything about it?"

"Because . . . because . . . I was the guy in it," Ross blurted out.

"You and Sandi made a sex video?" Nick's voice cracked at the word *sex* and echoed through the showroom. The hot-cocoa-drinking salesman snapped his gaze to them, drawing Ross's attention. He sent a little wave to the guy. "Hey, Darren, I can close up. You go on home to that sweet family of yours."

"You got it, boss. Thanks!" Darren tossed the Styrofoam cup into the trash bin and zipped out. Ross turned his attention to Nick.

"Just friends, huh?" said Emily.

"Hey, I didn't know we were being filmed." Ross was indignant. "How'd you find out?"

"James came up to me at the gym that afternoon and showed me. He blackmailed me with it."

"What did you do?" said Emily.

"I ripped the phone out of his hands and I threw it against the brick wall. It shattered. And I nailed him one. I mean, I sent him to the floor."

"That's how he broke his nose?" said Nick.

"Yeah. It wasn't a stray baseball like he told everyone."

"Why would he make a sex tape of you and Sandi?" Emily could not wrap her head around the motive here. Sandi was dating James and sleeping with Ross? What else was going on?

"He knew Sandi and I had been seeing each other. And she—we—were in love. It made James crazy angry."

"I'm missing something here. If she was in love with you, why was she still with James?" asked Nick.

"He had this weird hold on her. He could be sweet. And he was rich. He bribed her with nice things. Purses. Jewelry. New jeans. He made her feel special in a way I couldn't."

"But that's not real love." Emily still didn't get this mess.

I wanted to show her I would be there for her.

"But she was dating someone else. Didn't that bother you?" said Emily.

"Dating isn't exactly what I would call her and James. And I know she wasn't sleeping with him."

Nick cleared his throat. "What did you think happened to Sandi?"

"For a long time I believed she ran away. I kept hoping I'd get a call from her. I just wanted to know she was safe."

"How long did you hold on to that?" asked Emily.

"I guess I knew after a couple weeks she was gone."

"Gone?" asked Nick.

"Dead."

"Dead how?" said Emily.

"Murdered."

"And who do you think killed Sandi?" The wash of sadness sweeping over Ross did not escape her.

"Honestly, I had the same thoughts as everyone else. The stepdad."

"Never James?" asked Nick.

Ross shrugged. "I don't see it. He was controlling, manipulative, but not violent. He never even hit me back that day in the gym."

"He didn't fight back?" asked Emily.

"Not with punches. He got up off the floor, gave me this cocky little smile, and walked out."

Nick and Emily exchanged a quick glance.

"Turning the other cheek? That's not very manly," said Emily.

"James didn't like to get his hands dirty," Ross said.

"Or his designer clothes," added Nick.

"I don't get how you guys were friends with him," said Emily.

"We weren't," they said in unison.

"He was one of those guys who just showed up and inserted himself into everyone's business," said Nick.

"James was someone you tolerate."

"Maybe he didn't fight back because he knew he could get into big trouble for what he had done?" suggested Emily.

"He liked to let his daddy fight his battles with money and lawyers," said Ross. "I half expected to see a lawsuit the next day on my doorstep. But he just drifted away from all of us after Sandi was gone."

Nick was about to say something, but one look from Emily and he pressed his lips shut. Emily put on her best empathetic face and waited. Sometimes a moment of silence was all that was needed for someone to continue the conversation on their own. People hated silence. She didn't have to wait long before Ross filled it.

"I got to thinking about it. I spent a lot of time with Sandi and her kid sister, Tiffani. She was always hanging around us. She was this really sweet kid sister one minute, and then after Sandi was gone, she turned into a hellion. It's weird, right? I just think she's hiding something."

He stopped, and the three of them let that thought hang over them for a moment. Emily tried to imagine Sandi's little sister as a killer. How would she have had the strength to strangle Sandi, unless she knocked her out first? What would be the motive? Was she jealous of Sandi? Had Sandi promised her something and then backed out? Was it just a sisterly spar gone awry?

"Can you give us a minute?" Nick asked, motioning with a flick of his hand for Emily to leave.

Rude. "Fine." She disliked his dismissive attitude but didn't want to break their solidarity on the matter at hand. She smiled sweetly and strolled into the showroom to look at the selection of vehicles. As Emily passed a Lexus sedan, it triggered the image of the black Lexus in Pinetree Slopes at Sandi's site. Unlike Nick, who'd brushed it off, Emily was convinced that the two people in the car had been at that spot because they knew something about Sandi's murder.

Ross had access to cars. Unregistered cars. Cars without plates. Cars that could come and go easily off a showroom floor. If Ross had been one of the people in that Lexus, what was his motive for returning to the site of Sandi's grave? Emily started to roll a new circle of thoughts through her brain. If Ross had loved Sandi so much, why hadn't he put James in his place before the video incident? There seemed to be a very real possibility that since Sandi wasn't leaving James, Ross might try to take James down again. Would Sandi turn against Ross at some point if that happened? Would James fight back? Maybe not with his fists, but if he had such a hold on Sandi, wouldn't he try do everything in his power to sully Ross's reputation, shatter his chances of university scholarship, his varsity status, his shot at graduation? And did Ross have reason to believe there were more sex videos? Ross knew James and his father had the power to dismantle his whole life. Maybe he was lying about his love for Sandi? Maybe he'd been using her, too. Maybe Sandi wasn't worth the risk of losing his whole future. Getting rid of Sandi would send James the message that Ross had the upper hand and that he'd better not mess with him ever again. It was extreme, but maybe that's how far Ross would go to protect himself. It was a theory they needed to consider.

Emily glanced over at Nick. He was standing and shaking Ross's hand, like old friends. She thought Nick was being very naive right now. Ross had told a nice story, and Nick was immediately ready to cross him off the suspect list. Same with stepdad Gordon Ghetts. Emily had been deceived by well-intentioned stories before, and it had made her wary of feel-good tales.

Emily looked up to see Nick give her a quick nod. He was ready to go. She made her way to Ross's desk to say goodbye.

"Ms. Hartford, nice to meet you, again. I'm sure our paths crossed at school," said Ross, the tail end of his sentence getting cut off by a loud sneeze. Emily cringed as he blew his snotty nose into a tissue and then reached out to shake her hand.

"It's Dr. Hartford." Emily gave him a polite smile and kept her hands to herself. "And if you want some free medical advice, you should take two aspirin, plenty of water, and get a good night's rest."

23

Emily forgot to set an alarm and woke Sunday at eleven AM feeling groggy, but she didn't have the luxury of staying in bed. She had accepted an invitation from Anna to meet her and the family in Rock River at the ice arena at one. Flora and Fiona were both competing in a local freestyle competition, and Anna thought this would be the perfect way for Emily to be introduced to her new nieces.

Two hours later, a cleaned and caffeinated Emily joined Anna and her husband, Kyle, in the bleacher seats overlooking the ice rink, where a dozen girls were warming up.

"Flora is the one in the royal-blue outfit. And Fiona is the yellow one," said Anna, pointing them out in the rink. Emily glanced out across the rink to see the waify figures in yellow and blue whirling in their warm-ups.

"They're adorable." Both had long, sandy-brown hair and lean extremities. They definitely took after their mom. Emily hadn't noticed in their first meeting how beautiful and elegant Anna really was. Emily looked down at her short, dirty nails and compared them to Anna's manicured ones. It wouldn't hurt to step into a nail salon now and then.

"I'm so glad you could make it." Anna was beaming. "I've been telling the girls all about you. You're joining us for lunch after the competition, right?"

"Of course. I'm glad to be here. It's been quite a whirlwind, and it's so nice to spend time with . . . you." *Family* had been the word on the tip of Emily's tongue. But it didn't come out.

"I still can't believe I gained a sister."

"Me neither. Or a brother-in-law. And nieces." Emily leaned over to acknowledge Kyle, who was pecking at his smartphone. He glanced up.

"My apologies. Work. It never leaves you," said Kyle as he took an incoming call and stepped down the bleachers to talk off to the side.

"What does he do?" asked Emily.

"Investments. Mostly real estate. And a lot of overseas travel."

"Nice. Do you ever travel with him?"

"Sometimes. When the kids are off school," Anna said, flashing a smile. "I'm just dying to know more about my father and . . . and you and I . . . we have a lifetime to catch up on!"

"What do you want to know?" Emily felt a cherry pit of guilt plant in her gut. What did she know about her dad's most recent years? Virtually nothing. Now would definitely not be the right time to dump all that onto Anna's lap.

"How did your mom and dad meet?"

"College. They got married after sophomore year. After graduation, Dad went on to med school." And two years later I was born. After med school he set up his practice in Freeport, and that's where they settled. He and Mom always wanted more kids, but after a couple of miscarriages, it was pretty clear it wasn't going to happen."

"Oh my goodness. I'm so sorry."

"I'm sure they were sad about it, but it never came across that way to me. We had a good life. They were really happy. Really in love. And then . . . Mom's accident. Dad and I both kinda fell apart.

I ran away from home end of my sophomore year. To Chicago. I lived with my aunt Laura for the next two years until I enrolled in university, premed, and then I moved out to live on my own. From there, medical school. Surgical residency. And that's where I'm at now. I have two more years to go."

"Wow. Incredible story. So you actually live in Chicago, then?" Emily noted a slight disappointment in Anna's tone.

"Technically, yes. I mean, that's where my address is." She didn't want to get into the whole dynamics and dramatics of her complicated love life. Wow. She really was a tangled ball of dilemmas, wasn't she?

"Well, I hope you'll come back up and join us for Christmas," said Anna. "We really do it up. We put a tree in every room. And we spend all Christmas day eating and opening gifts and listening to Christmas music. We have an extra room. You're welcome to stay. We'll even put up a tree in your room for you!"

"It sounds very . . . celebratory. I'll definitely consider that. If I'm not on shift . . ."

"Oh, right. Of course. Well, just know you always have a place in our home."

"Thank you."

Emily was about to ask Anna how she and Kyle had met, but Anna turned to dig for something in the girls' gym bag. Emily realized this was the perfect opportunity to get the stock papers rightfully back into Anna's hands. She saw Anna's purse on the floor and tucked them deeply into the side pocket while Anna was still turned around. If Anna protested later, she would insist that the money be used on the girls. A college fund, for one. Or skating lessons. Those couldn't be cheap. When Emily looked up, she saw Flora and Fiona clomping their way up the stairs in their skates to greet her.

"Girls, this is your aunt Emily that I told you about," said Anna. Both girls came up to her with shy hellos and polite handshakes.

"It's so nice to finally meet you both." She matched their nervous smiles.

"Did you see us skate?" asked Flora, the twelve year old.

"I did. You're very good," said Emily.

"Aunt Emily, are you getting cupcakes with us?" asked Fiona, the eight-year-old, in a squeaky kid voice.

Aunt. I'm an aunt now. She tingled inside at the title.

"Ah, am I?" Emily looked over at Anna.

"It's tradition."

"You have to come," said Fiona.

"Then it's decided."

She wished Dad could be here to see these little darlings. Her heart sickened, knowing he would never know these two beautiful, gangly grandchildren. Or hers. She was quickly pulled from the thought as a little hand tugged on hers.

"Come on, Aunt Emily." said Fiona. "What's your favorite kind of cupcake? Mine's peanut butter and jelly!"

"No way! That's my favorite too," said Emily, suddenly feeling the warm little hand take hers.

24

A text from Nick pinged her phone. *Meet me at my house at 9 pm.*

Meet for what? She glanced at the clock on her dashboard. It was 6:56 PM and she was almost to Freeport. She was hungry and tired. Grabbing a pizza to go and staying in sounded more her speed. As she was about to voice-text Nick back, another text came in from him.

And wear something sexy.

Emily immediately called him. He picked up after the first ring.

"Thought that would get your attention," he said.

"I'm gonna pick up a pizza and head home. And I was planning to stay there. In cozy pants and a sweat shirt. So this better be good."

"Were you this boring in Chicago, too?"

"It's Sunday night. I'm exhausted." And no, she hadn't been this boring in Chicago. Brandon had had her out on the town every night off they could get. He loved city action, and she'd loved experiencing it with him. But that's because there was always something new and different to do. Not so in Freeport.

"I'm not going to tell you, but I will give a hint. It's a reconnaissance field trip for work."

"Okay. Interesting. But all my sexy clothes are still in Chicago," she said.

"Jeans and heels'll be fine."

"That I can do." She hung up and dialed for pizza. She knew Nick would want some. Besides, it would be a shame, and pure gluttony, to eat it all alone. She didn't mind being single right now, but she hated eating alone.

* * *

Quarter to eight, Emily arrived at Nick's house with pizza, heels, and a fresh blouse. He opened the door dressed in jeans and a crisp white T-shirt, and his hair was wet with that just-showered look. And he had put on cologne.

"You look great," he said, taking the pizza box.

"And you smell great." Emily stepped inside. Since when did Nick Larson wear cologne?

As they ate, they chitchatted about the past few days, but despite her subtle—or not-so-subtle—hints, Nick would still not let on what their secret errand entailed.

At nine o'clock they left in Nick's truck.

"Okay, I've tried to be good. What are we doing tonight?"

Nick held up a finger. "You'll see when we get there."

"Can you at least prep me? It's not every day I put heels on."

"I don't want you overthinking this."

Emily and Nick rode in silence for the next ten minutes as he took them outside Freeport. They were coming up to the Silver Slipper when Nick slowed down.

"Seriously?" said Emily.

"Don't judge. Yet."

The parking lot was full as Nick pulled in and tried to find a spot.

"What are we doing here?"

"Just trust me."

"Are you kidding?"

He parked his truck on the far end of the lot. Emily was surprised Freeport could sustain a place like the Silver Slipper. Then a thought raced across her mind. What if she saw someone she knew? One of the county commissioners? What if word got back to them? Or any self-respecting person in Freeport? She crossed her arms and held her ground.

"I'm not going in there."

Nick turned off the ignition. "Tiffani Parkman works here. I thought you could use your feminine wiles to see if you can get her to open up about where she was the day her sister disappeared."

"You couldn't have brought her into the station as per normal protocol?"

"She'll tell you more than she would me."

"These kind of girls can be pretty cagey." Two of Emily's med school friends had danced for their tuition. And there was no messing with them.

Nick unlocked the doors, but Emily didn't budge.

"We go in separately. I'll point out Tiffani and you approach her when she takes a break."

Emily shook her head. "That's ridiculous. I'm not going to stalk her. I'll come up with my own plan."

"Which is?"

"I'll figure it out."

"Like you did with the Dobson case? How'd that work out, huh?" He was referring to her tangle with the killer who, a couple of weeks back, had murdered teen equestrian Julie Dobson. If she pressed firmly enough into her side, she could still feel the bruised rib where she had been struck as she defended herself.

"I caught the killer, so I'd say it worked out pretty well."

Emily pounced out of the truck, heels pounding toward the entrance. It was a trek across the uneven parking lot, and her ankles were feeling the torque.

"I'm not letting you go in there by yourself." Nick had caught up with her.

She stopped and faced him. "Wait in the truck. I'll be right back."

Emily diverted her path to the back of the building. She waited near the dumpster, as much out of view as she could manage. Just in case someone should exit. A dancer. A busboy. A patron.

Emily almost laughed out loud. If these covert operations were going to become a thing with them, they would definitely have to work out a better code.

She quickly entered and slipped down the sticky floor of the black-walled hallway. It was lit with three exposed bulbs. She could feel the music pumping through the balls of her feet. There was only one large dressing room at the far end of the hall next to a tiny, one-seater bathroom. Emily poked her head in. She recognized Tiffani from a childhood photo on Mrs. Parkman's wall. Now, there she stood bared in her thong and pasties in front of a mirror as she wiped a layer of baby oil off her shoulders and arms.

"Tiffani?" Emily said.

"Yeah." She didn't even turn around. She swiped the towel over her legs to degrease them.

"I was told you could show me the ropes," said Emily, taking a step in.

"You new?" Tiffani glanced in the mirror and saw Emily standing behind her in the door.

"I hope to be."

"Weird. Wanda never said anything about a new girl." Emily was tongue-tied for a second. "But whatever. Probably slipped her mind. We could use a couple more girls. Who sent you?"

"Just . . . a friend."

"Friend's name?"

"I don't think he'd want me to say." She smiled coyly.

"Doesn't matter. I'll figure it out."

Tiffani studied Emily up and down.

"You have a good figure. What do you do?" asked Tiffani, rubbing off oil and sweat from her chest.

"I . . . I'm in school." It wasn't a complete lie.

"No, I mean moves."

"Oh. I can . . . I was in gymnastics," Emily lied. "And I was a cheerleader."

"I can work with that. Wanda give you the paperwork?"

Emily shook her head.

"You look a little deflated. Up there." Tiffani pointed to her chest. "Get a boob job."

"Oh." Emily swallowed hard. "Yeah. Maybe." Tiffani pulled the hair from her brush and tossed it toward the garbage pail. It missed and landed in a clump on the floor.

"What's your stage name?"

She hadn't thought about that. Right. Okay. "What about Doctor . . . Dazzle?" That sounded so stupid! No way was Tiffani gonna buy it.

Tiffani dropped the towel on a nearby chair and turned around. "If you're going with that, you should also get a racy doctor costume."

"Good idea. I didn't think of that." Emily bobbed her head in agreement.

Tiffani slipped on a pair of sweat pants over her bare cheeks. Emily wished she would cover her upper half for dignity's sake. "I'm heading out to take a smoke break. Talk to Wanda about the hiring papers, and then get back to me so we can schedule a practice session."

"Yeah. Sure. Thank you."

Tiffani was about to step out the back door.

"Tiffani?" Emily said, stepping in and closing the door to the club.

"Oh no, keep that open. Management doesn't like us to have it closed."

Emily cracked the door. She needed to get to the point fast. Before anyone came in.

"I heard about them finding your sister, and I'm real sorry."

Tiffani's face didn't flinch. "Thanks." She pawed through her bag for her smokes.

Emily had to up her charade game. "It's probably pretty stressful. I can only imagine what you've been through."

"Yeah, well, it's no surprise to me. I always figured she'd been killed or something," said Tiffani, tapping her cigarette pack on her palm.

"When was the last time you saw Sandi?" asked Emily.

"I dunno. You from around here?"

"I grew up here, but then left for a while." Also not a complete lie.

"Did you know her? You look about her age," asked Tiffani.

"I was a couple grades older. I knew who she was."

"Well, I'm out," Tiffani said, lighting her cigarette as she opened the back door.

"Do you ever replay that day in your mind?" Emily said.

"I don't get what you're driving at here, Doctor Dazzle. What's with the deep dive into my personal life? I don't even know you."

"Sorry, I don't mean to pry. It's just that I lost . . . someone close to me, too. I guess I kinda feel like a bond with you or something."

"We're not bonding." Tiffani looked up at Emily with a suspicious glance. "You sure you aren't with the police, Miss Nosy?"

"No. Of course not." Emily forced a giggle.

Tiffani took a drag of her cigarette. Emily backstepped toward the door. She was walking a fine line, and she wasn't sure where to go from here. She drew in a deep breath. "I better go find Wanda."

Tiffani peered at her. "You look too put together to be a dancer in a strip club."

Emily feared her gig was up. She had to think fast.

"You a cop or something?" Tiffani asked again.

"What? No!"

"You don't look like the type who really wants to dance."

"The . . . the truth is, I need to dance to finish college. I'm a bit broke at the moment, so I came home to save up," said Emily with an air of confidence as she put her hand on her side and thrust her hip out a couple inches. "There. My dirty secret." She threw her hands up and let out another squeaky giggle to break the tension.

Tiffani exhaled, filling the room with smoke.

She gave Emily a wry smile.

"I just hope they arrest that cop."

"What cop?"

Tiffani took a step closer to her.

"Nick Larson. She went to his house after she got home from school. And that is the last time I saw my sister."

"You think he killed her?" Emily feigned. "Why?"

"To protect the pack."

"What pack?"

"If you don't know, you're dumber than I thought. You went to Freeport High. You know exactly what I'm talking about." Tiffani mopped her moist brow with the back of her hand and took another drag. "Your little boyfriend, Nick Larson, sent you in here, didn't he? Doing his dirty work."

Emily had to keep her jaw from dropping. "I don't know what you're talking about."

"Don't act dumb, Doctor Dazzle. I mean Dr. Emily Hartford." Tiffani's triumphant face turned to Emily. "You're that crazy girl who ran away from home after her mom died."

Emily felt sucker-punched.

"Someone needs to look into Nick as a suspect."

"Nick has an alibi for that afternoon," said Emily with a cool tone.

"Of course he does. He's not going to admit he got rid of my sister to save his name. And the names of the pack."

Emily's mind flashed back to the image of Nick and Ross talking together secretively the night before. As farfetched as this theory might sound, nothing at this point could be dismissed. Truth and lies were strange allies. A queasiness rippled through Emily's stomach.

"I'm sure Nick didn't kill your sister," Emily clarified.

"Maybe. Maybe not. But he knows who did. That's how the pack operated. They all know. And they're protecting Sandi's killer."

Tiffani looked away with a half shrug that didn't exactly instill confidence in her belief. Yet it did raise a flicker of doubt in Emily. Was Rosy Ross one of the pack members?

Tiffani caught Emily looking at her and glared back.

A topless curvy redhead in silk hipster briefs poked her head into the room. "Hey, Tiff, I need to run out a second. Cover me?"

"You got it."

"Thanks, I'll be right back." The redhead ducked out.

"Oh, God . . . Carly . . . wait!" Tiffani grabbed a T-shirt and flung the door open, jumping into the hall to stop her. "Put this on, for God's sake. It's chilly out there." She wadded up the shirt and threw it at the half-naked girl. She held the door open and turned to Emily. "Now that you've used up my entire break, I'm gonna take a piss and you're gonna get outta my sight. Got it, Doctor Dazzle?"

Emily stepped into the hall. Tiffani wasn't rattled an iota from this conversation. When she stepped back into the dressing room, she closed the door and locked it.

Utter failure and embarrassment.

Emily hoofed it back outside and across the parking lot. She glanced over to where Carly was shutting the back passenger door of a black Lexus. The same car Emily had seen at Pinetree Slopes. Carly clicked the fob and the lock alarm sounded once, and she pranced back toward the club. Emily watched until she disappeared inside. Then she hustled to Nick's truck, where he was waiting for her.

"You saw that, right? Tell me you just saw that," Emily said breathlessly as she dove into the passenger's seat. "It's our Lexus."

Nick started the engine. "How can she afford a Lexus on stripper wages?"

"Tips?" Emily raised a brow.

"She must be good at what she does," said Nick.

"Not Lexus good. These aren't your Miracle Mile clients. She has to have a sugar daddy," Emily ventured.

"More likely," said Nick, holding a concerned gaze on Emily. "So, what happened in there?"

"Later." She peeled her feet out of her heels. Felt so good.

Nick pulled out of the drive, and they sped away.

"Nick, have you hired that attorney yet?" Emily asked after they rode in silence a few minutes.

"Not yet."

"Have you inquired into getting another detective from the state police post to take over this case?" She wasn't going to back down on this.

"I was thinking about deputizing you."

"Ha-ha. Let's also see about getting you a shrink."

"I'm serious. You did a great job on the Dobson case."

"No, Nick. Tiffani thinks you killed Sandi."

"Ridiculous. Based on what proof?"

"She said Sandi went to your house after you dropped her off. She said you were part of the pack."

"She's lying. Case closed."

"Why would she lie?"

"That's what we need to find out," said Nick.

"And this is why you can't bring Tiffani in to talk to you about it, isn't it?"

"It's her word against mine."

"This is exactly why you need an attorney," said Emily, feeling the heat rise up her back and into her neck.

"Sandi never came over that day."

"What's the pack?" asked Emily.

"A stupid high school urban legend."

"Enlighten me. I love a good tale." The sarcasm spilled over.

"It was a stupid name designation. It meant nothing."

"Were you part of it?" she asked.

"There was nothing to be part of." Nick pressed his lips together and clenched his jaw until the muscles flexed. "Was Ross part of the pack?"

Nick's silence told Emily what she needed to know. There was more to this pack stuff than he was admitting. And he was still sworn to its secrecy.

25

Emily wrestled with sleep all night, unable to quiet her spinning thoughts. How big was this pack, and how many others knew about it? Was Nick afraid he'd lose his job if people found out? And why was Nick afraid to hire an attorney?

After sickening herself with worry, Emily fell into a half sleep an hour before sunrise. Her cell phone woke her up. She cleared her throat and hit *accept*. Before she could get out a hello, Jo's voice spewed from the receiver.

"I'm absolutely furious right now!"

"Jo? What happened?" Emily sat up and stretched her legs out.

"I kicked Paul out last night."

"What? Why?"

"I just learned he was part of the pack."

Emily's stomach lurched. Not Paul, too.

"I don't even understand what this whole pack thing is," said Emily, jolted awake by the news. "Nick refused to tell me anything last night."

"Get over here and I'll tell you everything."

* * *

Emily found Jo in her kitchen hunched over her oak dining room table, staring blankly at the cross-weave fabric of her olive tablecloth. Normally bubbly and upbeat, today Jo had dark, swollen circles under her eyes and faint worry lines etched in her forehead. Jo was barely holding it together. Emily didn't say hello; she just started a pot of coffee in Jo's percolator.

"How did you hear about the pack?" Jo asked.

"I was with Nick last night visiting Tiffani Parkman at the Silver Slipper."

Jo shot a glance at Emily.

"Yeah. I know. Story for another time. Anyhow, Tiffani mentioned the pack and said that Nick was in it. And that she thought Nick had something to do with Sandi's murder. When I asked Nick about it, he shut me down."

The coffeepot stopped gurgling. Emily poured the steaming coffee into their mugs and brought them to the table. Jo teaspooned sugar into her mug with a shaky hand and stirred. Emily was dying to jump right in with a million questions. Information about this pack could be one of the keys to Sandi's murder. But she held back until her friend was ready.

Jo lifted her gaze to Emily only after she had taken several more sips. Then she let it all out.

"Paul says Nick knew about it but wasn't really into it—at least not like he and the other guys were."

"Nick said it was a name designation. What does that even mean? What did this pack do?"

"Apparently they had a pact of secrecy. And they did things they shouldn't . . . to girls."

What? "What kinds of things, Jo?"

"At first it was stuff like hiding in the girls' locker room and watching them dress for practice."

"Disgusting!"

"No, it gets worse. They would hide a camera in the locker room after swim practice."

"And no one ever knew about this?" Emily felt sick. Had this been going on when she'd been at Freeport High?

Jo shook her head. "I never knew. None of my friends knew. They would hide cameras on the stairs and film up girls' skirts."

"And what would they do with this footage?"

"Paul said they just passed it around to each other."

"And they never got caught?"

"Apparently not. Pact of secrecy."

"How many in this pack?"

"I don't know. Paul wouldn't budge."

Emily ground her teeth.

"I guess things took a turn during their senior year. James Van-DerMuellen wanted to take it to another level. He came to school one day with a super-secret video. It was Sandi having sex with some guy. James cut the frame so they couldn't see who it was."

But Emily knew who. Rosy Ross. She held it back from Jo.

"I feel sick. And so angry."

"Me too. Paul said that if the pack wanted to see it, they had to pay. Pretty soon, he was charging people outside the pack for a view."

Disgusting. No wonder Ross had been furious with James. Emily's heart sank.

"Paul said that in the video, Sandi looked really out of it. This wasn't consensual, Em."

Emily's eyes went wide as the sick realization came to her. What if Ross had drugged and raped her and this was all part of the pack's plan?

She didn't know how to respond. It was unthinkable what Sandi had suffered. She must have been so alone in her suffering all those years, hiding her stepdad's abuse. Then to be betrayed by James and used by Ross. The truth was so filthy and ugly.

"Why would James do something like that?" said Jo. "His family was rich. He didn't need the money."

"The rich always want more. Money makes them feel powerful. And power breeds the hunger for more power."

"He was always so cocky." Jo made a face. "How far do you think James was going to take this? How many times with Sandi? How many more girls?"

"He must have known that once she found out, she wouldn't keep quiet."

"I just don't see pretty-boy James VanDerMuellen actually doing her in," said Jo.

"Tell that to every Ted Bundy victim." Emily raised an eyebrow.

"I see your point. But James was one of those guys who got other people to do his nasty deeds."

Rosy Ross had said the same thing. "Where is James now? Does Paul know?" asked Emily.

"No." Jo wetted her lips with her coffee, then in a daze, set the mug back down without taking a sip.

"Paul knew about all of this, didn't he?" Emily asked quietly, hoping not to unleash a maelstrom of tears.

"Yes! And he did nothing! How can I ever let him back in this house as a husband and father? What kind of example is that to my kids?" The fury was taking hold of Jo again, and the blood rushed to her cheeks. "He betrayed me! Almost ten years. I hate him right now! I hate him for doing this to us!"

The roller coaster of emotions was cresting the hill. Between her punctuated breaths, Jo sputtered out her deepest fear. "And what if . . . Paul is liable for . . . conspiracy to kill Sandi? What if . . . he goes . . . to jail?" She broke down sobbing.

Emily wrapped her arms around her best friend. She didn't want to give her false hope, but she had to say something to get her to calm down. "We're going to get this figured out. I'm not going to leave you alone. Paul is a good man. A good father. Focus on that for a moment. Okay?"

"I just blew up. I've never, ever gotten that mad before at him, Em. I screamed and yelled. I was throwing clothes at him. The kids ran to their rooms and didn't come out all night. They've never seen us fight like that. It was awful. Really awful," she said, dabbing her eyes as they began flooding with tears. She took a tissue and tore it to itsy-bitsy shreds.

"Where are the kids now?"

"School. But I have to pick up Jaden from preschool at eleven. And look at me!"

Emily handed Jo a fresh tissue, and she dabbed it under her puffy eyes. "I can pick up Jaden. You take a shower and pull yourself together."

Jo nodded and blew her nose into a fresh tissue. "Okay. Thank you." Her face scrunched into a disconsolate expression, and fresh tears welled up. "What am I gonna tell the kids?"

Emily's gut was on the floor. She had no answer for that. "We'll figure something out."

Jo melted into her shoulder and burst out with a fresh round of sobs. Emily hugged her friend as she heaved in despair. After Jo quieted and was able to sit upright and hold her coffee mug again, Emily went in for the bold question she had been dancing around. If there was one thing Jo valued most in any relationship, it was honesty and open communication. And really, she should be asking the same thing about Nick.

"Do you think Paul is involved somehow in Sandi's death?"

Jo drew in a deep breath and answered with slow, weighted words. "That's the thing. I just can't fathom . . ." Her eyes got teary again. "We weren't even together back then, but still. To know that I married someone who had the capacity to . . ." The rest of her words got caught in her throat.

"I don't mean to scare you by telling you this, but I would advise Paul to get an attorney."

Jo nodded, but Emily could tell from the cloudy look in her eyes that common sense was not registering with her right now.

26

Emily knocked on Nick's front door. Paul answered, and Emily met him with a stern look.

When she saw his face, all she could think of was that if Paul was guilty of collusion in Sandi's disappearance, then Nick was harboring a criminal. But at best, Nick was taking sides—pinning her and Jo against him and Paul.

"Nick's at work," said Paul, who looked like he hadn't slept all night.

"I'm not here for Nick." Emily brushed past him and inside the house. Paul closed the door and joined her in the kitchen, a bright windowed room that overlooked the lake. The sun was peeking in and out of billowy clouds reflected on the calm lake waters. Peaceful. Serene. Nothing like the storm brewing in Emily. Or Jo.

"Jo already filled me in on a lot of details, so we're gonna short-cut this conversation," Emily started, turning to face Paul, whose brow crinkled in a forlorn look.

"You saw Jo this morning? How is she? Is she okay?" he said. "Can you please tell Jo that I'm sorry and I want to talk to her?"

Emily glared at him. *Not a chance.*

"Who are the members of the pack, and where can I find them?"

"How bad does she hate me?" pleaded Paul.

"Who are they?"

"Nick's dealing with it."

"What can you tell me about the sex video?" Emily wasn't about to back down, and she held no empathy for Jo's husband right now. She bored a look right through him until he slumped into a chair at the kitchen table.

"I'm not proud of what I did, Emily. I'm mortified. I just didn't think it was a big deal back then, and . . ."

"And you never thought it would come back to haunt you," Emily finished.

"I wasn't even with Jo at the time."

"That's not the point. You stood by and did nothing when a young girl was being sexually exploited. You can work out your marital issues later; right now you need to be concerned about how this looks in light of Sandi's disappearance and death."

"I didn't kill her," blurted Paul.

Emily strutted to the window. "But you didn't exactly do anything to help her, either. You were part of this, Paul."

"Sandi and James were a thing, so I thought she was in on it. I actually thought she was getting paid for it."

"Clarify. Paid for what, exactly?"

"Sex with other guys."

"Are you saying James was her pimp?"

"Anyone with a brain can put two and two together. How else did she get the new phone? Or the designer handbags?"

"Was anyone else from the pack sleeping with her?"

"I don't know."

"Were you?"

"No." He answered quickly and defensively. Emily drew her eyes sharply at him and held his gaze to see if he would break it.

"No," he said again. "I was not sleeping with Sandi."

"Do you know who killed Sandi?"

"No, Em. Of course not!" he groaned. Emily drew in a long breath. Ross could have fooled Sandi into thinking he cared for her. He could have colluded with James to make the videos with Sandi and sell them. He certainly hadn't been living in riches. And Sandi would never have been the wiser. It would explain why she looked drugged in the video.

Emily unlocked her gaze from Paul, and his drifted out the window toward the lake. With shoulders slumping, he moaned, "God, Emily, I was such a stupid kid!"

"Do the right thing."

Paul kept quiet for a moment and clenched his jaw. "We were sworn to secrecy."

"That was over ten years ago. Are you telling me that your loyalty is to a bunch of dumb jocks instead of your wife and kids and this community?"

"What am I supposed to do?"

"Make a statement to the cops and then give them the other names."

"Look, I don't believe Sandi was a hundred percent the victim here," said Paul, taking on a more authoritative tone. "She liked the attention. Dating James elevated her from country bumpkin to popular girl."

He certainly had changed his tune quickly. "That doesn't give him the right to film her having sex and sell it around school!"

His eyes darted to the floor. "I understand that—now."

Emily cocked her head at him in dismay. Where was Paul Blakely, the model husband and father? Did he really care more about saving his reputation than his marriage? Jo would be raging with anger if she could hear him right now.

Paul rose from the table and went out the French doors that led to the deck overlooking the lake. He was acting like a sniveling, stubborn jock. Jo had been justified in kicking him out.

"If you want any chance at making this right with Jo and this community, you'd better come clean and cooperate with this investigation," she called out to him.

Emily marched out the front door. She was shaking with fury as she got into her Nissan Leaf and drove away. What a bungle of events! She tried to imagine how Sandi must have felt when she learned that Nick, her good friend, had discovered her sex tapes were circulating. Confused. Angry. Shamed. Embarrassed. She must have wanted to confront James. And then what? Most likely Sandi would have called James and asked him to come over. James knew Nick would snitch on him. No doubt with this much at stake, he would have wanted to go after Nick. So he showed up at Nick's house to address the matter. Maybe he tried to lure Sandi away. Maybe Sandi didn't want to go? Emily pictured a fight breaking out between James and Nick—with Sandi trying to intervene and . . . getting caught in the crossfire. A misdirected punch. A violent throw to the floor. And Sandi suddenly dead between them. Neither knowing who had caused the fatal damage. Or one knowing the other had done it, but both were culpable. Was that the secret of the pack?

27

Emily bolted home and paced around the house for about an hour, trying to clear her thoughts, but was interrupted when a flower delivery van pulled up. She went outside to meet the driver. He handed her a vase of two dozen long-stemmed white lilies and white roses. Her favorite. The card simply read: *You're always on my mind. Love, Brandon.*

She thanked the driver and took them inside. They overwhelmed the kitchen table but made the room look light and cheery. She wished her spirit felt the same.

Emily looked at the date on the delivery card. November nineteenth. It had been two months since her engagement day. Immediately her thoughts drifted to Chicago.

Chicago. Sweet home Chicago. She smiled as the line from the blues song drifted through her mind.

She texted Brandon a quick thank-you and a picture of the flowers. They were lovely, and had come at just the time she needed a pick-me-up. Here was proof that there was still a lot of beauty to be had in the world. Here was proof that he still cared for her. Here was a glimmer of hope that things could be worked out.

Emily looked down at her duds. She had worn the same pair of jeans since she'd gotten to Freeport. She could no longer put off a trip to Chicago to pick up her things. She needed sweaters and her winter jacket. She was also missing other sundries and personal items she had left behind in her rush to Freeport.

Yes, things were heating up with the Parkman case, but there would be no better time. Besides, a trip to Chicago to leave all this behind her for thirty-six hours might provide some clarity and perspective as she sorted through everything Jo had told her.

Emily texted Brandon. *Heading for Chicago shortly. Will you be at the house?*

Technically it was a brownstone. A remodeled, four-story, single-family home that Brandon had bought without her after they'd gotten engaged. A source of irritation. Was it forgivable? Sure. Was it the right way to start a life together? Red flag.

It was only seconds before he texted back.

Be at hospital til 6. Key code 569010. Dinner?

Sure. What time?

Eight. My treat.

Sounds good.

R u spending night?

Emily thought about it a second. It would beat having to find an overpriced hotel room and paying through the nose for parking. She could sleep on the couch. Or the guest room. She didn't want things to be weird or give Brandon the wrong impression.

Yes. She texted back. And left it at that.

* * *

Thirty minutes later Emily locked the house and jumped into her car with an overnight bag. She let out a huge sigh of relief as she pulled out of the driveway. No sooner was she a mile past city limits than she heard a police siren behind her. She checked her rearview mirror. The blue and reds strobed and the cop was flashing his lights at her. She looked at her speed. She was actually under the limit by a couple of miles per hour. Was there smoke coming from her vehicle or something? Wait. Nick had done this to her before, when she'd returned to Freeport late on the night of her father's first heart attack. Emily sighed at the inconvenience and pulled over, unbuckled her belt, and jumped out of the car as Nick approached.

"Hey, what are you doing? You're supposed to stay put," Nick said.

"No, what are you doing? I wasn't disobeying any traffic laws. There's no reason you should be pulling me over," she snapped back.

"I knew you wouldn't pick up any of my calls," he said.

"So you followed me?"

"Not exactly. I went to your house and your car was gone. I just started driving toward town and guess I got lucky."

"What do you want?"

"Just to talk. Paul told me about your little visit."

"Yeah. And now I know why you shut me down when I asked you and Ross about the sex video." She folded her arms across her chest and stared him down. Emily was not in the mood to have this talk right now, but here it was. "What else are you hiding?"

"Em, I can't always share every detail of a case with you."

"Were Ross and James colluding to sell Sandi's sex tape?"

"That's an odd reach."

"Not if James was pimping Sandi and Ross was in on it."

"Also a big stretch."

"And are you sure Sandi didn't come over to your house? It's not adding up, Nick. Tiffani was gone at a friend's. James claims he was home alone. And so were you. Maybe James and Sandi came over. Maybe you and James got into a fight and Sandi accidentally got in the middle? Maybe one of you killed Sandi?"

"What? Whoa!" Nick shuffled his feet on the gravel in protest.

"Is that the secret of the pack you're hiding?"

"Em. Hold on. Where is this coming from?"

"I'm not dumb, Nick. None of the stories are connecting."

"So you drew some conclusion that I accidentally murdered Sandi with James?"

"You. Paul. Ross. You're all so cavalier and covert." She was aware from Nick's reaction that her flushed face and bulging eyes were conveying the depth of her distress.

Nick dropped his tone and held her gaze. "I want you to know I that I was never a part of the pack."

"Yes, you were."

"Not like that. We were in sports together. But I never participated in the stuff they did."

"But you did. By association," stammered Emily.

"I'm not going to argue semantics. I did not kill Sandi. And I am going to make this right. I'm going to do everything in my power to stand up for Sandi and find out who killed her."

"Great. Good. I hope so, Nick. I really do. But how on earth do you explain what happened before that?"

"I was . . . it was . . . just a weird high school guy thing."

"Boys will be boys?" she said with a sneer.

Nick's eyes diverted from hers, and that's all she needed to know.

Nick sighed, and the color drained from his face. "Ten years this side of it, I get that kind of defense doesn't really hold up."

"You knew. Even if you didn't participate. You knew," she said.

Sins of omission. Pack or no pack. He had kept silent. He had kept their secrets. In that way, he had been a part of it. Emily didn't know what to say to excuse it or make him feel better. She didn't want him to feel better. Their increasingly depraved behavior had led to Sandi's murder. It didn't get any worse than that.

"I think you better find an attorney and reconsider that badge," said Emily, turning to head back to her car.

"Running away again without telling me?" Nick's tone held venom.

Emily whipped around. "I still have a life in Chicago."

"If you're going back to Brandon, the least you could do is have the decency to tell me." Nick's words stung again.

Emily would not dignify this comment with a response. At least Brandon, from the moment she had met him, had always been a man of the highest integrity. That she could count on.

28

Emily was immediately charmed when she stepped foot into their brownstone. The pristine living room was a mirror image of the one she had seen on Brandon's phone when he'd first showed her. The rug was square. The throw pillows were fluffed and stacked in a row along the back of the L-shaped couch. Knickknacks and picture frames were free of dust. Brandon had a housekeeper. No doubt about it.

Emily set her bag down and wandered through the expansive four-story home. It was, down to the last detail, everything she could have ever wanted in a Chicago residence. What moved her most was a large wall heading up the second flight of stairs leading to the third floor that held dozens of empty picture frames. Written across the white paper inside the frames were the names of places they had talked about going. The Great Wall of China. Prague. Costa Rica. The Great Barrier Reef. Machu Picchu. Canary Islands. Amalfi Coast. Places Brandon wanted to take her. Place she would have willingly gone. Memories in waiting.

Emily went out the back, across the small yard to the garage in the alley. She thought it was the most logical place to find boxes of her things. But all she could find were Brandon's bike and toolbox.

She went into the house and into the master bedroom. She looked into the closet, surprised to find her clothes, not packed, but perfectly hung on one side of the walk-in. Her sweaters, jeans, and workout clothes were folded on the shelf above it. And her shoe collection lay in color coordination from whites to creams to nudes to blacks on the shoe rack. Jackets and coats were hung in a separate, smaller closet in the room, with boots on the floor under the coats. He was expecting her to come back and move in.

Her heart pinged with pain at this tender act of taking such good care of her things. After a few more moments of admiring it, she went to her car and dragged up a large, empty suitcase of her father's. One by one, Emily took the pieces off each hanger and rolled them into the suitcase. It didn't take long before it was filled. Emily made a quick mental calculation of what was left. Over half done. Not including coats and boots. She would need boxes. She started to text Brandon to ask if he would bring some from the hospital. There were always stacks of them down by the incinerator in the basement. Before she had a chance to press send, the closet door creaked.

"Hey, you're here." Brandon greeted her with an eager smile.

Emily spun around, sweater in hand. "Hi." He looked great in his scrubs, hair disheveled. "Good day?"

"They're always good," said the gorgeous optimist leaning against the doorframe. "But they're better when you're here."

She didn't know what to say. So she wadded up the sweater and tossed it back onto the shelf.

"I . . . sort of underestimated the size of my wardrobe. I was just texting you to bring some—"

Before she could finish, Brandon slid a stack of boxes from the bedroom into the closet. "I thought you might need these."

"I also didn't expect you to have unpacked all my stuff. Thanks, I think." She realized now that it had been a colossal waste of his time. "I appreciate the thought behind it anyhow."

Brandon nodded. "Obviously I expected things to go a little differently."

She nodded. Neither wanted to touch the unhealed wounds between them.

"May I help you?"

"Ah, please."

"Otherwise you might be here all night. And I have some special plans in mind."

"What are you cooking us?"

Brandon was a self-taught chef who loved to showcase his creations for one or twenty.

"Actually, I decided not to cook tonight. There's a new place I want to take you," he said, putting a box together.

"Where's that?" Emily grabbed the sweater she had just tossed onto the shelf and rolled it. This was also a trick Brandon had taught her when they'd started traveling together. Rolling the clothes kept them from wrinkling.

"I say no more. Let's finish this up. Shower. Change. And we'll be off. Sound good?"

It did sound good. Brandon had a plan per usual. It would feel wonderful to shut off her brain for an evening and just go along for the ride.

While Brandon showered, Emily freshened up in the guest bath where Brandon had thoughtfully laid out towels and toiletries for her. This was the kind of caring, thoughtful man Brandon was. The consummate host. Always wanting to make sure everyone felt comfortable and taken care of. At least, when he wasn't working. Or preoccupied with his nose in a textbook. As long as Brandon was in charge and his plans were on the table, everyone could relax and have a good time.

Emily, now in a fresh change of clothes, waited on the living room couch for Brandon to come down. The couch felt amazing on her tired legs and back. She sunk in, remembering how much she loved this piece of furniture. She had helped Brandon pick out this couch for his former apartment. She had sat and slept on it more times than she could count. It made this new habitat feel like home.

As she scanned the room more carefully a second time, she noticed that most of the items were new. New lamps. New artwork. New window dressings. Brandon had taken care of it in his way. On his terms. She hadn't been consulted about her preferences. How would he feel if she wanted to change the rug? Hang different curtains? Paint the walls turquoise instead of Dapper Tan?

She heard Brandon coming down the wooden staircase from the third level where the master bedroom was located. When he arrived in the living room, she expected him to clap his hands together twice and announce, "Ready!" like he usually did. More of a command than a question. But he didn't. He smiled and took a seat next to her on the couch.

"How have you been?" he said in a steady voice.

"Moving forward. You ready?" She started to rise.

"No, wait. Have a seat. I mean, really, how are you? With everything?"

Emily paused. It was unlike Brandon to be so reflective. What was he getting at?

He read her blank stare and filled in. "What's been going on in Freeport? How are things with your dad's estate? And this new case they threw on you? That was crazy. I think I woulda told them to shove off." He laughed a little. She did, too. It was crazy, but she didn't want to talk about it. She wanted to leave Freeport in her rear-view mirror for the moment.

"I'm getting through it." That was honest.

Brandon seemed disappointed. "Come on, Em. It's me. I still care."

"I can't really disclose anything about the case. And my dad's estate is complicated and detailed and . . . time-consuming."

"Is there anything I can do to help?"

She thought for a second about how to respond. And about the irony that he was asking now. Much, much after the fact. A huge part of her was gone, and he would never understand it.

"No. I'm just trying to adjust to the idea that I don't have any more time with him," she said.

"I thought I'd have more time, too," he said softly. "Emily. I'm sorry I didn't come up sooner. I'm sorry I didn't get to know him better. I'm sorry I wasn't there for you."

He reached for her hand, and she let him take it. He rubbed it between his own, dry and rough from surgical gloves and frequent washings. "I want to try. I am . . . trying to try. Will you let me?"

She was stunned by his confession and believed he was sincere. This was the conversation she had wanted to have two months ago.

"Do you still want a life in Chicago?" he asked.

"That's a big question right now."

She had invested so much in her training.

"Do you still want a life with me?" he asked.

"That's an even bigger question."

She had invested so much in their relationship.

He smiled. "Maybe I should start with a smaller question. How do you like the house?"

Emily glanced around the room, her eyes coming to rest on a large potted palm branching out from the corner. She liked the tropical flavor it added—it reminded her of their trips to the Caribbean in the middle of harsh Chicago winters.

"Would you ever put twinkle lights on an indoor plant?"

"That's a funny question."

"Why? Just answer."

Brandon's voice remained calm, but Emily recognized the familiar tension at play when someone wasn't seeing eye to eye with him. "Twinkle lights, huh? That's more of an outdoor look, don't you think?"

"I like them all year round," Emily said. "There's something magical about them."

Brandon gazed over at the palm, then back to Emily. "But if we have them all year, then they're not special in the summer or at Christmas."

"But would you do it anyway? Just for fun. For me?"

"I mean . . . for a party, maybe? Why?" he pressed. "What are you getting at?"

"Never mind."

He took her other hand. "Are you hungry?"

"Definitely. Please tell me it's a Thai place."

"Only three blocks from here."

Emily pulled herself from the depths of the cozy pillow stack.

"You'll need your winter coat. Nights are getting nippy."

She realized Brandon had unpacked that, too. "Where?"

"Master closet. Top shelf. Next to the box with the winter scarves."

As she climbed the stairs, Emily again passed by all those empty frames with the names of far-off places.

She realized that these were the things that made Brandon happy. And she didn't really need any of those trips to be happy. Twinkle lights on indoor plants could be enough.

29

Brandon left for his shift at Northwestern before dawn, and Emily woke up to the smell of his coffeemaker wafting up delicious scents of caffeine goodness as she lay in the bed in the guest room. She would swing by the doctors' lounge on her way out after her meeting with Dr. Claiborne to see him.

Emily reached up in a huge stretch. Sleep had been good. Very good. Brandon had a knack for picking luxurious mattresses and bedsheets and she had melted into them, falling asleep within seconds of hitting the down pillow. For a change, her dreams had not tormented her; they had been nondescript and tonally gray. But when she opened her eyes, only one vivid image sprung to mind. Sandi Parkman's fifteen-year-old yearbook picture.

Emily made her way into the kitchen and poured herself a mug of coffee. She pulled her laptop from her handbag and hit the power button. She wanted to see what she could discover about James Van-DerMuellen from an Internet search.

She Googled his name and came up with several matches. She soon found the right James, recognizing him from a high school baseball team photo. He was listed as a broker on the New York Stock Exchange. But that job had ended over a year ago. She tried

LinkedIn. No record. She looked on Facebook. No account. Twitter and Instagram. Nothing. She found an old New York City address, but nothing current. It was like he'd dropped off the map. He didn't even have a driver's license. She hunted for about an hour, determining that he must have gone off the grid.

Emily wondered what Nick was finding out from Paul and the rest of the pack about James and his whereabouts.

Emily clicked over to Paul's Facebook account. His last post was from two years ago, but she thought it might send her on a trail to see who else was connected to the pack and if they were still in touch.

Click after click. Down the Facebook rabbit hole, deeper and further into one account linked to another and another. They all seemed to be connected through Freeport High School's alumni page. Some of the names she recognized, but most she didn't. None of them mentioned James. It was like Nick said. He had graduated and disappeared.

Through another series of clicks, Emily landed on Tiffani's page. Last post was sixteen months ago. She tried finding her on Instagram. Bingo. It was littered with GIFs and memes and animal videos. And tons of staged selfies of Tiffani. Group shots at the strip club with the girls. Selfies at bars doing shots. Selfies with her and a girlfriend puckering up in the stands with fans at a hockey game. On the ice with hockey players. Tiffani posing in a bikini next to a souped-up sports car. Tiffani posing in short cut-offs with a monster truck. With each vehicle she was with a different guy. So many guys! Was this business or pleasure? Emily thought. Or maybe a bit of both?

Emily scrolled down until she stopped at one selfie. Tiffani in short-shorts, a tank top with chest overflowing. The odd thing was that only half her body was in the frame, the rest centered on a lake-and-sunset landscape. Emily tried to place the lake. It was a vast body of water. No shoreline. Almost like an ocean. Cancun? Hawaii? Caribbean? The water was dark midnight blue. Not tropical. It resembled one of the coasts. Maine or San Francisco? Perhaps even right here near home, Lake Michigan. Emily stared at the picture and noticed a smooth-skinned, very tanned male hand draped around her shoulder. Tiffani had cut the guy out of the frame. Odd. Why didn't Tiffani want to show off this guy?

Emily studied the image more. There was a distinct ring on her left hand. Emily dropped the picture onto her desktop and zoomed in. The quality pixelated, but she could make out a brushed platinum band with a diamond-cut black onyx stone embedded in the band and surrounded by six tiny diamonds on each side. Stunning. Modern. Very unique. Custom design for sure. She grabbed a screenshot and filed it away as the sun broke into the kitchen, flooding it with welcomed daylight.

Emily checked the time. She had been surfing for almost two hours. She chugged down the rest of her cold coffee and closed her laptop. In an hour she was to meet Dr. Claiborne in his office at Northwestern University Hospital.

* * *

After a quick shower, Emily shoved her last few belongings into a paper grocery bag, slipped her handbag over her shoulder, and was out the door. Thankfully, Brandon had packed all her boxes in her Leaf the night before, and the car was crammed floor to ceiling. She buckled into the driver's seat, a little worried about the tiny sliver of visibility she had out the back window.

Emily kept checking the time. Dr. Claiborne was a stickler for punctuality. She grabbed a parking ticket and slotted her car into a narrow visitor parking spot. With thirty seconds to spare, Emily traveled down the familiar hallway on the seventh floor to Dr. Claiborne's office. At exactly 8:30, Emily knocked at the half-open door and poked her head in. Dr. Claiborne looked up from his desktop microscope and cracked a broad smile when he saw her.

"Emily! Come in, come in. How nice to see you." He rose to greet her with a firm handshake, never breaking from his professional demeanor. Dr. Claiborne was not the hugging type. A welcome relief to Emily, who was not a hugger either.

"It's nice to be back. Feels like a lifetime since I was last here."

"You experienced a lifetime's worth of adventure, that's for sure. Please sit down."

His hand directed her to the living room set up on the side of his office, where she had sat in his counsel before or after a surgical procedure more times than she could remember. He sat in his leather roller chair across from her, and she drew contentment from his excited expression. "They can't stop talking about your miracle appendectomy two months ago. You became an instant legend."

Emily laughed a little. During her last surgery rotation, she had discovered a burst appendix hiding behind the lower colon and saved a man's life. "I'm just glad it worked out the way it did. How's the patient?"

"Excellent. Full recovery."

"Wonderful."

"I would ask how you are doing, but I suspect you don't wish to discuss it, knowing you."

Emily gave him a weary smile. "You're right. But I'll be fine."

"You always are. Your father was a great man, and I'm glad you were able to be with him during his final days." His knowing smile brought her comfort.

"It wasn't enough."

"You reconciled, I take it?"

"We did." She felt her throat tighten.

"That makes me very happy. Family should be united." Dr. Claiborne rested a gentle hand on her arm. "I have a feeling you'll see him show up every time you lift a scalpel. You're quite his legacy. I'm sure he was very proud of you."

Emily nodded as a spasm of grief pulsed through her, and her smile faded. She was not accustomed to such sentiments from the stalwart mentor who rarely showed emotion.

"We would not be human if we did not suffer. One could say it is what gives life its deepest meaning," Dr. Claiborne said.

All she could manage was a nod.

"I understand you requested a twelve week family leave of absence?" he said.

"Yes. I have to get things in order with my father's business and estate. And, wouldn't you know it, I've been roped into another death investigation case—at least until the county can find a new medical examiner to do the autopsies. Eventually they'll have to elect a coroner position, too. Unless they can find someone fit to do both jobs, like my dad." *And, who knows, maybe that'll be me*, she wanted to add, but she kept it to herself.

"That's a tall order indeed," said Dr. Claiborne. "I'm glad to hear you'll be returning to Chicago."

"I'm not sure," Emily hesitated. "One day at a time."

"Well, perhaps I can sweeten the pot for you."

Emily lifted a hopeful gaze to his. "How's that?"

"Emily, you must know that your track record at U of C the past few years has been exemplary."

"Thank you. I . . . learned from the best."

Despite the fact that most surgeons had egos the size of Lake Michigan, Emily couldn't imagine anything about Dr. Claiborne being selfish. Devoted husband, father, grandfather. Head of the surgical department. He was always putting his family, his patients, his residents, and his desire to advance surgical research ahead of himself.

"I'm planning to retire next year. And I have a few people in mind to take over my position as surgical department head."

Certainly he wasn't going to ask her to throw her hat in the ring? She would need decades of experience before anyone would ever consider her.

"Then there's my private surgery practice. Out in Rolling Brook Hills. I want you and Brandon to take that over. If you like, you'll be able to complete the last two years of your residency at the surgery clinic under my supervision."

Rolling Brook was in the suburbs where Brandon's parents lived and a good thirty miles from downtown Chicago. What about the university hospital? The perfect brownstone? Thai food within walking distance? Emily felt her eyes getting dry. When was the last time she'd blinked?

"Does Brandon know about this?" Emily could already hear Brandon's mother's cries of joy. She would have a plot of land picked out and a contractor on-site before tomorrow morning to build her and Brandon's mega-mansion next to theirs. And babysitting. Oh, she would be all over babysitting. And she would be all over their lives. Twenty-four/seven. Emily felt her esophagus closing. *Breathe. Breathe.*

"I have not asked Brandon yet. I wanted to talk to you first. What do you think?"

"I think . . . I think it's very generous."

"Well, understand you would be buying into the practice, of course. But it's in the black. Well established. No start-up costs. You could both hit the ground running."

"Yes. Wonderful. Thank you," was all Emily could release from her pinched throat.

"You two are the best I've ever trained. And I know you have a promising future together. How are the wedding plans coming along?"

"I . . . they . . ." She was suddenly very grateful to Brandon for not having said anything at work. Emily decided not to let Dr. Claiborne know that their promising future had been downgraded in status from certain to mere possibility.

"Oh, I didn't mean to put you on the spot. Of course you've been a bit preoccupied lately."

"I'm so honored by the offer," Emily said, putting on a confident tone to cover her shock.

"Of course, talk it over with Brandon. Formulate your questions, and we'll meet soon to get formalities started."

He was already getting his hopes up, and she wasn't about to dash them. She was glad her next stop before leaving was to see Brandon. They needed to nip this in the bud. Now. Emily wondered if this was the kind of opportunity Brandon would take. It would be in line with everything he had said he wanted. She was sure he would jump at the chance.

Emily thanked him again, and he walked her to the elevator and made her promise to check in every week.

As she traveled down to the doctor's lounge to meet Brandon, her mind fixated on what had just happened. It was the first time in her professional career that the doors of opportunity were opening in all directions. Before now, her hardest choice had been which medical school to attend. There had been only three top contenders she had wanted to consider. Two of which were in Chicago. And she hadn't wanted to leave Chicago. So it had come down to scholarship money. The University of Chicago had a better scholarship package. Decision made.

Now, multiple offers—good offers!—were being thrown at her. All of them were great. She could see herself thriving as a professor, a surgeon, or a medical examiner.

Who did she want to become?

Her fifteen-year-old self would have answered that in a heartbeat. Stay in Freeport County working with Dad.

But how did she define herself now?

The Emily in her twenties had found her identity as an up-and-coming top surgeon.

Now, with her thirties peeking out on the horizon, she found herself considering more altruistic paths. How might she best use her talents to shape the future and future generations? Where and how could she give back?

* * *

Emily's thoughts took her all the way to the doctors' lounge, and she was about to turn the handle when her gaze drifted through the small window in the door to a scene happening on the couch. Brandon and another resident, Elizabeth, a woman Emily had gone through med school with, were sitting close. Legs touching. Brandon was showing her something on his phone, and their heads were tossed back in laughter. Elizabeth brushed her hand against Brandon's. He stopped laughing and turned to her. Emily's stomach dropped. Was there something between them? She knew that look. Brandon had looked at her like that a million times. Even last night.

Emily let go of the handle and it unlatched with a click, snapping Brandon's attention to the door. For a brief second, their eyes met through the window. Then Emily bolted, her feet slapping the cement floor, her eyes laser focused on the elevator doors as she bound past patients in wheelchairs. She nearly ran into a nurse exiting a room.

"Emily. Emily!" Brandon's voice belted through the hallway. Staff and patients turned their heads to see what the commotion was all about.

Emily slowed remembering that she wasn't supposed to be running in a hospital. Only during emergencies. *This is an emergency!* She reached the elevator and lunged out with her index finger for the down button.

"Emily, can you wait? Please. What's going on?" She glanced over her shoulder. Brandon was marching toward her.

Why is this darn elevator so slow! It would never make it here before Brandon pounced on her. Emily spun around toward the exit to the stairwell and busted through the door. The door slammed closed and she raced down the stairs. Seconds later she heard the door open two flights above her.

Brandon was on her tail by the time she reached the bottom.

"Emily. Stop. This is silly."

She whipped around.

"I thought you were going to text me when you were on your way," said Brandon, his face flushing red.

"So you could hide your little tryst?"

"Please . . . there's nothing . . ."

"Why didn't you just tell me last night?"

"There's nothing to tell."

She barreled out the side door that led to the parking garage. For a second she didn't know which way to visitor parking.

Brandon pointed east. "It's that way."

"There's nothing more I have to say to you," she told him as he followed her.

"Em, it's not what you think."

"What is it, then?"

"Friends. You know Elizabeth."

"It looked intimate," said Emily.

"What? I can't have a laugh with a good friend? Besides, look me in the eye and tell me you haven't been hanging out with Nick what's-his-name."

She hated that he'd brought up Nick. She had drawn clean lines in the sand between her and Nick.

"I'm not seeing Nick!"

"I swear to you, there's nothing romantic going on between me and Elizabeth."

Emily knew what she had seen. "You know what? Even if there is, we're not together, right? So no worries, okay? Do what you want."

She pressed on toward her Leaf.

"Em, please. Thanksgiving is right around the corner. I was hoping you would join us?" Brandon asked.

"You're kidding, right?"

"My mom would love to see you."

Of course. It was always about pleasing his mom.

When Emily didn't answer right away, he added, "Is that a yes? Mom wants a head count for the caterer."

"You haven't told them about us." It hit her. "That's why you didn't cancel the Palmer House."

Brandon shrugged. "I'm an optimist, Em. You know that. I want you. I always have. And especially after last night. It was like old times again."

Old times were gone.

This was a new day. New choices. New Emily. Whatever those meant. What she decided to do in the future would be hers. And hers alone. She would not be made the fool.

30

Emily drove back to Freeport with the radio blaring. She wanted to drown out every thought and emotion that kept bubbling to the surface. After three hours she was so exhausted from trying to avoid her feelings that she pulled over and sat in silence for a moment.

Her phone buzzed from its mounted perch on the dashboard. The caller ID announced Dr. Charles Payton. She realized it had been days since she had thought about him. He might be the only person in her life right now who wasn't tangled in some drama.

She pressed accept and answered with a cheery voice.

"Charles. Hello!"

"Emily. Did I catch you at a bad time?"

"No. A perfect time. Driving back from Chicago."

"How were the old stomping grounds?"

"Uneventful," Emily fibbed. "Just needed to pick up a few things."

"Why don't you just keep heading along Ninety-Four and extend your trip to Ann Arbor?" She could hear the smile in his voice. Highway 94 connected lower Michigan to Chicago, but she had made the turnoff north on 131 over an hour ago. "Any more thoughts on joining us next fall?"

"Don't I have to apply first?" Emily allowed herself a soft smile that relaxed the tense muscles of her face.

"Formalities."

"I've thought about it some. And I have a lot of questions."

"Shoot. I'm all ears."

She rattled off. "Okay. Well, is this a new position? Who's actually heading the program? What exactly would I be doing? Do I report to you? Will I have lab duties? Am I overseeing a full department? Is there a curriculum in place, or am I creating that?"

"Whoa, yeah. Why don't you come down. We can discuss everything. Students will be just finishing fall term; you can meet a few. It'll give you a good taste of Wolverine hospitality."

"I'll see."

"Don't overthink it. Just come," Dr. Payton said with a beguiling tone. "I was actually calling because I have something new in the Parkman case. I examined the hairs you collected from Sandi's body and had them tested here at the university lab. Eight of the nine hairs shows a DNA match to Sandi. But one of the hairs did not."

"Okay. Interesting. Was there enough of a sample to get a match?"

"There's ample DNA present, but when I ran it through CODIS, there was no match. And as I'm sure you're aware, the other databases—ancestry types and government databases—are untouchable."

Emily knew that unless there was probable cause, you couldn't just go digging through the host of nonincarcerated persons' DNA databases trying to find a suspect.

"I'll have the report sent to you. You can share it with Sheriff Larson. Or he can request his own copy."

"Thank you." Emily was already deep into her thoughts on this. Who's hair was it, and what had it been doing on Sandi's body?

"Where did you say you found the hair?" Emily asked.

"Under the third fingernail of her left hand."

"Could have been transferred in a defensive act."

"See that. We think alike already," he said.

"Keep me posted?"

"Of course. Let me know when you can make the trip to Ann Arbor."

"I will." Rain began to pelt the windshield, and she could see a downpour ahead. "I should probably concentrate on the road."

"I'll see you soon." It came across as a claim more than a farewell.

As Emily hung up, something fierce stirred inside her. An emotional fuse tripped and ignited, as it often did so quickly in this bereavement season. She tried to pin down the feeling so she could try to make sense of it, but it eluded her. She gripped her hands on the steering wheel and slowed as she hit a whitewash of rain.

Worry thoughts filled her mind. Just as she served up one and swatted it away, another one spiked at her. She couldn't dodge and duck fast enough. They volleyed around her, vying at her concentration. Emily slowed and pulled over to the shoulder until the torrents of rain passed and she was able to clear her mind.

Heading back onto the highway, Emily pressed steadily on the gas pedal. She kept her speedometer at nine miles above the speed limit the rest of the way to Freeport. Nick had told her cops didn't stop drivers until they were at least ten over.

Before she knew it, an hour had passed and she was approaching the windy, hilly roads outside Freeport. She slowed, forcing her full attention on the road. This was the stretch where her mother's accident had taken place, and Emily was respectful of the danger these roads could present if one didn't heed the curves.

As she came out of one curve and was headed into the steep turn of another, she sensed another car coming up on her rear. She tried to get a better look in her rearview mirror, but her belongings blocked the view. She adjusted her speed, slowing down just a hair, and felt a tap on her bumper.

"Hey, back off!" she voiced.

She checked her outside mirrors, but the offending vehicle was out of her view. Emily tapped on the brakes, signaling the driver to get off her bumper. A few seconds later, he tapped her again. This time with greater impact. Emily's heart raced.

She craned her neck to try to see around the piles of boxes through her back window. It was no use. The sliver of unobstructed glass was too narrow to make out anything. Emily returned her gaze to the road.

As she did, she felt the bump at her rear again. Harder than the last time. It jostled the steering wheel from her grip, and her car veered toward the shoulder. On the other side of the shoulder was a steep embankment, straight down at least seventy-five feet into a dense woods. Emily struggled to gain control of her light, little electric vehicle as she weathered another bump that would have sent her off the edge of the road if she had not slammed on her brakes and pulled hard to the left. She skidded to a stop along the gravel shoulder. Her heart was pounding and her legs were shaking. She was safe. But where was that other car? Emily rolled her window down and stuck her head out. The road was silent. No car. It must have gone around the next bend. There was no way on that steep, narrow road it could have turned around fast enough to disappear in the opposite direction.

Emily cranked the steering wheel toward the road and stepped on the gas. She was going to chase down that SOB and make him pay! Emily tore down the road, going as fast as she felt she could while remaining at a safe speed. For three miles, her eyes searched side roads and driveways. Not a single other car passed her until she passed the Freeport city limits sign. Her chase was a lost cause. The car who'd hit her had mysteriously disappeared.

31

Emily drove directly to the Freeport County Sheriff's Office. She parked and trotted to the back rear driver's side to inspect the damages. There were two significant dents, about basketball sized, in the bumper where she had been hit. And lots of scratches. She strained to see if the other car had left any paint, but she found nothing.

Emily dashed inside and headed straight to Nick's office along the back wall. He was eating lunch at his desk when Emily barged in.

"Someone nearly drove me off the road just now!"

Emily stood on the other side of his desk, bracing herself so she wouldn't buckle. Nick met her flustered face with a piece of lettuce hanging from his mouth. He sucked the lettuce into his mouth and swallowed the bite in one gulp.

He got up from behind his desk and put his hands on the sides of Emily's arms and sat her in a nearby chair. She hadn't realized until this moment that her whole body was trembling. A quarter percent adrenaline. A quarter fear. And the rest pure anger.

"Describe the vehicle," Nick said, grabbing a pen and paper.

"I can't. I didn't see it."

"Try to remember something. What color was it?"

JENNIFER GRAESER DORNBUSH

"I don't know."

"Car or truck?"

"I don't know."

"Were you sleeping?" He attempted a joke.

"My car is packed to the roof with all my stuff. I had no visibility."

Nick sighed. She didn't care for his blasé attitude.

Emily went on to explain what she remembered about the incident and how she had chased after the disappearing vehicle. Nick took it down.

"Sounds like a common case of road rage."

"In Freeport? There is absolutely no traffic here to get mad at!"

"You'd be surprised at the impatience of people who get caught behind poky drivers or tractor combines."

Emily began to pace Nick's office. She hated that Nick stood so calmly at the side of his desk.

"What if it wasn't? Word gets around. And after what I did during the Dobson case, I'm not surprised if I've made a few enemies."

"You're being paranoid. I'm going to write up a report, but I doubt it's anything other than a pissed-off driver."

Emily's trembling had melted, leaving anger in its place.

"What if it happens again?"

"If it makes you feel better, I will follow you home. For your safety," Nick offered.

Emily nodded. Fine. She would be going home to an empty house. It was a good idea to have Nick come and check it out with her when she arrived.

"Did Dr. Payton get in touch with you?" she asked him.

"Haven't heard from him. Why?"

"Eight of the hairs collected were from Sandi. The ninth one that was under Sandi's fingernail has no criminal database matches."

"Another dead end. Great."

Nothing about Sandi's case was going to be easy, and Emily could see the worry lines etching themselves across Nick's brow.

Emily tried to combat the little doubts creeping in. None of the pack members had criminal records or DNA samples registered in CODIS. But that ninth hair could belong to any one of them.

"I did a pretty thorough Internet and social media search this morning. There was hardly anything on James VanDerMuellen."

Nick nodded. "I found out that James' family is living in Miami. I got a number and left several messages. His dad finally called me back when I threatened a subpoena."

"Oh. Good. Some progress."

"Apparently, James lost his job on Wall Street earlier this year and moved to Miami to live with his folks for a few weeks while he figured out his next steps. They had a falling out. James stormed off. And his dad claims he hasn't seen or spoken to his son in over six months."

"Did he say what happened?"

"He didn't go into it. My guess is he was broke. Wanted money but Daddy finally put his foot down."

"Did you tell his dad why you were trying to find James?"

"I kept it vague, but I'm sure he did a little research, and with the recent news about finding Sandi's body, it wouldn't be hard to piece two and two together."

"He knows his son will be questioned again now that there's a body and a case lining up," said Emily.

"He told me the next time I wanted to call, I would be speaking to his attorney. We can't squeeze blood from that turnip without legal action."

"Nick, you need to test DNA from the pack to rule out if it matches that ninth hair."

"I'm a step ahead of you, Doctor Death. I took Ross' tissue from the trash when we were there."

"What about you and Paul?"

"Do you honestly think I have anything to do with this, Em?"

"To rule you out as a suspect."

She wanted nothing more than to encourage him not to worry. But Tiffani's conviction that Nick was involved, James's track record, and Paul's confession had seeded this soil with suspicion. She didn't want to admit that maybe she didn't know Nick as well as she thought. But truth was, she had left home during the tail end of their sophomore year. So much could have happened during those next two years.

"The problem here isn't my DNA. It's that you don't trust me."

Emily drew in a deep breath. Why did they always find themselves arguing whenever they saw each other?

"Are you still housing Paul?"

Nick nodded. "Jo won't let him back."

"You could be housing a criminal," Emily said. "How does that look to a jury?"

"I'm not housing a criminal. I wouldn't do that anyhow, Em. Even if it was a good friend."

"Prove it by ruling Paul out. Send in his DNA sample."

"I'm working on it, Em. Now, just take a breather. You've done your job. I got it from here."

Emily bristled at Nick's tone. He had told her that on the Dobson case, and she hadn't stepped down. *When you push Emily away, she just pushes back.* And she had solved the case. Still, Emily understood how much she had offended him, and she couldn't expect him to react with graciousness. She certainly wouldn't have if someone had done the same to her. But she also didn't think he was seeing this situation with objective eyes. "I know you don't want to hear this, but for your own good, Nick, I think *you* need to step down from this investigation and let someone else take over."

He returned a look that told her there was no way he was leaving his post.

"Anything happen in Chicago I should know about?" He glanced at her ring finger.

Emily met his eyes with a vexing look and refused to water this conversation.

This case and Nick's persistence were starting to drive a wedge between them. How had that happened so soon after they'd shared a life-and-death moment just a couple of weeks before during the Dobson case?

"Nothing you need to worry about," she said. "You ready to go?"

Emily heeled out of the sheriff's office before he could answer. But she heard his footsteps trailing her. And neither uttered a single word as they got into their cars.

32

After Nick made sure the house and property were safe, he helped Emily unload the boxes from her car. They worked in tandem without so much as a word to each other.

"I doubt you're being followed. But keep the doors shut and locked," he said, setting down the last box. "Call if you hear or see anything. Got it?"

Emily felt uneasy being home alone now.

"Thank you," she managed, then locked the door behind Nick.

Nick went back to his patrol car without a glance in her direction. Emily shrugged it off and headed into the kitchen.

She fished bread, meat, and cheese from the fridge, smelling it to confirm it was still edible. She slapped her sandwich together and stood in the kitchen. She was too antsy to sit at the table. After playing the scene back in her mind, Emily conceded that Nick was right. It was road rage. Her imagination and emotions had been in overdrive. She needed rest.

So she slept. And holed herself up in the house. And poured herself into organizing her father's things. By midweek, Emily was tired of being alone in the house and looking at what her dad had left behind. She dialed Jo's number.

All she could hear were three kid voices yelling at the top of their lungs in the background. "I'm about to pull my hair out—or theirs. Kids. Outside. Now!" said Jo.

The screams and laughs dissipated as Emily heard Jo open the slider door to let three rambunctious kids out to the backyard.

"It sounds like you're preoccupied. I can call back later."

"No, Em. It's okay. Hearing your voice is sanity to my soul."

Jeremiah Blakely, Jo's ten-year-old son, screamed an order to one of his younger sisters to "Gimme that!"

"Jeremiah! Give that back to your sister!" yelled Jo. "Go play outside. Now."

"Hey, go deal with that. I'll call you later."

"No. They'll work it out. What's going on?"

Emily heard the slider door close and latch. Jo had had it! "I was wondering if that offer is still on the table for some help with my dad's things."

"Of course. You want me to come over now?"

"You sure? Sounds like you have your hands full."

"No. Now. I need a break now," Jo's frazzled voice begged.

"Bring the kids. They can play outside. Or we can give them a rake and they can make leaf piles."

"No way. Paul may not be living here at the moment, but he's not off the hook for fatherhood. It's his turn."

Emily could hear a small fist pounding on the sliding door and the middle daughter, Jessica's, muffled whine from the other side of the glass, "Mom! Jaden won't let me—" Jaden was Jo's youngest daughter of four going on fourteen.

"Jessica, you march right back into that yard and push your sister on the swing."

"Quick. Call Paul!" Emily laughed. "Get out of there while you still can."

"I'm on it. Give me thirty."

"I'll get a bottle of red breathing."

Emily smiled as she ended the call. She wolfed down the last few bites of her sandwich and glanced around the kitchen. She would commit to staying in Freeport through the holidays. That would give her enough time to figure out next steps. And in the meantime, she would fight for Sandi Parkman as she saw fit. Sandi deserved justice. Her mom deserved retribution. And Freeport needed this black mark erased from its history. Nick, Paul, and the pack would have to find their own way to make amends for their sins.

33

I t was the little things that wrenched at Emily's heart as she wrapped them and Jo organized them neatly in plastic bins. Dad's razor. His mismatched socks. A mustard-colored cardigan with a hole under the arm. Emily made sure they left out photos and his books. She wasn't erasing her father from the house. She just didn't want to be tripping over his ghost every time she went for something in the kitchen or bath.

"It still has your dad's touch," said Jo as they scanned the house a third time for anything they might have missed. "But there's also room now for your stuff."

Emily loved that Jo always knew exactly the right thing to say.

Next, they tackled the office. Emily had already packed up most of his files, but the desk and outlying areas were littered with medical and office supplies.

"So what's the deal with you and Paul?" said Emily, knowing that Jo wanted to get it off her chest but wouldn't dream of burdening Emily with it in the midst of what they were doing.

"The fact that I'm finally able to speak to him without blowing up or bursting into tears is progress."

"You're a woman of great grace."

"Hardly. I get that he was young and impressionable and trying to fit in and be a cool jock and whatever," Jo droned. "But I mean, he's still culpable." Jo's eyes began to water. "It's just careless and mean, what they did."

"Has he apologized?"

"To me? A million times." Jo wiped the corners of her eyes with her sleeve. "But I'm not really the one he should be apologizing to."

Emily nodded. "Do you think they realize they have some major atonement to do?"

"I don't think any of them see it that way. And I just keep thinking, what if that were Jessica, or Jaden—you know, thinking ahead ten years when they're teenagers . . . if someone was doing that to them and the guys at school were using them for pleasure . . . Oh, Em. It makes me physically sick to my stomach."

Emily's own stomach turned over, and she tried not to imagine it. "What's it going to take for you two?"

Jo shrugged. "Therapy. A lot of it."

"He'll go?" Emily had always seen Paul Blakely as the stoic, farmer type who handled his emotions in private. Or not at all.

"He'll go because I've told him he's going," Jo said.

Emily grinned and refilled Jo's wineglass. "It'll just take some time. I have faith in you two."

"Some nice jewelry would be a good start." Jo's face brightened; Emily realized she had found her sense of humor through all this.

"Jewelry's nice to look at. But how about a warm Caribbean getaway?"

"But not with Paul. I want my bestie there. We need a break, girl! From everything. Husband. Ex-fiancé. Kids. Work. Death." Jo smiled and Emily picked it up.

"Beaches. Spa. Piña coladas."

"What are you doing this weekend?" Jo picked up her phone and pretended to check her calendar. Emily laughed, and their holiday dreaming cleared the tension in the air.

Then Jo fell quiet. "I heard about the ninth hair."

"Does Paul have an alibi?" asked Emily.

"He says he was in the weight room after school. But how does he prove that? There was no trainer. No coach. No sign-in sheet. I told him he needed to submit a DNA sample."

Emily nodded. There were no words.

"I'll admit, I've already looked into an attorney. From Rock River. I didn't want it to be anyone local," said Jo.

"Does he know?"

"Not yet. He'd be livid. But I want to be on the offensive about this," said Jo, dusting the lip of a bookshelf.

"I wish Nick would get one, too."

"Doesn't the state office supply him with one?"

"I suspect they would, if he asked."

"What's it going to take for him?" Jo sounded as frustrated as Emily felt.

"Probable cause," Emily hated to admit.

Jo took down a stack of slim volumes with glossy covers. "You probably don't want these packed."

Emily took a look at them. Yearbooks.

"Your dad kept them for you. That's so sweet. Well, all two of them. Freshman and sophomore year."

Emily and Jo sat down on the floor, each taking one of the books. Emily cracked open the stiff spine of the sophomore yearbook and started to flip through its unfamiliar pages.

"You know, I never actually saw this book."

"You didn't?"

"No, they were delivered in June, after school was out. I was gone by then."

Jo nodded with a sweet smile. "I don't like thinking about your grand disappearing act."

"Me neither."

"I'm so glad you're back," said Jo. "I hope you stay."

"Jo, I never said it, but thank you for being my friend, even when we . . . weren't."

"We were never not friends," said Jo as she folded her book closed and hopped back to the shelf with her dustrag.

Emily was about to close her book when a photograph caught her eye. The shot was of one of those "Hands-in!" huddles athletes did before a game. The caption read, *United to win!* She couldn't tell what sport the players were from, because the image was a close-up of elbows and hands. She studied the male hands. A good handful were wearing class rings. One ring in particular stood out. It was a black onyx stone in a diamond cut. The only one in the huddle. The high school mascot was engraved into the left side and the graduation year into the other side.

"Jo, hey. Look at this picture. Do you know who that is?" Emily brought the book over to her and pointed to the hand with the black-onyx ring. Jo glanced at it.

"Nope. Don't recognize it." Jo went back to her dusting.

"Well, do you know who at Freeport had a black-onyx class ring?"

"Seriously? Out of six hundred students?"

"Just seems like a unique choice. Most people just get their birthstones."

"Unique people make unique choices," quipped Jo. "Wait. Do you think it belongs to one of the pack?"

Emily took another look at the ring. She was thinking of the guy in the picture from Tiffani's Facebook page. They were clearly two different rings, but the same stone. Coincidence or connection? Why on earth would Tiffani be with a guy from the pack? These guys had violated her sister, and most likely one of them had killed her. They would be the last people on earth she would want to associate with. If it was true, it would be a truly sick twist.

She dog-eared the page and slid the yearbook back onto the shelf.

When Emily and Jo were finished packing, dusting, and polishing the multiple pieces of wood furniture, the office did not look empty by any stretch, but it had tidy appeal, ready for a new occupant. They took all twenty boxes into the storage area and stacked them next to Emily's mother's things. As Emily pushed a box on top of the shelf, her eye caught the corner of a box she knew well. Her mother's sealed wedding gown.

"How about you? Anything spicy happen on your trip to Chicago?" Jo sent her a wry grin as they wedged the last two boxes into the storage cubby.

"Caught Brandon with a med resident."

Jo gasped. "Are you kidding me?"

"He denies there's anything there, of course."

"Appearances don't lie."

"Exactly."

"That sure ripped the ringer out of the wedding bells."

"Better to know now than after the wedding knot is tied," said Emily.

"Even then, can you ever really know someone?" Jo raised an eyebrow. "You're in the sweet spot. Ready for change and choice."

Emily liked the sound of that. This was her season of change and choice. She should embrace it.

"Where's that wine, by the way?" asked Jo.

"We finished it. Another bottle?"

"Please. I'm not ready to face my three hooligans just yet."

Emily led Jo into the kitchen and pawed through her father's kitchen cabinets. "Something I just can't get rid of," said Emily.

"I was going to ask, but I didn't want to push."

"A lot of my mom's stuff is still here." Emily opened a bottom cupboard stuffed with bakeware.

"I'm starving."

"Help yourself."

Jo reached for a half-eaten bags of chips on the counter and slid into a chair as Emily used a step stool to reach the cupboard doors over the fridge.

"I think there's more wine in here." She tugged on them, but they didn't budge. She tugged again, and the left one gave way and flung open, sending Emily back. Jo grabbed Emily to steady her. Regaining her balance, Emily peered into the cabinet. Bingo. There was a three-quarters full fifth of gin and an unopened bottle of champagne staring back at them. Emily saw a tag hanging from its neck. She turned it over and read aloud: *To Robert and Cathy. May you have many years of happiness together. Here's something to celebrate the first.*

Jo saw it, too. A quiet moment passed between them.

"They made it only six months," said Jo.

Emily nodded. Life was fleeting. Love was not to be squandered. And champagne was to be drunk. Emily pulled it down.

"Let's get this chilled, and someday soon we're going to pop the cork on this in celebration of finding Sandi Parkman's killer," said Emily.

Jo nodded. "Sounds right to me." Emily handed her the bottle and Jo put it into the fridge.

"For now, gin?"

"I'll get the glasses," said Jo.

Emily poured two generous shots over ice. They toasted and tossed them back. Emily's body warmed from throat to belly to toes. The smooth gin relaxed her tense muscles and the light taste of juniper berry lingered on the roof of her mouth.

Jo slid her glass over to the bottle and clinked it twice.

"I'm not stopping at one," she smiled. "Hey, I never get to do this at home. Let me live a little."

As Emily poured a second round and topped it off with tonic, an idea popped into her brain.

"Jo, do you have time to help me with something?"

"I'm all yours."

Jo lifted her glass, and she and Emily did a second toast.

"To best friends forever."

"No matter what the future holds, we will always have each other," said Emily.

They clinked glasses and drank.

"So, what do you need?" asked Jo, licking the gin from her lips.

"A makeover."

"For your date with the doctor?" Jo giggled.

Emily's face crinkled into a sly smile.

"Em, what are you scheming?" Jo crammed two more crackers in her mouth.

Emily shook her head. "I appreciate your solidarity, but you've got enough stake in this case already. The less you know, the better."

"If you want my help, I need the four-one-one."

"I can't. Sorry." Emily sucked down the rest of her drink. "Don't worry. I got this. I shouldn't have asked."

"Oh no, no, no." Jo shook her head. "We just toasted to our undying friendship. I'm not helping you until you tell me what you're up to."

"Fine. I'm applying for a job."

"Sleuthing in Freeport not paying the bills?" Jo joked.

"Promise you won't say a word. Not even to Paul."

"Of course not. But I don't want to be an accomplice to anything sordid or dangerous."

"I just need a way to get to Tiffani." Emily raised an eyebrow. "Undercover-like."

"Em, you just barely recovered from being left for dead the last time around."

"Jo, it's going to take everything we have to find Sandi's killer. Please."

"What do you have in mind?"

"Something club-like?" Emily posed.

"Where are you applying for a job?"

"The Silver Slipper."

Jo's brow wrinkled. "Then you mean something slutty."

"You were always good with using your assets to get guys to notice you."

"Is that a compliment?"

"It's a gift."

Jo sighed. "Emily Hartford. I will help you. But we're gonna need a shopping trip to Rock River."

"I don't have time." Emily motioned to her boxes from Chicago piled in the foyer.

"Somehow I don't envision a clubbing outfit in one of those."

"Brandon liked buying me sexy clothes and taking me to fancy restaurants."

"And you left him why?" said Jo.

Emily pried the lid off one of the plastic bins and dug inside, pulling out a cheetah-print cocktail dress and black heels with spiky brushed-silver grommets.

Jo admired them. "Well, I can definitely work with that."

And she held out their glasses for a third round.

34

At half past midnight, Emily tottered into the Silver Slipper, completely disguised thanks to Jo's makeup skills and a Marilyn Monroe wig Jo had trimmed into a short bob. The place was teeming with people, and she strained her eyes to the front to see who was up on stage. No Tiffani. The music changed. Dancers on stage collected their tips and exited. A new group of dancers entered. Tiffani was one of them. She took her place at one of three poles and began her routine. Emily watched for a moment, then set her sights on finding Wanda, the manager, who turned out to be a beefy broad in a black muscle shirt. Her jet-black, waist-length hair, pulled back into a thick ponytail, was streaked with tasteful purple and blue strands.

Emily watched and saw Wanda sail behind the bar, yelling something at the bartenders that Emily couldn't decipher. Whatever it was sent them scurrying back and forth as she barked orders. Emily lifted her chest and made her way toward her target.

"Excuse me, are you the manager?" Emily sang in a sweet voice.

The woman turned to Emily. In her spike heels, Emily was a good four inches taller than Wanda.

"Lemme guess, you're looking for a job?"

Emily swallowed, plastered a fake smile on her face, and mustered up her Chicago wits. "I am. And it looks like you could use some more talent on that stage."

The woman looked her up and down. "What's your experience?"

"Diamond Rhino." Emily made up the name on the spot.

"Never heard of it."

"It's in . . . just outside Chicago." Betting that Wanda didn't cross the Michigan state line very often.

Wanda bought it and looked her up and down. "You class up the joint too much and I lose my regulars."

"I can be whatever you need," Emily said with a wink, holding her persona.

"What's your name?"

Emily's mind flicked skittishly through a couple of possibilities. Pepper? Cinnamon? Anise? Why did she have spices on the brain? Were spices sexy enough? She hoped she hadn't paused too long when she croaked out, "Cardamom."

"Unusual." The woman gave her a curious look. "I like it."

"I bake a lot of cookies," Emily blurted. *Ridiculous.*

"I'm Watch Your Ass Wanda. Meaning you'd better keep it in line, or I'll be on yours."

Emily nodded coolly. "No worries. I'm easy to work with. I don't get in anyone's way."

"When Tiffani finishes her set, go up and introduce yourself. She'll show you the ropes."

"Oh . . . ah, Tiffani. Okay." She had to think fast. She needed time to work her way more covertly to Tiffani. "I was wondering if I could shadow that girl instead." She pointed to a leggy girl who couldn't have been a day over seventeen.

"Lexi?"

"I like her style."

"Sure. Whatever. Lexi's a strong dancer."

"So, I start tonight?"

"Not dancing. I need you in rehearsal first so I can see what you do and know what shift to give you. If you suck, you'll be working Monday afternoons."

"What time do you want me here?" Emily held her moxie.

"We hold dance rehearsals at four tomorrow."

"I'll be here. Thanks." Emily reached out her hand to thank Wanda. She slapped a dirty, wet rag into Emily's hand.

"Wait. When you're not dancing, you're serving. Consider tonight your table audition." Emily nodded as Wanda pointed to a set of tables in the corner where a quad of biker dudes chugged cheap beer. "Start there."

Emily made her way to the tables in the back. She had actually never waited tables before. Tonight would be total improv. *How hard can it be? Smile. Bring beers. Take tips.*

It was hard. Really hard. Customers shouted names of drinks at her that she had never heard. With no pen or paper, Emily had to commit orders to memory. Thank goodness for years of medical school memorization tactics.

The Wild Goose. Grey Goose vodka and grapefruit juice.

Tito's and Tonic. Tito's vodka and tonic water.

Grandma's Whiskers. Whiskey, grenadine, and a spray of soda water.

Emily was relieved when the orders were simply beer or shots. As she served, Emily did her best to keep her focus on Tiffani, who moved on and off the stage in short shifts. If a guy leaned in to tip her, Emily would try to get a look at his hand for the black-onyx ring. Often Emily would wedge her way up toward the stage, tray in hand, pretending to scan for empty bottles to clear.

As the night wore on, the sweaty crowd multiplied and kept her busy in the back corner. After four hours of music pumping through every cell of Emily's body, she was exhausted. She needed a break and wanted to check in and make friends with her new mentor. And her feet were killing her! How did these girls do it night after night?

At four thirty AM, customers from her section cleared out and made their way to the stage. Emily drew in a breath and took a seat at an empty high-top in the corner. Meanwhile, the action onstage never slowed. As the music transitioned, indicating a dancer exchange, Emily saw her newly appointed mentor, Lexi, slip offstage and head to the back. Tiffani was still onstage. Now would be the perfect time to introduce herself.

Knowing the way to the dressing room, Emily trailed Lexi. But she found the dressing room empty. Strange. Emily popped her head out and looked down the hall. The exit door was cracked. *Of course. Smoke break.* As she hoofed toward the door, she heard girls' voices. She opened the door, and three girls holding cigarettes looked up at her.

"There you girls are. How's it going?" she said with a confident smile as she hobbled down the rickety wooden steps toward them. "I'm Cardamom," Emily said. "The new girl."

"Yeah, we've been watching you," said a girl in a pink wig with wisps of her real red hair poking out. "First time in heels?"

Emily feigned a laugh and turned to Lexi. "Wanda said she wants you to train me."

"Tiffani does the training." Lexi lit her cigarette and inhaled.

"Guess she's promoting you," said Emily.

"What's your real name?" Lexi asked.

"Cardamom."

"Uh-huh. Your mom must have been on the good stuff when that birth certificate came around." Lexi took a drag on her cigarette.

"Spare one? I said I was going to quit, but . . . maybe tomorrow." Emily forced a laugh. Lexi was not amused.

Lexi handed her a cigarette and a lighter. In a rebellious phase during her freshman year, Emily had learned to smoke at parties. She lit the tip and inhaled, trying not to cough. How had she ever thought this was pleasant?

"How long you ladies been working here?"

"Long enough," said Lexi, clearly not in the mood to train anyone.

"Got any tips for me?" Emily bluffed.

She must have hit on the right question, because names and descriptions of customers started to fly from the girls. Emily let the cigarette burn down a couple of centimeters before she drew it to her lips again. She did a lot of nodding and took note of the endless list of guys who were causing trouble for these girls.

"No bouncers?" said Emily.

"We have Bulldog and Jax," said Lexi.

"Two's not enough for a place this size," said the girl wearing fishnet stockings and Mary Janes.

"But all Wanda cares about is profits," said Lexi.

"You ever say anything?"

"We've tried. The money's good, and there's never been any real trouble."

"What exactly do you consider real trouble?"

The job sounded a lot more dangerous than Emily had imagined.

"Real trouble is—well, you know . . ."

Emily assumed they were talking about sexual assault. "Rape?"

Lexi nodded and took another drag.

"How far does it go?" said Emily.

"We can hold our own," said the pink-wig girl.

Emily tossed her butt to the ground and stamped it out with the toe of her shoe. "You're kidding me about all this, right? It sounds awful. Illegal. When I worked at the Diamond Rhino—"

"Where's that?" said Lexi.

"Chicago," Emily fibbed.

"Oh my God. Why on earth are you up in Podunk Freeport?"

Emily sighed. "Long story. How do these guys get away with all this crap?"

"Who's gonna stop them?" said fishnet stockings.

"Watch Your Ass Wanda? It's her job to keep you safe."

"Telling your customers no is bad for business," said Lexi.

A wave of compassion struck Emily. These were young women, just like her, who were trying to earn a living. It wasn't right that they were being taken advantage of.

"Well, that's gotta end. You should be able to say no. It's your right."

Lexi smiled at Emily. "I like you. You have spunk. But good luck changing anything around here."

"If I were you, I wouldn't stir up the waters. Snitches get short-shifted," added fishnet stockings.

Emily would talk to Nick about this place later. These girls needed protection. Maybe some undercover surveillance. One or two arrests and some bad publicity would strike the fear of God into Wanda or shut her down.

Emily shook her head. "Don't worry. I have a few ideas."

At that moment Watch Your Ass Wanda stuck her head out the door. "Hey, I'm not paying you for your ideas. All of you. Get back in here. We've got another two hours until close."

Two hours! Emily didn't know if her legs would make it that long. The girls snubbed out their smokes and made their way to the door. But as Emily turned to head inside, her gaze landed on that familiar black Lexus she and Nick had seen at the club before. It was parked just twenty feet from the back door in the staff lot at the back of the building. Something about it gave Emily pause. The front passenger side bumper was dented in.

She marched over and turned on the flashlight app of her phone so she could scan the light over the front bumper. Dealer plates. This was definitely the Lexus she'd seen at Pinetree Slopes.

"What are you doing?" Lexi yelled.

"Does anyone know who's car this is?"

"Tiffani's."

"Really?"

She moved the light across the bumper and around to the passenger side, where she saw a large dent near the tire wall. The dent matched the height of her Leaf's rear bumper, and she noticed red paint flecks embedded in the center of the indent. Emily pounded the spike of her right heel into the ground, trying to gain composure.

"Did she say how it happened?" Emily's cool tone crusted the ladies standing around watching her.

"She said she ran into a mailbox," said Lexi.

"What do you care?" said Wanda from the back door. "Get back to work!"

Adrenaline surged through Emily. She growled under her breath and pounded to the back door. The girls stood back bewildered as she stomped past Wanda into the back of the club, down the hall, and into the main arena. The club was thumping, and Tiffani had moved to center stage. Emily didn't hesitate a second as she pranced herself onto the stage, garnering strange looks from the other dancers. Emily wove her way to Tiffani, hands on her hips.

"It was you! You tried to drive me off the road!" she yelled over the music. Tiffani didn't hear or notice Emily until she spun around the pole and her leg caught on Emily's, sending Emily off-balance and Tiffani sprawling to the floor. Emily grabbed the pole to keep from falling, but she couldn't keep a grip on its greasy exterior and she crumpled next to Tiffani.

"What are you doing? Who are you?" yelled Tiffani over the music.

Emily crawled on her hands and knees over to Tiffani and got in her face. "The red Nissan Leaf you nearly ran off the road—that was me!"

Tiffani shook her head. "Get off my stage, crazy lady!"

Emily could see from the corner of her eye that they had drawn the attention of the entire crowd. Some of the men were cheering them on. The other dancers had stopped their routines and huddled off to the side of the stage. She and Tiffani had become the main attraction.

"Cardamom! What are you doing?" screamed Lexi from the sidelines.

Tiffani must have seen her car at Pinetree Slopes. Had she been tracking Emily ever since? And how?

"What were you doing at Pinetree Slopes the other night?" Emily hissed. Tiffani tried to grab at Emily's mane, but Emily managed to dodge her, swinging her legs around to sideswipe Tiffani with a kick. In the process, one of Emily's heels went flying.

"I don't know what you're talking about." Tiffani seemed untouched by the kick. She body-slammed Emily to the floor, then pounced on top of her, pinning her down. Emily clawed at Tiffani, trying to break free.

"You know more about your sister's murder than you're letting on!"

Tiffani grabbed Emily's hair and yanked her head back, leaving her blonde wig in Tiffani's grip. Tiffani shrieked. She looked down at Emily with wide-eyed incredulity. "Doctor Dazzle." She grinned. "Cute disguise."

"Stop this! Now. Stop it!" yelled Wanda, slapping her hand on the edge of the stage. Immediately Jax and Bulldog stepped in. "Take her out! Now!"

"Eat this, Doctor Dazzle!" Tiffani rose, Emily's wig in one hand.

"Who's Doctor Dazzle?" Emily heard Lexi exclaim from the sidelines.

Jax grabbed Emily's arm and leg on one side, and Bulldog latched on to the other. Splayed out, Emily could do nothing to resist as they dragged her away.

"You keep away from me and my family!" yelled Tiffani.

Emily opened her mouth to respond, but the music pumped up several decibels and her response was drowned out. Her defeated gaze back at the stage was timed perfectly as Tiffani, playing up the part of victim vixen, waved Emily's Marilyn bob over her head like a victory scalp. The crowd roared with excitement. Tiffani, a seductive smile plastered on her face, danced her way to the edge of the stage to collect a shower of fives and tens.

Emily was delivered and set down outside the back door. Jax went back inside, but Bulldog stayed.

"I'll make sure you get to your car safely," Bulldog said with the utmost respect. Emily was sure she wasn't the first broad he'd had to escort from the premises.

Emily walked to her Leaf, and he trailed her. But when she got to her car, she didn't get into it right away. She went around to every tire well and bumper, running her hand underneath until she found what she was after on the driver's side rear fender. Ripping the little tracking device from its magnetic hold, she held it up for Bulldog to see.

"Oldest trick in the book," she said. She had learned a thing or two about tracking devices from the days when her father was being followed by a killer he was testifying against.

Bulldog's expression didn't waver. He just stood in place, staring at her, as she got into her car.

"This is illegal, you know," she stammered, slamming the car door closed. Bulldog remained expressionless as she pulled away.

Emily drove out of the parking lot and down the street a couple of blocks. She pulled over and threw her car in park. Kicking off her remaining heel, she rubbed her swollen feet. She looked in the rearview mirror, barely recognizing herself. Emily ripped off both sets of fake eyelashes and ran her fingers through her tangled hair. Besides completely embarrassing herself, she had just shown her hand to Tiffani.

Emily rested her head into the steering wheel. It wasn't like her to let her emotions get the better of her. Her irrational mind had snapped when she saw Tiffani's fender, unraveling everything that had happened in her life in the past month. She was officially losing it. And the only thing she could take comfort in was that her little stunt had unearthed proof that Tiffani had some deep, dark secrets that were now were surfacing with her sister's remains.

35

Despite the fact that she was still ticked at Nick, Emily picked up his call the next morning. She was hoping he'd have some word about Sandi's case.

"Heard you had an interesting night, Cardamom," said Nick as soon as Emily said hello.

She grimaced. So, word about the fight had already reached him. At least she didn't have to explain how she had completely humiliated herself.

"You're a real piece of work, Emily Hartford. I didn't know you had *that* in you."

"Not my finest moment. And before you suggest it, yes, I am considering therapy." *The kind where I disappear to a spa in the Caribbean.*

"I only wish I coulda been there to see it." He let out a full laugh.

"This is funny to you? I totally botched things up," she said.

"I'm just glad you're okay." He was still on her side. He always was.

"She had a tracker on my car," Emily said. "I could press charges."

"How are you going to prove it was her?"

"The paint on her Lexus is from my Leaf."

"And you'll need to collect it and get it sent to the crime lab for proof," said Nick. "But under what cause am I supposed to make an evidence collection? Besides, now that she knows, what are the chances it's even going to still be on the car anymore?"

"Good point," said Emily. Tiffani was probably having it buffed out as they spoke.

"I'm more concerned as to why she was tracking you in the first place," said Nick.

"Because she knows stuff about Sandi's murder. Call her in for her statement," asked Emily. "Tell her you need her DNA sample to rule her out."

"Can't I just get that from under one of your fingernails?"

"Touché."

"Or maybe you still have some of her hair on your dress?"

"I deserve that. But yes, good point. I'll comb my dress for her hair."

"Shame she got your wig. I would have loved to see you in it."

"Have you checked her Facebook for any more clues?" Emily could hear him clacking away at his keyboard. "Nick? Did you hear what I said?"

"Yeah."

"Yes, you did check it?"

"Check what?"

"Tiffani's social media. To see who she's been hanging around with."

"I'm looking right now."

She waited. More clicking and typing.

"Nick? You there?"

"Yeah."

Another pause.

"Nick!"

"Sorry. Busy morning. Busy week. And it's only gonna get busier as the holidays start."

Thanksgiving was just a week away. The weather was worsening, and that meant more traffic accidents. Shoplifting would be on the rise. Drunk driving, of course. And the increased suicide attempts as holiday depression set in.

Emily knew from her father's work that there was always an increase in deaths around the holidays. She and her mother had never been able to enjoy a whole Christmas Day without Dad getting called out on a death investigation. The holidays certainly were not happy times for all. Including her.

But even though she hadn't spent the last twelve years of holidays with her father, they had always at least sent their greetings on Christmas morning with a short phone call. Where would she spend her holidays now? It wouldn't be with Brandon and his family. Aunt Laura in Chicago always went to Colorado skiing, and that didn't feel right this year. Or Jo and her clan? That might not be the best idea, given the fragile state of their marriage. Maybe with Anna and her family? She warmed at the thought of Anna's offer to join them for the holiday.

"I'll let you go," she said.

"Wait. Before you go, you're invited to my annual Friendsgiving turkey roast this Saturday."

"Thanks. I don't know what my plans are yet."

"You should come. All work and no play makes Jane a dull girl."

"Fine." *But only because I don't want to sit in my dad's empty house all weekend.* "What should I bring?"

"I always leave that up to the guests."

"What happens if you end up with, like, five hash brown casseroles?"

"Somehow it always works out."

Yeah. Somehow everything always works out for you, doesn't it, Nick? "Can it be store-bought?"

"No, city girl. It cannot. Why don't you just bring a beverage?"

"That sounds like something you assign the kid from your class who you're not sure is going to show up."

"If the shoe fits," said Nick. "Guests start arriving at noon. We party till the last one leaves. Which for some means after the Sunday football game."

Emily grinned. Nick knew how to keep things in perspective, even when the world around him seemed to be crumbling.

"And Emily, one more thing."

"What?"

"Do me a favor and keep your hands by your side for now. Can you do that, please? I have enough on my plate with the holidays coming up."

Emily sighed, and with double crossed fingers replied lightly, "As you wish."

36

Emily did find several strands of Tiffani's hair on her dress sleeve. She didn't really believe Tiffani had killed her sister. Nonetheless, she bagged and labeled them carefully and drove to Nick's office to deliver them. He wasn't around. She signed them in with the officer on duty to be registered in the evidence locker for Sandi's case.

Then, for the next two days, Emily kept her side of the bargain and laid low. She distracted herself with cleaning the house, organizing the kitchen, and sleep. Much-needed sleep. Whenever the pressure of her future mounted beyond what she could stand, she watched movies and made apple pies. Emily also volunteered to babysit when Jo took a few extra shifts at the hospital. Jo hadn't let Paul home yet, and the kids were starting to ask a lot of questions.

Emily, concerned about her friend's sanity, suggested a shopping trip to Rock River on Friday, Jo's day off. She owed Jo a little black dress and wanted to give her a distraction from her woes.

"Look at us," said Jo as they browsed a department store. "Two women, not even thirty, our love lives in shambles. It wasn't supposed to be this way."

"No, it wasn't."

Jo pulled a dress off the rack that looked similar to the one Emily had ruined.

"What's up with that Dr. Payton guy? Any bites?"

"Heard from him earlier this week. It was just a professional call."

Emily grabbed a second and third black dress and held them up for Jo's thoughts.

"The first one," said Jo, pointing at Emily's left hand, the dress with the ruffled collar. Emily slung it over her arm.

"Jaden told me her daddy has a brand-new house on the lake. Did I miss something and you kicked him out for good?" asked Emily.

Jo glanced at Emily with a pained look. "That's just kid talk. They see things literally."

"How are things going between you two?"

"No change. But that's because of me. I'm holding back until we get some real answers about Sandi's death."

"Start therapy yet?"

"I tried to set an appointment, but then he always has some excuse why he can't go."

"I'm sorry."

Jo shrugged and headed to a rack of cocktail gowns. "By the way, Emily Hartford, what happened at the Silver Slipper?"

"I can be a little overdriven at times," said Emily in an underplayed tone.

"You think? Did you accomplish what you had hoped?"

Jo's sarcasm washed over Emily. She didn't want to reveal the road incident. "I made everything worse," she said, joining her friend at the rack.

"You went on your instincts, and instincts aren't wrong," said Jo. "Don't apologize for wanting justice for Sandi."

"What am I supposed to do now?"

"You'll figure it out. It's your superpower, Doctor Dazzle. Or do you go by Cardamom now?"

Emily laughed, encouraged to hear her friend had such confidence in her.

"In the meantime, dress therapy," insisted Jo.

Emily snatched a couple items from the rack she would never be caught dead in and followed Jo to the dressing room.

37

The next day, Emily arrived at Friendsgiving shortly after one PM and found it in full swing. Nick's recently remodeled lake house was teeming with people. There was the crowd from high school, some married, some sporting a kid or two, the rest single and a few drinking more than they should. Many were friendly faces from Freeport, but not ones Emily recognized. She smiled at the stream of people as she made her way into the kitchen with one of her apple pies, which now seemed like a very underwhelming contribution as she set it down on the crowded counter next to six more pies just like it.

"Jaden, out of the kitchen. Go find your brother and sister." Jo entered with Jaden shuffling behind her. She took her by the shoulders and pointed her in the direction of the living room. "Mommy's gonna hang with the adults now."

Jaden skirted off, and Jo grabbed a red Solo cup from a stack on the counter and penned the name *Cardamom* under the lip with a Sharpie.

"Here. Let's get you something to drink." She shoved the cup into Emily's hand. Emily read the name.

"So, does everyone here know?"

"Pretty much. You're getting a reputation of being a real badass. My advice—go with it." Jo took Emily by the arm to a pair of kegs chilling outside on the deck, where Emily selected the lighter of the two beers, a pilsner. Jo did the same and then motioned for her to fol- low her down the steps that led to the lakeshore in front of the house.

"Wow, you can really feel winter setting in," said Emily, pulling her hood over her head.

When they got to the deserted sandy shoreline, Jo turned to Emily with an apprehensive look.

"Nick and Paul have something cooked up to collect DNA sam- ples from the members of the pack today," said Jo in a whisper.

"Paul told you that?"

Jo nodded. "We went out for a bite after therapy."

"He showed up. Good."

"Said we had to do it for the kids." Jo rolled her eyes.

"It's a start," Emily said pulling on her gloves. "The members of the pack are here?"

"Some of them. He wouldn't say who."

"It would be so much easier if Nick just called them into the sta- tion for a statement."

"That's what I think, too. But Paul said that Nick wants to pro- tect the innocent until proven guilty. You know how Freeport is."

Emily could see his point. Stir up any suspicion and it would immediately assume blame.

"Or Nick doesn't want to spook the killer," said Emily.

"Understandable," said Jo, zipping up her jacket. "That wind off the lake is biting."

"Did Paul mention the plan?" asked Emily.

"The cups. They're going to collect their DNA from the cups after the party."

Emily nodded. It was a good plan.

"Is that legal? Can they do that?" Jo's voice thinned when she was nervous.

"It is if he can get samples they dispose of."

"I don't get it."

"Well, let's say you drink from a red plastic cup and then toss the cup into a public trash. Or one that doesn't belong to you. A police investigator has the right to collect it and run a DNA test on the saliva."

"Anyone can lift my DNA after I toss this cup?"

Emily nodded.

"You're like a Nancy Drew who drinks and dresses like a stripper," Jo joked, but Emily could see new creases lining her forehead.

"I hope Nick has sent in his DNA. Paul's results should be back right after Christmas. It can take up to eight weeks or more. The labs are always backlogged," Emily said, knowing this was on Jo's mind. "You're not worried, are you?"

Jo shrugged, discouragement lodged in her look. This time frame would eat into the stability of their fragile relationship. "Let's just focus on our plan?"

"My sleuthing sidekick." Emily grinned. "I like that."

"Jo? Em?" They turned to see Paul calling them from the deck. "Turkey's ready."

Jo waved to acknowledge him. "Coming!"

"When does he get to come back home?" asked Emily.

"Tomorrow. We've got a houseful of family for Thanksgiving next week, and I don't want questions."

Emily understood. It wasn't worth rocking the family boat while they were trying to work things out.

"Okay, so here's what I'm thinking. You stick close to Paul. I'll stick close to Nick. Observe and record. But they can't know we're onto them."

Jo took a swig of her beer and gave Emily the thumbs-up. "Let's get 'em, Cardie."

* * *

Emily grabbed a plate of food from the kitchen and took it to the garage, where a number of the guys were standing around drinking. A handful were smoking cigars or vaping. The garage door stood open and it was freezing, but none of them seemed to notice as they hung out in their sweat shirts and flannels. At first scan of the crowd, she didn't see Nick. Then she heard his laughter booming from a tight circle of guys surrounded by a cloud of smoke near the opening of the garage door.

She scanned the social landscape for a place where she could slip in unnoticed. There was a small ring of ladies talking in the corner. It was the perfect cover. She would integrate herself into their circle and resume her lookout. She greeted them and started to make small talk. Every so often she would glance over to Nick's group. She didn't recognize the guys he was talking to. In fact, she didn't recognize many of the people in the room. Had she gone to school with them, or were they work friends? Were any of them part of the pack?

She saw Nick collecting cups from the guys and head out of the garage and around the back of the house for a beer run. She made a quick excuse to the other women—nature calling—and wedged her way out of the garage in his direction.

The sidewalk led to an outdoor wooden staircase that brought her up to the back deck. She bounced up the stairs two at a time as Nick reached the top and disappeared to the deck beyond. When Emily hit the top step, she paused to watch him. He was at the keg, filling all the cups. Simple beer run. No DNA samples yet. Emily had taken one step backward, creeping slowly to get out of view, when a man wearing a bright-orange hunter's cap came up behind her.

"Hey, you okay? Didn't mean to scare you," he said, grabbing her by the arm as she nearly tipped backward. Nick looked over. Her cover was blown.

"Thank you," she said, steadying herself.

"Nick, I think you're out of napkins," the guy said as he took the last two steps up the stairs and went onto the deck.

Emily knew Nick had seen her, so she pretended she was heading for the sliding door that led into the kitchen.

"Em! You're here. I thought maybe you had ditched again." His cheery booming voice stopped her in her tracks. "Check the pantry, Pete. And hey, can you take these to the guys in the garage for me?"

"You bet," said Pete, taking the four full cups of beer in his large palms.

"I don't want a drop of that spilled," Nick joked. "Em, wait up."

"I'm not one to waste good beer," said Pete, disappearing back down the staircase toward the garage.

"Pete's a brewer. Owns Mash Up, the microbrewery in town," Nick told Emily.

Emily nodded. "I've just gotta go check on . . . a thing that I brought."

"Oh, what did you make?"

"I made one of the half a dozen identical apple pies. Not very original."

"If you used your mom's recipe, then it's probably the best one of the bunch," said Nick, placing a hand on her forearm. "I'm glad I ran into you right now. Would you mind coming with me a sec?"

"Sure?" This tracking plan wasn't panning out exactly how she had hoped.

Nick drew her back into the house, through the kitchen, and toward the stairs leading to the second floor.

"Where are we going?"

"Shhh." He slipped her upstairs to his bedroom.

"What are we doing here?" Emily asked, standing firmly near the door.

"Can you shut that, please?" Nick waved his hand at the door.

She shut them in, wondering what this might look like to the casual partygoer. She didn't need to add steam to the Freeport gossip train. Emily glanced around the room. It was tastefully decorated in a nautical theme, navy and yellows. One whole wall was a window overlooking the lake. Breathtaking. Peaceful. She had a hard time diverting her eyes from the captivating view, but quickly turned to Nick. "Why are you being so secretive?"

"Look, Em, I need a favor. I'm collecting surreptitious DNA samples from some of the pack who are here, and I need to get them expedited at the lab."

Well, no use sneaking around anymore now that he had just admitted to the plan.

"That would be nice, but that's not how it works. There's not a single lab in the state or the country that isn't backed up."

"What I'm saying is that I don't have the clout to put a rush on them. But you . . . I was thinking maybe you could take them to Dr. Payton's team."

"I see." So this was it, huh? Her mind was already ahead of itself. Leverage.

"He seems into you. Not that I want to encourage that."

"But you're willing to throw me at him in this circumstance." She was half joking. But Nick didn't see the humor.

"For the sake of the case? Please."

"I thought you wanted me to keep my hands at my sides."

"It's a need-to-know situation, and now you need to know."

Finally.

"Who are you tracking?"

"Brett Tillerdale. Rick Bayfield. Landry Patrick. You remember any of those guys?"

Emily thought she had been in an English class with Landry freshman year. It was hard to recall beyond that.

"Just vaguely. But I'm not sure I would recognize them if I saw them now," she said. "What happened to them?"

"Brett doesn't live in the area anymore. Landry and Rick are in Freeport. There, happy?"

"I am," said Emily, relaxing her stance. "Any alibis?"

"Landry says he was out running the track after school."

"Can you get anyone to confirm that?"

"Almost impossible. Landry didn't remember that many people who were at the track that afternoon."

"If no one can place him at the track at the time of Sandi's disappearance, that doesn't bode well for him," said Emily.

"You're right. And Landry was probably the closest friend to James because their parents were close. They spent a lot of time at each other's houses."

"Interesting. That sounds like a conversation you need to expand down at the station."

"I'll call him in if I have to."

"And Brett? Rick?" Emily continued.

"Brett was working at Icy Cup. I doubled-checked the employer records. Rick was helping his dad at the family dairy. Paul confirmed with the dairy-farm foreman, who went back and checked the time cards."

"Paul checked them?"

Nick employing a friend as a sleuthing sidekick was probably not the best investigative prowess.

"Paul's dad is friends with the foreman," he said.

She was annoyed. "The foreman could be lying."

"He has nothing to gain from being dishonest."

"What about James? Any luck finding him?" Emily asked.

"He's a ghost. None of these guys kept in contact with him after graduation."

"Nothing more from his dad?"

"His dad said he got home a little after five, had dinner with the family, and then went upstairs to his office for the night."

"Did he mention anything about a broken nose?"

"No."

"You'd think he'd remember his son coming home with a banged-up nose."

"I'm not sure his parents paid him much attention."

"What about Tiffani?" suggested Emily. "Why has she stayed so quiet? If your sister got murdered and her body was finally found and the case was reopened, wouldn't you be hounding the police, the detectives, sheriff, anyone you could to crack the case?"

"Of course I would."

Nick walked over to his bed and sat on the side that overlooked the water. He pressed his palms to his temples and squeezed. "I'm doing the best I can, okay?"

"I'll take the samples to U of M."

"Drop by the station Monday morning."

Emily held him in her gaze. "Nick, you need to submit your sample, too."

"Hands by your side, Hartford." He turned his gaze out the window.

She went to sit next to him on the bed. Together they stared at the lake, now surrounded by barren trees. The late-November winds stiffened the water into whitecaps rippling onto shore. The afternoon sun was waning across the sky into a formation of dark clouds billowing on the horizon. Storm clouds. The first snow, perhaps. It was expected any day. Tomorrow they might wake up to a white blanket on the ground.

"Where are you spending Thanksgiving?" Nick asked, stirring them back to the present.

She was about to say *at home with Dad*, then gulped down the response before the words escaped. Tears watered in the corners of her eyes. Nick put his arm around her and squeezed.

"I'm going to my folks. And you're welcome to join me. I'm sure they'd love to see you."

"Thanks," she said, inhaling and taking one last look over the lake. "We better head down. Or people are going to start to talk."

"I'll go first. Make sure the coast is clear."

"We're sneaking around like we're fifteen," said Emily.

"Except no parents around."

"Freeport gossip is way more intimidating than parents catching you."

They both let out a small laugh.

Nick stuck his head out of the bedroom. "Coast is clear. See ya down there."

When he disappeared into the hallway, Emily walked into the en suite bath. She spied his overflowing garbage can next to the toilet. Several used tissues and a dirty Q-tip were of special interest to her. Emily carefully plucked the items from the trash and placed them into an unused trash bag from under the sink.

38

The excitement in Dr. Payton's voice practically leapt from the phone when Emily called him Sunday and asked if she could drive down on Monday morning to deliver the DNA samples.

Putting a rush on it would be no problem. But he couldn't produce official results until the week after the holiday because the staff and students had already left for Thanksgiving break.

Waiting only one week was a gift, seeing as most testing could take up to two months. Emily expressed her gratitude and agreed to meet him in his office around noon. He promised her a tour of the facilities and dinner out if she could stay. She definitely would. A snowstorm was predicted and she didn't want to return to Freeport on dark, slippery roads. So, Dr. Payton had graciously set her up in guest housing.

After she arrived late Monday morning, she dropped her things in her room and headed and walked through the expansive campus to Dr. Payton's building. The sidewalks were wet with fresh snow and tree branches were lined with white, but the campus was quiet at the start of this holiday week. It brought back memories of her own years at the University of Chicago and holidays spent in the dorms. She'd never minded being on her own those first couple of undergrad years. If she wasn't skiing in Colorado with her aunt Laura, she would just crash at her aunt's flat in Chicago for a staycation. It was cozy, quiet, and in the center of the theater district. She could sleep or play her music loud, and no one was there to wake her or complain about noise. And then came Brandon. After him, her holidays had been spent with his family in their ten-bedroom mansion in the tidy north suburbs. Or on the ski slopes in the Alps. Or the beaches of Aruba. It all just depended on what mood Brandon's mother was in each year.

Entering the medical building, Emily shook off the cold and stomped excess snow from her boots. She stepped into the atrium and paused to gain her bearings. There was a winding staircase in the middle that led to the second floor, where she found Dr. Payton's office. His door was cracked open.

"Charles? It's me. Emily."

She heard a chair scrape against a wooden desk, and then he was at the door greeting her with a huge smile.

"A pleasure to see you again." He gave her a hearty handshake, holding on a just a bit longer than was customary.

"I have the samples," said Emily, removing them from her handbag.

"Oh, not here. Let me take you to the lab."

He grabbed a set of keys from his desk and whisked them down the hall. At each doorway he told her the name of each professor and their specialty, although only a few were actually in for the day.

They arrived at the lab on the third floor, and Dr. Payton unlocked the door and let them in. While the walls and floors were traditional brick and mortar from a hundred years ago, the equipment at each station was at least three to five years ahead of anything she had seen at the University of Chicago. Outstanding. Dr. Payton must have read her amazed expression.

"Yes. We're very lucky. We secured a large grant a couple years ago that keeps us funded," said Dr. Payton. Emily let her eyes drink in every detail of the massive scientific power this lab held. "Just think. You would have your own research assistant. Access to state-of-the-art equipment. Summers off."

Emily grinned at Dr. Payton. "You know how to sweeten the pot," she said.

"I can log in those samples now, if you want. Show you how these bad boys work," he added.

Emily handed them over. He took them to the back, where he processed them and logged them into their computer system. "We'll be a bit backlogged from the Thanksgiving weekend, but I'll make it a priority to get to these first thing next Monday."

"That's perfect. We're just really grateful for the expediency." Her eyes were drawn again to the beautiful instruments before her.

Dr. Payton laughed. "Can't stop staring, can you?"

"Caught me."

Dr. Payton logged in the last sample. Nick's.

"Nick Larson? The sheriff?" He gave her a curious look.

Emily struggled to respond and settled on, "It's complicated."

"Is he a suspect?"

Emily smiled and decided to change the subject. "The guest housing is really nice. And thank you for the orchids in my room."

"My pleasure. Want to make you feel at home here."

She squirmed inside and diverted her eyes from his to her surroundings. It was a dream lab. "Tell me more about the work you're doing here."

"I have several grad students working on a machine I developed that will swab DNA from mass casualties on-site for instant results. Can you imagine how much time that would save in victim identification?"

"What a huge relief for families. How does it work?"

"The theory is that you swab the samples and place them on the well of this small microplate. You can then run the direct DNA amplification process in less than two minutes."

"Has it been tested? What's the accuracy rate?"

"We're over ninety-seven percent accurate. But to really put it to the test, unfortunately, we would need a real mass disaster. So we're prepped and ready to go on-site, but of course, it's a sad reality to have to wait for."

Dr. Payton printed out a report of the log for her. "Here's yours. I'll call you with the results next week."

Emily tucked it into her bag. He led them from the lab back to his office, and they talked for some time about the department's needs and future direction. Emily could see that she would fit in nicely here. She and Dr. Payton had similar views about pedagogy and what they expected in student participation and research methods. She would have the freedom to experiment and work with some of the top law enforcement in the country to help them develop tests she and her father had dreamed of years ago—like X-ray machines that let you examine evidence at the site of the crime. Never had she imagined in med school that her life might take this turn.

Dr. Payton walked her back to guest housing. It was just past one, but the sky was dark gray and foreboding. Snow had started coming down hard by the time they reached the building.

"What do you think so far?"

"I'm impressed. I've always loved university life almost as much as I loved forensics. It's all very tempting."

"Then I've done the first part right. I was hoping the shiny gadgets would lure you. In part, anyhow."

She laughed. "You've given me a lot to consider," she said as he opened the door for her.

"I'm glad we've made it this far in the process."

"No promises just yet."

"I can't help that I've had my fingers crossed since our first morgue meeting."

"I have to ask. How did you find me? And why me?"

Dr. Payton chuckled. "I've sort of been stalking you. But in a professional way."

"Okay?"

"I've read a lot of your dad's articles in the *Journal of Forensic Science*. He mentions you in some of them. I started to dig and discovered you were only fourteen when you helped him with a murder-suicide. I was intrigued. So I searched a little more. Discovered your background, med school, surgical residency. When Sheriff Larson phoned, I jumped at the chance to come to Freeport. But I sure didn't expect to see you. That was pure bonus."

"And you decided to offer me a job? Just like that."

"I know talent when I see it."

Emily was touched by his compliment, and a little wary. No one had ever pursued her so doggedly before. For a slot in school. For a job. She had been an excellent student, but that had held little water when she'd been faced with the fierce competition of others as gifted as she. Emily had always excelled, but not without hard work.

She glanced beyond him to the snow outside, falling so thickly it had covered the footprints they had just made.

"You don't have to walk all the way back to your building for your car, do you?"

"Actually, yes. It's a good thing I don't mind a brisk walk in the snow."

"Too bad you don't have a pair of cross-country skis. Please be careful."

"I'll pick you up ten to eight. The restaurant's not too far from here. Wait in the lobby. I'll escort you to the car."

"I'll be ready."

He took off, disappearing within seconds into the white whirlwind. She liked being put on a pedestal. She liked being pursued. She really liked his caliber and his style. He was a hard worker, persistent, and serious. And he didn't make her feel overlooked. He offered potential and possibility. On her terms. It was tempting.

* * *

Dr. Payton picked her up from guest housing that evening in his Audi SUV. They valeted at Chateau Le Bleu just a few minutes down the road. Given the snowstorm, Emily and Dr. Payton virtually had the place to themselves, barring a Chinese family seated near the window at the front.

The host seated them at a two-top in a darker corner with a tea light candle casting a soft glow over the silver and linens. A bottle of red was on the table, and the waiter arrived to pour a small taster sample in a red goblet. Emily swirled the liquid a few times and inhaled. She had learned how to taste wine from her many wine tastings with Brandon, from Napa to Bordeaux.

"It's nice. Smooth. No tannins," said Dr. Payton. He swished the wine in his mouth to spread the flavors. Emily did the same. "I taste blackberries and—"

"Tobacco on the back of the tongue?" added Emily.

"Yes. Exactly." He sounded suave. "Actually, I don't know a thing about wines."

The waiter poured more into her glass, then into Dr. Payton's. He recited the specials and left them to mull over the choices.

"I'm thinking scallops. How about you?" She looked up from the menu to find him staring at her.

"I'm thinking about you."

Emily didn't move or breathe for a long moment as they held each other's gaze. There was an underlying assurance in him she had never seen in Brandon or Nick. Maybe it had to do with maturity and age. Finally, she took another sip of her wine.

"Emily, I know you're not obtuse to the situation here. You know I like you. As more than a candidate for the department."

"There must be rules about professors dating," she said boldly, knowing she had clearly read his intentions.

"Nothing we can't overcome."

"I guess I have to get the job first."

He smiled and enjoyed another swig of the wine.

"You already have a strong résumé, but there is something that could really put the feather in the cap of your application."

"Oh, what's that?"

"Have you published before?"

"On a resident's schedule? No." And then she quickly remembered that Brandon had published half a dozen times with Dr. Claiborne before he'd completed residency.

"Would you consider publishing a journal article with me on the Parkman case?"

"A journal article? Oh, is that what you had in mind when you were talking about using this case for your research?" she asked.

"I've been thinking about it, and yes, I think it has great merit."

"What angle would you take?"

"Case study. On rural investigations of clandestine graves."

It was a good angle. "Sounds like it will require a good deal of research." She tried not to lead with her wariness, but it leaked into her tone.

"All you need to do is give your report and expert opinion as medical examiner."

Emily hesitated, trying not to be influenced by the flattery of the ask. "It might be a bit premature," she started. "There's so much going on with the case right now. Don't you think it would be better to get some closure on it before publishing? I would just be afraid of leaking some piece of information that might harm the investigation."

"No. We would take a purely scientific and sociological approach. The article would focus on aspects of the injuries, how long the body had been left to the elements, if similar cases from rural areas have yielded investigations that led to arrest and trials."

"I don't know if I feel comfortable about this. There are a lot of personal angles involved in this one." Emily didn't want to divulge how many in her own circle of friends were on the brink of being accused as suspects or accomplices. She wasn't sure she wanted this case and its backstory to go public.

"I get that it's a sensitive case, but we wouldn't be pointing fingers. Just presenting a case study."

"I don't think it's a good idea. Perhaps we can revisit this another time." She put her foot down.

"I'm not trying to pressure you. I'm only offering because I want to give you a leg up on the competition."

"What competition is that?" she asked.

Dr. Payton stuttered over his answer. "You aren't the only one being considered for the position. I'm sure it doesn't surprise you to hear that the other applicants have more specifically related experience in the field."

"I see." She was not surprised, but she was put off by the slight threat he was insinuating. And she didn't like the casual manner in which Dr. Payton had not considered the people involved in this case. These were her friends. Her community. This was her home.

*   *   *

The waiter arrived with the entrées and they sunk their teeth into the first delicious bites. Emily couldn't remember the last time she had eaten such a gourmet meal. She had been promised one by Brandon for her birthday over two months ago. But her father's heart attack that day had dissolved those plans instantly.

"If you don't mind me asking, why did you get into surgery instead of following in your father's footsteps?" said Dr. Payton as he poured the last few drops of wine into her glass.

"I loved helping my dad with death investigation. But I knew I would need a medical degree if I wanted to pursue it."

"Normally I would say that seems like an odd choice for a young girl."

"People don't understand that it's so much more than cutting up dead bodies."

"I've never thought of it as more than just a procedure."

"No one is ever prepared for a death of a loved one. It can be scary and upsetting and confusing. My dad gave people answers as to why and how their loved one died. When someone can sit down and really explain this with compassion, it gives a lot of comfort and peace of mind to victims' families. He helped them during their darkest hours so they could focus on the meaning and purpose of the life of their loved one."

"That's beautiful, Emily. So, why surgery?"

"Life brings us detours sometimes." And she left it at that. "I bet you always knew what you wanted in life."

"I did," he said with confidence. "And gratefully, it's all worked out the way I had imagined." His whole body was still as he said it, his gaze unflinching on her. "But you . . . you're much better than I ever imagined."

She warmed under his smile, and before she knew it, Emily asked him, "What are you doing for Thanksgiving?"

"No plans yet."

"How would you like to spend Thanksgiving with me and my sister's family?" she said, making a snap decision to spend the holiday with her new family.

The words purred from him. "I would love to."

"Great." The wine had drained all the problems from her head. Change and choice. Potential and possibility. It was hers for the taking.

Now she just needed to confirm with Anna that she was, in fact, still invited for family Thanksgiving. And with a date.

39

I t continued to snow for the next three days. No one in Freeport, including Emily, could remember a time so much snow had collected before New Year's. There was at least a foot on the ground by Thanksgiving morning.

Emily awoke and pulled back the curtain, expecting to find the driveway buried in another six inches. But her driveway was clear of fresh powder, and the sun had melted away any remaining snow into small puddles.

Dr. Payton came up early Thanksgiving Day to Emily's house, and she drove them to Rock River to Anna's. She felt differently about this Thanksgiving than she had about any other since her mother passed. She wasn't nervous about things being stuffy or awkward, as they often were with Brandon's family. Anna made her feel comfortable. And being with her sister and brother-in-law and nieces felt like having a real family—her family! Dr. Payton brought no expectations or pressure to please. He was easygoing and chatty. The perfect guest. Together they navigated this unfamiliar territory as newcomers.

After dinner, Emily helped Anna wash dishes in the kitchen while Dr. Payton and Kyle took the kids outside to play in the snow.

"I love that you're here. Let's always do this," said Anna. "Whether you stay in Freeport or go to Ann Arbor or back to Chicago, you always have a place here with us."

"I like that idea." Emily glanced out the kitchen window and noticed that gray sky had overcome the blue. Snow was starting to fall again. The two men and sisters were rolling giant balls of snow to make snowmen. "I always wanted to have a sister to do that kinda stuff with."

Anna followed her glance. "Yeah. Me too."

"I suppose you have a lot of questions about Dad?"

"It's funny. I was looking at you and Fiona at dinner. You two have the same nose. Same lips. Even the same little laugh."

"Mom always said I resembled my dad more," said Emily. "Genes have an interesting way of expressing themselves." It made her happy that she and her little niece shared family resemblance.

Anna's face dropped, and she turned away from Emily to wipe the suds off her hands. Emily wasn't sure where to carry the conversation from here. How much did Anna want to know about her dad? Emily wiped down a few more plates and waited for Anna to take the lead.

But Anna remained silent until the last dish was dried. She then slung the towel on the countertop and declared in a chipper voice, "Why should we be in here doing all the work and they get to have all the fun?"

"Yes. You're right." Emily glanced back outside. The snowman had a base and a torso now.

"We have lost time to make up for," Anna stated, untying her apron and tossing it on the kitchen counter. She grabbed Emily's hand, and they dashed out the back door without their boots and coats.

*   *   *

By dusk, another snowstorm was rolling in on the horizon. Emily and Dr. Payton hastily said their goodbyes and got on the road back to Freeport. They were too late. The incoming storm billowed up and overtook them, unleashing its frozen fury. Crawling along the two-lane road with whiteouts and drifting gusts, it took them almost two hours to make the usual one-hour trip from Rock River. It was nearly ten o'clock when they pulled into the driveway, and it had been decided miles before that Dr. Payton would spend the night instead of making the treacherous trek to Ann Arbor. There was no way she would send him back on the road tonight.

She made up the bed in the guest room in the basement while Dr. Payton made a fire. Soon they were cozied up on the couch in front of the fireplace with a bottle of wine.

"What a perfect day. Right down to the snow angels," said Emily.

"That was really cute. And I have the pictures to prove it." He whipped out his phone and scrolled to the series of Emily and Anna in the yard. She devoured them, stopping on one where she and Anna were sandwiched between two snowmen with their arms around each other, clothes wet, hair messy. A real sister picture. Like the ones she had seen so many times of her friends and their sisters.

"What was your mother like?" asked Dr. Payton.

"Strong. Supportive. Independent," said Emily, reflecting on her memories. "She was always there for me and my dad. Whenever I needed to work something out, I would crawl up next to her and we would just talk it out. Dad was the teacher, but Mom was the listener. What's your mom like?"

"A lot the same. She's a widow now. My dad died three years ago. Heart attack. She found him lying in his study. Doing what he loved."

"Which was?"

"Watching the stock ticker on the business channel. He was an investment banker."

"I'm so sorry," said Emily.

"My mom travels a lot with her friends. Keeps busy."

"Does she ever come to visit you at the university?"

"Every semester."

Emily yawned. "Oh, dear. That was so rude." She yawned again. "I'm sorry. All that fresh air."

"You don't have to fight sleep for me. It's been a long day," said Dr. Payton.

"Thank you. I think I'm going to head up." She stretched out her legs and sat up. "I put extra blankets at the foot of the bed. It can get a little cold down there."

"It's been a wonderful day, Emily," said Dr. Payton, taking her hand. Emily noticed how warm it was as it enveloped hers. "Thank you for including me in your new family."

He cupped his other hand on her cheek and drew her face toward his. She could feel his light breath, touched with the scent of red wine. He leaned in and his lips touched hers. They hung there for a moment as he pressed them lightly into hers for a kiss. She wanted to kiss him back, but found herself paralyzed. He was the first man whose lips had touched hers since she and Brandon had started dating. She'd thought she'd never kiss anyone else ever again. *It's okay to move on. Brandon certainly has. You're not doing anything wrong here.*

Dr. Payton put his lips to hers again, and this time she returned the kiss. With both hands, he cradled her head and drew her deeper into the kiss. But it didn't feel right.

Emily pulled away. *And this is no way to start a new job. If I even want it.*

"Good night," she said in a whisper as she pushed the blanket off her lap into a heap. He sunk back into the couch, and Emily thought she could detect a slight frown in the waning firelight.

"Good night, Emily," he said in a return whisper that held no judgment or disappointment. "Sleep well."

She rose from the couch and slipped out of the living room into the dark hallway that led upstairs. Dr. Payton's tone had told her he was not upset or offended that she had cut off the kiss. But Emily was upset about her own lack of decisiveness. Life was pulling her in all sorts of directions. And they all looked promising. Dr. Payton included.

She wished she could cozy up to her mother to talk it all out. In the early teenage years, when every day had seemed to bring some scenario of unsure footing in Emily's life, she would find her mother reading in bed. She would motion for Emily to come lay by her side and wrap her arm around her as Emily dished about the day's problems. Somehow the solutions were so accessible when Mom was there to steer her.

Drifting up the stairs, wrapped in this memory, Emily bypassed her own bedroom and went into her parents'. She pulled back the heavy quilt that a trio of great-aunts had made them for their wedding. Emily slid under the covers and curled into a fetal position. The day had been so full of life and fun and family. Why did she feel so very much alone?

40

Emily awoke as day was breaking the next morning. White light seeped around the edges of her blinds, and she struggled to shake the hangover of last night's melancholy. She had not yet touched anything in her parents' room. She wondered how long she could avoid facing the memories of this room before she had to either get the house ready to sell or remodel it into her master bedroom.

Emily crawled out of bed with a shiver and slipped her feet into plush mule slippers. She drew open the blinds to see the sun cracked over the sparkling white horizon. At least a foot of snow had fallen, burying her Leaf and Dr. Payton's SUV. It held her motionless as she watched the sky change in minutes from pink to tangerine to faded blue. These were the mornings and moments she would never encounter in the city. *Amazing.* She could think of nothing as important right now as drinking in the scenery framed before her . . . with a hot cup of coffee.

Emily pulled a sweat shirt over her head and padded downstairs to start a fresh brew before Dr. Payton arose. With snow this thick, she knew he would be stuck here until the snowplow came through, which could take several hours to get this far into the county.

As Emily approached the kitchen, she thought she heard a slight shuffling of paper from the office. Was he up already? She crept closer and saw the door cracked open. Emily peered through the sliver in the doorway and couldn't believe what she was seeing. Dr. Payton was sitting at her father's desk, paging through paperwork and taking photographs of each page with his phone. She reeled back out of view and clasped her hand over her mouth so she wouldn't gasp audibly. *What is he doing?*

Her first instinct was to barge in and bust him. He was breaching her privacy—and that of the medical examiner's office! But her investigative prowess took over, and she paused for a moment to observe and weigh her options.

She craned her neck for another look to assess the situation fully. Sure enough, he was positioning a photograph from the file folder to get the best angle for a good picture. She weighed her possible plans of action. She could step in and catch him in the act. It would be awkward and embarrassing, and he would for sure deny it. She could ask to see his phone, but he might not give it up. And then she might feel compelled to call the police. And that would get super awkward. He would probably leave before the police could arrive, and then she'd have to take the next steps to get him arrested for stealing. It would be a huge deal involving the Ann Arbor police and the university. He'd probably lose his job.

Why kill an ant with a sledgehammer when you can squash it with your thumb? her father had always said. Emily found a better plan hatching and she let him dig his own grave as she tiptoed back into the kitchen to make coffee and breakfast with a satisfied smirk. He wouldn't get away with this.

After a few minutes Emily heard the floor creak as he exited the office and went back to the basement. *Snake!* Emily turned on the small radio her father had installed under a cabinet to listen to the morning news. Her mind reeled with her plan as she took her time making coffee and stirring up a batch of coffee-cake batter, one of the few breakfast delicacies she knew how to bake because it came in a box. She poured it into a Bundt pan and slid it into the oven and then took fresh fruit from the fridge.

While she was slicing pears, Dr. Payton emerged, fresh faced and dressed for the day in slacks and a sweater. She greeted him with a smile.

"Good morning. Sleep well?" she said, putting on a gleeful voice.

"I did." He glanced out the dining room window to the back-yard. "Wow, it looks like we're snowed in."

"Yes. But who doesn't love a snow day? Especially when there's nothing on the agenda. Can I get you some coffee?"

"I'd love some." He sat on the barstool at the counter opposite her. "When do you think they'll have the roads cleared?" He turned his gaze to the picture window that faced the country road in front of the house.

"Are you in a hurry?" She thought she detected impatience in his voice.

"Not entirely. I just . . . don't want to overstay my welcome."

Emily set a piping-hot coffee in front of him. "Sugar? Cream?"

"Black." He brought his lips to the rim and took a quick sip to test the temperature.

"It's probably going to be a few hours before you'll be able to drive out. I have a coffee cake in the oven and a bowl of fresh fruit. I can make some eggs, too." Emily was studying him for the slightest tell.

"Wow. Impressive. A real bed-and-breakfast."

There was no tell. He was calm and cheery. Not an ounce of guilt. Her heart sunk. What if he was just using her? *Of course he is. Who spends Thanksgiving with a first date and total strangers?* Now that she was single again, she really needed to brush up on her dating savvy.

"I was wondering if you could AirDrop the pictures you took yesterday at Anna's? Before we forget."

"Of course." Dr. Payton was careful to hold his phone away from her. "Turn on your Bluetooth."

She did, and soon the pictures came through. She pressed *Accept*. Dr. Payton set his phone on the counter, the screen now black.

"Thanks. These are great. The very first pictures I have of me and Anna." She sprinkled sugar in her voice.

The kitchen timer beeped. Emily pulled the cake from the oven and set it on a hot pad. "It just needs five minutes to cool, and then we can cut it." She set a plate and fork on the counter. She couldn't stand to be in the presence of this liar one more second. "Fruit first?"

"I'd love some."

She scooped some into a small bowl and slid it toward him with a force that knocked his coffee cup down like a bowling pin. The coffee spilled over the counter and onto Dr. Payton's lap. The mug landed with a crash and splintered on the floor.

"Oh my gosh, I'm so sorry! I'm a klutz!" she exclaimed.

"Don't worry." Dr. Payton bent down to pick up the pieces, and Emily took the opportunity to switch his phone with hers, pocketing it in the kangaroo pouch of her pullover sweat shirt.

"I'm gonna grab a couple towels to mop this up." Emily disappeared into the laundry room off the kitchen. She quickly pulled his phone out. Darn. It had gone into lock mode. She tried a few generic sequences. No go. Then, remembering the address of his building, she punched in the number. Access! She clicked onto the photo app and found the photos she was after. There were at least three dozen he had captured from the Parkman case file. *Snake times a hundred!* She deleted every single one, before emerging from the laundry with a couple of old towels.

"Here you go." She tossed him the towels. As he knelt to the floor to mop up the coffee, she deftly placed his phone back on the counter in place of hers.

"Oh, look. There's the snow plow. Wow, they're really on top of it today. Usually takes hours," Emily said, pointing to the road, where the massive machine sent a wave of powder into the ditch. Dr. Payton bobbed his head up, and Emily could see the relief on his face.

"I think I'm going to head off before we get any more snow."

"I totally understand. I'd probably do the same thing." Emily couldn't wait to get rid of him.

"Thanks for everything, Emily. I enjoyed our time. And I'm looking forward to the football game tomorrow."

"Me, too. If I don't get snowed in," she said.

"So, I'll call you later and we can make plans?"

"You bet," she said with a calm smile.

Emily walked him to the front door. He gave her a hug, but she didn't hug back.

"I don't . . ." he said. "Did I miss something here?"

"What do you mean?" She liked that she was channeling her inner Scarlett O'Hara. She wished she could be there to see the look on his face when he opened his photo app.

"I thought maybe there was something between us. Sorry if I misinterpreted."

"We should probably keep things professional for now." She pressed her lips together with a quick raise of her eyebrows to show her absolute confidence in this decision.

He nodded. There was definitely disappointment in that frown this time.

"Drive safely," she said.

He slipped out the door, and it took some effort for him to shuffle his way through the slippery terrain to his car. And when he got there he would have to warm it up and brush off a foot of snow before he could drive away. Emily didn't wait to wave goodbye. She shut and locked the door behind him.

41

"Emily, I need to tell you something." Delia Andrew's urgent command over the phone pulled Emily out of her lazy afternoon nap.

Forty-five minutes later, Delia arrived at the front door, a power-house of purpose in a cherry-red puffer jacket. She stomped the snow off her boots and entered the foyer.

"How was Thanksgiving?" said Delia.

"It took an interesting turn," said Emily, hanging Delia's coat in the front closet. "That Dr. Charles Payton is a snake. I caught him taking pics of my ME files with his phone!" She handed Delia a spare pair of pink slippers and marched into the kitchen with Delia trailing behind.

"What do you mean, doll?"

"I caught him in Dad's office stealing photos of the Parkman file?"

"He was here? Overnight?" Delia's eyebrows raised.

"It wasn't like that." Emily *tsk*ed.

Delia sat herself on the barstool at the kitchen counter. "Well, this confirms it. I did some checking on Dr. Payton with a couple of my colleagues. He has a track record of 'borrowing' research to construct journal articles. It didn't cross my mind he would do that to you, seeing as he had an interest in you."

"That's exactly why he took an interest in me." Emily grinned. "Don't worry. I took care of him, Hartford style."

"You are your father's daughter," Delia said with an approving smile.

Emily fired up the flame under a teakettle on the stove. "Green tea?"

"Read my mind."

Emily prepped loose tea into two tea bags.

"Where's Nick?" asked Delia in a delicate tone that shifted Emily's gaze to her.

"How should I know?"

Delia sighed. "We need to find him."

"Why? Is something wrong?"

"This morning Pepper Cave Construction was doing more excavation on the site where Parkman's bones were found, and something else came up."

"If it were more bones, I would have been called," said Emily.

"No. Maybe worse. It's a letterman jacket. The name *Larson* is on the back."

"What?"

"And if that's not enough, Nick's graduation year is on the sleeve. And the initials *NL* in black marker on the inner tag." Delia's gaze didn't move from Emily's as her brain struggled to put the information together.

"What was it doing out there?"

"When the foreman found it, he called the sheriff's office. Nick couldn't be reached. Not even on his cell."

Emily felt a cold shudder run up her spine. What did this mean?

"The cop on duty processed it and placed it in the evidence locker."

"How did you find out about this?"

"I know the foreman's wife, Melany. She stopped in the bakery this morning shortly after her husband found it."

Even a snowstorm couldn't stop the Freeport gossip train from speeding along its tracks. Emily paced the kitchen. Where could he be?

"This doesn't look good for him," Delia said.

"Do you think he killed Sandi Parkman, Delia?"

Delia shrugged. "I don't want to believe that any more than you do."

"They were friends, but—" Emily's tone wavered. But this was corollary evidence. Not good.

Emily grabbed her phone and dialed his cell. The other line rang until voice mail picked up. Emily didn't bother to leave a message. She pressed end.

"What do we do, Delia?"

The doorbell rang.

"Maybe that's Nick!" Emily darted for the door. But when she opened it, a familiar figure dressed in a long black wool coat and suit greeted her.

"Ben Bishop! Aren't you supposed to be in Phoenix?"

"Good afternoon, Dr. Hartford. How are you?"

His presence made her panic. Why would he show up dressed like an undertaker? *Oh no! Cathy!* "Is everything okay? Is your mom okay?"

"Yes, yes, she's great. Never better."

"What are you doing in Freeport?"

"Lily and I drove back this week," he said. "She missed her family here, and with the baby coming, she—well, we—wanted to be closer."

"And your mom?" Emily bobbed her head around Ben to get a glance at his car.

"She's in Phoenix. Loves it. We did a house swap. We're planning to go down for a few weeks every winter."

"I see. I'll have to give her a call."

"If you can catch her at home."

"What do you mean?"

"She jumped right into retired life. Water aerobics. Golf. Pickle ball. Shopping trips across the border. Happy hours at the community pool."

Emily was glad to hear she was moving on.

"And let me guess, you took over Bishop and Schulz?"

"I did. Guess I kinda missed Freeport, too."

"Being called up in the middle of the night? Dealing with feuding family members? Waiting for death to pay your bills?" Emily was happy to hear the business would stay in the family.

Ben chuckled. "I know. But you get it. We're there to help people in their greatest time of need."

Emily smiled. He had Cathy's optimism. And he would do just fine carrying on the family torch in Freeport. "Sorry, I should have offered to let you in."

Ben procured a paper from his inside coat pocket. "No need. I came to deliver this. I just need your signature."

Emily unfolded the page. As she scanned it, her brow furrowed. "A release for cremation of Sandi Parkman's body?"

"Yes. It was faxed to me this morning by the police."

Emily looked at the signature. She couldn't make it out. "Who signed this?"

Ben pointed at the squiggle of a signature. "Sheriff Larson."

"How can you tell?"

"See?" He pointed to the name. "That's an *N*, and the second word starts with an *L*."

She didn't see. "Were you there when he signed it?"

"No."

"Did you call him to confirm?"

He shrugged. "It's on police letterhead."

Delia looked over her shoulder and shook her head, confirming what Emily had already deduced. It was forged.

"I don't mean to rush you, but it's opening day and the guys are gonna head out again at dusk. I missed the morning hunt, and I really don't wanna miss this one."

Hunting.

"He's at his blind," said Delia, reading Emily's mind.

"But where's that?"

"I have no idea."

"Look, Ben, I'm not signing off on this release for cremation." Emily took the orders and ripped them in two. "This isn't Nick's signature or official police letterhead. I don't want that body released yet."

Ben's face scrunched up.

"I . . . I . . . can you do that?"

"She sure can," said Delia.

"Happy hunting, Ben," said Emily, closing the door.

42

elia left, and Emily paced the house until she couldn't stand being alone with her thoughts any longer. Then she dialed Nick's number twenty times. Finally, she plopped down in her father's armchair and closed her eyes. The stack of evidence against Nick was a sandbag smothering her every moment she sat in silence.

Oh Dad. What would you do here? What am I missing?

She lay on the armchair motionless while she tried to still her mind. After wrestling away a string of unhelpful worry thoughts, Emily focused on inhales and exhales. It was a technique Dr. Claiborne had taught her when she was facing a particularly challenging procedure. It helped her stay in the present and keep her mind from wandering five steps ahead.

As she breathed, her mind slowly unblocked, and soon she recognized a small voice as it trotted across her thoughts like a ticker on the bottom of a screen. *People don't change*, Dad had always said. *Look for the patterns in behavior. They are consistent in how they think and act. We don't usually see the real person in public. We see their persona.*

Her mind shifted from Nick and his jacket to Tiffani.

After Sandi's disappearance, Tiffani had gone from being the good, studious little sister to a rebel, high school dropout, and stripper.

Tiffani had created a persona to deal with the trauma. A big, splashy persona. But what was the specific trauma? What was it that had caused Tiffani to change so much after Sandi's disappearance?

People suffered deaths all the time and they didn't turn from moral to iniquitous without significant reasonable cause.

What terrible thing had happened to Tiffani?

43

Emily wrapped up a plate of coffee cake and hopped in her car. She drove straight to Mrs. Parkman's home without calling first. *Homebound* was the word that came to mind when Emily got to the door. She peered into the small window and saw Shirley Parkman wrapped in an afghan on the couch staring at a game show on TV. It looked like she hadn't moved for days. Would Emily find cobwebs fastening her to the seat cushions?

Emily rang the bell, but it didn't sound. She rapped on the door four times, shaking Mrs. Parkman from her trance. Emily waved through the window.

Mrs. Parkman labored to come to the door.

"Hi, Mrs. Parkman. I've been thinking about you with all this snow and thought I'd stop by to make sure you're okay and bring you a treat."

"Thank you, dear. Would you like to come in?"

Absolutely.

Emily stepped in and almost gagged. The house smelled of stale popcorn and moldy mushrooms and body odor and urine. *Is this how she spends every day? Is this how she spent Thanksgiving?*

"How was your holiday?" She didn't know why she felt the need to raise her voice.

"Shhh. Quiet. I'm not deaf," said Mrs. Parkman, leading Emily to the living room. She lifted a stack of newspapers from a rocking chair and pointed. "There you go."

Emily sat, cringing when she slid back in the chair and something sticky tugged at her pant leg from the seat cushion.

"Did you have Thanksgiving with Tiffani?" said Emily.

"No. She had to work," said Mrs. Parkman, settling into her couch. "When I saw you at the door, I was hoping you had some news about Sandi."

"I wish I did. We're all working very hard on the case." Emily handed her the plate of coffee cake.

"Thank you. Just set it there on the coffee table."

Emily looked for a spot, landing on a stack of magazines, the top one dated nine years ago.

"I was wondering about Tiffani. You said you remember she went to a friend's house that day after school. And you said that the friend was kinda tiny and scraggly. Any chance that name came to mind since we last talked?"

Mrs. Parkman's attention was back on the game show. "What's that, hon?"

Emily wanted to tell the television, *Shhh. Quiet.* It was at least ten decibels louder than it needed to be.

"Tiffani's friend. Where she went after school the day Sandi disappeared?"

"What about her dear?" said Mrs. Parkman.

"Do you remember who that friend was?"

Mrs. Parkman shook her head. "No, no, I haven't got a clue."

Emily smiled. "I just keep thinking about Tiffani. You said she changed a lot after Sandi's death. Can you tell me about that?"

"I dunno. I guess we all have our ways of grieving. I just kinda left her alone. She was one of those self-sufficient types."

Emily nodded. She could tell this wasn't going to be an easy nut to crack.

"Did she start hanging around a different set of friends?"

"Couldn't say. Like I said, I really didn't know her friends." Mrs. Parkman leaned forward and peeled back the foil on the cake. Her chunky thumb and forefinger selected a piece, and she crammed the whole thing in her mouth. "I was working a lot in those days."

Maybe this was one big, fat waste of time.

Mrs. Parkman chomped away, making no attempt at conversation as Emily patiently watched her stare mindlessly at five minutes of commercials.

Mrs. Parkman went for the last piece, and stuffed half of it into her maw. It didn't seem as if she had anything helpful to offer about her daughter's disappearance. Emily cleared her throat to excuse herself from Mrs. Parkman, when a commercial for skinny potato chips cued up. Mrs. Parkman watched for about fifteen seconds before her glossy eyes found focus on Emily.

"Skinny chips. You know what? I do remember this one friend Tiffani had. Skinny Minnie," said Mrs. Parkman laughing. "Skinny Minnie."

"Was that her real name?" Emily asked.

"That's what Tiffani called her." Mrs. Parkman turned back to the screen. Her recollection was final.

Skinny Minnie. Emily rolled it around her brain a few times to seal it into her memory.

"Is that where she went that day . . . when Sandi disappeared?"

"You asked if I knew any names. There you go." The second half of the cake disappeared. "That was delicious."

"Thank you." Emily smiled politely. "Does she still live in Freeport?"

Mrs. Parkman shrugged. "I gotta hit the crapper." Mrs. Parkman pushed herself off the couch and tottered into a hall, using the walls to steady herself. Emily heard the door shut and rose from her seat to take a little tour of the living room. This place could definitely be a featured home on that TV reality show about hoarders. She found the remote tucked into the couch cushion where Mrs. Parkman had just been sitting and notched the volume down on the TV. When she did, a soft *scritch-scritch* turned her head to the opposite wall. *Scritch. Scritch-scritch.* She followed the noise, moving across the room. *Scritch-scritch. Scritch.* Then it stopped. She froze in place, listening. Just when she was tempted to believe her ears had deceived her, the scratching started up again at the base of the wall. *Scritch-scritch-scritch.* Emily's skin crawled. *Scritch-scritch.* Mrs. Parkman had rats!

Emily backed away and scanned the room, trying to drown out the sound with her mind. Soon her eyes came to one uncluttered wall shelf that displayed a set of four tarnished three-by-five frames with a layer of dust coating the glass. In each frame was a picture of Sandi, a life span. Sandi as a baby. Sandi's first day of school. Preteen Sandi on a horse. And prom-picture Sandi. With a young man. Emily did a double take. She picked up the frame and wiped the grime off the glass. A clean-cut, tuxedoed James stood out. She leaned in to get a closer look. He was holding up Sandi's hand in one of those awkward posed-portrait shots. And that's when she recognized the black-onyx class ring. James. Odd as it seemed, it could be no coincidence that Tiffani possessed the same black onyx stone cut in a diamond shape. Why did she have the same stone? Did it belong to the guy in the Facebook picture? And was that guy James? There was most definitely a connection between James and Tiffani. This proved it.

If Nick had any hope of proving his innocence of this crime, he would need to hunt James down. Emily quickly captured the image of the prom picture on her phone seconds before Mrs. Parkman waddled back in.

"Would you like to stay for dinner, dear?" said Mrs. Parkman, heading toward the kitchen. Emily's stomach curdled at the thought of the rats in the wall and what might emerge from the Parkman fridge.

"I think you have rats in your house, Mrs. Parkman," Emily said.

"Oh?"

"I heard scratching in your wall. You should call an exterminator."

"Oh?"

"They could be carrying diseases. And that's not safe for you."

"I've never heard them," said Mrs. Parkman.

"Maybe because you have your TV turned up?"

"I've never seen any droppings."

"Maybe not. But I heard them just now."

"Oh. Okay. I'll tell Tiffani. She'll know what to do," Mrs. Parkman said, opening the fridge. The smell of curdled milk and rotting vegetables wafted out. And Emily quickly thanked Mrs. Parkman and made her exit.

* * *

Emily waited in her car in Nick's driveway until his truck pulled in an hour after dark. She got out of her car and walked over to his as he shut off the engine and hopped out, dressed in his hunting gear.

"I know what it looks like," he said with a tired lilt in his voice.

"Who told you?"

"I was with Paul. A text came through from Jo as soon as we were in signal range."

"Nick." Her voice was trembling. "What was your jacket doing buried in that woods?"

Nick reached into the back of his truck to unpack his gear. Emily could see the lifeless form of a buck under a black tarp in the bed of his pickup. Nick popped the gate down.

"She was cold. I lent her my jacket."

She scrutinized him. "Look at me and tell me that again."

He turned to face her, leaning against the truck. "I'm not looking for your trust or approval. I know who I am and I know what I did. Or didn't do."

"Then what are your theories? Because you'd better start producing some in light of this new evidence."

"I don't know. Okay? I've talked to everyone I know to talk to."

"I think Tiffani knows where James is." Emily whipped out her phone. "Look at the ring from the Facebook photo. Now look at the picture from the Parkman's. James' ring from high school. Same stone." She held up Sandi's prom picture.

"How do you know that's the same stone?"

"It's a very unique cut."

He took a look at the photo. "That's not definitive."

"I have a gut feeling."

"'She has a gut feeling, Your Honor!'" he mocked.

"Come on, admit it. It's not a coincidence."

"You're right. It's an impossibility."

"If you can't find James, at least start with Tiffani."

Nick didn't respond. "I know how to do my job, Em."

"Why won't you call her in for questioning? What's the problem?"

"I did. After you told me about what the girls from the club said, I went to check it out, and there's shady business going on. I put some undercover cops in place to watch Wanda."

"Good. Thank you. And what did Tiffani say?"

"Nothing I don't already know."

"I talked to Mrs. Parkman. Skinny Minnie," blurted Emily. "She was one of Tiffani's best friends. I thought that might ring a bell, since you're the king of nicknames."

"You should stop looking into this."

"You need help, Nick."

"You're undermining me and making me look ineffective."

Nick went around to the back of his truck. Emily took a deep inhale.

"I gotta get this thing hung and dressed."

How could he spend the day traipsing around the woods with his buddies when his head was about to be placed on the chopping block?

Nick proceeded to tie a rope around the deer's hind legs. A pulley system was in place to lift the deer from the back of the truck. Emily didn't want to stick around to see the rest. She huffed back to her car as more snow began to fall. His stubbornness would be his downfall.

44

Emily didn't hear from Nick on Saturday. Or Sunday. Today was Monday, and the passing days without word made her nervous. But this morning, Skinny Minnie was on her mind as she took to the high school library and searched the yearbooks for the years Tiffani had been at Freeport High. There was a waif of a girl in Tiffani's class named Mina. Did Mina translate to Minnie? It was worth a shot. Mina DeBoer. Emily found her profile listed on LinkedIn. She was a family therapist practicing with a private agency in Pittsburgh. The head shot accompanying her page showed a thin-faced, young woman with a bob and a plain brown sweater tastefully accessorized with a gold necklace that held a small cross pendant. She wore her makeup simple. She expressed a small, sincere smile. No teeth. No exaggeration in the facial lines, but she looked relaxed and confident. Her profile page listed only the agency's 800 phone number and a generic email, most likely for privacy reasons. Mina wasn't on any of the other social media platforms. Again, probably to protect her privacy. Smart gal.

Emily left a brief message via the agency contact page but wasn't hopeful that it would be received, as so many weren't. Why did people use contact pages and then never check them or have their emails forwarded to their inboxes? She made a note to remember to call the practice later that day. Then she relaxed with a walk on the property to clear her mind and think about the future.

When she got back to the house, Emily left another message for Mina and then cracked open her surgical textbook to refresh herself. If she did decide to slip back into residency after the new year, she didn't want to seem rusty.

Before dinner, Emily was about to call Mina's office again when her phone range. She recognized it as an Ann Arbor area code.

"I'm Samantha, Dr. Payton's research assistant," said the voice on the other end. "Dr. Payton asked me to reach out to you."

"I see." Hiding behind an assistant. What a snake move. "How can I help you?" said Emily.

"Dr. Payton wanted me to tell you about some lab results."

"Okay. Go ahead." Emily grabbed a pen and paper.

"We were able to get a DNA sample from the root of the hair that was submitted." Her voice was clinical. "From the sample, we looked at twenty-one loci points. And we came up with a match."

Emily held her breath. A match. A real lead in the case.

"The match that was detected belongs to a Nicholas Larson."

Emily's pen hit the paper, leaving an asymmetrical blue dot of ink seeping into the white page. Her hand became limp as she dropped the pen.

"Hello? Are you there?" said Samantha. "Ms. Hartford?"

"Dr. Hartford," she mouthed, and then found her voice. "Yes, I heard you."

"Ah . . . yes. Um, could you read that name to me again?"

"Nicholas Larson."

"I . . . are you . . . sure?"

"We are positive it is the sample from the remains." Her voice remained emotionless. "The database shows his address is in Freeport."

"Um . . . right. Okay."

"I'll send this all in my follow-up email so you can review it yourself."

Emily's mind whirled to process what she had just heard.

"Ms. Hartford? Are you still there?"

"Did you send the report already?

"Yes. I just emailed it to the investigating officer listed on the paperwork. Sheriff Larson at the Freeport sheriff's office." She didn't seem to see the connection at all. It was just a formality to her.

Emily's throat was pinched. It was only a matter of time before Nick would see it. Maybe he already had.

"Is there anything else I can—"

Emily hung up and grabbed her keys.

Her hand was on her car door handle when her phone rang, startling her. The screen announced, *No Caller ID*.

Was it Mina? She dove for the phone.

"Hello. This is Dr. Emily Hartford," she said, getting into her car and starting the ignition.

A wispy voice answered. "This is Mina DeBoer, returning your call."

45

"Thanks for calling me back, Ms. DeBoer. I'm sorry if this call seems rather out of the blue. I'm the acting coroner in Freeport, Michigan . . ."

"Oh my God!" Panic immediately shot through the phone line. "Did something happen to my mom?"

"No, I'm not calling with bad news."

"Okay. Thank God."

Emily heard a sharp exhale on the other end and made a mental note to work on her conversation leads. "I just need to ask you a few questions regarding a case I'm working on."

"Oh. Will this take long? I have a client in five minutes."

"I'll be quick. I've been working on the case of Sandi Parkman. Did you know Sandi and her family?"

"Yes."

"Were you aware that Sandi's remains were found recently?"

"My mom sent me a news link about it."

"I was wondering if I could talk with you about your relationship to Sandi and the family."

"Am I . . . am I being questioned or something?" More tension in Mina's voice.

"What? No. Nothing like that. I'm just trying to fill in some of the blanks. Mrs. Parkman mentioned that you knew the family."

"Well, I knew Tiffani mostly," Mina said, exhaling.

Now Emily was anxious. There was so much at stake here, and it would be only hours—or less—before Nick was arrested. She was desperate to discover if Mina might offer something, anything, that might direct suspicion away from Nick and toward a real suspect. She tried to keep the calm in her voice.

"There's nothing to worry about. It would be really helpful to the investigation."

There was a sustained pause on the other end. "I can call you back?" said Mina in a flat voice.

"Ah. Sure. Of course. When is a good—"

But Mina had already hung up.

* * *

Emily called Nick's cell to see if he was home or at his office or maybe out on a call. No answer. She phoned the department next, and the assistant on duty said he had taken a sick day. Nick was never sick.

She made the trek to Nick's house over snow-covered roads. How had everything tumbled so quickly into such a great tribulation? Her world was spinning. And she felt like she was losing grip as everything unraveled around her. Her eyes went hot with tears. *Pull it together. Now is not the time to fall apart.*

Her car didn't handle well on the slippery country roads, and it took twice as much time to get to Nick's as it normally did. Nick would have checked his emails for the morning and seen the report. That's probably why he had called in sick. She felt the ticking of the clock with each bump on the snow-packed surface. Her heart was pounding through her fingertips as she gripped the steering wheel. She wanted to deliver the news in person and explain what she had done.

Nick's house was the fifth one on the right after she turned onto the road that circled the lake. Through the bare tree lines, she could see the flashing red strobes from a police cruiser parked in his driveway. She was too late.

Emily pushed on the accelerator, and her car gently slid to the right shoulder. She corrected in time to avoid sliding off the road. She slowed the last twenty feet and pulled into his driveway.

Through the giant picture window at the front of the house, she could see Nick and two of his officers standing in the living room talking. There was nothing animated about their gestures. It seemed a friendly visit between colleagues. But Emily knew differently. They were there to arrest him.

Emily coasted to a stop and threw the car in park. She jumped out and shuffled through the snow to the front door.

As she went for the knob, the door opened. She could now see that his hands were cuffed behind his back.

Emily's mouth gaped. "Nick!"

Each officer had an arm as they turned him toward the door to guide him out of the house. Emily thought they looked horribly uncomfortable and apologetic. It had to be awful to be arresting your own boss. Nick's face was expressionless.

"Nick. It was me. I was in your bathroom—"

"Not a word," he commanded.

"What do you want me to do?"

"Stop talking."

"Is there someone I can call?"

"An attorney," he said, without turning back to look at her.

The officers helped him down the slippery front steps. All she could do was watch as they escorted Nick to their squad car and drove away.

Emily stood there, looking into his empty house. From her vantage point she could see the kitchen counter, where she noticed Nick's phone. She certainly didn't want the cops coming back to confiscate it. She slipped off her wet boots and went inside. She grabbed the phone and started to guess the passcode. Nick's birthdate. His street number. His badge number. Denied. Denied. Denied. She had one more try before it would lock her out. On a whim, she punched in her own birthdate. The phone lit up. Emily elbowed her shock to the side and found Nick's dads's number in his contact list and called him. She explained what had happened so his parents wouldn't hear it from the cops, a friend, or worse, a news source. Then she called Delia.

Emily did nothing to hide her panicked tone as Delia bombarded her with questions. No, she couldn't say over the phone what had happened. No, Nick was not okay. Yes, Nick was alive. No, Nick was not injured. Could she just please come to Nick's house.

Emily shuddered after she ended the call. For the first time, the question of Nick's innocence suddenly became very real for her.

Her thoughts somersaulted around her brain. She pressed her palms against the sides of her head and wandered over to the giant slider doors that led onto the back deck from the kitchen.

She stood there, staring out toward the frozen lake. The white-washed landscape had a clearing effect on her mind. And a single thought was set in place. She had betrayed him.

46

While she waited for Delia to arrive, Emily dialed Mina's number at least a dozen times. It was borderline harassment, but Emily didn't care. The current situation had left her a little crazy. On the last try, Emily left a message. Although she didn't leave any details, she knew she sounded desperate. Because she was.

Instinctively, Emily grabbed Nick's phone and pressed her birth date. She couldn't help herself as she began to scroll through Nick's email and texts, just in case there was anything that might . . . No, wait! She couldn't. It would be tampering with evidence. She could go to jail. Lose everything. She set the phone down and wiped her fingerprints off it. She paced around the kitchen. Then she returned to the phone and picked it back up. She would peek. She wouldn't delete or change anything. *No harm in that. Right?*

She found that Dr. Payton's assistant had sent the same email she'd sent Emily to Nick's personal email three hours earlier. Dr. Payton had waited to call her until he was sure Nick had received the news. Snake!

She also found multiple emails, texts, and phone calls that correlated with Nick's search for James VanDerMuellen. He had researched the high school class ring company and gotten his hands on a copy of the receipt for James's ring. He had hired a digital forensics expert to conduct a deep-dive Internet search on James that had turned up nothing in the past couple of years. It was like James had scrubbed himself from the Internet. Nick had contacted countless family members and friends by text, email, or phone. The same message echoed through each response. "We haven't seen him. We don't know where James is. He's disappeared. He owes me money. We're worried."

Nick had done his due diligence.

Delia came bounding through the front door without ringing the bell. Emily nearly jumped out of her skin.

"Don't you knock?"

"Maybe you should lock the door," said Delia. "What's going on, doll?"

"The ninth hair. It's Nick's," she blurted out, struggling to hold back her tears. "They just arrested him."

"Oh, God. I can't believe this." Delia held Emily for a moment and then gently led her to the kitchen table.

"I'm making you some tea. Sit there and tell me everything." A little mom treatment was exactly what Emily needed.

Emily handed her the lab report she had meant to give Nick. After a moment, Delia looked up at Emily with a slight terror in her eyes that Emily had never seen before.

"I can't believe . . . are you sure?"

She nodded. "But the worst part is, Nick didn't know his sample had been submitted. I did it."

Delia left a long pause between them, filled by the sound of the gas flame hissing under the kettle on the stove. She stood motionless by the kitchen sink, staring into it with a disbelieving gaze.

"With that and the jacket . . . I'm just afraid . . ." Emily didn't know where to go next. "What am I going to do?"

"Do you honestly think Nick is guilty?" Delia asked her, straight faced.

Emily was quiet for a moment before saying, "I want to believe him. I know his character. He's not like that. But Jo didn't think Paul was like that either. So, yeah, I don't like it, but I do have some doubts. Sins of omission are still sins."

"And now it's coming back to bite him." Delia leaned against the kitchen counter with her mug warming her palms. She looked at Emily with resolve in her brow.

"With a little push."

"Are we not all capable of evil?" said Delia, who had seen her fair share.

Emily had learned this, too, in her cases with dad. Even the best of people could be tempted into dirty deeds if the right circumstances presented themselves. Silence passed between them.

"I'm testing you, doll. Doubt is an essential duty to this job. You're right to have it."

"It feels awful."

"Of course it does. Especially given this situation. You care very deeply about Nick. Maybe you even love him. I know you thought you were trying to help."

Emily glanced away. She could hear her mother in Delia's words. But she hadn't been able to give her and Nick's relationship a fair shot—in high school or now. The timing had just always been off between the two of them. What if he was convicted for Sandi's murder?

"I did it because I wanted to find out the truth," said Emily.

"And now you don't like the results." Delia snapped Emily from her emotional introspection. Her eyes flitted back to Delia's determined gaze. "But you are likely the only person who can help him right now."

It was bitter medicine to swallow. She would do everything she could to free him. He would do the same for her. He'd saved her life. Now, she had to save his.

Delia took a sip and joined Emily at the table. "I heard about your escapade at the Silver Slipper," she said with a soft smile.

Emily let out a little chortle. "Not my brightest moment."

"But a fearless one. That's heroine material."

The anxiety began to trickle from Emily. "Where do I start?" She drew in a deep breath.

"We're going to put this together logically." Emily felt a wave of relief as Delia clicked into her investigative mode. "Let's talk this through. What do you have so far? What do you know?"

As Delia served more tea, Emily explained where she was so far with the case, how unhelpful and odd and disconnected Mrs. Parkman had been. Paul and the pack and their dirty deeds. Her lack of conversation with Mina. The DNA evidence. How Tiffani had almost run her off the road.

"Tiffani definitely knows something," said Emily. "But besides the fact that she's acting all weird, the only real evidence I have is these rings."

"You think they're somehow connected?"

"I know it seems like a stretch, but what do you think?"

"Why would she be protecting the man who killed her sister?" asked Delia.

"Exactly. I can't wrap my head around that one,"

"Well, let's take a look." Delia enlarged the images of the two rings on Emily's phone screen to get a closer comparison. Delia's lifetime of experience in the FBI with investigation and tool identification gave her a distinctive edge in seeing the finer details that clinched a theory and corroborated evidence. She spent the next few minutes taking measurements and jotting down a set of computations on scratch paper.

"Your instincts are impeccable, my dear. Unbelievable. You see here—they are the same stone. Right down to the defects. See that vertical scratch on the left side, about half a millimeter in length? It's the same one in this photo."

Emily was elated and in awe of Delia's skills.

"My guess is that James or Tiffani had the stone remounted in a new band," said Delia. "Now you need to find out why Tiffani and James were together. And if she knows where he is."

"How? I've totally blown my cover with her," said Emily. "She doesn't trust me or want to see me."

"We'll just have to approach this differently," said Delia.

"How?"

"Melany."

Emily gave her a quizzical look. *Who?*

"My friend. The contractor's wife. Her husband owns Pepper Cave Construction. Remember?"

Emily nodded, but she wasn't seeing the trees for the forest here.

"Don't you think it was odd that of all the plots on Pinetree Slopes, the first one to be excavated was the one where Sandi's body was found?"

Of course. It was so obvious when Delia said it!

"Can you get Melany to tell you who has the deed on the land and who's building there?"

"Now you see it, doll," Delia nodded. "I think this may yield some interesting results. In the meantime, you keep working on Mina and pay Nick a visit in jail. Bring him an extra sweater and a blanket. The mayor doesn't like to waste money on heating the city cell."

"Thank you, Delia."

Delia rose from the kitchen table and set her mug in the kitchen sink. "I'm going to head out. You okay?"

"Yes. Much better." Emily felt hope rising in her chest. "I'll just clean up a bit here, grab a few of Nick's things, and close the house."

"Good girl." Delia gave her a hug. "It's going to be fine. And someday you and Nick will tell this tale around the campfire to your grandchildren."

"Don't get ahead of your skis, Ms. Andrews," Emily cautioned. She knew Delia was just trying to lighten the mood, but there were still so many hurdles to jump. If Nick was proven innocent and released, would he forgive her?

Delia left, and Emily collected herself as she bustled about the house, gathering the items she needed for Nick. She ran upstairs to Nick's closet and grabbed a sweater, socks, and fresh pair of jeans. She was about to switch off the closet light when a glint caught her eye. A small plastic picture frame. She recognized it because she'd had the same one once. Her own fifteen-year-old face smiled back at her. Nick had his arm around her, and they were standing in her front yard under a red-leafed maple. Her mother had taken the photo just a few weeks before her crash. It was September nineteenth, Emily's birthday. The four of them— her, Nick, Mom, and Dad—were on their way to dinner to celebrate. Nick's freshly shaven face still glowed with a summer tan. None of them looked as if they had a care in the world. All so blissfully unaware how much life was about to change. She loved that Nick still had this picture. Still holding on to hope. Something she had given up long ago.

Emily trudged downstairs in a daze. She shut off all but one living room light and turned down the heat. Tomorrow she and Delia would collect their new pieces, and soon the entire puzzle would be complete. She had to have faith in that. Not just for her own sake, but for Nick's.

47

Later that evening, Emily slid a blanket, sweater, and several bottles of water through the cell bars to Nick. He nodded his thanks, but didn't say much more for a few minutes as he slipped the sweater over his head and chugged down a bottle of water. The officer on duty was a good friend of Nick's from the department and had let Emily bring everything in without batting an eye. Emily had gotten the feeling that the officer felt worse than Nick did about the arrest.

"I'm sorry, Nick. I really am." She gripped the cell bars with both hands and drew herself closer. "Talk to me, please."

"You were always headstrong. Even in high school. But the stakes weren't as high back then."

"You seemed so dead set on not providing a sample. And anyhow, I didn't think there'd be a match. So it would all go under the radar—"

"And you would have your peace of mind," said Nick, wagging his head.

Her voice went to barely a whisper. "Nick. The hair. The jacket. What's going on?"

"I've been running everything through in my head." Nick matched her volume so the guard wouldn't hear. "The day Sandi disappeared was one of those days in early spring that changes its mind. You know? It starts out warm but then drops ten or fifteen degrees as a front comes in."

Emily nodded. She had often been caught in the city in late April or early May underdressed in sandals and a lightweight blouse as a quick-forming storm sprung from Lake Michigan and whipped frigid wind through her bones.

"Sandi had worn a short-sleeved shirt to school that morning, but by afternoon when I brought her home, she was shivering."

"You lent her your letterman jacket."

Nick nodded. "It was in my back seat. She put it on, and when she went to get out of the car, she started to take it off. I told her just to keep it. I'd get it back later. The last time I saw her, she was wearing the jacket."

"And you never said anything? To anyone? You never asked for it back?"

"Worrying about my dumb letterman jacket was the last thing on my mind after she went missing. Tiffani told police that the last time she saw Sandi, she remembered she was wearing a short-sleeved shirt, so I figured . . . I don't know . . . I guess I figured she had left it at home. And I certainly wasn't going to ask the Parkman family if they could look around for my jacket and return it to me. It just didn't seem . . . appropriate. By that time, I was graduated and I didn't care about a stupid high school jacket I would never wear again."

"And the hair?"

"Locard exchange principle." Nick was resigned. "I'm sure that there were hairs of mine stuck to the collar of my letterman jacket. If she grabbed it by the collar, then my hair was transferred under her fingernail."

It made perfect sense. Transference of matter, particles, material, fibers, hair. It happened all the time without anyone noticing or knowing.

"But it doesn't mean you had anything to do with Sandi's death. Or were even with her when she was killed," insisted Emily.

"I know that. You know that. But how is this gonna look to a judge and jury?"

She looked him in the eyes, still gripping the bars with both hands. "Nick. Don't get mad when I ask you this, okay? You are innocent, aren't you?"

Nick's eye never flickered or flitted from hers. "Emily, I did not kill Sandi Parkman."

"Thank you." Her gaze bounced to the wall and then the floor. "I hate that I have to ask that."

"I know. I hate that you did." His eyes bounced back to her and held. "But I would have too."

"Nature of our work, I guess," she said softly and without judgment. "Will you forgive me for . . . everything?"

He nodded and lifted his hands to wrap them around hers, and they gripped the cell bars together. After years of being apart, here they were, face to face. Hand to hand. But it still felt so far.

Nick's hands warmed hers. She could feel his pulse through his fingertips. It was elevated. He was anxious. She started to count the beats and time his heart rate. A hundred and thirty. She looked at his pursed lips, his tight throat, and the slight crinkling in his brow. His eyes didn't leave hers. They were wide and round like the ones in the closet picture, but lacked brightness. They were dulled with exhaustion and worry.

In this moment, Emily knew she could trust Nick completely. Any doubts that had surfaced in the past couple of weeks and hours were only emotions or imagination on overdrive. All the mistrust, secrets, and disappointments that had lingered between them since they were sixteen melted away as their hands clutched each other around the cell bars. No letting go this time.

She had to get him out of there. At any cost.

"How much is bail? I have a little money set aside."

Nick shook his head. "Judge set bail at half a million."

"What?" Emily shrieked, causing the officer on duty to glance up from his phone and look over. "That's a ludicrous amount!"

"I think he's just trying to make a point. No favoritism. Or some such political move like that." He sounded frustrated. "He's up for reelection next year."

"That's not fair."

"Fairness has nothing to do with it. Welcome to county politics." She groaned, and he snugged his sweaty grip around her hands. "What's the next step for you?"

"I get an attorney. Like I should have done from the start."

She leaned into the bars with a whisper. "Don't worry. I have a plan too."

"Please don't do anything stupid." A worried look wrinkled the corners of his eyes. He was thinking about her near-death experience with the Dobson case.

"Delia's helping me. Certain things have come to light, and we're getting close to breaking something big."

"Care to fill me in?" Nick whispered, and rested his face on the bars. She leaned hers in close enough that she could feel warmth from his face radiating onto hers.

"I can't right now. For your own protection." She gave him a small, reassuring smile.

"You sound like a spy. I like it." He raised an eyebrow. "It's sexy."

She let out a little laugh. If he could flirt with her at a time like this, there was still hope.

"Nick Larson. We're getting you out of here, and we're going to find Sandi's real killer and prove that you had nothing to do with her murder. And when that's over . . ." Her voice cracked and a lump swelled in her throat. She willed herself to stop getting choked up. But the lump only grew bigger, and she couldn't force the words out.

"It's okay, Em. You don't have to say anything. I get it." He held his grip on her, and she dipped her head toward his. Their foreheads touched between the bars. For a long moment, Emily and Nick stood there, eyes closed, transferring unspoken hope between them.

A thought appeared to Emily with the same clarity as the one she'd had at Nick's house overlooking the lake. There was no other place she'd rather be than with Nick. She didn't need to travel down any more roads with any more guys. When this mess was all over, she was ready to take him up on his offer to start over.

48

Early the next morning, before Emily's alarm went off, her phone rang. Emily, who had only been half sleeping anyhow, rolled over instantly and reached for it. She recognized the number immediately.

Skinny Minnie Mina.

She tapped accept. "Hello? Mina?"

"Is it true?" squawked Mina's voice. "Has Nick been arrested for Sandi's murder?"

It was the first time Emily had heard anyone say those words out loud, and it gut-punched her.

"Yes." Emily's throat and eyes felt dry as she sat up in bed and tried to be fully present.

"I can't believe it. I can't believe! It's not true! It can't be him! It's not Nick."

Emily waited for her to continue. She found it best to let the hysterical talk themselves down.

"It's ridiculous! Someone's got this really backwards! What's the evidence? Why do they think he did it?" Mina took a breath and finally paused.

"I'm not really at liberty to divulge that. I can understand why you're upset."

"Yes. I knew Nick in high school. He wouldn't do this."

Emily liked the resolve in her voice. Mina would make an excellent character witness. She goaded Mina to see where she would lead. "Sometimes we think people are one way in public, but we really don't know how they act when no one's looking."

"I understand that. But not Nick. You should know that. You dated him. He stood up for people who were being teased. Like me and the Parkman girls."

Nick the Prick. Emily finally understood his nickname. Not everyone saw Nick as the outgoing, easygoing, cool kid. The jocks. The pack. They hated a guy who stood up for the underdog. Jerks.

"Niceness isn't a character trait that excludes people from becoming murderers," said Emily, hoping to incite more information from Mina.

"I know . . . but he wasn't . . . Tiffani was with me the day Sandi went missing."

Emily's spine tingled. She grabbed a pen and paper from her nightstand.

"She was?" Emily prompted.

"Yeah. She showed up to my house a little bit before dinner. She was a mess."

"A mess how?"

"Shaking. Crying. Or I mean, she had been crying. Her eyes were all red and she didn't want my mom to see her. I told her to go wait in my room until dinner was over. I asked if she wanted to eat with us, but she wasn't hungry."

"Okay. And how long did she stay in your room?" Emily was scribbling it all down.

"All through dinner. I went to my room after and she was laying in my bed all curled up with my stuffed animals. I knew something bad had happened. I thought maybe her stepdad had come back to the house. He was out of prison, you know."

"Did she say what was wrong?"

"Am I gonna get in trouble for not reporting this sooner?" asked Mina.

"What do you mean?"

"I mean . . . like arrested?"

"Why would you think you might get arrested?"

"Because . . . I'm about to tell you that . . . look, she didn't want anyone to know . . . but now that Nick's being accused of something I *know* he's not capable of . . . what I mean is that Tiffani Parkman is the victim of a rape."

Emily did her best to hold in her surprise and keep a calm demeanor.

"I see. What do you know about this incident?"

"James VanDerMuellen raped her." Mina's voice held conviction on the matter.

What? Emily's pen punched through the paper.

"What did Tiffani tell you?" Emily kept a calm tone as she dislodged her pen.

"James had come to her house after school before anyone else was home. He basically seduced her. She didn't want to, but he'd said Sandi was okay with it. He filmed them and told her not to tell anyone."

Emily gulped down the horrible news. Thank God Mina couldn't see the look of disgust on her face right now.

"Did she tell anyone besides you?"

"Not that I know of."

"And what about Sandi? Did she know?"

"Tiffani said that Sandi had come home right after it happened and went ballistic. She and James got into a huge fight. Screaming. Yelling. Then they sort of made up. James apologized and they took off for a drive."

A drive to her death. This was getting so, so ugly.

"And that's when Tiffani came to your house?"

"Yeah. She rode her bike over." Mina drew in another deep inhale and then exhaled. "I never told anyone because I'd promised Tiffani I wouldn't. She had been through so much with her stepdad, and then James, and then Sandi disappearing. I just didn't want to make things worse for her," Mina broke down in a sob.

Emily gave her a moment until she heard Mina blowing her nose. "Mina, are you okay?"

"Am I in big, big trouble?" she sniffled.

"Not at all. You did the right thing." Emily assured her she would be safe and asked if she would go in to the police station to give her statement.

"I have to think about it. I'm afraid to go alone," said Mina. Emily agreed to set up a Skype call later that afternoon with the two of them and the Freeport police. She would walk her through every step of the process.

As soon as she got off the phone, Emily saw that Delia had texted her two hours earlier at four AM.

Stop by Brown's. Surprise info.

Emily swung herself out of bed and leapt into her clothes. *Hang on, Nick! We may be finally getting somewhere.*

49

Emily knocked on the alley door of Brown's Bakery. Delia opened it, greeting Emily with a plate of freshly baked cinnamon rolls. Emily's stomach growled at the sight of them.

"Good morning," said Delia with a freshly lipsticked smile. Emily might be this chipper too at six thirty in the morning if she were surrounded by baked goodness.

Emily took a roll off the plate and stepped inside. "You know you're never going to get to truly retire if you keep making these so insanely delicious." She sank her teeth into the cinnamon-y soft bread and icing.

"I've already had several offers to franchise," Delia told her as she marched them through the kitchen.

"Tempted?"

"If they can duplicate the local friendliness of Freeport, then we have a deal. But so far, I haven't seen it. Latte?"

"Absolutely." She licked the sticky from her fingers.

"How's Nick?"

"Unflappable on the outside. But last night his heart rate was elevated . . . and the look in his eyes. Stone-cold worry."

"There's a box of rolls ready for you to take to him this morning—and the rest of the guys over at the station." Delia pointed to a delivery counter. Emily nodded. Delia was a softie.

They entered the front café, and Delia went to the barista station behind the counter. She grabbed two mugs and flipped on the authentic commercial-grade espresso maker she had imported from Italy.

"I have some rather disturbing but case-breaking news," Emily began.

"As do I, doll. You go first," said Delia.

Emily quickly explained to Delia how Tiffani had run to Mina's after James sexually assaulted her and then blackmailed her with the video.

"This case gets worse by the minute." Delia steamed the milk and poured it atop two shots of espresso. She handed it to Emily and leaned against the counter with her mug.

"There's no doubt in my mind James killed her," said Emily, finishing off the last bite of her roll. "We have to get Tiffani to tell us the truth about that afternoon and why she was with James six months ago."

Delia nodded as a timer buzzed from the kitchen, and she heeded its call. Emily followed her to the commercial ovens that lined one of the walls. "What's your news?"

"That the plot of land in Pinetree Slopes was purchased about six months ago by Hendrick VanDerMuellen."

Emily, who was taking a sip of her latte, almost sprayed it all over Delia.

"James' dad? Wow!"

Delia slid out a rack of bread, took one cursory glance, and slid the loaves back in, setting the timer for another five minutes.

"You don't think they were planning to move back to Freeport?" Emily asked.

"Not at all. Hendrick invested money with the land developer. Well, his company did. They own Lexington Investments, and his company made the purchase. So no actual human names are on the deed."

"Lexington was building the house on that parcel where we found Sandi's remains . . . but who was going to live in it?"

"Melany didn't know." Delia pulled a lever on a large mixer, and the giant paddle slowed to a stop. She pulled a batch of stringy dough onto the ceramic counter and began to roll it into one long log. "Melany says her husband never came into contact with any representative from Lexington. It was a corporation-driven transaction."

Why was it that no one, including she and Nick, had put this together until now? Emily watched as Delia cut the long dough roll into twelve pieces.

"Can I give you a hand?"

"That'd be great, doll. Just shape these into round loaves."

"I bet Hendrick knew about his son's dirty deeds," said Emily.

"Very likely," Delia entertained. "As I recall, the VanDerMuellen family moved south the fall after James graduated. I think after Sandi's death and the investigation, they wanted to close the door on this chapter of their life and hope their past never came back to haunt them."

"I just don't think it's a coincidence that the family corporation purchased the plot of land where James buried his murder victim," Emily mused.

"Nor do I," said Delia. "But be careful about making assumptions. There's always more than meets the eye."

Good point. As Emily formed her dough pieces into symmetrical round balls just like Delia's, she thought back to the Facebook picture with the black onyx stone. In light of what James had done to Tiffani, why on earth was she in a recent photograph with him? How had he made it back into her life? Why had she allowed him? Maybe he was blackmailing her again. Perhaps Tiffani was in more danger than she was letting on.

Stranger still, Lexington had bought a plot of land in Pinetree Slopes around this same time. Did Tiffani know her sister was buried there? There was no way James was planning to return to Freeport and live on that parcel. But he was going to let some other unknowing family live in a house with a dead girl buried underneath.

Emily handed Delia her loaves, and she placed them evenly onto a large tray. She slit a crisscross on each of the tops and then lay the tray in the oven, setting the timer for twenty minutes. Brown's would be open before it went off, and Delia would soon be hosting a stream of regulars.

Emily's mind kept reeling with insights and impossibilities.

It all boiled down to Tiffani.

She had to find a way to pry Tiffani's life open and get to James.

"I know your train of thought right now. Do what you need to do, but be careful." Delia nudged her and handed her Nick's box of cinnamon rolls.

"What do you mean?" Emily tried to layer her voice with innocence. But there was no fooling a former FBI agent.

"Sometimes the best disguise is no disguise at all."

50

Emily delivered the cinnamon rolls to Nick and reassured him that there were new developments in the investigation, but she didn't want to divulge them. Nick revealed that another detective was going to be assigned to the case within the week. Someone from the state police post. Both he and Emily knew what this meant. It would be a slow-moving machine to get the new person up to speed. And it wouldn't be the only investigation this person would be working. Sandi's case would lie dormant, and could become stagnant if there were no new leads. All the more reason for Emily to put her plan into action.

Nick's case was being assigned to the county defense attorney, who he believed would do a competent job. Emily could tell that Nick's nerves were shot, and his bloodshot eyes were a dead giveaway that he hadn't slept a wink. He asked her to bring him a few more things from home. A toothbrush, deodorant, and more socks. Looking into his pained eyes made her gut twist. The only thing she could do for him was to keep her spirits light and get Tiffani to crack.

"Please be careful. I'm not out there to save you from the crazies," said Nick.

Emily grinned and took his hand. "I'm ready this time. And no one is going to out-crazy me."

* * *

For the next few days and nights, Emily camped out in a hidden spot near Tiffani's apartment and watched her coming and going. There was nothing unusual about her activities. She got home late, slept in late, and then usually rolled out of the house midafternoon to run a few errands in Freeport. Emily trailed her every time. Tiffani returned home and then headed off to work around seven or eight. Emily would follow her to work, too. While she waited, she reviewed her father's medical examiner case files to see what she had missed in twelve years. It was a good use of time and kept her from nodding off.

One file in particular caught her attention. She hadn't found it with the others. Her father had placed it in the top drawer of his desk for easy and frequent access, Emily surmised. She read the details of the autopsy with shock. It was dated June the summer after she left for Chicago. A family of four—mom, dad, and two twins—had been shot to death in their lake home on a summer weekday afternoon. No weapons, bullet casings, or suspects had ever been found. The autopsy report was rote and clinical, but it was her father's hand-written notes, scribbled on several sticky sheets tacked to the inside of the manila file folder, that gave her pause.

McClelland estate. Detroit. 2 guns used. Revolver. Glock. Oldest child missing. Possible witness. Kidnapped?

She closed the file and sat with her troubled thoughts. It was the third night of her watch, and lack of sleep was catching up to her. She felt her head bob back on the seat rest as sweet sleep overtook her. But not for long.

The grumble of a diesel truck awakened her as it pulled into the strip club complex. She checked the clock. Two AM. Inside the club, patrons had already been hours deep into the entertainment, as the club was closing soon. The truck parked next to Tiffani's Lexus at the end of the lot. An odd spot, when so many vacant ones were closer to the door. Emily could make out the form of a man in the driver's seat, but given the way he had parked in the shadows, she was unable to collect any identifiable detail about him.

Emily trained her binoculars on his rear bumper and jotted down the numbers on his Florida plates. *Florida. Miami. James. Is James in the truck?* She was dying to leap out and run over there. But she kept still.

He didn't get out. He didn't move at all, just stared straight ahead.

She watched. And watched. Over the next hour, Emily witnessed several of the girls trickle out as their shifts ended. A few patrons also left. By three AM, only a handful of cars remained in the lot. Emily always made a point of parking down the street so she wouldn't stand out when the crowd thinned.

A few more vehicles exited, leaving only three in the lot. The Florida truck. Tiffani's Lexus. And an SUV.

A half hour later, Tiffani emerged with Watch Your Ass Wanda. They chatted for a few minutes, and then Wanda took off for her SUV. Tiffani walked toward her Lexus, a duffle bag slung over her shoulder and a tiredness in her step. Her head hung, eyes to the ground. She seemed unaware of the truck and driver.

Emily's heart raced for Tiffani, but she continued to watch. When Tiffani was about fifteen feet from her car, a man opened his truck door and got out.

Tiffani's head jerked up, startled, and she stopped in her tracks, clutching her bag. From Emily's view, she could see Tiffani's face light up with shock.

The gentleman's appearance bespoke wealth. His thick, well-styled, silver hair, tailored shirt, and fitted jeans showed he paid attention to his looks.

The man, probably in his early sixties, came a few steps toward her. Tiffani backed up. It wasn't a friendly conversation. Emily pulled up the keypad on her phone. Her finger hovered over the nine. She had a feeling this could get ugly fast.

As if on cue, the man started gesticulating and had his hands in Tiffani's face. Tiffani backed up again, her bag dropping to the ice-packed parking lot. She shouted something at him, and he grabbed her by the arm. She wiggled to get free. He grabbed her other arm. Tiffani tried to knee him in the groin.

The man removed his grip for a second, and Tiffani rushed for her car. He lunged after her, taking her down by her coat hood and throwing her to the ground. His hands clenched around Tiffani's neck as he lorded himself over her. Tiffani kicked and punched, but she was losing to a greater strength.

Emily slammed her accelerator to the floor and peeled into the parking lot with three quick, successive horn honks.

"Hey. Hey!" Emily called out from her driver's side window.

The man's head jerked up, and he released his grip. He lumbered to his feet.

Emily sailed up alongside Tiffani as she scrambled to her feet with a look of sheer terror.

Emily's face was flint as she turned to the man. "Who are you?"

The man turned and scampered back into his truck. He didn't bother to back the truck up. His tires spun out on the slippery parking lot as he barreled forward out across a snowy patch of lawn and over the sidewalk. His truck bounced down off the curb onto the street as he laid a patch of rubber.

Emily caught her breath, then turned her gaze to Tiffani, who, shaking and flustered, was darting toward her Lexus.

"You okay?"

Tiffani didn't respond at first.

"Tiff? You okay? Talk to me." Emily paced toward her.

Tiffani nodded without looking back. She pulled her keys from her coat pocket. Emily jumped to her side. She wasn't letting her off the hook.

"Tiffani. Who was that?" Emily demanded.

"No one."

"He nearly killed you."

"He wasn't going to kill me," she said in an unconvincing whisper.

"So his hands clutched around your neck were just a friendly, little hug?" Emily was furious. "Who is that guy?"

"Leave me alone." Tiffani's keys slipped from her hand, and she dove to retrieve them.

"Don't be a jerk about this. I just saved your life."

The force of Emily's words had no effect on Tiffani, who plowed past her to get to her car. Emily saw that she was lost in shock, and she calmed her tone. "Why was he trying to hurt you?"

Emily trailed Tiffani to her driver's door, blocking her from getting in. Finally, Tiffani lifted her gaze to Emily.

"He thinks I know where his son is."

"That was Hendrick VanDerMuellen?"

Tiffani nodded.

"And do you know where James is?"

Tiffani didn't answer. She tried to wedge Emily from the driver's door, but Emily planted herself.

"What the— Get away from my car!"

"This won't be the last time he'll come after you."

Tiffani lunged at Emily, but she braced herself and pushed back. Tiffani was not going to win this one!

"I know what James did to you that day," Emily blurted. "And I know he killed your sister." She searched Tiffani's calcified expression. "I wanna see James rot in hell just as much as you do. And I can help. But I need your story."

Tiffani wouldn't lift her eyes to meet Emily's, but Emily could see she had shattered something inside Tiffani. She had done it. She had wedged her way in.

"Move," said Tiffani, pressing the fob to unlock her Lexus. "And get in."

51

"He came into the club early last March. I was totally shocked," said Tiffani, sitting at the wheel of her parked Lexus as the heater warmed the interior. "He said he had lost his job in New York and was visiting some buddies up here."

Tiffani took a couple of long swigs from her flask and passed it to Emily. Emily politely declined.

"When was the last time you saw him?"

"Right before he left for college."

Emily nodded. "How did you feel when he showed up now?"

"Furious. He acted like nothing happened. Like I should be happy to see him after ten years." Tiffani went quiet for a moment. "I knew this was my chance to do something."

"Do something?"

"He was drunk, and I got him to buy a private lap dance. And I danced for him. He liked it. He kept coming back for more. I saw my way in."

"How could you stand to do that with someone who had . . ." Emily couldn't bring herself to say the words.

"Raped me? Used my sister as a sex slave? Then threatened to kill me every day until he left Freeport?" Tiffani's face was hard.

She explained to Emily how she'd turned the tables on him. She'd lured him in like she did all her top clients. But with James, she took it further. Made it personal. Special. He was the only one who got to have her. Really have her. But it came at a price. She charged. And he paid. Whatever she asked. She got him to buy her new clothes. And jewelry. And the Lexus they were sitting in. She used their pillow talk to get him to confess that he had killed her sister. Every gory detail.

Emily sat riveted to Tiffani's story. "He just confessed? Like that?" she said.

"He was really high. I don't even think he remembers all the things he told me. I recorded everything," Tiffani added.

"It must have been so hard to hear all that."

"It was all I could do not to vomit or shoot him in the face."

"What happened? Why'd he do it? Why'd he go so far as to kill Sandi?"

"Sandi had found out about the sex video. I heard them fighting when she got home from school. She was screaming at him. She said she was going to go to the school. His coach. The police."

Nick. He had told Sandi about the tapes just moments before and triggered the whole explosion that day. If James hadn't been at home with Tiffani, would things have turned out differently? Would Sandi still be alive?

"They were in the living room. I was in my bedroom. Cowering. Hoping they would forget I was there. But after a while, things quieted down and I heard a knock on my door. She came in, took one look at me, and knew James had gotten to me. She went ballistic. I had never seen her so . . . possessed. She ran for the phone to call the cops, but he dragged her across the living room and hit her. And that's when I ran from the house into the garage and got on my bike. But then . . . I was just paralyzed. I sat there on my bike, staring out at the driveway. At his car. I wanted to do something. But what? Pop a tire? No, then he'd be stuck there. Drain the gas tank so he would get stranded? No, what if Sandi got in the car and then ended up out in in the middle of nowhere with him? I don't know how long I'd been out there when they came out of the house. Sandi was calmer and James was being really nice to her. He even opened the door for her. And then they drove away. And I just kept staring. They never saw me. And then I got on my bike and—"

"Went to Mina's."

Tiffani twisted to look at her. "How did you know?"

"Your mom said you went to a friend's," said Emily.

She was astounded by Tiffani's account, and yet she knew she had to stay quiet, hoping more secrets would spill out.

After a moment, they did.

"I left her. I abandoned my sister," Tiffani said with a lower lip quivering.

"You were scared."

"But I never called for help. I never even told my mom."

"He threatened to kill you," Emily reminded her.

"I should have gone to the police right away."

"You can say that now, but things look differently when you're thirteen and an older guy is threatening your life."

"I was never strong like Sandi. I was the bookish one. You know? The shy one. She always stood up for me. She never let my stepdad . . . get to me. You know?"

Emily gave a single nod. The gravity of it all was almost more than she could take, but she had to remain still.

"The next day, James came to the junior high. He was so angry."

"Did he hurt you?"

"He got one hit in. He threatened me every single day, until one day . . . he was just gone." Tiffani drank from her flask again.

Goose bumps ran up Emily's arm. "I'm sorry. I'm so sorry this all happened to you," said Emily. How different might Tiffani's life have been if James hadn't shattered it into so many pieces? It had broken her. She was sick. She needed help.

"Here's the thing. I let it happen. I let him treat me that way. I actually played along. Afterwards, when he'd calmed down, I showed him I was on his side. And, ten years later, it was all worth it." A smile of secret revenge spread across Tiffani's lips.

Emily felt a shudder of terror. Tiffani had been plotting this since junior high. Revenge had seeded itself and grown deep roots. She needed to get out of there. Now.

Tiffani shook her head and reached for Emily's arm. "Have a drink, Doctor Dazzle." She shoved the flask at Emily's face and held it there.

"I should get going." Emily put her hand up.

Tiffani wagged the flask at Emily, and whiskey splashed onto her face and into her eyes. She squinted and blinked. Tiffani laughed. She pressed the flask to Emily's lips, and Emily wriggled away.

Tiffani laughed.

"Your secret's safe with me," said Emily, desperately wanting to escape. She glanced at the sunken locks. She was trapped.

"Pinetree Slopes. I knew the land was going to turn into a housing development because one of my clients was a contractor who had just been hired by the developer over there."

Was that Melany's husband? Was he having an affair with Tiffani?

She turned to Tiffani with a stoic expression as she put the last puzzle piece into place. "You got James to tell you where Sandi was buried. And you persuaded James' family's company to invest in Pinetree Slopes so James could buy select plots of land. One of those being where Sandi was."

Tiffani rocked her head back and forth. The alcohol was taking effect. "James said he would dig up Sandi's remains before excavation."

James *had* been the person with Tiffani that night at the parcel. Emily had to admit she had never seen such expert skills of persuasion.

"After he got his father to invest, I could tell he was pulling away. He stopped coming to the club. He was getting bored. Maybe with me. Maybe with Freeport. He was getting job offers. LA. Tokyo. He has wanderlust." Tiffani turned her head toward the window. "But I didn't want him wandering away. I convinced the contractor to start excavation sooner than planned."

"And the skeletons came out of the closet, so to speak," said Emily, sweat running down her spine. "You must have known he'd run. Have you tried to reach him?"

Tiffani shrugged, "Who cares? I'm taken care of. House. Car."

Tiffani's cavalier attitude didn't make sense. Why would Tiffani have done something to make James run? And why wouldn't she want him to pay for the injustices he had caused?

"Where is he? If you know, we can have him arrested."

"Let Nick find him. Or whoever else is in charge now."

"Nick shouldn't be in jail over this."

"He damn well should be. And the rest of the pack. They could have stopped this long before Sandi ended up dead!"

Emily felt herself go red hot. Tiffani wasn't wrong. "Mina made a statement."

Tiffani's jaw clenched, and she gripped the steering wheel with both hands. "She shouldn't have done that."

"You're clearly in over your head," Emily said.

Tiffani started the engine. Emily reached to unlock the automatic doors. Tiffani countered and the locks clicked down.

"Let me out, Tiffani."

"You don't really want to help me. You want to help Nick."

Tiffani grabbed the gearshift, and Emily saw a glint of gold metal. The platinum ring with the black onyx stone was rubberbanded around the shifter stick. Emily quickly diverted her gaze, hoping Tiffani didn't notice, and tried the locks again. Tiffani was quick.

"Let me go!"

Tiffani didn't budge. With her hand prepped to unlatch the door handle, Emily hit the unlock button again, and before Tiffani could relock it, she released the handle and sprang from the car. No sooner had Emily shut the door than Tiffani threw the car in reverse and floored the gas pedal. Emily jumped back just as the side mirror nearly smashed into her.

Emily sprinted to her car before Tiffani could come back to run her over. She jumped in and started the engine. The wheels spun on the ice as she saw Tiffani's taillights disappear down the street. Emily made her way carefully out of the parking lot. As she drove, she replayed Tiffani's conversation in her head.

Tiffani knew where James was. Otherwise Hendrick would not be tracking her down and trying to kill her.

And then it hit her.

Tiffani's ten-year plan was about to reach resolution.

52

"I know this is going to sound crazy. But you have to trust me," said Emily to Jo and Paul at their dining room table the next morning after breakfast. It was after eight and the three Blakely kids had gone off to school.

"You want me to send my husband to the Silver Slipper? In broad daylight?" Jo shook her head. "You've lost your mind, Emily Hartford."

"I know it doesn't make sense, especially after what you two just went through, but please. It's really important to the case. And getting Nick out of jail."

"You have to give us more to go on, Emily," said Paul, taking his wife's hand in his. Emily was glad to see this loving gesture. She wanted nothing more than for her friends' marriage to recover and thrive. And she felt awful about what she was asking.

"I can't divulge every detail. Just yet. I just need you to keep Tiffani Parkman engaged while I check on something."

"Just how *engaged*?" demanded Jo, eyes piercing Emily.

"Hang out at the club and keep an eye on her. You don't have to talk to her or anything—I mean, unless she looks like she's leaving. Make sure she doesn't leave the club before I text you the all clear."

"This is really weird," said Paul, discouragement in his brow.

"Are you putting yourself in danger again?" Jo was adamant.

"No, of course not." Emily's voice lilted, and she knew Jo could hear right through the lie.

"I know you, Em," Jo said. "And I don't like this."

"Why don't you go to the police?" asked Paul.

"It's complicated." Emily wrung her hands over her full mug of coffee. She had been so nervous, she hadn't taken a single sip, and now it had cooled to undrinkable.

"You don't trust the new detective, do you?" said Paul.

"I'm at a delicate stage, and I don't want any screw-ups."

"We're not doing it," said Jo firmly, "unless you tell us what's going on."

"I will go to the police. I'm planning to. Of course." Emily hesitated. "But I need to be sure about something first. I'm just corroborating evidence."

"You being so cryptic is not helping convince us," said Paul.

Emily searched her brain for some better way to convey things. "If I tell you this, you have to keep it to yourselves. At least for now."

"We're not gonna blab, Em. We want Nick out of jail as much as you do. You need to trust us, too."

Emily looked to Jo. "Remember the black-onyx ring from the yearbook picture? It was James's class ring. Tiffani used the stone and had it set in a new mounting. I saw it on her finger in a Facebook picture and in her car. Delia confirmed it's the same stone."

Jo's eyes went wide.

"Does Tiffani know where James is?" demanded Paul.

"I can't say."

"You'd better say," said Jo.

"I'm not putting either of you into any more jeopardy over this. You have enough to deal with," said Emily.

"Ever since you came back to Freeport, your sleuthing has really stirred things up," said Jo. "I love you, but maybe you should just stick to surgery."

Emily didn't argue. Jo's emotions were warranted.

"Paul, can you go to the club or not?" asked Emily.

Paul looked to Jo, who crossed her arms and turned to Emily with a serious look.

"He can go. This one time." She got up from the table and paced a few steps. "You both owe me big-time."

"I know. And thank you." Emily hoped it came across as sincere and grateful.

* * *

Emily waited incognito at Tiffani's apartment complex the rest of the morning.

Tiffani emerged from her apartment at eleven thirty, and Emily texted Paul.

She's on her way.

Emily pulled out slowly and trailed Tiffani. She soon realized Tiffani wasn't going directly to the Silver Slipper. Emily trailed her at a safe distance through the streets of Freeport and then outside the city limits into the country. It didn't take long before Emily realized that Tiffani was heading to her mother's home. It would be harder for Emily to hide herself in the open landscape of the county. She drew back far enough that she could just see the form of Tiffani's Lexus cresting and dipping over the gentle hills of the road to Mrs. Parkman's.

The Lexus soon approached Mrs. Parkman's driveway and turned in. Emily then passed the driveway and pulled her car over to the shoulder, parking far enough away to be hidden from Tiffani's view by a cluster of trees down the road past the house but still within good view of the Parkman home. She was about to exit her car when she realized she could be stepping into more danger than she was prepared for. Thinking fast, she reached under the passenger seat for her portable toolbox and grabbed the sharpest object she could find—a Phillips screwdriver. She stuffed it into the interior pocket of her winter coat and exited.

Climbing down the gently sloped embankment into the ditch, Emily was able to get even closer by walking the ditch alongside the road back toward the Parkman home. She found a private perch behind some shrubs where she could survey undetected.

She watched Tiffani get out of her car and slip into the side door off the garage.

Why would she not use the front door? Why wouldn't she go right in to see her mother?

Ten minutes passed. Emily imagined Mrs. Parkman on the couch in the living room watching TV. She would never think to glance outside, because the TV would be blaring and she couldn't hear a darn thing.

TV blaring.

Rats in the walls.

Have Tiffani call the exterminator.

There was no exterminator.

There were no rats.

I let him treat me that way. I actually played along.

The scratching she had heard was . . . human.

I showed him I was on his side. And, ten years later, it was all worth it.

A human clawing to get someone's attention. Clawing to get out.

James.

The side door of the garage opened, and Emily felt the air being sucked from her lungs at what she saw. Tiffani shuffled out backward, tugging with all her might on the rope of a red sled as it bumped over the threshold of the doorway and onto the drive. On the sled was a human-shaped object wrapped in a faded blue sheet. Tiffani jerked the sled across the snow-covered driveway toward her car.

Emily glanced toward the picture window. She saw Mrs. Parkman get up and head into the kitchen. She still had no idea what was going on outside her house.

Emily stood motionless in a patch of tall, dead weeds poking through the snow, trying to decide what to do. Go after Tiffani? Call the police? Follow Tiffani? Was there any chance James was still alive under that sheet? Her stomach grew nauseous and twisty.

Tiffani parked the sled by the trunk as she opened it. How on earth was this slender woman going to lift this dead weight of a man? An image flashed into Emily's brain. Tiffani onstage during her pole dance at the strip club. She could lift her entire body parallel to the floor, inching it down to within centimeters of the dance floor in an ever-so-graceful manner, never even breaking a sweat.

Tiffani effortlessly grabbed the bottom half of James's body and lifted, flinging his legs over the lip of the trunk. She didn't waste a second positioning herself under his upper body. With a heave, she shoved the rest of him in. Then she threw the sled on top and slammed the trunk closed. Emily pressed her lips together hard and bit down on her lower lip. She tasted blood as she licked away the pain. She willed her frozen limbs to move.

Emily jammed her hand into her pocket for her cell phone and realized she had left it in the car. *Darn it!*

Emily unfurled her stiff legs from a crouched position. They tingled as the blood flowed back into them, causing her to stumble on her first few steps toward her car.

Tiffani hopped in the driver's side, and a second later the engine fired up. At a glance back through the front picture window of the house, Emily could see Mrs. Parkman waddling back into the living room, holding a soda and a bag of potato chips. She never turned her gaze toward the action happening outside that window.

Incredible. That TV must be so loud!

At the house, Tiffani barreled her Lexus in reverse down the driveway, skidding and slipping left and right on the snow-covered dirt drive that no one had bothered to shovel or have plowed. She swerved out onto the empty country road in the direction of Freeport.

Emily's mind raced. Where would be the most likely place to dump a body between here and Freeport? There was Rock River, which flowed from far north near the upper peninsula through the city of Rock River and eventually into Lake Michigan. Or there was Freeport Lake.

Emily could hear the Lexus's tires skidding on the icy pavement as Tiffani was getting away. Soon her car summited and disappeared over the hill. Emily had scampered the last few steps to her car when she heard a rumble from a truck coming around the curve in the road, facing Emily. She didn't get a good look at the driver, but she was certain from the make and model of the truck that it was Hendrick VanDerMuellen. She ducked into her car as the truck sailed past.

Emily watched in her rearview mirror. The truck slowed as it reached the Parkman house. There was wrath in the way Hendrick cranked his truck and plowed down the drive. He knew his son was being held captive and was about to take punitive action on the unaware, innocent Mrs. Parkman.

She couldn't let that materialize.

53

Emily sprung from the ditch and plowed through the foot-high-snow-covered field toward the Parkman house. It would have taken longer for her to get the car started, turn it around, and drive the slippery road into the Parkmans' slippery driveway than to just hoof it there. Besides, she didn't want to call more attention to herself with a vehicle. As she ran, she managed to dial Paul.

"Where are you?" she huffed, out of breath.

"I'm sitting in the club parking lot. I don't see Tiffani's car."

"There's been a change in plans. I think she has James in her trunk and she's going to dump the body."

"She what? Where?" Paul's panicked voice shot through the receiver.

"Can you get over to Freeport Lake? It's on the way to the club, so I'm just taking a stab in the dark here, but I think that's where she'll go first."

"The lake's frozen over, Em. I heard from a buddy of mine who went ice fishing over there this morning."

"Okay . . . okay . . . then she'll be heading to the river."

"Got it. I'm on my way."

"And call the police! Tell them I need backup at the Parkman place. I've got a fire to put out here."

"Em, no—"

She hung up on him.

It would take the police at minimum ten minutes to arrive. And she wasn't about to let Hendrick get away.

Emily drew in a deep breath for courage and moved toward Hendricks's truck, taking the screwdriver from inside her coat. White-knuckling the handle, she bent down next to the rear passenger tire. With all the force she could muster, Emily thrust the pointed end of the screwdriver deeply into the rubber. It tore a hole through the stiff material, releasing a hiss of air.

After puncturing all four tires, Emily took a stand a safe distance from the garage but close enough so she could see inside through the half-opened door. Hendrick VanDerMuellen was kneeling by a pile of blankets that Emily guessed had been James's makeshift bed.

"You won't find your son here," Emily called into the doorway.

Hendrick spun around to face her.

"His body is on its way to the lake."

"Sonofa—" He methodically walked out of the garage toward her.

Emily took a few steps back, still gripping the screwdriver.

He lunged toward her, but Emily sprung back, maintaining her safe distance.

He lunged again. She dodged him deftly, drawing him out into the open driveway. His ruddy face grew red. She had awakened the beast. A very unfit beast.

"You've known since high school what your son was involved in. Haven't you? You knew he killed Sandi Parkman. You managed to sweep it all under the rug. And you just kept sweeping, all the way to Pinetree Slopes."

The sins of omission stared back at her with steely bloodshot eyes. A guttural growl emerged from the back of his throat. Even though her heart was racing, Emily's courage grew and she didn't back down as he approached.

"Your money and lawyers can't buy you out of this now."

He put one relentless foot in front of another, locking her in his gaze.

Emily raised her screwdriver, aiming it at his head, and took several steps back, drawing him from the garage. This wasn't the first time she'd looked death in the eye and survived. She would not back down. For Sandi. For Nick. Even for Tiffani.

"I will jab this right into your eye if you come any closer," she warned.

But Hendrick proved a coward. As soon as he was just feet from her, he buckled, rushed around her, and sprinted to his truck. Emily spun around, staying in place. Hendrick hopped into his truck and tried to drive off. Emily grinned as he got only a few feet on his squishy, flat tires.

Police sirens peeled in the distance. Emily felt an inner relief as she watched Hendrick try to run across the expansive yard, thickly blanketed in snow.

Hendrick ran and fell. Got up and tried to run again. It was comical.

As the cop car pulled in, Hendrick gripped his hand over his chest and collapsed in the snow.

The officers quickly subdued Hendrick, cuffed him, and pulled him up from the ground. He trudged along with them, slowly but showing no signs of a heart attack. It had all been a ruse.

54

Emily knocked on Mrs. Parkman's front door. An outburst from a laugh track on her TV pumped through the exterior walls. Emily knew she couldn't hear her, so she tried the door handle. It was unlocked. How unsafe and trusting of her. Mrs. Parkman didn't see Emily until she was standing in front of her and nearly jumped at the sight of her.

"Hi, Mrs. Parkman," yelled Emily over a loud commercial for a new pharmaceutical treatment for eczema. "Do you remember me?" She reached for the remote on the coffee table and turned the TV to mute.

"Oh. Oh . . . hello. Miss Emily Hartford? Of course."

Dr. Hartford. But Emily didn't bother to correct her. "I'm sorry to barge in like this. I did knock."

"Did you? I didn't hear it."

Emily sat down next to Mrs. Parkman on the couch. Outside the strobe lights from both cruisers flashed red and blue over the white yard. The woman had not been aware of anything outside.

"How are you doing, dear? I hope you brought me more of that delicious coffee cake."

Emily shook her head. "I just wanted to let you know that I caught those rats. They won't be bothering you anymore."

Mrs. Parkman reached for her glasses on the coffee table. She slid them on and batted her eyes into focus.

"Oh. Well. That's awful kind of you," she said as Emily took her plump, chapped hand. "I'll tell Tiffani to cancel that exterminator."

"That won't be necessary," said Emily.

55

Emily wanted to go straight to the city jail to Nick, but Paul's text changed her course.

Tiffani arrested. James recovered. At hospital.

Emily zipped down the country roads into Freeport, arriving at the hospital morgue first so she could confirm James's body and start the death certificate paperwork. Of course, an autopsy would be mandatory.

But when she got to the morgue, his body wasn't there.

Perhaps his body was still in the emergency room. They probably hadn't transferred it downstairs yet. She took the elevator from the basement level to the first floor and hurried toward the ER. A handful of cops meandered near the entrance, watchful and wary. They stopped her when she tried to enter.

"Excuse me, miss. You're not allowed in there at present," said one with gray sideburns and a paunch.

"I'm Dr. Emily Hartford, Freeport County coroner. I'm here to transfer the body of James VanDerMuellen to the morgue."

"Body?"

"Em! Em!" Jo's voice cut through the crowd, as did her slender figure, now dressed in her scrubs. "He's not dead! Come with me." Jo took Emily by the arm and pulled her into the ER.

"He's not?"

"He's *barely* not dead." Jo pointed to a curtained area, where two cops stood guard outside.

Emily broke from Jo's light grasp and marched over to the curtain.

Jo swept up next to her. "One peek." She turned to the cops. "Officers, this is Dr. Emily Hart—"

"We know who she is," said one Emily recognized from the jail. "Yeah, she's Nick's gal."

"What? No. I'm not Nick's . . . anything . . ." She said with junior high impertinence.

Jo pulled the curtain back a few inches. The cops stepped aside, and Emily took a look. An emaciated figure covered in bruises and gashes lay on the hospital bed. His hair was covered in dried blood, and he was hooked up to more tubes and monitors than Frankenstein's monster.

"Oh my god. What did that woman do to him?" said Emily, closing the curtain.

Jo spoke in hushed excitement as she drew Emily to the nurses' station. "When Paul got to the boat launch down by the river, Tiffani was already there. He saw her dump his body into the river! He dove right into that freezing river to pull James out. It wasn't until the ambulance came that the paramedics discovered he was actually not dead."

"Will he make it?" asked Emily in a hushed tone.

"He will. But there's a lot of damage to his brain."

"How are you doing?" Emily said, knowing the ethical corner Jo was backed into in having to care for a killer.

"You have no idea how much I'm struggling with this one."

Emily hugged her best friend. "You're amazing. Thank you for trusting me."

"I'm just glad we can all put this behind us and start to heal."

Emily nodded. "Where's Tiffani?"

"Jail. She tried to bolt after she dumped the body, but Paul had already alerted the state police, and they chased her down."

"Wow. I'm just . . . so grateful." Jo hugged Emily again. Satisfaction stirred in Emily. James, Hendrick, and Tiffani were going to be able to stand trial in the future.

"Emily Hartford!" boomed a large male voice from behind her. "What have I said about letting the cops do their job?" She whipped around. *Nick!*

He was charging into the ER with Paul at his side, carrying a tray of to-go coffees and a bakery bag from Brown's. When their eyes met, Nick broke into a relieved smile.

It was so good to see him out from behind bars!

She skipped a few steps toward him, and they met in an embrace.

"See, I told you. Nick's gal," she heard the cop say behind them.

"Did you lose weight in the slammer? You look a little gaunt," she said, giving him a once-over.

"Prison food. Goes right through you." He pulled her close. "I don't know if I should be grateful or hateful that you are so incredibly stubborn and strong-willed."

"I tend to bring out a lot of mixed emotions." She grinned. "How'd you get out so fast?"

"Due process works a little faster when you're the sheriff."

"We are a pretty great team when we're not quarreling," said Emily.

"Team Doctor Death and . . ."

"Good St. Nick!" She shook her head. "I'm retiring that nasty old nickname."

"Ho, ho, holy smokes, I'm so glad you saved me, Emily Hartford," Nick said with a cheesy belly laugh as he slipped her hand into his.

"Now we're even," she said, squeezing his hand.

56

"Delia told me that Pepper Cave Construction has decided to donate the Parkman parcel to the community and turn it into Parkman Playground. Complete with a swing set, slide, sandbox, picnic tables. There's even going to be a memorial garden planted for Sandi," said Emily as she and Nick walked hand in hand through the frozen cemetery a week later. She was grateful that a place of peace had been preserved in Sandi's honor. A place where community could be nurtured. Where neighbors could get to know one another. Watch out for one another.

"Paul asked if we wanted to join them for a bite to eat afterwards," said Nick.

"Sounds good."

Nick gripped Emily's arm as they made their way through the packed snow to the grave. They were officially a couple. Doing couple things. Like going to funerals. And dinners with friends. And planning for Christmas in two weeks.

"Do you think any of the other pack members will be here?" asked Emily.

"As a matter of fact, yes." Nick caught Emily's cold glance.

"They deserve jail time," Emily said, burn in her voice.

"They're not exactly off the hook yet."

Good. "It's going to be a while before I can forgive and forget."

"You forgave me."

"You were repentant."

"More than you know," said Nick in a tone that revealed his heavy heart. "There's something I still need to do. And I don't know how it will affect my future. Our future."

"What is it?"

"You'll see."

As they wound up a small hill that led to Sandi's grave site, Emily noticed how the sky had cleared and the sun warmed the earth, melting patches of snow. She looked ahead and was surprised to see trails of people heading toward Sandi's burial plot.

"This is incredible," she exclaimed. "I had no idea so many people would turn out."

"Between the police department and Delia's campaign, we raised over ten thousand dollars to give Sandi a proper memorial," said Nick.

"I'm stunned. The park. Now this."

"Small towns at their best."

Emily smiled and hugged Nick to her.

Emily and Nick made their way to Delia, who had already arrived and reserved a few spaces for them near the casket.

"Thank you for making this possible," Emily said to Delia.

"That's what we do, doll." She looped her arm through Emily's. "I'm hosting a reception at Brown's after the service. Spread the word."

A pastor dressed in a parka and heavy gloves stood at the head of the grave as several hundred mourners formed a giant crescent around Sandi's gravesite. Dotted through the crowd, Emily noticed a few members of the pack standing solemnly with dutiful spouses or significant others at their sides.

Emily shifted her gaze to Sandi Parkman's casket and was saddened that Mrs. Parkman could not be here. She had suffered a minor stroke the day after receiving the news about Tiffani and was in the hospital.

No mother and no sister to send a daughter home. But in their places, an incredibly compassionate community of people who would not let this unspeakable tragedy remain blemished with misery and suffering.

At that moment, Emily renewed the vow she had internalized as a junior coroner watching her father. If there was anything she could do to prevent lives from ending like Sandi's, she would seek to do it. It was essential to send the message that justice would be served. Everyone's life had importance and significance. No one was disposable. No matter where they came from or what ill fortunes they got tangled into.

For the next hour, under the high December sun, she and Nick stood hand in hand as the pastor gave his prayers and message. When he finished, he asked if anyone else had words to offer. Nick's hand slipped from Emily's as he stepped up right away to the head of Sandi's casket. From the periphery, she saw the members of the pack trickle up to the front. Paul. Ross. Landry. Brett. Rick.

They gathered in silence, and Nick stepped forward to address the town.

"What I'm about to say is hard, but it has to be said. As your sheriff. As a son of this community. As Sandi's friend. Over the years, you have all heard secret whisperings about Sandi's life. We were part of the urban legends and stand before you today to confirm that, unfortunately, they were true. By manner of omission, I played a part in what happened to Sandi. I want to ask your forgiveness. I stood by when I knew Sandi was being abused and suffering and I did nothing." He paused to clear the catch in his throat.

"I should have intervened. I should have confronted James. I should have stepped up and said something to her mom, to teachers. I should have gone to the police. There are a million things I should have done to save her. But I didn't. And I'm deeply sorry for my inaction and what it caused."

The next words came with calculated purpose.

"Freeport deserves a better role model for your sheriff. You need to start this next chapter with a clean slate. So, I'm stepping down."

An audible gasp escaped from Emily, joining the shocked expressions of everyone around her. She glanced at Jo, whose face registered her own surprise at the announcement as she reached for Emily's hand.

Nick then stepped up to Sandi's casket. Emily watched spellbound as he silently mouthed long sentences full of emotion. Little changed in his body movements, but she saw his lips quiver and a tear escape. He brushed it away with his sleeve and set a bouquet of yellow roses on her casket.

After he stepped back in line with the others, one by one, the rest of the pack members made their public confessions. But Emily could barely concentrate on their words.

When they were finished, Nick led them away from the grave site, and they trailed down the hill and out of sight.

Soon, small clusters of families and couples peeled away from the grave in complete silence as they all pondered what they had just witnessed. Emily stood frozen in place, hand in hand with Jo.

When they were finally able to remove themselves from Sandi's grave, Emily and Jo walked together to the main drive to join Nick, Paul, and a few other friends, who they could see flocked together talking.

Emily glanced up the hill to a barren maple tree that overlooked the west section of the cemetery.

"I'll be right back," she told Jo, breaking away.

"Want some company?"

"No, it's okay."

Her parents shared a gravestone under the maple tree where her father's date of death had been recently chiseled in. She brushed the snow that had collected on top and stood there looking at it, still finding it hard to believe that her father had passed just weeks ago.

"Hey . . . so, I was just in the neighborhood . . . couple plots down," she started, finding her voice. "It's a pretty interesting story. For another time. Just thought I would catch you up. Um . . . Brandon and I are not engaged anymore . . . but it's okay. Better a broken engagement than a messy divorce. Right?"

She paused, imagining that her mother would be nodding her head in agreement right now as she fired a million questions at her. *Are you sure? What makes you so sure? Is this something you might regret five years from now? How did Brandon take it?*

Emily laughed a little to herself.

"Yes, Mom. I'm sure. And no, I'm not going to regret it."

She searched her brain for what to say next.

"Oh, yes . . . how could I forget? Anna! We found each other. You would really like her, Dad. She's smart and witty like you. But has a dry, sparse humor. Like you're not sure if she's joking. But then you realize she is . . . and she's really sweet too. A total hostess. Like Mom. And her girls . . . your granddaughters are darling. We're becoming family. So thank you. For her. I just wish . . . you would have told us a little sooner." Her throat caught and she swallowed hard. Tears began to form warm trails down her cheeks and neck. She let them come.

Sounds of friendly laughter across the cemetery drew her back to where Nick and his friends were huddled. Nick's gaze left the group and caught hers. His smile absorbed a piece of her sadness as she turned her gaze back to the gravestone.

"Oh, in other news, I've almost finished packing up the house. Mom, don't worry. I'm keeping all your bakeware. I've made like four apple pies since I've been home. Of course, they taste nothing like yours. But I'll keep practicing." She laughed to herself and could hear her father butting in to inquire about more serious matters— like her plans.

"My plans? Yes, my plans. Dr. Claiborne offered to sell me his practice. But I'm going to decline. I'm not ready to make any big decisions. One-year rule, remember?"

She cracked a small smile, thinking about Cathy Bishop wearing a sombrero and drinking margaritas. They were all going to be okay. In their own time.

"I'm gonna go now." It came out all raspy. "Don't worry. I won't wait another twelve years to visit. Love you both."

Emily padded from the grave, head lowered to the ground. When she stepped onto the pavement and looked up, Nick was just feet away from her with an outstretched hand.

57

December seventeenth. Today was the day Emily was supposed to have married Brandon Taylor at the Palmer House in Chicago among four hundred or more of his family's guests. She woke up with it on her mind and then realized there was no longer a single bit of bitterness or resentment attached to her memory of him, of them, of anything they had shared. In her heart, she wished Brandon well, then jumped out of bed with a huge sigh of relief.

Choice. Change. Potential. Possibility. They were all hers now. And last night, before drifting to sleep, she had confidently decided on her next steps. She just hadn't broken the news to Nick yet.

As she drew back the curtains and looked outside, a fresh snow was falling again from the ominous gray sky. It was perfect Christmas weather.

She dressed and rushed to the kitchen for coffee, running over a list of things she could do today. Should do today. At the top of the list was decorating the house for Christmas and baking cookies. She had offered to host Anna and her family this year. Her first hosted Christmas. And Nick, the host-with-the-most, was not just making the ham but roasting a whole pig. Emily had gasped when he'd suggested it. *We'd better see about inviting some more people.* And so the list had grown. Delia Andrews. Jo and Paul and kids, who had decided to spend a quiet Christmas together, rekindling their flame. And a few odds and ends from the sheriff's office—folks who didn't have family nearby or had to be on duty later that day.

Yes, there was much to do. But instead, Emily found herself swaying to Caribbean holiday music coming from a radio app on her phone as she bustled about her father's office packing the last box of his files. The walls of her father's old medical office were now bare and in need of a fresh coat of paint. The shelves were empty, exposing little scratches and indents in the wood. It required some touching up. But not now. Unless the renter insisted.

As she scanned the bookshelves for any remaining objects, her gaze caught the corner of a picture frame shoved to the back of a top bookshelf above her reach. She slid over a chair, climbed up, and retrieved it. It immediately tore at her heart. It was her favorite family photo, taken at the beach at Lake Michigan the Labor Day before she had started her sophomore year of high school. She, her mom, and her dad were standing on the shore with the dark-blue water and clear sky on the horizon. Dad was in the middle with his arms around both of them. The wind was blowing her mother's hair out from under her sun hat. She looked so pretty and carefree. Emily remembered, and could tell from the shape of her mouth, that she had been laughing. She was always laughing. Next to Dad, Emily was in her one-piece suit, squinting into the sun with a broad smile as she leaned onto her dad's shoulder.

She pushed the regret of a dozen years out of her mind as she touched the faces in the photograph. She would take this one with her.

Just then, the office door swung open with the force of a frigid gust. Nick entered quickly and sealed them in against the next blast.

"I think it's getting worse out there," he said, stamping off his boots on the snow mat. In one hand he held a shopping bag, in the other a potted something-or-other wrapped in brown packaging paper. "It makes me wonder why we live in this arctic tundra." He peeled away his scarf, draped it over a chair, and shook snow out of his hair. "I love this music."

"Helps you forget what's going on outside," said Emily.

"And it's a perfect segue for this," said Nick, tearing at a corner of the packing paper. "I thought you could use a little early Christmas gift for your new office."

"I thought we weren't doing gifts."

Emily watched as he unwrapped the potted plant, which was at least a foot taller than he was. As the paper peeled off, the branches of a baby palm splayed out.

"Wow. It's . . . big."

"Really brings the room to life," Nick said. "And there's more."

"This is already too much already."

"What? No. It's perfect in here. And . . . just wait!" He ran to the light switch and turned off all the lights. The dimmed room reflected the stormy sky outside. It felt more like evening than midday. Then he reached into the pot of the plant and extracted a plug. He inserted it into the socket, and the tree lit up in twinkle lights.

Emily's lips parted to let out "Oooh!" but the expression was silenced by the uneasy anticipation of news she had yet to break.

"Nick, it's lovely," Emily said. "But . . . I can't keep it. Here."

Nick looked around the office. "Sure you can. There's plenty of natural light."

She gave him a playful punch as the music shifted to a calypso rendition of "O Holy Night." He grabbed her by the waist and tucked her into his chest. "I love you, Dr. Emily Hartford. Do you know how long I've been waiting to say that?"

As the melody reached the chorus, Nick took Emily's face in his palms and drew his lips to hers.

"I love you, too," she whispered. "And I'm . . . returning to Chicago after the new year."

His forehead touched her shoulder, and he took a long inhale. He tried to respond, but couldn't get a full syllable out.

"I love being back in Freeport. But I need to finish my residency strong—in Chicago."

"And then?"

"Then, I'll see. But whatever the next steps, they will be uniquely my own. Not decided by Brandon. Not by my father's death. Not by you begging me to step in as coroner," she grinned.

Emily pulled Nick in for a hug, but he stiffened.

"I thought we . . ."

"Of course we are. You do realize you don't need a visa to visit Chicago." She smiled.

"No, but I'll need a plane ticket."

"What? Why?"

He buried his head in her long blonde hair and whispered into her ear, "I'm heading to Virginia. Quantico."

She tilted her head back and looked at him with wide eyes. She mouthed the letters *FBI*.

"Delia convinced me. And put in a good word."

"I'm so happy for you," she whispered back.

Emily nestled in Nick's warm embrace, and they held each other and swayed as the steel pan drum plinked out the beat of "The Little Drummer Boy." Outside the storm quickened and raged. Close to an inch of snow had already accumulated in front of the office door since Nick's arrival. It was Christmas Eve, and they needed to savor this holiday spirit, because Emily knew it would only be a matter of time before the phone would ring, requesting the services of this coroner.

ACKNOWLEDGMENTS

This particular story, as most of mine are, sprung from an amalgamation of experiences and cases that I observed growing up with death investigation under my nose 24/7. Was there a Sandi Parkman in my past? Yes. There were Sandi's being abused by family members. There were Sandi's being sexually exploited by so-called boyfriends. There were lonely, wounded girls seeking attention and admiration at often great costs to them.

There are still far too many Sandi Parkmans.

There doesn't have to be. We can each be part of the solution. If you see something or suspect something; say something. It can be as simple as letting that someone know that you see, you care, and you will confidentially help them.

Additionally, sexual exploitation and trafficking is right under our noses. We can see it in our most vulnerable populations, but also in the most unlikely. In the big cities, but also in the smallest towns and most rural country sides. Learn the signs of someone in distress. Give someone a lifeline, before it's too late.

US Department of Health & Human Service, Office on Trafficking In Persons

https://www.acf.hhs.gov/otip/about/what-is-human-trafficking

ACKNOWLEDGMENTS

National Trafficking Hotline: 888-373-7888.

A special thank you to those who read, edited, resourced, and lovingly nitpicked this story as it went along. Ryan, Sidney, Amy, Gordon, Mina, Gail, and Ron. For my spunky and ever-encouraging agent, Julie Gwinn. And thank you to the amazing staff at Crooked Lane who helped shape this novel from its inception: Jenny Chen, Matthew Martz, Ashley Dio, Melissa Rechter, and Rachel Keith.